W9-CJM-819

For Nance

Prologue

1945

NIGHT CROSSING

Robert Ryan

review

First published in 2004
by Review

An imprint of Headline Book Publishing

10 9 8 7 6 5 4 3 2 1

Cataloguing in Publication Data is
available from the British Library

ISBN 0 7553 0179 X (Hardback)
ISBN 0 7553 0180 3 (Trade Paperback)

Typeset in JansonText by
Letterpart Limited, Reigate, Surrey

Printed and bound in Great Britain by
Clays Ltd, St Ives plc

HEADLINE BOOK PUBLISHING
A division of Hodder Headline
338 Euston Road
LONDON NW1 3BH

www.reviewbooks.co.uk
www.hodderheadline.com

NIGHT CROSSING

The London Cage: July 1945

The murder trial was drawing to a close after a week of eyewitness evidence, expert testimony and legal wranglings. Even after being in the so-called court for five days out of the seven, Uli found it hard to believe that men were fighting for their lives in such an incongruous setting. It had once been the grand dining room of a Kensington mansion, and every day she tried to picture the huge formal meals that must have taken place here, the gleaming silverware, sparkling crystal decanters of wine, the inevitable brandy and cigars and politics.

Wartime, however, had taken its toll, and the tableau refused to come to life. Now, cracked linoleum covered the floor, protecting the prized parquet that shone through the larger gashes. The enormous fireplace had been crudely boxed in, the flowers and cherubs of the ceiling plasterwork were blurred by endless coats of distemper and the towering windows scarred by the gummy remains of anti-blast tape. The oak panelling on the walls was scuffed and scraped from one-sided combat with army furniture. It was hard to imagine that the space would ever see its glory days again.

The empty long metal table where the six-man tribunal would take their places and pass judgement was at one end of the room. The defendants and their counsel, two army officers appointed by the military court, were to the left of it, along with a pair of translators. The three-man prosecution team, led by scrupulously correct Major Hansard, sat opposite to the right. Uli was at the rear of the room, perched on the first slat of her seat, as if ready to flee at any moment, an impulse that always grabbed her when the three young men accused of the murder were led in.

Now the trio sat just eight metres from her, all staring straight ahead, upright on their folding wooden chairs, lost, like everyone else in the hushed room, in their own thoughts. At first, a week previously, they had been slumped, indifferent to the opening proceedings, which, after they had been advised of the regulations they were being tried under, mainly consisted of challenging the legality of those very statutes. Their leader maintained that what had happened was no business of this court. Gradually, as their lawyers' petitions were refused one by one, and they began to appreciate what was at stake, they became more animated, scribbling notes and appealing to the translators for clarification. Now they were slipping back into torpor once again, as they came to grips with the fact that British justice was going to be done, whether they recognised it as such or not.

Just a few more minutes and it would all be over, Uli hoped. She had forced herself to sit here day after day, almost as a penance, simultaneously trying to grasp and to shut out the grisly details of that night when the three men set upon one of their own, beating him with an iron bar until his eyes were

4

closed, and his lips were split and his voice was too weak to raise the alarm, then dragging him across the compound to the bathing block where—

The door at the far end of the room snapped open and the six members of the tribunal marched in. The Presiding Officer, a gaunt, expressionless Guards colonel, nodded as those already in the room rose to their feet, and there was a scrape of chairs and a brief expectant murmur as all sat once more. Uli examined the faces of the other five men at the front table, two lieutenant colonels and three majors. They no doubt thought that their expressions were unreadable to those present in the courtroom.

Uli, though, could see in those grim eyes what the sentence was to be, and she glanced over at the three defendants for the last time. She imagined first the black hoods and then the intricately knotted ropes passing over their heads and she was surprised that the thoughts gave her no pleasure at all. As a bitter taste soured her throat and her stomach heaved, she rose from her seat and hurried from the court, conscious of the clacking of her heels on the linoleum as the NCOs moved quickly aside to let her pass.

Part One

1938–40

One

Berlin: October 1938

The alley where Ronald Draper of Imperial Chemical Industries had bled to death now smelled of carbolic and ammonia, thanks to the civic-minded *Hausfrau* who had scrubbed away the large stain of blood and excrement at the far end of the passage. It was, thought Inspector Cameron Ross, admirable that anyone who lived in these dank Weimar blocks could be so conscientious.

The Inspector knelt down and examined the cobbles of this short cut that linked the street to one of the inner courtyards of the complex. Berlin had baked throughout the summer and even now, when autumn should have staked its claim and the first *Winterhilfe* – winter relief – collection-box-rattlers had appeared on the streets, the days were warm and humid. The smell from Draper's leaked body fluids must have built over the forty-eight hours while the crime scene was sealed, hence the need for the carbolic.

Something from the human spillage had been absorbed by the rough stones, because Ross could just make out an inch-wide ribbon that marked the route of Draper's slow crawl towards the street. The stain on the cobbles represented the last few minutes of his life.

Ross looked at the notes that he had been allowed to copy from the mortuary report. The Englishman had been stabbed nine times. The four wounds in his back were large, diamond-shaped punctures, probably made by a sharpened file. They had not been fatal. The blade that had entered his chest had been the one that had killed him. This weapon had been flat and wide, and had slid easily into his tissue and between his ribs, thrust upwards again and again until one of the edges snicked the aorta, filling Draper's chest cavity with blood.

Ross carefully examined the brickwork of the wall. The Neuköln tenements only dated from the 1920s but were crumbling already. He used his pencil to work at the individual bricks on the lower striations, hoping to find one loose, to discover the kind of hiding place that a desperate, dying man might choose. There was nothing, just a molehill of poor-quality mortar at his feet.

The policeman became aware of someone silhouetted at the street entrance of the alley and looked up. Ross was expecting one of the hard, snot-faced Berlin street kids who had pestered him when he had first arrived, but it was a uniform that greeted him. He squinted and checked the colours of the sleeve insignia – orange and green – and the jacket piping: orange. He relaxed. It was a young *Anwärter* of the *Ordnungspolizei*, the Orpo, the regular uniformed police. The *Anwärter* was the Berlin equivalent of a British bobby on the beat. Except the latter displayed no equivalent to the twin lightning flashes, the *Sigrune*, that adorned this tunic's breast pocket.

'And what do you think you are doing?' the young man barked.

'You are blocking my light,' said Ross, softly. 'Could you move aside, please?'

His calm, practised authority meant that the Orpo did as he was told and moderated his harsh Berlin accent by switching to *Hochdeutsch*. 'What are you doing here?'

Ross stood, grunting as his knees clicked. He walked forward into the main street, blinking in the light. The road was busy, the streetcars packed, the air filled with the rattle and spark of the *S-bahn* trains as they clattered over their wooden trestles. Friday afternoon, and the weekend had started in earnest. Across the street, a gaggle of startlingly white dresses, girls from the *Bund deutscher Mädel*, the League of German Maidens, many of them clutching pictures of Hitler to their nascent bosoms, skipped along the sidewalk, on their way to or from a Faith-and-Beauty dance rally.

Close up, the Orpo was a good-looking kid, a decade younger than Ross, barely into his twenties, and most of his bulk came from the pockets and belts and epaulettes that puffed out his uniform. Finally Ross said: 'I'm doing my job. What are you doing?'

Ross could see the confusion in the chiselled face. Ross's German was good, but a slight sibilance from his vestigial Scots accent suggested an *Auslandsdeutscher* of some description, possibly a Colonial German. 'I need to see the notebook. And your identity card.'

Ross took a step forward. 'Are you arresting me?'

'I don't need to arrest you to see the papers or your notebook,' said the young man, his hand sliding across the belt towards his whistle. Ross held up a placating palm and reached into his jacket pocket. He produced the *Ausländer Dienstausweis*, which had taken him a whole day of form-filling – and string-pulling – at the *Polizeipräsidium* on Alexanderstrasse to obtain. It

11

allowed foreign policemen limited powers, mostly enabling them to enter official buildings, even if it didn't usually get them much further than the reception desk.

The Orpo took it, examined the four-page document and handed it back before saluting smartly. 'My apologies, Inspector.'

'None needed. I should have identified myself immediately.'

'*Anwärter* Schuller at your service, sir. This is a former murder scene, Inspector. Is that why you are here?'

Ross nodded, biting his tongue. *No, I just like poking around in piss- and bloodstained alleys*, he wanted to say. 'This is your beat?'

Schuller waved an arm. 'From the canal to the park.'

That covered a hefty swathe of working-class districts, taking in the fringes of Hallesches Tor, once famous for its seedy boy-bars, now long suppressed, and all of Treptow. 'Big patch,' he said sympathetically. 'You know much about the case?'

The young man shook his head. 'The Kripo won't let us near anything interesting. I get to stop the traffic. Block people going into the bars while they take statements from the owners. Fetch them coffee and cake from Kranzler's.'

'They get anything from them?' Ross indicated the scruffy café up the street and, opposite, the bar-cabaret. The latter was the sort of place that would be closely monitored by the Sipo or one of the other police agencies charged with suppressing internal unrest. There were still a few establishments brave enough to take the Führer's pronouncements and recycle them as subtle satire and sarcasm. It was one of the many reasons why Hitler hated Berlin so much.

'You think the Kripo'd tell me if they'd got anything, sir?' said Schuller ruefully. 'But I gather not. Nobody saw anything. Probably just another drunken brawl that got out of hand.'

'I'm sure you're right.'

At the edge of his vision, Ross saw the dark Horch saloon detach itself from the orderly flow of traffic and draw to a halt level with him. Two thick-necked bulls in plain clothes stepped out from the front. Schuller sprang back and straightened up, distancing himself from the foreigner.

'Inspector Ross?'

Ross nodded.

Both produced their glazed-linen identity cards. '*Ober-regierungs und Kriminalrat* Pohl would like a word.' The back door of the saloon was opened wide to show him the figure within.

Ross had a rule about getting into cars with strange police-men, but you didn't take a summons from a Kripo *ORuKR* – a rank equivalent to lieutenant colonel – lightly. He slid into the rear seat and the door slammed shut.

Pohl reminded Ross of a bloodhound, all eye-bags, jowls and wet mouth. His hair was greased back from a sharp widow's peak with a perfumed pomade. He offered his hand and introduced himself as *Herr Doktor* Pohl.

'My apologies for not seeing you at the Alex,' he said, using the slang for the Kripo headquarters. 'The reorganisation of the force takes all my time now. But I thought I would bring the good news personally. We know who killed your man.'

'Really?' asked Ross warily. 'You have the culprits?'

'Culprit. A man called Eickhoff. Not a Berliner. Already known to us.'

'You have him, in custody?'

Pohl nodded.

'Tegel or Plötzensee?' The two main Berlin prisons, although these days the latter held more politicals than criminals.

'Prinz Albrecht Strasse.'

That might make things trickier, thought Ross. The old

13

university building was the heart of the Reich Security Service's ever-expanding fiefdom. 'Any accomplices, *Herr Doktor*?'

Pohl shook his head, setting his cheeks flapping. 'We believe he acted alone.'

Ross hesitated, wondering how to react to this nonsense. 'Can I see Eickhoff?'

'Not now. Monday perhaps.'

'Why not now?' He tried to keep the irritation from his voice.

'Inspector. We have to complete our own inquiries using our own methods according to German law before we can allow a . . . guest to intervene. It is also the weekend and *Reichsführer* Himmler's birthday, which means a big parade on Unter den Linden to police. We will be short-staffed. Monday, perhaps.'

'Morning?'

'Afternoon.'

Ross opened the door to get out. 'Very well.'

'You have friends in Berlin to entertain you over the week-end?' asked Pohl, as if he genuinely cared.

'Some, yes.' All Ross really had planned was a round at the Wannsee golf course, which his father had recommended. Or rather, he'd said, 'If you manage to miss the trees, even you should get round on par.'

'Excellent. You know I am so glad that everything was sorted out at Munich between our countries. Aren't you?' he said, referring to the humiliation of Chamberlain by Hitler. Ross thought of his father's profanity-fuelled indignation at the news, but said nothing. 'Fighting over people like the Czechs . . . I have nothing against them personally. I drive a Tatra, a fine car. But . . .' Pohl shook his head dolefully. 'We can't let them dictate our two countries' destiny.'

'Indeed,' said Ross. 'Thank you, *Herr Doktor*.' They shook hands. 'Monday, then.' As he stepped out of the Horch, Ross turned and poked his head back inside, unable to stop himself adding: 'I'll be curious to know how this lone man managed to stab a big chap like Draper in the back with one weapon, then switched to another to stab him in the front.'

Pohl didn't skip a beat. 'Oh, so will I, Inspector. So will I.'

Ross caught a cab north, then walked the last kilometre back to his hotel, down poor butchered Unter den Linden, its trees a victim of subway construction and, subsequently, the width of the latest generation of tanks. He thought about Draper.

All he knew was that Draper had claimed to be on his way home to England with information of the utmost importance. That message had been left at the British embassy the day before he was murdered. Draper's hotel room had been searched thoroughly by embassy security before the Germans could get there. They had found nothing, which had infuriated Colonel Ross. So the old man had decided to call in what he called 'a few outstanding favours' from Scotland Yard, and to have a detective from the Met sent over.

Which was where Ross came in. Despite his protests, the Colonel wanted to keep it in the family, and requested that his son should be the one chosen for the mission. As usual, he had assumed that the Inspector had nothing better to do than wait for him to snap his fingers. Still, as Ross knew, his father was not an easy man to dislodge from an idea, and he simply went higher and higher up the chain of command until his request was granted.

Fat lot of good it had done the Colonel sending him, for he, too, had turned up nothing. Perhaps the information had only been in Draper's head. In which case, it was lost to Colonel Ross for ever. He didn't relish breaking the news to the irascible old goat. Bringing his father bad tidings still reminded him of being summoned to the library with Nanny for a behind-the-ears inspection before bedtime.

He looked to his left down Wilhelmstrasse, at the lights blazing in the British embassy and beyond, imagining he could see number 8 Prinz Albrecht Strasse, although it was actually masked by other buildings, and tried to imagine the fear and pain that the arrested man must be going through in the basement cells. No matter that he was probably innocent of Draper's murder, the Gestapo would have found another reason to put him through hell.

At the Hotel Adlon, Ross walked across the lobby, past the lounging SS officers who seemed to be a permanent fixture, collected his key and was told there were no messages. He was therefore surprised to see an envelope on the floor as he opened the door to his room. The Adlon rarely got such things wrong. Unless whoever had delivered it had sneaked by the front desk.

Inside the envelope was a thick printed card, with the date filled in using a heavy Gothic script. An address in the western, more affluent, section of the city, an invitation to afternoon tea on Sunday, and a little checklist underneath. No uniforms. No ranks. No politics.

There was also no RSVP number, but by the time he had called the concierge and booked himself a table at Uckhurt's on Ku'damm for dinner that night and slid into a hot, soapy bath, Ross had already decided to accept. He had a hunch that there was a connection to the brutal death of a salesman in a Neuköln alley.

Two

The address on the card was on the southern side of Tiergarten, the so-called Alte Westen, a short walk through the chaos of Potsdamer Platz and west to the Matthäikirche, the Nazi church of choice. The house that Ross was seeking was not one of those villas done 'in the English manner' as Berliners said, with huge gardens and porticoes, the kind of places that housed either high-ranking officials or embassies, but in a more modest street – at least, by Alte Westen standards – of tall, flat-fronted edifices with refreshingly clean lines.

Ross found himself hesitating at the bottom of the steps to the house's rather sombre entrance, wondering whether he had made the right decision to come. His anxiety made him look across the street, to where a portly man in an ill-fitting uniform was watching. The man turned away and hastily scribbled something on the notepad he yanked from behind his Sam Browne-style belt.

'Don't worry about him,' said a voice. 'Just the local *Block-wärter*.' He turned to find a lady almost as substantial as the house in front of him. 'Sundays he gets to wear his uniform. Rest of the time, he's the local handyman. Which is a useful profession for a Party stooge. Here for tea?'

'Yes.' He showed his invitation.

She held out her hand and he took it and introduced himself. 'Gertrud Ritter,' she said. '*Vossische Zeitung*.' Ross smiled, thinking that she looked like no journalist he had ever seen, with her copious jewellery, flouncy dress and flamboyant hat. Nor did she seem much like a Party member, although most scribblers were these days. There was something too tart about her tongue: Party members didn't make disparaging remarks about *Block-wärter*. 'Come along, then. Not been here before? A word of warning . . .' She paused, her hand on the bell pull, and grinned. 'It's rather informal.'

The hall was more impressive than the exterior suggested. The floor was highly polished teak, the walls covered with murky portraits of various grandees and landscapes, the furniture heavy and ornate, and everywhere the giant potted plants so beloved of middle-class Germany. From behind white doors decorated with gilded inlays came the sound of animated voices. The young maid took their coats. Ross's new companion indicated the room beyond the closed doors and whispered in his ear, 'Would you like some help with who's who in there?'

'I'd be very grateful, *gnädige Frau*.'

They were ushered into the salon, a sensitive fusing of what had once been two separate rooms to form a space large enough to throw a decent ball. A row of floor-to-ceiling windows covered in surprisingly delicate gauze curtains let in shafts of the soft afternoon light, although flanking them were tightly curled swathes of dark velvet that could be swished across for a complete blackout. At one end of the room was a highly polished piece of ebony that even Ross's untrained eye could tell was a serious piano.

There were perhaps thirty people in the room, each holding a plate of pastries or cake in one hand, and coffee or wine in the other.

'Dutch ambassador over there,' Gertrud whispered in his ear. 'Klaus Blemberg, Deputy Chairman of *Deutsche Bank*, nice man, Jurgen Telling, of the *Staatsoper*... well, formerly of the *Staatsoper*, that monster Tietjen got rid of him.' She took a breath, as if suppressing her anger. 'Goering's doing, of course...' The list went on, mainly, it seemed to Ross, people associated with the arts, and especially music, although most of Gertrud's asides and explanations went over his head. 'And this gentleman,' she said loudly as a figure detached itself from the feeding frenzy around the table, 'is our host.'

He was a tall, thin man, slightly stooped, his entire sharp-boned face seeming to peer over the half-moon glasses hovering at the end of his nose. He gave Gertrud a kiss on her heavily powdered cheeks before turning to address Ross, extending a hand as he did so. No stiff-armed *Hitlergruss* here, even though its omission was risky at any gathering, even in one's own home.

'Hello, Inspector Ross. Cameron. My God, how you've grown. But then, it would be strange if you hadn't, wouldn't it?'

Ross scanned the face for clues. The use of his Christian name took him aback completely. Informal indeed.

'Oh, I'm not surprised you don't remember. Windhoek? And the veldt? Your father was liaising with the German Farmers Union. You must have been... fourteen or fifteen?'

The image of a younger, happier man flashed for a second in Ross's mind and was gone. But a name stayed. 'Fritz?'

'Fritz Walter! Yes. Well done, Inspector. And how is your father?'

'Well, thank you.' Ross recalled Walter and his wife, also a travelling musician, brought over to entertain the disenfranchised German population of South-West Africa, a troupe only too glad at the time to get away from the chaos in the shattered and demoralised Fatherland. His wife had played . . . cello, an instrument that had seemed far too large for such a gamine creature. Ilse, that had been her name. Even to a gawky fourteen-year-old she had seemed such an exotic flower out there, pale and delicate among the big, rough-skinned pioneers and their beefy *Frauen*.

He looked around and saw her flit through the middle of the small knot of people at the table: a quick glimpse of dark hair cut unfashionably short, cropped almost, exaggerating a pair of large brown eyes that flashed his way. He thought he caught the beginning of her smile before the curtain of people closed around her. She hadn't changed a bit.

As Walter made his introductions, Ross kept trying to get another sighting of her, but she seemed to have left the room. 'Herr Walter—'

'Fritz. Please.'

'How did you know I was in town? To invite me here?'

'What? You think staying at the Adlon is hiding? Most of Berlin knows that a British policeman is here – you forget that underneath all the bluster and posturing this is still a provincial town. Are you all right?'

He realised that he was still scanning the room for her. 'Yes. Sorry.'

'Ah, Ulrike. Coffee, Inspector?'

She was in front of him now, holding a silver tray with an ornate coffee pot and tiny quatrefoil porcelain cups, those large unblinking eyes staring into his.

'Ulrike?' he stumbled, thinking his memory had let him down.

'Yes, you remember her, don't you? I think she must have been two. Possibly eighteen months—'

She was their daughter, the cheeky little girl that Ilse would place in his charge while the musicians tuned up. He remembered them standing, hand in tiny hand, her blowing raspberries every time her mother put her bow to the strings, causing both of them to collapse in giggles.

'My God – I thought . . . How do you do?' he corrected himself.

'Hello, Inspector. My father told me all about you. I enjoy meeting anyone who knew my mother . . .'

She let it tail off and Ross looked up at Walter. 'Ilse?'

His host shook his head. 'Second child. It was what they euphemistically call a difficult birth. Neither of them survived, Inspector.'

Ulrike swept in with a well-timed diversion as her father's eyes filled. 'How do you take your coffee, Inspector?'

'White, no sugar.'

He helped himself from the tray and thanked her.

'You are welcome, Inspector. Careful.'

He looked down. His hand was shaking.

'Uli, you've got him all flustered,' said a new voice. 'She does that to me sometimes. Even at my age. She looks right into you. It's unnerving.'

The speaker was, Ross estimated, in his early fifties, a handsome man, although his blond hair was yellowing and the grin sent a web of laughter lines streaking down his face. He was dressed in a sharp double-breasted pinstriped suit, with a Party badge prominent in the lapel. A gold Party badge, no less. Another handshake, but preceded by the quick flick of the less extreme form of *Hitlergruss*, merely showing the right palm. Ross realised with regret that Fritz and Ulrike had faded away and he would have to make small talk.

'Otto Vedder.'

Ross cocked an ear to catch the accent. Austrian. 'Cameron Ross.'

'Inspector Cameron Ross,' Vedder corrected.

'You don't have a title?' asked Ross, knowing full well he would have. The man's bearing screamed military background.

'Well, strictly speaking I am a Staff Colonel.'

'With . . . ?'

'Shall we walk in the garden? Bring your coffee, Inspector.'

Ross gulped what was left in the cup and handed it to one of the staff, feeling the world shift in strange ways once more. He wondered what his father would have done in this situation, and knew that he would have grasped and mastered it, but no solution came to him.

They took a turn around the walled garden. Vedder made polite conversation, telling him of his stint in the K&K, the old Austro-Hungarian army, and his time at Austria's *Kriegschule*, the school of war.

'And now?'

'I work at Tirpitzufer. Not far from here. You know it, Inspector?' A questioning eyebrow flicked up.

Ross nodded, blood draining from his face. He could only be referring to one section of the street. Numbers seventy-two to seventy-six Tirpitzufer formed the headquarters of the *Abwehr*, German military intelligence. Ross smelled a rat about this whole soirée, and the motives for inviting him. The affable Otto Vedder was a high-ranking Nazi spy. The sort of spy who might well have had Draper killed.

After fifteen minutes of quizzing him about the murdered man, the Kripo investigation and the suspect now in custody, Vedder ushered Ross inside. As he did so Ross felt Vedder press something, which he quickly pocketed, into his hand.

'Nice talking to you, Inspector. Good luck with the case.'

He walked off into the crowd, which had grown while they had been away. From the far end of the room came the rich resonance of the grand piano. It reminded Ross of his time on a student exchange in Hannover, when his family had held a weekly *Musik Abend*, an evening of recitals.

There was a rude blowing sound in his ear. He spun around. Ulrike smiled up at him. She no longer held the coffee tray. She blew another soft raspberry.

'You remember doing that?' he asked in amazement.

'Oh, I used to do it till I was five or six. Every time mother played at home. I am sure the joke had worn thin with her by then, but she never let on.'

'I seem to recall that I thought it was rather hilarious.'

She cocked an ear to the music. 'Chopin,' she said. 'The room has lovely acoustics, doesn't it?'

'Yes, now you mention it—'

'Did you like Uncle Otto?'

Ross laughed. 'Hard to say, given that we have only just met.'

'Come, come, Inspector. A man in your line of work must make snap judgements. Tell me about Uncle Otto.'

'I thought he was very charming.'

Ulrike dropped her voice to a deep whisper. 'Liar.' Before he could react she said: 'Ah, listen . . .'

The piano playing grew louder, faster, more ferocious, highly percussive. Ross put a hand to his chin. He could feel those wide eyes raking him.

'Karl Hartmann. The *Jazztoccata*. Do you like it?'

'Well, it's a little modern for my taste,' he said. 'I feel safer with Chopin.'

'Modern? Oh, that's a dangerous word. Hartmann has had to move abroad, you know. Too much jazz, too many Jewish

23

melodies for the RMK.' Ross indicated that the initials meant nothing to him. The Reichs Musik Kammer? They decide who can play and who can't. What can be performed, and what can't.' She lowered her voice and pointed at the ceiling. 'Father shouldn't even be playing it here. But those idiots are tone-deaf.'

Ross looked up, puzzled, imagining men on the floor above, ears to the carpet. 'I think I am too,' he said, as the piece clattered to a conclusion.

'Nonsense. It just takes some getting used to. Like Stravinsky.'

Ross grunted. He hadn't quite assimilated that, either. 'So what do you play? Piano like your father? Or cello like Ilse?'

'Neither. Violin. Or did, until the accident.'

Before he could ask for an explanation the maid was bobbing in front of Ulrike. Her face was drawn tight, the manner jittery.

'Excuse me, miss, but you have a visitor.'

'Who is it, Anna?'

'Herr Erich.'

Ross thought he detected a fizz of irritation. 'Tell him to come in.'

Frida hesitated. 'He's in uniform.'

'Ah.' Ulrike turned to Ross. 'Erich is my fiancé.' Ross tried to keep his face impassive, to hide what was an unreasonable pang of disappointment, but the little smile she flashed suggested he hadn't succeeded. 'My father has a rule about Sundays and uniforms . . . would you walk with us?'

'I can't just leave.'

'Oh,' she said mischievously, grabbing his arm and leading him towards the door. 'You're finished here, Inspector. Come, tell me what you remember about my mother. Erich would want to hear that, too.'

The severe-looking Erich Hinkel with his jutting cheek-bones

24

and savagely cropped fair hair was resplendent in a startlingly white uniform with matching beret, a swastika armband and a polished belt with a prominent *Blut und Ehre* dagger. The big lad looked a little old for the *Marine-Hitlerjugend* uniform, although his face still bore the fading evidence of a young man's spots and pimples.

Ulrike had introduced them at the door and Erich had given a stiff-armed salute before shaking hands. He called Ross 'Sir', which made him feel ancient.

'Shall we walk? To the Tiergarten?' Ulrike had asked.

The streets en route to the park were full of a baffling variety of uniforms. Men and women alike were dressed in all shades, from the lightest khaki to crow black, as citizens made their way back from the military parade on Unter den Linden, which had been part of the *Reichsführer*'s birthday celebrations. Ross wished that his police colleagues who, even now, thought the communists were more of a threat than the fascists, could see the end result of the road that they had allowed Mosley to start down with his thuggish rallies at Olympia.

Ross tried to speak of Ilse, but in truth there wasn't much to say, little that he could summon up from the memories of eighteen years previously, except one journey by ox-wagon to play in front of ten bored and drunk farmers and another to a village where seemingly every soul within a hundred-mile radius appeared. Ross had not really known back then why they were chaperoning the musicians. Only when Ross was inducted into what his father considered to be the family business was he told that it was to ensure they really were musicians, not seditionists in disguise, trying to sow dissent among the newly disenfranchised Germans.

Ross could sense during these reminiscences that Erich was bursting to say something to Ulrike in private, and Ross tried to find an excuse to get away.

When they reached the park gates he said, 'Look, I'm quite tired. I played golf yesterday with the Wannsee pro. If you two want to talk—' he began.

'Nonsense,' Ulrike protested. 'All you need is some air. There is a tent just a few hundred metres from here.' The tents – *Zelte* – were the park's refreshment stalls.

'Uli,' blurted Erich as they strolled down the path through the woods to the clearing. 'Today they announced our postings. To honour Himmler's birthday. I have been selected for the *Reichsmarine*. The submariner section.' His chest swelled. 'U-boats, Uli, U-boats!'

'Mutineers! Mutineers!'

The cry came from behind them, and Ross felt a body barrel into him, and caught the scowl on the young face as it flashed in front of his. Another runner, this one dressed in regular *Hitlerjugend* uniform, bowled past and turned. 'Mutineers,' he hissed at Erich. 'If you're up for it, sailor boy.'

Erich looked torn for a moment between joining the athletic boys and young men who were bursting out of bushes and along the small, twisting pathways that criss-crossed Tiergarten and waiting for Ulrike's reaction to his momentous news. Finally he shouted: 'Stay here. At the shelter. I'll be back soon.' And he turned and sprinted as fast as he could towards the wall of trees at the far end of the lawn.

'The Mutineers?' asked Ross.

'The damn' idiots, if you ask me,' she said, her voice quaking.

A flight of ravens burst from the branches of the oaks ahead of them, cawing loudly. A shrill police whistle sounded from the direction of the Victory Column. Most of the strollers had paused, anticipating violence.

'They pick fights with the Hitler Youth,' Uli explained. She gasped as a cobblestone dropped onto the path ahead of her, bouncing once with a flat thud. Then a second was thrown, arcing high over the refreshment shelter. From their left came a wild-eyed figure, his tweed suit shredded on one arm, face bleeding, his arms pumping. Behind him, fifteen or more Hitler Youth, faces scrunched into hatred, a low growl emanating from them. Their prey swerved and headed directly for Ross and Ulrike, and the pack followed.

A large rock hit the Mutineer in the back and he stumbled forward with a yelp of pain.

'Don't do anything,' said Ulrike, gripping his arm. 'Please. It's best.'

Ross nodded, knowing that she was right, but as the injured boy leapt into the undergrowth he felt a prickle of shame.

The Mutineer was flung from the bushes. He was followed from the undergrowth by two of the *Streifendienst*, the *Hitlerjugend* Patrol Service, a kind of Gestapo *manqué* who swarmed around parks and gardens at weekends looking for anti-social behaviour. Both had truncheons raised as the unfortunate lad collapsed and rolled into a heap.

'Stop!' shouted Ross.

The first blow must have broken the boy's upraised arm, such was the sharpness of the crack. Now the pack had arrived, a swirling mass of young bodies, fired up with fanaticism, jostling for position to land a kick, a punch, a stab.

'Stop!' Ross repeated, hoping his voice wouldn't crack.

'Keep out of it.' Erich grabbed his sleeve. Ross shrugged him aside, pulled the nearest kid from the ground and flung him away with surprising ease. He found he could do the same with the second and third and he began to bellow, stoking his fury. As he moved to the centre of the scrum the bodies became harder and heavier, the wall of flesh denser.

An arm went round his neck and Ross felt his windpipe close.

He leaned forward rapidly and Erich lost his grip, his nails raking across Ross's Adam's apple.

As Ross straightened, the group closed in on him, their hot breath on his face and neck. One of them landed a punch on his bicep, deadening it, then there was a kick to the shin. Something cracked against the back of his head.

He imagined the cornered antelopes he had seen on the bushveld, struggling as the wild dogs tore at their flanks, pulling them to the bloodied earth. He lashed out with an elbow, cracking a nose, gave a stab into an eye with a finger, all the dirty tricks his father had taught him. But, like a tired old *gemsbok*, the young, hungry dogs were dragging him down.

Three

Uli swabbed a patch of dried blood from Ross's eyebrow, pulling a few hairs out as she did so. 'Ow.'

'Serves you right.'

'For standing up to those brutes?'

'For not trimming your eyebrows,' she sniggered.

They were in the wooden shelter that was part of the *Zelt*, the refreshment kiosk, in a darkening park lit by hissing gas-lamps. He had been saved from the pack by the appearance of the regular Berlin police, who had stopped the frenzied youths from tearing Ross limb from limb. He'd been let off with a warning to stay out of internal affairs, and had watched powerlessly as the battered Mutineer was handed over to two SS who had also arrived on the scene. They marched the boy off, administering their own repertoire of slaps and kicks.

After a loud row with Erich who was furious about Ross's intervention, Ulrike had fetched a first-aid kit from the proprietor of the kiosk. She cleaned the scratches on Ross's throat and forehead while Erich, his white uniform besmirched with grass stains, the beret missing in action, had skulked off with his friends. As she dabbed at his face, Uli told Ross about her time with the BdM, the League of German Maidens.

'Are you still in the League?'

'No. The accident stopped that.'

It was the second mention of a mishap, so he asked: 'Which accident?'

She held up her hands. The left was bent at an odd angle. 'At one of the week-long winter camps. Skiing. I broke both wrists, but this one set funny.'

'Ouch.'

'Yes. They were very embarrassed. When I asked permission to attend a music-appreciation class rather than BdM duty, they leapt at it. So no more marches or rallies for me, thank God. There. All done. Sure there's nothing broken? No dizziness? Nausea?' She laughed. 'BdM first aid. See, it was good for something.'

He stood, aware their voices were carrying through the still evening, and she was talking sedition.

'Come on, I'll take you home,' he said.

'No. Let's get a coffee. I know where.'

They walked quickly, Uli with her arms folded under her breasts, Ross with his collar turned up to try and hide the livid red marks at his throat. 'Did the breaks affect your violin-playing?'

Ulrike smiled. 'Just about completely. Father had a concert lined up for me. A recital, really, to show me off to his friends and colleagues. I was to play Handel. The Sonata for Violin and Piano in F major . . . well, it doesn't matter. I turned up at home with wrists swathed in bandages and the joints of a seventy-year-old. At least, that's what father told me when the splints came off.'

'That doesn't sound too sympathetic. Was he disappointed?'

She nodded. 'Heartbroken, more like. It's part of the reason he dislikes Hit—' She stopped herself. 'He blames the BdM. He'd be even more heartbroken if he knew the truth.'

'Which is?'

Ulrike stopped for a second and examined Ross's face, as if assessing whether she could trust him. She held up her crooked arm. 'It was no accident.'

The café that Uli chose was in a street on the edge of the park and so full of pungent smoke from Turkish cigarettes that they took a table outside. Ross had pressed her for more information about her not-so-accidental injury but she parried and batted like an expert, letting his questions drift off into the gathering night. He was glad that he hadn't had to face this one across a table in one of the Yard's interrogation rooms.

'Down there–' she pointed suddenly to an ornate house, bristling with columns, cupolas and a host of rooftop statues outlined against the blue-black sky – 'was the home of Joseph Joachim . . .' She waited for some sign of recognition, but Ross shrugged. 'Famous violinist? Hungarian Concerto for Violin, opus 11?' He shook his head. 'He was born in 1831, but lived long enough to make recordings. His Brahms . . .' She sighed dreamily.

'Go on. Brahms – yes, heard of him.'

'Well, what's interesting is that Joachim's house later became the Institute for Sexual Science.' Ross concentrated on spooning sugar into his coffee, adding three more than he normally would. 'Apparently it was full of the third-sexers and intergrades – neither men nor women. The locals didn't know where to look most of the time.'

Neither do I, thought Ross. Uli's attitude to talking about sex was as modern as the music in her house, it seemed. Ross cursed his primness, but he knew it was a cultural thing. None of the

English girls he knew would talk like this. He looked up and saw the gleam in her eye, as seductive as the little raspberry-blower who had captured his affections all those years ago.

'Talking of violins,' he said. 'Your wrists.'

'Hmm. Change the subject if you must.'

'I must,' he said with a laugh. 'What did you mean about it not being an accident?'

She drummed the table with her fingertips. 'I've never told anyone else this.'

'Well, don't, if you feel—'

'No, I'd like to . . . what's your expression? Get it off my chest?'

Ross nodded.

'Shrug the monkey, as we say. But then we all have monkeys we ought to get off our backs, haven't we, Inspector?'

He could feel himself being reeled in, but he couldn't help himself. 'Such as?'

'Such as what you are really doing in Berlin.'

'I—' he began. 'I'm investigating—'

'Stop. Let me explain one thing. I have an unfair advantage.' Uli hesitated, relishing the moment. Oddly enough, so was he. 'I can tell when you're lying.'

'You can what?'

'I can't tell what you are lying about, but I know when something isn't quite right,' she added hurriedly. 'I'm what they sometimes call a Duchenne? You know of him?'

Ross's head whirled with the sudden switchback changes of topic. She was pulling some of the tricks straight from the textbook his father had written on the art of interrogation – never allow the subject to settle down into a rhythm, don't give him time to formulate a planned answer. 'A composer?'

'Not this time. Faces.'

'Faces?'

'Do you know how many muscles control your expressions?'

He took a guess. 'Ten?'

'Forty-three. And they work all the time, betray your every emotion. If you know how to read them. Don't move.'

Uli reached across and put her hands on either side of Ross's face, pressing against the cheeks. 'I can see embarrassment. Anxiety. Don't worry, I'm not going to hurt you. Amusement. You think this is a trick, don't you? A parlour game?'

'I don't know what it is,' he said truthfully, although he was enjoying the sensation of her fingers on his face. He looked into her unblinking brown eyes, and felt fear and excitement.

'Did you like my mother?'

'Yes.'

'Did you lust after her?'

'Uli—' he protested.

'Yes or no?'

'No.'

She laughed. 'A lie, I think. But you are quite good at hiding your thoughts, Inspector. It must be your British reserve.'

She uncupped his face and leaned back. 'Let's see if you register shock.'

'How do you do that?'

Uli put her elbows on the table and rotated her hands in the air. 'You were wondering about how I broke my wrists. I got Erich to snap them for me.'

Erich stood just outside the yellow cone of light from the street lamp, watching Uli and the Englishman together at the café. The afternoon had gone all wrong. He had known that by turning up in uniform at one of her father's precious soirées with their insulting rules, he would force her to come out to see

33

him. But she'd brought this old man with her. *Must be at least thirty.* And when he finally did tell her about the honour of training for the U-boats, the moment had been swept aside by those cowardly Mutineers. He had fetched those policemen to rescue the stupid Englishman and what thanks did he get?

Erich flinched as he saw Uli reach out and touch the man's face. It was ridiculous for him to be jealous, he knew. Uli and Erich went back to kindergarten, to being wheeled side by side by their starched nannies, and they shared a bond, a secret that the Englishman could only guess at. That day on the slopes when she had raised her arms and closed her eyes and he had pushed her forward, three times in all, until there was a snapping sound and Uli began to scream, even louder than when she'd thought the Englishman was about to be coshed in the park. That subterfuge in ski week, the drastic action she saw as guaranteeing her freedom from her father, that would keep and bind them together for ever. It had been the only reason he had done it.

Erich looked at his watch. He couldn't stand there all night, and he could feel the panic draining away from him as he watched the man. It was foolish to think that the old boy could look at Uli as anything other than a child. Even more so to contemplate Uli falling for a foreigner. God, he'd be a candidate for the Dalldorf lunatic asylum if he continued thinking that way.

Having reassured himself, Erich turned for home, to settle down to his project on *Kapitän* Hans Rose, commander of U-53, one of the boats that had nearly brought Britain to its knees in the Great War. Daring, a brilliant tactician, ruthless in the pursuit of victory, yet humane once he had achieved it. A role model for all Germans.

Ross ran the bath deep and hot and sprinkled in the salts that the Adlon's concierge had magicked up. Gingerly he lowered his battered body into the bubbles, sucking air between his teeth as his skin reddened. As he lay there, he pondered the strangeness of the day. Finding himself hanging on the every word of someone with whom he had last played childish games twenty years previously. Someone who now seemed to be able to second-guess him, to know intuitively what he was about to say before the words came from his mouth. The dozen years that separated them had seemed like a vast gulf in Africa. Here it had shrunk to nothing. Or perhaps the adolescent crush that he had had on the mother had transferred itself to her almost identical – in fact, more attractive – daughter.

She's engaged, said an unwelcome voice, *so stop that now.*

She's engaged to a mindless thug, he insisted back. *And there was something about those eyes when she held him . . .*

Was all that stuff about Duchenne genuine? Was that how she had deduced that he was in Berlin on something other than straightforward police business? Then there was the enigma of her father's party, with Uncle Otto and his note – which, he realised with a start, he hadn't even looked at.

Ross heaved himself from the bath, donned a robe and rummaged in his jacket pockets. Why a note? Notes were dangerous things in the world of subterfuge. Unless . . . unless someone was listening. That was what Uli had suggested. She hadn't been pointing at the room above, she was pointing at microphones. Was that why Uncle Otto had taken him out into the garden, because somewhere down the road men with headphones and notepads were scribbling down snatches of conversation, hoping to catch an indiscreet remark?

Ross found the note and unfolded it. The letterhead featured the ubiquitous German eagle sprawled across the top. The message was handwritten, the signature stamped and smudged but legible. There was a time – nine-thirty a.m. – and an address. To his surprise he found his hand shaking. It must be delayed shock after the park, Ross reasoned. But then again, it wasn't every day a British spy, albeit a casual one, was invited to meet the head of the *Spionageabwehr*, the German military intelligence organisation.

Four

The row of brown stucco-fronted town houses that had been pressed into military service on Tirpitzufer had been divided and subdivided over the past four years, so that the interiors were baffling rat-runs, with staircases that led to blind walls, and seemingly endless rows of tiny offices.

Ross was chaperoned through the dark, creaking bowels of the *Abwehr* HQ to a rear staircase, and shown up to the fourth floor. He passed through several ante-rooms before being ushered into a cramped office. It appeared to be empty, but the curtains blew and he spotted his host on the balcony, gazing over the Landwehrkanal.

'Inspector,' the man said in his excellent English, striding into the room with his hand extended. No formal stiff-armed salute, Ross noted with some surprise, and a business suit rather than a uniform. There were other unexpected touches. The required picture of Hitler was present and correct, but positioned high behind the desk, where it would not be seen, at least not by the desk's occupant. A long-haired dachshund sniffled on a bed in a corner. Ross was standing on a threadbare carpet, and the room's only ornamentation was the model of a battle cruiser on the desk and a signed and dedicated picture of Franco, displayed rather more prominently than the Führer's. It was far removed from the over-embellished gilded lair, of the kind that Fat Hermann might prefer, that Ross had been anticipating.

'I really must take Seppl out.' He pointed at the dog, which opened one eye in anticipation. 'Would you care to join me?'

He was a small man, not five foot five; even so, Admiral Wilhelm Canaris affected a stoop, which made him seem even shorter. He had piercing blue eyes under a wild tangle of eyebrows, white hair shaved high above the ears, and a disarmingly casual manner for the Fatherland's chief spy. As they left the building the Admiral grabbed a rather grubby mac and placed a trilby on his head.

They crossed north over the canal, the dog sticking close to Canaris's heels, to a small private garden square, where Seppl instantly squatted. Ross was thinking that he must watch where he stood when Canaris said: 'Don't worry, a contingent of Hitler Youth comes in three times a day. They are only too pleased to clear up our shit.'

Ross followed the Admiral around the gravel path while Seppl risked a scamper on the grass. 'I was very honoured by the invitation to meet you, Admiral. But confused . . .' His words were drowned out by the engine noise of one of Lufthansa's Junkers tri-motors coming in low over the city. The plane's corrugated sides made Ross think of a flying Nissen hut, an image he hadn't been able to shake when he'd boarded one of the aircraft at Croydon a few days previously.

'The party invitation was a clumsy way to get your attention,' said the Admiral when the plane had passed. 'I discovered your connection to the Walters. It was a perfect excuse for Otto to look you over in an informal setting.'

'Did I pass muster?'

38

A grin. 'You're here, aren't you?' He stopped suddenly and turned to look up at Ross. 'Your suspect in the Draper case was taken before a People's Court yesterday. He was sentenced to death. He will be beheaded . . .' He looked at his watch. 'Well, by now, actually.'

Ross's jaw worked but no words came out.

'It was easier for them just to blame one man, clear it up, send you home. Best not rock the boat just now.'

'I . . . I shall put a complaint through the embassy. I was not even—'

'Don't waste your time,' said Canaris, with a wave of his hand. 'They suspected what Draper was, just like they suspect you. You know your room at the Adlon is full of listening devices? Be careful.' From his pocket he produced a silver cigar canister. 'This is what your man had hidden.' He wrinkled his nose. 'Only an Englishman would consider where he put this a decent hiding place.'

It was a second before Ross realised what Canaris meant. 'As a Scot, I don't mind agreeing with you. How—?'

'The post-mortem was performed by one of ours.' He held out the canister. 'Here. Don't worry, it's been disinfected.'

Ross took Draper's tube and unscrewed the cap. He peered in. 'Was it empty when you found it?'

Canaris shook his head. 'No.'

'So what he found out was valuable?'

'Possibly.' Canaris ruffled the neck fur of the dog, which had decided it had done enough for one morning and was panting at his ankle. 'I hear that you, unlike your esteemed father, are a friend of Germany, Inspector Ross.' Canaris was demonstrating the depth and breadth of his knowledge. 'Is that right?'

Ross shrugged. 'I . . . yes. I like Germany, I like its culture, music . . . and I like Germans,' he said truthfully. He felt his mouth go dry. This next sentence could be the biggest mistake of his professional life. 'Or at least, I did.'

'Oh, you don't have to approve of the present incumbents to be a friend, a true friend to Germany, Inspector Ross. Am I correct?'

Ross hesitated. The man they called the White Fox was certainly not above playing games with him. He said cautiously: 'I think so.'

Canaris looked around to make sure that they were unobserved. 'You know what Heydrich is recruiting now?' Reinhard Heydrich was Canaris's protégé turned arch-rival, the ambitious head of the *Sicherheitsdienst*, the Reich's Security Service, the Gestapo's Siamese twin. 'Lip-readers. If you are registered deaf in Berlin, you are likely to get a call from the SD, seeing if you can be of use. So many people are meeting outdoors, you see, that eavesdropping is becoming difficult. Lip-readers, though, can operate through binoculars at a distance that would render microphones useless.'

'That makes deafness an enviable disability. If you have to have one in this day and age.'

Canaris raised an eyebrow and smiled. 'Unless it's a club-foot. Club-feet are also very fashionable, I hear.' Ross didn't reply. It was a dig at Goebbels. 'Look, a man can serve two countries, Inspector Ross, if the aim is to make sure that those two countries don't go to war. If a man was to have assurances that what he gave would go no further.' The blue eyes stared at him. 'Not to the *Wehrmacht* or the *Luftwaffe* or the navy. To here.' He pointed back at the *Abwehr* town houses.

'Assurances?' asked Ross. 'What kind of assurances?'

Canaris lifted his battered trilby and swept back his hair. 'I don't suppose my word would count for much?'

Ross looked the former U-boat commander up and down and

tried to read the vast script lurking between the lines. 'It might. What do I get in return?'

Canaris tutted and shook his head, as if to indicate a trifle. 'Why, what was in the tube, of course.'

Ross shrugged with feigned dismissiveness. 'Is that all?'

The Admiral fell silent, and Ross feared that he had somehow overstepped the mark. However, he knew that his father would never accept the first offer on the table, so he too refrained from speaking. After a few minutes Canaris said softly: 'Seven, seven, zero, nine, S for sugar. Can you repeat?' Ross did so. 'Barclays Bank, London. Should you activate the account, then I will know we are speaking the same language.'

'If not?'

'It will close at the end of November. A missed opportunity.' He raised an eyebrow. 'For all of us.'

Canaris took out a pack of cigarettes and offered Ross one. He refused. 'Forgive me, Admiral, but you haven't really told me what you want me to do.'

Canaris signalled to the dog and they began the walk back to his office. He waited a while before he said, smiling slyly and with a note of disappointment in his voice, 'Oh, Inspector Ross, I think you understand me only too well.' Canaris picked up the dog to carry it the last few hundred yards. 'If you have any doubts, you can always ask your father.'

Ross knew he was being goaded. 'As you said, my father doesn't share my views on Germany.'

'No, but he is a very pragmatic man. He'll understand. Good day, Inspector Ross. Give the Colonel my regards when you report back.'

Canaris disappeared into the Tirpitzufer complex, leaving Ross alone on the street, feeling as if he had just been played like an old fiddle.

41

★   ★   ★

Back at the Adlon, Ross was patched through by the continental trunks to London. The duty officer answered and Ross said very simply, for the benefit of the SD's listeners, 'Can you tell the Chief Superintendent that I'm coming back early? Yes, case closed, all tickety-boo.'

No, it bloody well wasn't. Canaris had as good as told him that the death of Ronald Draper in that Neuköln alley was an execution disguised as a murder. That the Kripo had then used it as an excuse to behead a third party – someone they needed a trumped-up charge to dispose of – thus avoiding a diplomatic incident in the immediate aftermath of Munich. However, they had failed to find whatever it was that Draper had hidden up his arse. His father had told him that, according to his travel expenses, Draper had been to Bremen, Kiel and Hamburg as part of his ICI business. What had he picked up there? Ross had no way of even guessing.

So what about the offer from Canaris? If he promised to start a tit-for-tat trade, Ross would get the document that had been in the tube. But what would Canaris want? His head was pounding. Catching criminals for A Division was so much easier than this. He was doubly glad to have disappointed his father by becoming a copper, rather than a professional sneak, one of his 'casuals' spying for Churchill and Dansey on the QT.

Still, he had to keep up appearances, to act the outraged policeman, so he caught a cab to the Alex to protest about the execution, but, unsurprisingly, nobody of rank was available to see him. Certainly not the lugubrious *Herr Doktor* Pohl. He left a strongly worded note and walked down to the Tietz department store. Opposite was a perfumery, one of the few Jewish businesses on the street that hadn't been Aryanised. All around the little shop, signs that had once said 'Kochmann' and 'Rosenberg' had been torn down or painted over. Alone along the block was Max Goldschmidt. Max was safe because nobody could replace him – no Aryan could do his job so well – and SS officers used him to supply their wives and mistresses with his exquisite bottles of perfume. Nazis could be very pragmatic in their pogroms.

The shop was filled with dark wood shelves, holding stoppered bottles of liquids, some vividly iridescent, others merely tinted by whatever mysterious ingredient lay within. Behind the counter the walls were hung with boxes studded with tiny compartments, each one holding a miniature bottle of crystal or powder. Elsewhere, glass-fronted cabinets contained rows of brown bottles with thick yellow-ish labels, the contents named in a cursive script that had faded to an almost illegible beige. It all suggested a last bastion of alchemy.

'A bespoke scent?' asked Max, an etiolated man with perpetually flaring nostrils that made him look as if he was picking up millions of odours that mere mortals were unable to detect. 'Of course. I have a backlog, however. A week, ten days.'

'I'd like it express,' said Ross, using the Berlin shorthand for paying over the odds for swift service.

'How express?'

'This afternoon.'

The perfumer made a noise as if this were an insult to his art. 'Why the rush?'

'I have to leave the country.'

'Don't we all?' Max said with a heartfelt sigh. 'So. Tell me about her. I will see what I can do.'

'I beg your pardon?'

'If it is bespoke, I need to know about her character, so I can match the components to her personality. I suppose bringing her here is out of the question?'

'It's meant to be a surprise.'

Max fetched his pad, placed a pair of glasses on the end of his twitching nose, took down Ross's name and contact details and then said: 'Go ahead.'

For ten minutes Ross stuttered through a description of Ulrike, trying to pin down the qualities that he had deduced from one meeting: the sparky, teasing sprite, the hint of inner steeliness tinged with sadness, possibly guilt, whenever she spoke of her father, the strange unblinking eyes that seemed to peer deep inside your head, the unfeigned love of music, despite what she had done to herself, the odd and unsettling intuitiveness she displayed. A Duchenne. He must find out more to see if he'd been had. He wouldn't put it past her.

'Is that enough?' asked Ross at last.

'It might be,' said the perfumer as he scribbled down some options to try.

'What do you think?'

'What do I think?' Max Goldschmidt laughed, took off his glasses and rubbed his eyes. 'I think, Herr Ross, that you are in love with this lady.'

Five

Winter was already biting deeply on the German coast. The four towering sheds of Krupp's *Germania Werft* shipyards in Kiel shook as the bitter north wind whistled through the corrugated iron sides and steel girders, eddying around the quartet of conning towers within. The noise of the gale was accompanied by a steady tattoo of hammering, punctuated by the crackle of welding or the sudden whirr of a drill. Twenty-four hours they were working now, round the clock to get the boats off the slipway and out into the waters of the Baltic and, after that, into the Atlantic, where they belonged.

Oberleutnant zur See Günther Prinz pulled his greatcoat collar around his neck and patted the cold steel hull in front of him. Of the four U-boats being assembled at the yards, his was by far the most advanced. They had even reached the stage of bolting the 88 deck-gun in position. True, the boat still looked scabby and rusty in places, oddly naked without insignia or radio wires; even the 'asparagus', the periscope, was missing, but the end was in sight.

The boat had been laid down in February 1937, eighteen months previously, and it was but a few weeks away from completion. Already Lutz, Prinz's Chief Engineer, and his team had done their *Baubelehrung* – the familiarisation tour – making sure that the boat was bolted together to their satisfaction. Prinz wanted to do his own personal inspection before the crew arrived in Kiel over the next month or so. He had only thirty of the boat's complement of forty-eight confirmed. Volunteers for the undersea boats, it seemed, were in short supply. Just the thought of the steel tube gave many regular sailors the *Blechkoller*, the chest-constricting fear experienced only by U-boat crews. Conscription and callow youths too stupid to know any better than to volunteer would be needed to fill up these hulls, he knew, and that would make the commander's job – his job – trickier, at least until he won their trust and respect.

Prinz turned to Hans Schepke, the yard's chief designer, and, using the slang for torpedoes, asked, 'How many eels?'

'Fourteen,' said Schepke proudly. 'Four bow tubes and one stern. Same as your old one.'

Prinz had served on a VIIA boat during the Spanish Civil War, one of several subs used for reconnaissance, minelaying and blockades in that conflict. This was the 'B' version, incorporating what they had learned from the experiences. He nodded. 'What type of eel?'

'The G7a.'

Prinz tutted, disappointed. It was the model of torpedo that left a trail of tell-tale bubbles all the way to the target. A sharp-eyed enemy lookout just might save the day. It wasn't good enough.

'But by the time she is commissioned,' said Schepke, seeing the look of displeasure, 'the next generation will be on trial. No bubbles. And there will be magnetic detonators, not impact ones. A proximity explosion is far more effective.'

Prinz thought about it. 'So the ship's metal makes the torpedo explode a few metres beneath the keel?'

'Exactly. You will see other changes in these boats. More fuel in the saddle tanks – thirty-three tons more. More powerful engines. Here, look. Twin rudders for manoeuvrability. Top speed on the surface will be eighteen knots.'

'And submerged?'

'Eight. Perhaps nine. Trust me, you will like this boat.'

'I'd better, or else I'll be back,' said Prinz, flashing a wry smile. They both knew why this boat had to be as perfect as possible, and why Prinz's Chief Engineer had spent hours looking at every rivet and weld and bulkhead – very few submariners got the chance to return home and complain about shoddy goods.

'You want to go on board?'

Prinz hesitated, savouring the moment when he would see the cocoon of his own command. He could smell the diesel and sweat already, even though the engines hadn't run and it still possessed a well-ventilated interior. Within its first week at sea, though, it would stink like every other U-boat, a stench at once nauseating and oddly comforting.

'When will she be commissioned?'

Schepke looked at his clipboard. 'By the end of November. It has to be – we need the space to build the next one.' The designer couldn't keep the glee of a bulging order book from his voice. Both Kiel and the Bremen yards were working to full capacity turning out the Type VII U-boats.

'And does the boat have a number yet?' asked Prinz, knowing full well that it should have by now.

'Oh yes, they all have numbers, from when they are just a rack of steel plate and a box of rivets. *Werk* number five-eight-two.' That wasn't what Prinz meant and Schepke knew it and held up a hand to show that he was joking. He indicated the ladder leading to the deck hatch just aft of the gun ring. '*Oberleutnant zur See* Prinz. Would you like to step aboard U-40?'

The letter from the RMK, the Reichs Musik Kammer, was in a thick, embossed envelope. Ulrike's hands shook as she lifted it off the tray and dismissed the maid. Her mouth was dry. Should she wait until her father got home? No. It was her idea, her venue, her choice of programme. She had written the application, had pleaded, rather eloquently she thought, that much of this music deserved to be heard. Furtwängler had got away with conducting *The Magic Flute*, had even won praise from the Führer, when a year previously it had been frowned upon. And most importantly Georg Kulenkampff had played the Mendelssohn Violin Concerto with the Berlin Philharmonic within recent memory. Surely it was time to reconsider some of the decisions made in the past, those spurious distinctions between Aryan and degenerate music? It wasn't as if she was asking for Stravinsky or Hindemith or Egk.

Ulrike walked into the main music salon and tossed the letter on the piano, where it skidded along the lid, its raised eagle eyeing her menacingly. She knew her request to the RMK might have gone as far as Goebbels before a decision had been made. It was a shame that Richard Strauss was no longer at the RMK – at least he had shown some leniency. After all, one of his librettists had been Jewish.

Ulrike took a deep breath, snatched up the letter, ripped open the flap and pulled the single sheet out. She looked at the signature first. Paul Gräner, a man whose musical career was booming under Hitler, had scrawled his name across the bottom. The letter was curt and to the point. Schumann, Liszt, yes. Schoenberg, definitely not. But yes, a big loud yes, to Mendelssohn's Violin Concerto.

She let out her breath in a long sigh, feeling her eyes fill with tears, reading and rereading the line that after much consideration the RMK had decided to allow the performance, even though she must announce at the start of the piece that this was a Jew who had simply stolen Protestant church music and turned it into a sickly mélange.

For the first time since it had happened, Ulrike felt regret about her 'accident'. She would be cutting a disc in the wings of the small hall, monitoring the levels of the microphones, and not playing on stage, not bowing the *Allegro molto appassionato*, fully aware that she would be able to steer it away from the schmaltz it sometimes became, to bring out the lyricism. Her deformed left hand was automatically making shapes and she thrust away the shroud of melancholy. She had made her choice, and her choice had been to thwart her father and to regain her freedom, to have the suffocating shackles of practice day in, day out, removed.

She had also rediscovered the joy of listening, without over-analysis, and the pleasure in recording music so others could hear her father's piano-playing, her cousin's singing, Franz Haug's violin, the Müller quintet, their little circle of dedicated performers, as clear as it had been the night she switched on the cumbersome disc-cutter.

This time she might not have to use that monster. Erich's father worked for AEG and he had promised her the use of a Magnetophon, which could record a whole twenty minutes on tape, as opposed to the five she could get on a disc. Twenty minutes! And, so he said, the sound quality was wonderful.

She thought of Erich, of their future together, pre-ordained, it seemed, since the cradle. How long was an engagement meant to last in these troubled times? Both families were still irritatingly vague. When you're ready, her father said. Ready for what? She was probably as ready for Erich as she'd ever be. Was he ready for her? He was a good-looking lad, and if he had been turned into a blinkered philistine, he was hardly alone. Once he grew out of uniforms, parades, hero-worship and . . . submarines. She remembered with a jolt that he was going off to serve in some horrible tin can under the ocean. She stamped her foot in irritation. She must discover when he was due to leave.

Ulrike heard the front door slam. Father. Careful not to skid on the polished floors, she rushed to tell him the good news.

The weather had finally turned. Rain spattered down on the pavements around him as Ross leaned into a sharp headwind, pushing himself up the hill to Ulrike's house, wondering with each step if the gale was trying to prevent him making a fool of himself. In love? Him? He had no idea what that felt like. He knew what it wasn't, thanks to the near misses with girls when he'd been in his twenties, edging slowly towards betrothal because it was expected, then veering away at the last minute when the full implications dawned on him, the realisation that a couple of happy summer picnics were not the best preparation for a life together. His father claimed to have decided on marrying his mother within an hour of meeting her. Ross was sure that this was in rose-tinted retrospect. Since the Spanish-flu epidemic of the post-war years had carried her off, the Colonel had eulogised the woman whom he felt so guilty about surviving.

Ross had to admit to himself that he didn't have too many problems meeting women. One of his near misses had told him that if he grew a moustache and slicked his hair back he could double for the actor Ronald Colman. It was meant to be a compliment. Meeting was one thing, marrying another.

Max must be wrong. He wasn't in love, surely? This was just a gift for a young girl who'd patched him up after a foolish escapade in the park. One with whom he'd spent a strange but pleasant evening until it got dark and cold and the café had closed up around them, while she had explained to him why the National Socialists couldn't make their minds up about whether to ban Goethe or not. She told the story of them decapitating his statue in the park, and the hue and cry to find the head again when he was rehabilitated a month later. She insisted that, even though she couldn't play music any longer, she still got pleasure from singing, even if her voice was mediocre. And she sat there and had done her best to impersonate a hundred and fifty voices roaring out Bach's Mass in B minor, oblivious of the stares of tired waiters waiting to go home, and then had lowered her voice and offered him an intimate snatch of a Hugo Wolf lied.

This didn't make it love, even though Ross could still hear the poetry of Mörike ringing in his ears, still feel the shudder of pleasure as she half-sang and half-whispered the lyrics at him. None of his English girls had ever managed anything like that, none of them would even have heard of the Austrian composer and the poetry that he set to music. Mind you, nor would they have explained in quite such detail how venereal disease eventually took his mind.

Goldschmidt was a perfumer, not a clairvoyant. In fact, Ross wasn't even sure about the perfume that *Herr* Max had created. He'd let Ross sniff it before it was stoppered and wax-sealed, and it was light, fruity, not like the heavy, rich scent he had expected at that price.

He was already a fool, though. He should have been thinking about links, connections and messages. Why had Uncle Otto, clearly a long-term Nazi, used the Walter household to fix up a meeting with Canaris? What was Canaris up to? How much money was in that account? And what was his next move?

51

ROBERT RYAN

All these questions – but sitting immovable at the front of his mind was Ulrike. He was confused, that was all. He was glad his colleagues at Scotland Yard couldn't see him flustered like this.

The door was in front of him, his hand on the pull, barely shifting it a quarter of an inch, so that there was but the faintest of rattles within. Perhaps they wouldn't hear. Perhaps he should leave the parcel on the step. Then the maid was smiling and welcoming him in, and he was snatching the hat from his head.

Ulrike came running into the hall, her stockinged feet struggling to make a purchase on the teak, a letter in her hand, a smile on her face that faded when she saw him.

'Oh. I—'

'Is this a bad time? I'm sorry.'

'No. No. Just . . . I thought you were father. Come in. Take your coat off. Is it raining? Anna, can we have some coffee—'

'No, thank you, I'm not staying. In fact, I'm leaving Germany.'

She waved the maid away. 'Really? Case closed, Inspector?'

'Yes. Look, I wanted to thank you for the other day—' Ross fished in his pocket for the gift.

'You'll miss our concert if you leave.' Ulrike thrust the RMK letter at him.

'Which concert is that?'

'At the Schleehalle.' She couldn't hide her excitement.

'When is it?' At last he had the package out.

'November ninth.'

'I'll be long gone, I am afraid.'

She sighed, feigning irritation. 'Your loss. Mendelssohn's Violin Concerto. A real rarity.'

'Sorry,' he said yet again, holding out the daintily wrapped present in his palm. 'Here. This is for you. I had it made. He

52

made me describe you to get it right. It's just a token of my appre—'

He stumbled as she stared back at him, her face shutting down, the playfulness gone, back to a mask of Germanic correctness.

Ulrike's voice had dropped again, but there was none of the smokiness in there of the other night, just an uncompromising brittleness. 'I cannot accept this, Inspector.'

'It's bespoke.'

'I can see. Goldschmidt's. Very fancy. But it would be improper for me to take it.'

'I don't see why—'

Now, just a hint of a smile. 'Don't you, Inspector?'

'I . . . well, I suppose it could look . . . I didn't mean—'

'For a betrothed woman to accept an unexpected gift from an unattached man, it isn't quite the way we do things in Berlin, Inspector.'

Ross suddenly felt like the gauche Britisher abroad. 'Yes. Of course. I was forgetting my manners.'

Ulrike held out her hand, at once the icily polite hostess, leaving him flustered, unsure of exactly what he had done to upset her, but in no doubt that he had.

'Have a safe journey back. Boat-train or aeroplane?'

'Lufthansa. From Tempelhof.'

'Enjoy the flight. I will give my father your regards.'

'Yes, do that, please. And I'm sor—'

'Goodbye, Inspector.'

And he was walking down the steps, his face burning, knowing that he had achieved exactly what he had feared – making an idiot of himself.

Six

Anwärter Schuller of the Berlin *Ordnungspolizei* stood to rigid attention in front of *ORuKR* Pohl, who was slowly reviewing the young man's notes and his training file. Schuller's face was impassive as the pages were turned, but inside he was shaking. Pohl was in charge of streamlining the multi-headed police and security forces into something approaching a cohesive organisation. However, it didn't normally involve dealing with a lowly street cop such as himself. Schuller stared straight ahead at a large picture of the Führer shaking hands with the Mercedes driver Rudi Caracciola just before a Grand Prix race. There was a model of the Auto Union Silver Arrow on the large walnut desk. Schuller hoped the man didn't expect small talk. He knew nothing about motor sport.

'Your family originally Schwäbisch?'

'Yes, sir. From near Heidelberg. We moved here when I was two.'

'Good National Socialists, are they? Your family?'

'Yes, sir. My sister is a BdM group leader,' Schuller replied, even though he was certain that snippet would be in his file.

'Good. Your notes here about the meeting with the Englishman, Ross. They are complete?'

'Yes, sir.' He had taken great care with his record of everything that had happened in that alley. He knew that interacting with a foreigner would attract interest, although he hadn't anticipated it would be at this level.

'Nothing else was said? About why Scotland Yard saw fit to send its own man across for a straightforward murder case?'

'No, sir.'

'Very good. Your file has a red eagle, Schuller. You know what that means?'

'No, sir,' Schuller answered truthfully. It didn't sound good.

'It means . . .' Pohl hesitated. 'Promising. One to watch.'

Schuller couldn't help exhaling with relief.

'I am sure you are bored with pounding the streets of Neuköln. I am recommending your transfer to the Hackescher Markt station. And for promotion.'

'Sir. Thank you, sir.'

'Any questions?'

'What will my assignment be over there, sir?'

Pohl smiled. 'We are setting up a new Barrack Police Unit for special duties in the Mitte district. If you are interested.'

Schuller nodded. He was being transferred to the *Schutzpolizei*, the Schupo, the Protection Police of the Reich. Something big was clearly in the air. It could be, thought Schuller, his chance to shine.

'Of course, sir. Thank you, sir,' he said again.

The departure lounge at Tempelhof aerodrome was a world apart from the oversized garden shed that served the same purpose back at Croydon. Three of the four walls were panelled in heavy oak and adorned with huge photographs of Nazi dignitaries – many of them showing a beaming *Reichsmarschall* Hermann Goering – waving from the steps of various aircraft. A carved German eagle sprawled across one side of the room, its talons gripping a garlanded swastika, while finely detailed German aircraft swooped in attendance. The fourth wall was mostly glass, where travellers looked out over the airstrip itself and admired the Junkers and Focke-Wulfs of the Lufthansa fleet. It came as no surprise to hear that the *Reichsmarschall* himself had had a hand in designing the area.

Outside Ross could see the London-service tri-motor on the apron, the last of the luggage being loaded, the boiler-suited mechanics making their final checks. He couldn't wait to be home, to speed away the next five hours and be deposited in his flat, where he could bury his embarrassment about Ulrike in some deep recess of his mind.

Through the window, he saw what looked like his case disappear into the hold. The cigar tube was nestling in the hidden compartment at the rear of the lining. It was only incriminating if one knew where it had been and what it represented, but the presence of the tube still made him feel edgy. He glanced up at the lounge desk where the Lufthansa staff were still busy with the paperwork, willing them to get a move on.

'*Herr* Ross.' There was a hand on his shoulder. He looked up at a sallow specimen in a trilby staring down at him. The man produced his identity card. He was a member of the *Luft-Sonderpolizei*, the special airport police. 'If you will come with me, please.'

Ross looked around, his mind seeking some way out of this. One or two of his fellow passengers stared at him, but most had buried their heads in their complimentary copies of *Volkische Beobachter*, knowing it was the safest course of action.

They must have located the cigar tube hidden in the case. Idiot, Ross thought. Hide in plain sight, his father always said, that was the best course of action. Ross nodded and stood. He felt the guiding pressure of a palm in the small of his back, ushering him out of the lounge.

As they stepped through the glass doors, the policeman said, regretfully, 'I am afraid I had no choice.'

'No,' Ross agreed.

'She is not allowed through without a ticket, you see.'

Ross didn't understand until he turned and saw Ulrike, clutching an envelope to her bosom.

'Thank you so much, officer,' she said, beaming.

'My pleasure,' said the cop, touching his trilby.

'Uli,' said Ross.

'You forgot these documents, *Herr* Ross,' she said loudly for the benefit of the copper. 'So I took the liberty of bringing them down.'

She handed over the envelope and he said, 'How careless of me. Thank you very much, Uli.'

She lowered her voice. 'I had to apologise.'

'No. It is me who should—'

'Shush. I've been rehearsing this all the way over here. The least you can do is let me say it.' Ross nodded, trying to hide his smile. 'I was rude. I was simply taken aback by your generosity and forgot that you English, uh, Scottish—'

'British,' he offered.

'British. Do things differently. It was a lovely gesture.'

'And it's in my bag. On that plane. There.' As he looked back he could see a trail of passengers heading for the steps.

'Oh, I didn't come for that. Honestly. Is that what you think? I came for my perfume?'

Her face began to cloud and he said quickly, 'No, no. Just that . . . well, it's no use to me. I'm glad you came down, Uli. Really. And just let me offer my apologies.'

'Not needed. But accepted.'

A silence fell between them. A German man would have bowed and turned at this point, all honour satisfied for both parties, but Ross shifted his weight from foot to foot. She stepped close, raised herself on tiptoes and kissed his cheek. As she came away she remained close, near enough for him to feel her breath on his neck, and he imagined his arms around her, pulling her to him in a long embrace. Then she would kiss him again, and to the outside world they would just be two lovers having to endure separation, storing up the memories of each other's touch and aroma for the weeks and months ahead.

His arms, though, remained at his side. He hoped that on this occasion Uli really could read his mind, and the twinkle in her eyes suggested that she might have.

'Have a safe flight, Inspector. I hope we meet again.' She turned, a grin dimpling her cheeks as she did so, and strode purposefully off. Ross took a step after her, wanting to prolong the moment, to ask why she had turned cool on him when he had offered her the scent, but there was someone at his side, a Lufthansa official.

'Sir, the London flight is boarded. The Captain wishes to start the engines.'

'Yes, I'm coming,' he said softly.

When Ross, still feeling queasy after a pitching flight through the thick cloud cover nestling over Europe, arrived back at his flat in Fitzrovia, there was a terse note summoning him to a meeting with his father the next day. He could feel the disapproval leaching from the page into his fingertips. Ross had failed him. His own son had shown that he was better off in A Division than as one of the casuals of the Z organisation that Ross senior ran for Claude Dansey. Well, Ross had warned him that would be the case. It wasn't always a matter of like father, like son.

Ross put the note aside, undid the string around the parcel that he had picked up from the bookseller on Charing Cross Road and peeled aside the paper. He lit the gas fire in the living room and sat in the armchair, about to read through his purchases, when some instinct made him fetch from his coat pocket the envelope that Uli had given him. He had assumed it was empty, a ploy, but as he shook it a small piece of paper fluttered out onto the carpet. It was seven lines of poetry, by Eduard Mörike.

Night rises tranquil on the land;
Dreaming, she leans on the wall of the hills.
Her eyes behold the golden scales
Where time's at rest in peaceful vessels.
But bold the springs and the fountains rush forth,
They sing in the ear of Night, the mother, of day,
Of the day that is ended now.

Ross stared at it for a while, trying to fathom what Ulrike was trying to say. Was there a message for him here? He was lost. Eventually, he put on the kettle for tea and turned to the two volumes he had bought. Perhaps there was a clue to this strange but beguiling girl in the books.

The first, on human physiology, told him that Guillaume Duchenne de Boulogne was a nineteenth-century neurologist who had given his name to a form of muscular wasting disease. Ross closed his eyes at this, imagining what the knowledge of certain early death would do to a person. Would it make you grasp the remaining time with vigour? Or would one slump into a despondency?

He read on. The condition, it explained, was passed from mother to son. He reread the passage hungrily, making sure that he hadn't skipped any vital words. Only occurs in males.

He slammed the book shut and picked the second volume, on psychology. He found Duchenne de Boulogne in the index and thumbed through to a chapter on 'Physiognomy and the Inner Life', illustrated with photographs of often grotesque expressions, many of them displayed by the feeble-minded.

He read slowly this time, aware of his heart thumping. Could it really all be true? He looked at his watch. He called the Yard and got through to DS Fred Cherrill, the new head of the Fingerprint Bureau. Cherrill was held up as the epitome of the modern copper, bringing order and science to the detection of crime. He had also written a paper on the Yard's long-discredited Anthropometry Department – the one concerned with classifying criminals by their physical characteristics – that had been abandoned forty years earlier, claiming that, although much of it was bogus, some of the techniques merited re-examination.

After he got off the telephone with Cherrill, Ross knew without a shadow of a doubt that Uli had not been playing a parlour trick on him. And why she had refused the perfume. It was a good thirty minutes before his face stopped glowing.

Lehrter Bahnhof, situated across the Spree from Tiergarten and the scorched shell of the Reichstag, was Berlin's main station for departures to the north. It served cities such as Stendal, Hannover, Köln, Lübeck, Hamburg and Kiel, so it was usually busy, but Uli had never seen it so crammed with people and locomotives.

There was a train at each of the eighteen platforms and as soon as one whistled its departure and left the station, another slid to take its place.

60

Uli pushed her way through an entrance all but blocked by kitbags and suitcases, then navigated her way through the human throng. The air of the departure hall was thick with steam and raised voices. Over at one side, cordoned off behind a row of policemen, was a line of terrified-looking civilians – mostly Jews, she guessed – their papers being heavily scrutinised before they were allowed onto the platform to board.

Most of those about to depart Berlin from the station, however, were from the army or navy, and they were young, even the officers practising their swaggers.

Uli felt herself swamped by the uniforms as the crowd pressed around her, and she had to walk on tiptoe to try and spot Erich. She had promised to see him off, even though she was dreading another goodbye, especially this one. Hers was not the kind of news that you were meant to bring to someone about to go off and serve the Fatherland.

She found him at the news-stand, hastily scribbling her a note, and he beamed with relief when he saw her. 'Uli. I thought you weren't coming.'

He put his arms round her waist and there were catcalls and whistles from his new colleagues. Erich ushered them to a quiet spot between the mail trucks.

'I had trouble finding you,' she explained. 'So many people.'

'Yes. Exciting, isn't it?'

She stepped back and looked at him. He seemed changed, less awkward in the uniform, no longer a boy trying to fill a man's shoes. 'You look very smart.'

He plucked at his tunic and lowered his voice. 'I know. Mother altered it for me, so it fitted better. I'm glad you came . . .'

'So am I.' She paused to gather her strength and began. 'Erich—'

61

'Uli,' he interrupted, 'I have been thinking. I shall be away for months and, if the worst happens, I shall be at sea for perhaps years. I think it is unfair to ask you to wait for me as my fiancée.'

'Erich. You'll be back for Christmas.'

'Probably. Even so, I think the honourable thing to do would be to put our engagement in abeyance.'

'What? You're breaking it off?' she said, genuinely shocked.

'Don't be upset.'

'I'm not upset.'

'I talked it over with my father. He agreed. If we had named a date it would be different . . .'

'Erich. I don't know what to say.'

'It doesn't change anything, really. I still want us to be together. I still love you.'

She knew what the gesture meant. Erich's intention was to make sure that Uli would not be constrained by the conventions of being betrothed while he was gone indefinitely. He was giving her her freedom. Uli felt a rush of relief, and had to force herself not to tell him that she was going to break it off anyway. Exactly why, she wasn't certain, but she had divined over the last few days that Erich, with his blind obedience to a cause she loathed, was not where her future lay. However, not having to explain this was an unexpected bonus. *Let his noble sacrifice stand*, she told herself.

Erich's head snapped around as he heard shouted orders for his group to entrain. 'You aren't mad at me, are you?' he asked.

'No. Not at all. I think you are very brave,' she said truthfully. 'And considerate.'

'Good.' He kissed her gently on the mouth, turned and disappeared into the phalanx of white marching their way to platform four to board the train for Neustadt and its School of Anti-Submarine Warfare.

★　★　★

Colonel Donald Ross found the weather-beaten Senior Professional of the Stoke Poges golf course, near Windsor, in the back of his shop, winding a new grip onto a driver. As Donald Ross entered, the man looked up and wiped his fingers on a cloth before accepting the proffered hand.

'Hello, Charlie,' said the Colonel.

'Hello, sir. You don't get out this way much these days.'

'More's the pity. You seen my partner?'

'That would be the young man, would it?'

'Yes.'

Charlie gestured over his shoulder at the putting green. 'He's back here, practising.'

'What did he tell you his handicap was?'

'Nine, same as yours. At Huntercombe, though, so he may struggle a bit here. You're still playing off nine?'

'Yes. But these days it's a real nine, Charlie.'

The professional laughed. 'Good to see you again, sir. Been busy?'

Colonel Ross nodded. He'd been busy all right, feeding information into the great maw of Winston Churchill who chewed it up and spat it out faster than they could gather it. 'Busy, yes.'

'Well, you come here a bit more often, and I'd get you to scratch, I promise.'

'I think there'll be time to work on my golf after the war, Charlie.'

Charlie felt the colour drain from his face. He had two boys of call-up age. 'I thought after Munich—'

'Piss for our time?' said Colonel Ross with a sneer. 'Come on, it's a slow day – will you caddy for me, Charlie?'

Charlie pulled himself together, thinking he might get some

more information if he tagged along. 'With pleasure, sir.'

'Did the young man give his name?'

'Cameron, sir.'

The Colonel laughed. 'That's his Christian name. Cameron. Cameron Ross. We're about to give my son a good thrashing, Charlie.'

The quartet, two players and attendant caddies, met outside the extravagantly porticoed clubhouse. 'Hello, father,' said Ross, holding out his hand.

The Colonel gripped it hard for the briefest second, then waved towards the course. 'You haven't played here before, have you? Number seven's the hole. A four hundred and twenty-five, par four. It'll sort the men from the boys. Eh, Charlie?'

'How's that?' Ross asked the caddy.

'Pond, just fifty yards short of the green,' he explained. 'Rather punishes those trying to make up for a poor tee shot.'

'Charlie's going to caddie me,' said the Colonel. 'You can have Marks here.'

'That's fine, Colonel.'

Ross shook hands with Marks, and the quartet set off across the five hundred yards of immaculately shaved grass towards the first tee. The hole was a three-hundred-and-ninety-five-yard one, par four, with a chain of bunkers and a loop of the course's river guarding three-quarters of the green.

'What sort of man was he? Draper?' asked Ross.

Ross senior signalled for the caddies to drop back and slowed to a leisurely pace. Ross knew that his father got out of breath easily, thanks to a damaged lung from his gassing in the Great War. Now and then you could hear it, a strange wet slapping as the scar tissue tried to extract oxygen.

'Oh, the usual kind for a casual. A misfit. A dreamer.

Although this one had a silly sense of humour. Loved pranks. But–' his father paused and looked at him – 'a patriot, if I might use that unfashionable word. Prepared to take risks for his country.'

'Was he one of yours?' He was asking whether the Colonel had recruited him personally.

His father shook his head. 'Dansey brought him on board a few years back.'

Claude Dansey had set up his Z Organisation in the early 1930s, picking up operatives where he could – mostly toffs and businessmen of independent means, although anyone with a decent cover story for Continental travel was welcome. Draper, as an Imperial Chemical Industries free-roving salesman and purchasing agent, with good contacts in Germany, Austria and Hungary, was perfect.

'So, no sign of whatever it was that Draper had discovered?'

'No, sir,' replied Ross.

'Shame.'

'All might not be lost, though. I had a meeting with Canaris.'

The Colonel looked at him in amazement. 'For crying out loud. Wilhelm Canaris? Tell me from the beginning. Everything, mind.'

Ross began, his account interrupted only by the need to play some golf and to be circumspect around the caddies. On the first tee they tossed for honour, and selected their balls, the Colonel going with a Dunlop, Ross a Penfold. Ross's opening effort was messy – he pulled the ball way over towards the trees to the left. He shaded his eyes and watched it clip the edge of the rough and roll back onto the fairway. Still a long way short of the green.

Marks said quietly: 'Not bad. If you don't mind some advice—'

'Advise away, Marks, please.'

Marks gave him some quick pointers on stance and ball placement, finishing with an encouraging: 'Early days yet, though, sir.' Ross nodded his thanks.

The Colonel's shot was much smoother, his footing and swing more convincing, and he dropped a good twenty yards further on the fairway. As they strolled on, his son described the meeting with the White Fox.

'Are you sure it was Canaris?'

Ross suddenly had an attack of self-doubt. It never occurred to him he could have been an impostor. 'Yes,' he said, with all the conviction that he could muster.

'Well, well, well. Shall we play on?'

After they completed the first – the Colonel ahead by one stroke – they walked on to the second, a treacherous three-hundred-and-ninety-yard dog-leg, par four. 'Canaris is no fool,' said the Colonel. 'He knows you're soft on Germans.'

'That's not true. I like them as a people, but—'

The Colonel sighed. 'I should never have sent you on that exchange. It was meant to be a case of "Know thine enemy." Not give you some misty-eyed idealism about the country. The same country that has taken Austria and the bulk of Czechoslovakia.'

Ross stopped walking. 'That is unfair. I hate Nazis as much as the next man. Trouble is, you think the whole nation has gone over.'

'Haven't they?'

'No. The Walters, for instance. Good people—'

His father waved his club to dismiss this. 'Cameron. The Walters are related to Otto Vedder, you said. Vedder is a nasty piece of work.'

Ross knew that he was going to get nowhere. It would be a waste of his breath to explain that he had found a natural lie-detector in Uli, someone who might be very useful to the Colonel. But he would certainly suspect some sleight of hand, especially given her nationality. Nothing good could possibly come out of Germany, was the Colonel's current creed. 'What do you suggest I do? About the bank account?' asked Ross.

'Canaris wants to establish a dialogue with us somehow. In return, you get Draper's information. Or something that passes for it. You, flattered, fall for it—'

'Dad. That's not what happened.'

'Quiet. I'm running you through the scenario. You, flattered, fall for this "Friend to Germany but not the Nazis" nonsense. So, what do you do? You activate the account and play along.'

'Father, I have to be back on duty at A Division on Friday.'

The Colonel glared at him. 'I'll have a word with John Moylan.' He was talking about the Police Commissioner himself. His father always went to the top. Ross started to protest, feeling himself railroaded, but his father poked him in the chest with the handle of his club to silence him. 'There is going to be a war, Cameron. No ifs or buts. I know that. Your new chum Canaris knows that. And I'll make sure John Moylan knows it. He'll agree that the defence of the realm takes precedence over mere coppering. I went along with your choice of career when you argued that it was a more useful choice than Z. Well, the position's reversed. You've a link to Canaris, man. That's worth six A Divisions right now.'

The Colonel bent down and placed his ball on the tee, and Ross suppressed the urge to hit him with his wood. His father had always resented his son's choice to join the regular police force after university, where his facility with languages ensured a rapid rise in the fast-modernising organisation. This was his revenge, Ross was certain, his way of demonstrating to his son that it was possible – and preferable – to play on a larger stage than West End Central.

As the old man straightened he said quietly, 'Welcome to the spying game, m'boy.'

Seven

Berlin: November 1938

The Schleehalle was near Stettiner Bahnhof, at the unfashionable end of Friedrichstrasse. It had been built in 1903 by a Berlin philanthropist to bring music to the surrounding tenements, although once the family fortune had been lost high-brow culture had given way to crowd-pleasing cabaret.

In the last few years the place had mostly fallen empty, its audience taken by the three *kinos* within easy walking distance, and, thought Uli, the neglect was starting to show. However, the acoustics were passable, the stage was deep, and, after much cajoling, the ancient heating system had raised the temperature to the point where it was possible for Uli to take her gloves off.

She fussed with the Magnetophon, hoping that the chill wouldn't affect the mechanism as she spooled the fat ribbon of tape through the complex maze of recording heads, as directed by Erich's father. She had set up the machine in the orchestra pit, fed by three microphones through a device called a balancer.

Uli peered over at the rim of the pit at the sparse audience. There was an hour to go, so she shouldn't get anxious. She'd received her first letter from Erich that morning. He was at Wilmhelmshaven, undergoing his intensive training, and he described hours spent in a steel boiler, being rocked back and forth to try and simulate conditions on board a U-boat. She could tell from the tone that some of the perceived glamour of the *Bootwaffe* had been chipped away by the experience. What would the navy turn her former fiancé into? In normal times, she knew exactly what Erich would be. An engineer at AEG, like his father. But now?

She was still perplexed by him breaking off the engagement, and her own reasons for wanting to do so. Were her motives something to do with Inspector Ross? She found herself thinking about the policeman, imagining herself a little *Hausfrau* with him, in much the same way that she had with Erich. Except life in London, with a Scotland Yard detective, seemed more glamorous than settling for being an engineer's wife.

Yet that was ridiculous. What she had seen in Ross's face, in that hallway, hadn't had anything to do with domestic bliss. Her Duchenne ability – the freak of nature that enabled her to read expressions, no matter how fleeting – had picked up something altogether more base. She'd felt bad afterwards, of course. It wasn't the first time that she'd seen lust in a man's eyes. It was a while since it had shone through so strongly, however. She'd gone to Tempelhof to make it right, and had ended up even more confused.

Sometimes she wished she could just look away, ignore her Duchenne facility altogether, but God had given it to her for a reason, even though it had dogged her for years now. She still remembered catching the lie when her father had assured her that she could be one of the top violinists in Germany. Even as his voice said that, his face told her he thought she could be good, but not that good. It was then she knew that the years of

70

rehearsal and performance he had mapped out for her would, ultimately, result in failure and bitterness. All those hours and days of endless repetition, trying to master the nuances of the concert repertoire, the never-ending practice sucking the life out of her. It had taken her months of torment to realise that it was better to end it then, with two snapped wrists. Better to be a person, with room for living and loving, than a performing machine.

Uli felt someone staring at her and looked up. It was her father peering down from the footlights. He smiled, but the expression was strained. 'Don't you wish you were up here?'

She grinned back and said, truthfully: 'I'm happy where I am, father. I'll do you proud.'

He sat down on the boards, legs dangling into the pit, and held out another letter from the RMK. For a second she thought that permission to perform had been revoked, but she remembered the oily clerk who had turned up earlier and signed the documentation. As she read, her father said, 'Two violas down, the woodwind is short, too. No percussionist. People are scared, Uli. And they'll be even more scared when this gets out.'

'This is preposterous,' she said as she scanned the single page. 'This applies to a third, a half of the musicians in the city.'

He nodded. The RMK was proscribing any musician who had even a single Jewish grandparent. It meant that Fritz Walter's scratch orchestra, and the Müller quintet, would be decimated. She was shocked when she saw the tears in her father's eyes.

'Make sure you get everything,' he said quietly, pointing to the tape machine. 'This could be our swansong.'

The gramophone had a crocodile-skin finish and, so the sales-man had said, a Garrard Number 22 motor, an excellent soundboard and a supply of spare needles. Ross had paid ten shillings for it, rather a lot for a reconditioned model, he'd thought, until he recalled guiltily just how much money there was in that Barclays account. He'd asked his father's advice on what to do with the treacherous windfall: 'Spend it, you blithering idiot,' the Colonel had said.

The gramophone, his first purchase, was now in the corner of Ross's apartment, a ground floor flat with living room, kitchen, bathroom and bedroom, leading off a square hallway. Alongside the machine was a growing collection of recordings, mostly Beethoven and Bach, which he played when he needed reminding of Germany's gifts to the world, and some Hugo Wolf lieder when he needed to remind himself of Ulrike.

That morning, when he had realised that her father would be playing the concert at the Schleehalle, he had gone along to the music department upstairs at Foyle's on the Charing Cross Road. He had returned with a box of four shellac discs containing the Mendelssohn E minor and the Bruch G minor concertos recorded in Paris and London by Yehudi Menuhin.

With a sleet-filled November rain rapping at the window, Ross stoked the coal fire, took the first of the fragile black records from its crinkling sleeve, laid it on the turntable and lowered the arm before retreating to his armchair.

As he listened to the violinist's fingers skittering up and down the neck in the first movement, he pictured Uli watching her father's ensemble play the same piece, hundreds of miles away in Germany. He smiled to himself. *I know your secret now*, he thought. The book had hinted at it, but the fingerprint expert DS Cherrill had confirmed it, albeit in hushed tones, as if it were dangerous to speak of such black arts in the modern Metropolitan Police Force.

The physiologist Duchenne had discovered that some people can spot minuscule changes of expression. There are many thousands of faces we can show, often for the merest fraction of a second, that reveal our true feelings. Everyone, apparently, does it, but the vast majority of people cannot see them. Uli and her kind could. It wasn't mind-reading as such, but it was close.

The insistent buzzing finally broke through his thoughts and he was aware of the click of the needle on the record's exit groove. The door bell sounded again and Ross leapt up, lifted the arm from the disc and hurried into the hallway.

As he opened the door a gust of wind threw rain into his face, and it was a second before he could focus on the man in front of him.

'Well, Inspector Ross, aren't you going to invite me in?'

Ross nodded and stood aside to let *Oberst* Otto Vedder of the *Abwehr* step into the warmth.

The first half of the concert went by in a blur. Uli was balancing the microphones, making sure that the machinery didn't overheat, keeping an eye on the spool speed and trying to move as quietly as possible as she tiptoed around the installation. The opening Liszt was shaky, she thought, the sound too bright, and she had repositioned one of the microphones before the Schumann, which was an improvement and again before the Blacher, which made it as perfect as she could have dared hope. Now there was just the Mendelssohn and the Paul Winter Fanfare to come.

She was gratified to see the hall filling for the second programme. Her father brought her a coffee and she ran through the technical difficulties with him, but he shrugged them aside, his mind on other things. Fritz Walter checked his watch. 'I'm sure it will be fine,' he said. 'It's time.'

He stood, straightened his clothes, walked to the centre of the stage, and silenced the auditorium with outspread arms.

'Ladies and gentlemen. Thank you so much for coming. I hope you are enjoying the performance. I have been asked . . . told to say something about this music, which is about to be played by my colleague and friend Franz Haug.' There was a smattering of applause. 'But, to be honest, I think we should let the music speak for itself. Ladies and gentlemen, Felix Mendelssohn's Violin Concerto in E minor.' There was enthusiastic clapping and a few shrill whistles of approval.

Oh God, Uli thought. He'd skipped the RMK-approved intro. There'd be hell to pay for that if there were any officials out there. She hesitated over the tape control until she was sure that the orchestra and the lead violinist were ready. With just twenty minutes of tape, she was anxious about capturing the whole performance, and she hoped her father took the concerto at a brisk tempo. Slowing it down would be a disaster.

The needles on the circular dials flickered as the piece began, but almost at once she realised that something was wrong. The rear microphone was far too twitchy, its indicator stabbing right round over to the right. Then the sound reached her ears. They were yelling at the back: '*Arschloch, Beschissener, Sackratten,*' and other insults that she couldn't catch. She heard the normally unflappable Franz fumble, discordant notes issuing from his instrument. There was a low growl now, a hum almost, from the audience. She pulled herself up over the pit edge, hoping to silence them, but she could see that the newcomers were slipping off their coats to reveal their uniforms underneath. Their faces were contorted and angry, fists were being shaken, and a fight had broken out in the back row.

Uli didn't see or hear any signal, but as one the interlopers produced bricks and bottles and hurled them at the stage. Glass smashed next to her, sending shards into the machine, which began to squeal. On the stage the music stuttered to a halt, to be replaced by groans and yells and atonal protest from the strings as precious instruments splintered under the onslaught.

'Uli. Uli.'

It was her father, reaching down for her. There was a thin smear of blood on his forehead. She looked around for the tapes of the first half.

'Uli. We have to leave. They are coming.'

She glanced back again. The pack of thugs was pushing through the audience, sweeping those brave enough to protest aside, some leaping from seat-back to seat-back to reach the stage. Many were brandishing thick sticks or metal bars.

'Uli.'

Her eyes burning with tears, she allowed herself to be hauled up on stage and to join the musicians, some still clutching their instruments, all making a run for it, hoping that nobody had thought to block the stage door. As she reached the wings, the first of the mob clambered down into the pit and began to strike at the AEG with an axe handle. Another wrenched at one of the spools until it came free, the ribbon of tape unravelling.

Hands pushed at her and swept her into the gloom of backstage and into the smoky air of the side alley. From behind them they could hear the piano and the double bass being smashed.

Uli tried to tend her father's wound but he shrugged her off and pointed to the street. 'We all ought to get clear,' he said, 'as soon as possible.' He raised his cracked voice. 'Thank you all. I'm . . . sorry. Please, get home – quickly.'

Fritz put an arm round his daughter's shoulder and they joined the crowd of dazed patrons spilling out of the theatre, their faces lit by the glow from a fire down the street.

They headed north towards Stettiner, the nearest station, too numbed to speak, watching embers dance on the night breeze, feeling the heat as they got closer. Allowing them to play the Mendelssohn had been a trap, of course. Even if Fritz Walter had followed the RMK script, the thugs would still have stormed the stage. It was a warning to all other musicians. Uli wondered if any of Erich's friends had been among the roughnecks.

Ahead was a group of policemen encircling the newly arrived firecarts in front of the burning building, barring their way. They were being organised by a young man around her own age. She approached him. 'Excuse me, officer. I'm sorry. I know you have work to do. My father and I need to get to the *S-bahn*. We must go home.'

The newly promoted *Wachtmeister* Axel Schuller spun around. There was a scream of despair as flames spouted from the gilded dome behind him. Someone else cheered and there was a loud smattering of applause.

'My God, is there anyone in there?' she asked.

Schuller remained expressionless. 'Your best bet is to turn around and make for Friedrichstrasse station, miss.'

The smoke was thickening now, choking her, and she could hear the detonations of breaking glass coming from the *Höfe*, the courtyards across the street that housed workshops and stores.

'Can't we come through here? It would be quicker.'

Schuller's face hardened. 'Just go home,' he said. 'As fast as you can. Lock your doors. Don't go out, no matter what you hear.'

There was a hiss as arcs of water began to issue from the hoses, spouting towards the flames now engulfing the Invalidenstrasse synagogue. She noticed that the firemen's aim seemed to be off. They were dousing the neighbouring roofs to protect them, while the synagogue itself continued to burn fiercely.

Uli looked south and saw a second synagogue on fire, an orange inferno against the night sky. Then she heard breaking glass everywhere, an almost continuous crackle blanketing the city.

'Why aren't they dousing the synagogue?' she asked, tugging the policeman's sleeve.

'Get out of here! Now!' yelled Schuller.

'Come,' muttered her father, thrusting a folded handkerchief over his nose and handing her his spare one. 'We have to leave.'

Uli thought of the opening line to the verse that she had written out for the Inspector: *Night rises tranquil on the land.* A far from tranquil night was certainly crossing over Germany.

Yes, she decided, as the once-magnificent central dome imploded, spitting out a cloud of fiery debris that spiralled up into the darkness. *We have to leave.*

Eight

Ummanstrasse 48
Alte Westen
Berlin
November 21, 1938

Dear Inspector Ross,

Not knowing your home address, I am sending this letter via Scotland Yard. I assume you read about the terrible events of November 9th in your newspapers. Kristallnacht they call it here, because of all the broken glass. In many ways the aftermath has been worse. The RMK has banned my father from performing, pending a tribunal. Needless to say, we are fairly certain of the outcome. The fact is, Inspector, I need to get father out of the country. He is not a well man. His health degenerated rapidly following the disruption of our performance that night. He doesn't eat. I hear him pacing at night. He has lost weight.

As you know, it is very difficult to get into another

country without sponsorship. We are luckier than most –
with no J on our passport, we can take out monies and
goods, so would not be too much of a burden to the country
that accepts us.

I realise our meeting in the house was not a happy
one, for which I still ask your forgiveness. If we'd had
more time at the airport, I might have been able to
express myself better. I look forward to the opportunity to
explain myself.

However, if you could see your way to helping us with
the formalities, perhaps acting as one of our sponsors, I
would be eternally grateful. I would happily send you
details of the procedure. I hope this finds you well.

Yours sincerely,

Ulrike Walter

Flat 2,
Chaconne House,
78 Westerfield St,
London W1
MUSeum 2037
November 23, 1938

Dear Miss Walter,

I hope this letter reaches you and finds you in the
best of health. I read about the events in Berlin on the
night of your concert and have felt nothing but
concern since. Given your father's and your own
position in the world of music over there, it occurred
to me it would be much safer if you left Germany for

a little while. Would you consider coming to England? I have heard there are a number of Continental musicians settled in London, with plenty of recitals and concerts as a result of this new talent.

I also hope you do not think this forward or impertinent of me. My presumption with the gift was most regrettable. I think I now understand a little better why you reacted as you did (not that I deserved any better). I would welcome the opportunity to mend the bridges between us, to start again as friends. However, I can assure you that in this instance I am thinking of nothing more than your family's safety and security. If there is anything I can do to facilitate your wishes in this matter, please do not hesitate to contact me at the above address.

Yours sincerely,

Cameron Ross

Nine

Thorpeness: August 1939

Ross could see her at the far end of the beach, a flash of black hair, then she was gone, hidden by one of the great heaps of pebble and shale that the unseasonable storm had thrown up at the weekend. Today, however, the North Sea was uncommonly glasslike, its usual slate-grey hue softened by the blue of the cloudless sky, and the wind a mere whisper. It was a fine day for a walk along the section of shore between Aldeburgh and Thorpeness, away from the blankets and windbreaks of the holidaying families.

There she was again, scrabbling up to the top of a ridge, her feet sliding as she skittered down the other side. For once they didn't have this section of the beach to themselves. He was aware of small groups of busy men, some of whom paused and glanced over at him, then her, wondering if they were together.

Ross knew what they were up to with their maps, chains, theodolites and transit-compasses. Already there were steel beams lying just offshore, their ugly sharpened snouts poking above the water at low tide. 'No Swimming' signs had sprouted along the foreshore. Some of the seafront houses had been requisitioned, emptied and awaited the arrival of . . . who? Troops, very likely. The wire and the mines couldn't be far behind.

His own house, purchased by the Z Organisation for his 'mission' – as his father called it – was at the southern edge of Thorpeness. It was one of the basic black clapperboard bunga-lows built when the eccentric Ogilvy family ran out of money to create more Mock Tudor representations of what they thought of as Merrye Olde England.

Its simplicity suited Ross just fine, and the neighbours, who were mostly holidaymakers at this time of year, pretty much left him alone. Ross had a routine: a meal once a week at the golf club, a pint in the pub, just to put his face about – and his story about recuperating from an illness picked up abroad – so the locals wouldn't gossip too much about the young chap at number seven and his companion.

Ross looked out to sea, at the fishing boats scurrying back with their catch, wondering if they knew that somewhere beneath them, as well as the Continental telephone cable, there very often lurked a German submarine. Ross knew because once a week his task was to set up the transmitter that Otto Vedder had given him and to send his reports out across the ocean. Except he wasn't the usual kind of spy, because everything he sent had been written by Claude Dansey and his father. He supposed he was what they called a double agent.

In return for this treacherous work, Vedder had given him the document that had resulted in Draper's murder. Disappoint-ingly, the piece of paper from the cigar tube had turned out to be an indecipherable scrawl of numbers, a formula of some sort, that he had passed across to his father. Apparently the boffins had had no luck deciphering it either. When they did, he hoped it would be worth all this.

She reached him at last, panting hard, and he bent down to ruffle her silky coat. Bess responded with a wet lick to his face. He threw a stick for the retriever and watched her scamper after it.

He wondered what had become of Uli. She had never replied to his letters, so he assumed she was still in Germany, with her father, trying to weather the storm. Did she ever think about him? He hoped that she was all right, and not fallen foul of the persecutions he had read about. Above all, he wanted her safe and well.

Ross took the stick from the dog's wet jaws and struck out once more for Aldeburgh, where he would buy some fish for his supper. And something for Bess.

In the brittle cold of early morning, the fresh-faced crew of U-40 stood in three lines on the wharf next to the sleek shape of the newly painted boat. Their captain mounted a small podium in front of them, his back to their new home. Prinz had shaved and was in his best dress uniform. Erich felt his stomach heave at the sight of the boat.

In training he had experienced six days at sea in U-6, one of the oldest submarines in the fleet. A hundred and forty queasy hours, the boat lurching on the surface of a confused, foam-flecked sea, the diesel exhausts spluttering constantly as the waves washed over them. He was pleased to see that on the newer model before him they had positioned the exhausts higher, to avoid the wash. Erich hoped that they'd made the berths bigger, too.

He recalled the alarm bells, the first dive, the litany of instructions over the loudspeaker. *Clear the bridge, open the air-release vents and flood.* Then the ballast tanks started to fill, aft to stern, pointing the nose of the sub downwards. There was a change in sound through the pressure hull as clattering diesels gave way to the hum of electricity, the slap of waves on the deck gradually lessened until there was only the hissing of the tower cutting through the water. Then, a dry-throated silence as the cold steel of the sides appeared to shrink around them.

Twenty-five boys trapped under the sea with the same number of experienced crew, the latter smirking as they saw the reality of U-boat life finally dawn on the young faces. To his shame, he felt the urge to run up the ladder and unscrew the hatch and get to the surface before they got any deeper, before they trimmed off at fifty metres. He could still feel the ache in his fingers from the clenched grip he had kept on an icy pipe, willing himself not to weaken.

Erich shook the memory off. The panic had soon passed, and once he was at his allotted task, then time went quickly. Work, sleep, work, sleep, that was the routine that kept you sane. Being a technician, rather than one of the Lords – the sarcastic term for the regular crew – meant that he had a different cycle from the eight hours' rota (work, sleep, light duties) that most of his companions had. He would do six hours on, six hours off, day in, day out. His fellow *Maschinisten* worked the same shift, but out of phase with him, which meant, like most on board apart from the senior officers, they shared a bunk.

Now these boys would take this gleaming new specimen through the Kiel canal and into the Baltic for sea trials and then strict tactical exercises and an assessment before being allowed out into the major sea lanes. If you failed the tactical exercises, then you had to do it all over again.

Günther Prinz began his speech, his voice sometimes whipped away by the gusting wind, but there was no disguising his pleasure.

Erich could tell that Prinz wouldn't tolerate failing the tacticals. Any delays would mean spending the coming winter locked in the frozen ports of the Baltic. Not a good start for U-40's career.

Erich tried to catch Prinz's words. They seemed to consist of the usual platitudes of service, pride and comradeship. Erich recalled the parting sentiments of Scheer, the commander of the UAS (the School of Anti-Submarine Warfare) at Neustadt. 'Have a long life' had been his final admonishment, delivered in a regretful tone that suggested most of them would have anything but.

Beyond Erich's submarine he could see another, dieseling out of port, the tiny bobble hats of the crew just visible in the conning tower. This one had been in for repair, and the crew by now would have been shaken down, uniforms customised for warmth and comfort. Shadowing it was one of the supply ships that were intended to keep the U-boats on a fighting footing thousands of miles from base.

Erich stared at the bulbous hull of a Type VII. Directly aft of the free flooding space in the bow was the torpedo room, then the chief petty officer's quarters, followed by the junior officers' area, with its permanent mess and work table. Next came the commanding officer's room, the only area of privacy on the entire U-boat – being in charge got you a large curtain to separate you from the officers' wardroom. Just across from the commander's quarters was the sound room, where the *Funker* sent messages and scanned the undersea world with hydrophones. Aft of that was the control room, a mass of red and green valves for flooding or blowing tanks, and switches – many, Erich thought proudly, stamped AEG – with much of the floor space taken up by the twin shafts of the periscopes, the larger sky scope and the attack one. Clustered around the scopes would be the helmsman, two planesmen, navigator, captain and chief engineer.

Next came the accommodation and galley for the Lords, then the engine room with its supercharged MAN diesels, followed by the aft torpedo room and the electrical engines, possibly AEG but sometimes Siemens or Brown-Boveri. This was where Erich would be when they were submerged, an *Elektromaschinist*, tending the double commutators. On the surface Erich would institute the first and most important task of any U-boat – making sure that the batteries were rapidly recharged by one of the diesels, decoupled from its screw.

A cheer went up as Prinz finished his speech. There was to be a tour, followed by celebratory drinks on board for all. The crew broke ranks and began to stream onto the ship. Erich hung back for a second, not quite ready to give up daylight. He felt a slap on his back. It was Becker, the IWO, U-40's first officer.

'Look lively, Hinkel. You don't grab a bunk, you'll be sleeping in the bilges.'

Ulrike Walter watched the tears well in her father's eyes when he saw the upright piano in the corner of the apartment. The carpet stank of cats and the windows were grimy. The traffic in Archway Road produced a constant din of grinding gears and squealing brakes and what warmth there was came from a malodorous paraffin heater. The view from the rear rooms was obscured by clouds of steam from the laundry below, but Fritz Walter only had eyes for the piano.

They had arrived at Southampton with all the right documents and letters of sponsorship – their guarantor, the struggling composer Charles Gorton, had found a much-needed £50 to pay for the privilege of vouching for them.

Even so, Uli had been forced to sign an undertaking that she would only seek work as a domestic cleaner – a 'char' as they called it. Her father was forbidden from working at all until his residence status was confirmed. His savings had been small and, although the house in Berlin was up for sale, they could not depend on that. There were plenty of vacant houses in Berlin for the speculators to choose from.

They had, until now, relied on the kindness of fellow refugees and musicians like Henry Wood and Max Rostal. Now, with two cleaning jobs in the big houses on Highgate Hill, she could afford the rent on this small flat and to repay Gorton for his generosity.

Sometimes Uli felt like taking a bus to Scotland Yard, finding that Inspector Ross and slapping his face for not helping them. Other times, she thought long and hard about why he might not have replied to her three letters. She refused to believe that he could have ignored their plight so callously. That wasn't what she had made of the man at all.

Her father sat down on the stool and ran his fingers over the piano keys, frowning as one produced nothing but the dead thump of wood on wood. He looked up and smiled at her. 'Well, I must know some tunes that don't require a G.' She bit her lip and smiled back. Everything was strange to him in this country, from the light switches, which you had to flick rather than turn, and the direction of the traffic when you crossed the road, to the layer of grime that coated everything.

She took their bags and unpacked, making sure that she used fresh liners in the drawers before laying out his shirts and her blouses. They hadn't left Germany with much. She thought of all the books and music manuscripts left behind, the childhood diaries, the clothes and instruments abandoned or given away in those last few hectic, tortured days.

They were luckier then their Jewish friends, who had been unable to liquidate any of their property, had paid a fortune for the privilege of leaving, and then spent weeks or months sailing from port to port until they could find a country willing to accept them. Only when British Jews said that they would bear the full cost of their immigration and housing were many of the adults allowed into the United Kingdom. The trade unions were worried about the effect on jobs, of course, by the influx of any newcomers, Jews or Gentiles, which was why she'd had to promise to stick to drudgery. Thank God she no longer played the violin – her fingertips were so raw and chafed from the scrubbing powders the English loved so much that it would be agony to press on the strings.

Fritz Walter sighed and looked at his watch. 'Shall we eat out tonight? I noticed a café down the street. Didn't look too bad. And maybe a Dick and Doof film. I saw one advertised.'

Uli hesitated. They should save every *pfennig* they could. There were already rumours about what would happen to German nationals if war was declared. However, she could see he was craving small comforts.

'Of course. Yes, let's celebrate our good fortune.'

'Uli—'

'I'm serious,' she said quickly as she waved her hands around the room. 'It's a start, isn't it? A fresh start?'

'Are you off tomorrow?'

She nodded. 'Mostly. I have to do two hours in the evening for the Baxters—'

'Oh, Uli.'

'But how about we go to The Radio Show at Olympia in the morning? That would be fun—'

He shook his head. He was reluctant to cross London. 'No. You should rest. Tomorrow, I'll do some cleaning here.' He drew a finger across the top of the piano and frowned at the black oval on his skin. 'Who would have thought England would be so . . . grubby?'

'We must also register at the police station, remember. Otherwise someone will report us.'

There was a banging on the door. It was Mrs Herron, their new landlady, her pasty features screwed up in distaste. 'Sorry, miss, but there is one rule I didn't tell you about.'

'Yes?'

'No German. We only speak English in this house.'

'Oh. My father's English isn't so good . . .'

'I'd tell him to make it good as soon as he can, miss. I know what you are. But people can get very funny when they hear accents these days.'

'Yes. Thank you,' said Uli. She closed the door and went back to her father.

'What did she say?'

Uli raised her voice. 'She said we should speak English because if she's listening at the walls it's a waste of time if she can't understand a word we say.'

Fritz Walter chortled. Uli knew that the woman was right. Her father would have to get used to calling Dick and Doof by the English names Laurel and Hardy. Even so, she had to fight a flash of anger. They had been forced out of their country, their home, by a bunch of murderous fanatics and had landed in this place where, in order to survive, they had to deny their roots. They were the good Germans, the real Germans, yet they were the ones facing cultural extinction. It wasn't fair.

To pass the time before they went to eat at the café Uli turned on the wireless. While she waited for it to warm up she explained to her father that they were going to have to

89

adopt a new language as well as a new home. Once the radio's valves were glowing she caught the tail end of the news. The Radio Show at Olympia had been closed earlier than expected. At the time, it seemed little more than an inconvenience, rather than another shadow moving across their lives.

Ten

England: June 1940

'I met Hitler once.'

Ross nearly spluttered his pint of watery beer all over his father. The Colonel smiled, pleased with the response.

'What? When? You never told me this.'

Ross senior took his time answering. They were in the back bar of The Cross Keys in Aldeburgh, sitting in front of a dying fire. Outside a piercing wind seemed to be blowing most of the North Sea down the streets, howling as it went.

'When I went to visit in thirty-four.' Ross put his pint down and watched his father take a sip of whisky. The old man was uncommonly jovial, as if now that war had been well and truly joined he could relax and get on with it.

'I looked in on Brandt, an old chum – or so I thought – when I was in Munich. I took tea with him and he asked me lots of questions about South Africa. Then he asked me to come back the next day as he had a colleague who would be interested in my views on Colonial Germany. All rather puzzling.'

Ross sat enraptured as his father told of the silver tea service that was waiting upon his return and how, instead of his friend, it was Adolf Hitler – the 'colleague' – and two aides who entered the library. Hitler drank from his own pot of coffee and his own cup and nibbled his way through a plate of dry biscuits while he quizzed Ross's father on South-West Africa. It was clear that he was interested in the colony coming back to German control. 'I told him that the Germans there would not welcome any more stiff-necked officials. There was a pause. I thought he was going to storm out. "Stiff-necked?" asked Hitler. "Did you ever meet Governor Zeiss?" I asked. There was another pause. Hitler laughed. Laughed. He got up and proclaimed that Zeiss was, indeed, a stiff-necked Prussian prick. Then Hitler said something that makes my blood run cold every time I think of it.'

Ross waited while his father took a deep breath and said in a German accent: ' "I now understand our files on you a little better, Major" – I was still a major then – "Ross". The thought that Hitler had been reading files on me shook me. You understand? That even back then, the Germans had detailed documents about me, which the Führer had bothered to consult before meeting me. Remember, this was when those idiots at the *Daily Herald* routinely described him as a clown. He was no clown.'

'So, if not a clown, what did you make of him?'

During the Great War Ross's father had interrogated thousands of Germans, and the older man prided himself on being able to sum up anyone quickly and succinctly. He was struggling here. 'I didn't feel the charisma that others have spoken of. And there was no charm. Just a frosty politeness. But good God, the menace coming off the man. Oh, yes. I felt the danger all right.' The Colonel was breathless now, and wheezing. He pointed at Ross's empty glass. 'Another?'

Ross nodded and his father went to the bar. The pub was

almost empty – the government was advising relocation ten miles inland from the southern and eastern coasts – and the few remaining customers were grim-faced, unable to shake off the depression that had settled on the country with the news of France's defeat and the withdrawal from Dunkirk. Bess, curled around his feet, whimpered and moved her back legs, engaged in some dreamy pursuit. Ross scratched her neck, releasing the comforting odour of wet, musty dog.

His father sat back down, slid the pint over and raised his glass. 'Didn't think I'd find a decent malt in this neck of the woods. Damn' sight better than that muck you're drinking.' He sniffed, disapprovingly. 'Is that the dog I can smell? Needs a bath.'

'Dad, did you check? About the Walters?'

'The girl?'

'Well, not just the girl. The father as well.'

The Colonel shook his head. 'I made inquiries at Enemy Alien Registration. Not on the list, boy. A, B or C.' The three letters indicated how much of a risk you were considered by the interviewing tribunals, 'C' being none at all, 'A' being enough to have you locked up. 'She's still in Germany I would expect. Never made it here, anyway.'

Ross felt himself sag. The fact that she had never replied to his letters made him suspect as much. He had destroyed whatever chance there had been for them in an unguarded moment. Perhaps there had been nothing there anyway, perhaps it was just a confused memory from a time when he had been happy – a young boy on an adventure with his father, infatuated by an older woman. Maybe he was projecting all that onto Uli, the daughter. Yet, no matter how many times he played that one over, it simply didn't fit the emotional jigsaw inside him.

'The other thing is . . . I need to get back to the Yard. I hear that the crime rate is rocketing during the blackout. We've had a constable shot dead, lootings—'

His father raised his hand. 'You go back to the Yard, and you'll be straight out again. It's full of Specials and detectives dragged out of retirement. Able-bodied men are at a premium for things other than chasing forged ration books.'

'Well, that's fine by me. Because I am wasting my time here.'

The Colonel frowned. 'How's that?'

'Anybody could do what I am doing. As you said, I am able-bodied – the country needs me on the front line, not stuck in a backwater—'

His father's fingers sank into his arm, making Ross wince with pain. 'What you are doing, the link you have, is vital. You don't understand, do you?'

'I'm a detective inspector, not a spy, no matter what you wish, father.'

'Well, you'd better bloody well get the hang of it. Canaris isn't interested in you as a spy. It's a link to me. To us. Just in case.'

'In case of what?'

'Canaris is not pro-British. But nor is he in any rush to invade.'

'Why?'

'Because he thinks the Americans will come into the war if the Germans try that strategy.'

'Is he right?'

His father shook his head. 'If I knew the answer to that . . .'

'So I'm a glorified telephone line? A go-between, piggy in the middle, passing messages from one lot of spies to another?'

'Yet if the SD or any of the other services trying to get men into this country check you out, you're a greedy, run-of-the-mill traitor.' The Colonel took a deep breath. 'I tell you this in

94

utmost confidence. Canaris is no angel. It was he who persuaded Hitler to support the Fascists in Spain. But nor is he stupid. He thinks the expansion of this war is madness. He tried to warn us about France. He had a route to us through the Vatican. I hear that fellow Heydrich nearly uncovered the contact and it had to be shut down. Nasty piece of work by all accounts, Heydrich. Kills Jews willy-nilly, yet has Jewish blood himself, so they say. Anyway, you were a fall-back method of communication to us. He's not known as the White Fox for nothing.'

'So you knew about the invasion of Belgium and France? Through me?'

'He warned us that it would happen. Told us two dates for invasion, which came and went. Unfortunately my esteemed colleagues at MI6 decided it was all bluff, a ruse to get us off our guard while Hitler struck elsewhere.'

'So the White Fox cried wolf?'

'In a manner of speaking. But I don't believe it was deliberate. Something tells me that Canaris believed that information.'

'So the mundane messages I get . . .' began Ross.

The Colonel smiled. 'Are not always what they seem. Leave it at that.'

Ross pulled his arm free. 'Leave it at that?'

'When will you learn that coppering and espionage are not the same thing?'

'I didn't ask to learn the difference.'

Ross's father sipped his drink. 'For once, do as you are told.'

'For once . . . ? I've spent my life doing what you wanted. Apart from joining the Met, I agree. Fine bit of rebellion that was. It still led me here.'

'Cameron . . .'

Ross could tell by the ice in the voice that his father was about to lose his temper. He didn't want that. Not in public. 'Look, dad.

It's hardly maximising your manpower having me twiddling my thumbs between cryptic messages, no matter how vital you say it is. Don't you need German speakers? Couldn't I do something between transmissions?' The Colonel nodded, accepting the point. 'I could come to London—'

'No. Not London,' Ross's father said quickly. 'How about I send work up to you here? Things that need a grasp of the language. Nothing too hush-hush, of course, but things I'd value your opinion on. Would that help?'

A sop, clearly. 'It'd be a start,' Ross said. *Christ*, he thought: he would willingly jump into a crowd of Hitler Youth to try to save a stranger, tackle any villain in London, but put him up against his father and he crumbled.

'Good. That's settled, then.'

Ross calmed himself down, capping his frustration. He didn't want this to end badly, and he could see his father making the same effort. Eventually Ross asked in a more conciliatory voice: 'Isn't this a very dangerous game to play? For both sides?'

The Colonel leant across and slapped his son's knee. 'Yes. And that's exactly what makes it so much fun.'

Uli ran from the bus stop and up Archway Road to tell her father the news from a meeting of the *Freier Deutscher Kulturbund* in Hampstead. Over coffee and cakes, she had heard the plans for a concert series at Sadler's Wells in Islington. It was not the most salubrious part of town, but the recitals were to feature all the foreign talent now resident in London, organised by Fritz Busch who was artistic director of the Glyndebourne Festival. The week-long programme was to include at least two slots by her father. There would be Strauss, Brahms, Beethoven, Mendelssohn and more.

The tidings would help lift the despondency that they still felt about the humiliating experience of the tribunal, about the new friends who had found themselves in the terrifying, blacked-out halls of Olympia, waiting to be transported God knows where. She and her father, though, had managed to procure a precious 'C' rating, which at least meant they could carry on living and working in London, rather than face 'internment for the duration'.

Uli passed the little grocery by the roundabout where she had registered her ration book, but the queue was no shorter than it had been that morning and she hurried on.

She saw them about two hundred metres away, waiting outside her house, an older sergeant and a young constable. As she approached she unclipped her bag, ready to show her registration card and the classification notice from the tribunal.

She was aware of eyes watching her from the windows across the road. The neighbours knew, or had guessed already, that there was trouble. She reached the doorway and looked into the sergeant's face. 'We came down to let your father pack in peace.'

She shook her head. 'Pack? We . . . We've already had a tribunal. We are C. No threat.' She tried to remember the phrase they had used. 'We're friendly enemy aliens.'

'I'm afraid there has been a change of plan, miss.'

'Collar the lot.'

Uli looked at the young constable who had spoken. 'I beg your pardon?'

He flushed. 'It's what Churchill is meant to have said. "Collar the lot." After France rolled over for your mob, like. All of you have to report to detention centres. No exceptions.'

'*My* mob?' She felt like screaming, but bit her lip.

'I'm sure it's just a temporary thing, miss,' said the sergeant, and she could see that this wasn't a pleasant duty for him. It was clearly a knee-jerk reaction to the fall of France and the Low

Countries. But if England were to fall, wouldn't it be madness to have all the anti-Nazis and Jews locked up in one place for the invaders to find?

'Where are they taking us?' she asked.

'To the police station first, miss.'

'And then?'

He shrugged. Uli shouldered her way past the pair, fighting back the tears.

'I'd travel light, though, miss,' came the sergeant's voice down the hall after her. 'Just in case.'

Eleven

Slowly, U-40 shook itself down into a fighting vessel ready for the great campaign to come. The newly promoted *Herr Kapitänleutnant* Prinz was pushy, ambitious and, like all submariners, intensely superstitious. He had put one of the torpedo technicians ashore in North Africa when the man had proved to be dangerously clumsy, mangling three fingers in the torpedo-hoist chain. Blood on the decks of a U-boat was not a good omen.

To fill the empty post, Erich had been moved from electrical motors, which meant a different sleep-cycle and at least one tower watch a day, something that Prinz insisted on for all but the engine mechanics to help combat claustrophobia. Now Erich was quartered in the *Bugtorpedoraum*, the cramped forward torpedo room, where he and his fellow 'eel' operatives lived like cockroaches in the spaces left by the huge metal bombs, a giant tank of compressed air and its reserve cylinders and trim tanks, where the smell was of feet and the thick grease used to lubricate the weapons. Bunks had to be folded away when not in use, as did tables and chairs. Hammocks were used until at least some of the torpedoes were discharged and they had more room. It explained why those at the business end of the boat were keener than most to find targets.

The boat's first offensive patrol in the winter of 1939 had been a disappointing sail to the Azores. Pickings were slim. Steamers were sighted, but either they were neutral or they zigzagged efficiently. Prinz grew glummer by the day as he faced the prospect of returning to Kiel without flying the pennant indicating tonnage sunk. Worse, news had reached them from BdU, the U-boat command, that U-47 had boldly entered Scapa Flow, the British Navy's impenetrable stronghold, and sunk the *Royal Oak*. Prien, the commander of the boat, was being fêted all over Germany. Prinz retired to his quarters. They all knew what his problem was. An itchy neck. The Old Man wanted a Knight's Cross. The next day the depth rudders started to snarl, and then one jammed completely. It was time to limp home.

The ignominy of returning empty-handed was offset by the tans they'd acquired sunbathing in the warmer climes. On their return Erich was given an intensive course in the attack computer, the rudders were repaired and they took delivery of the next generation of eels, the ones with the new magnetic primers, which, Prinz told them all proudly, were designed to detonate a few metres under a ship's keel, a far more lethal blast than an impact explosion in the side.

Then, days into the second patrol, one of the propellers bent during an emergency dive drill. Another return, this time accompanied by withering sarcasm from *Konteradmiral* Dönitz, C-in-C of submarines, and with the added humiliation of having to stand to attention on the quayside as two other U-boats motored in with fresh flowers stuffed in their air vents and victory flags fluttering from their radio masts. After replacing the suspect props – Prinz insisted that both had to be changed, just to be sure – U-40 had skulked out from Kiel once more, round to their new base at Lorient, on the southern Brittany coast, from where they had struck out a third time, hoping for better luck.

With the e-motors fully charged and both diesels running, the grey North Atlantic spewed over U-40's bow and flecked into their faces as they went in search of vindication. The sea was coming in at an angle, the rollers causing the boat to lurch. Erich gritted his teeth and rode with it, hardly noticing the constant shuffling of his cork-soled boots to adjust his balance. Wind north-east, veering to the right, visibility fair but falling, barometer one thousand and three. Summer warmth was scarce up here. They had left to the sound of a military band, travelling in sunshine, the blue sky merely speckled with thin cloud. By the time they had passed Newcastle somewhere off their port, the greyness had begun to wrap itself around them.

It wasn't cold, exactly, more bone-chillingly damp. It was damp below deck, too, with every surface glistening with permanent condensation caused by the constant changes in air pressure, which meant everything that could rot did so. Very quickly the U-boat took on the signature smell of every other submarine in the German navy – a sodden concoction of mildew, stagnant bilge water and diesel fumes. Even the food tasted of it and by the end of the voyage every man would carry the stink ingrained in his skin.

The constant spray had soaked through the short jacket that Erich was wearing, part of the captured British Army kit redyed and issued to U-boat crews in the weeks after Dunkirk. As soon as he got the opportunity, he would switch back to the leathers and oilskins. They'd been promised a new spray-guard for the bridge while in dock, but it had never materialised. Next time. If there was a next time.

He went back to watching his quadrant, making sure that he

could tell where the sea ended and the sky began. There were three others doing the same with their portion of the ocean around them, while Becker, the IWO – first watch officer – scanned the sky for British bombers. Like their fellow hunters, the submariners' route took them north to Scotland, BdU fearing the mines rumoured to be blocking the passage around the south of Ireland.

They were through the Shetland–Faroes passage now and the sea would start running smoother soon, so the few old hands on board claimed. U-boat Command had them heading for Newfoundland, from where they would form part of a hunting *Rudel*, a pack, patrolling the eastern seaboard of Canada and the United States, the first in a series of choke-holds designed to starve the British into submission.

Erich scratched his scrawny beard – growing one was preferable to shaving in the dishwater from the galley – and thought of Uli. While on leave he had visited her house in Berlin but, as his father had warned him, she was no longer there. She had gone to Britain, the neighbours said, with a sense of shame that he was clearly meant to share. But he couldn't. He wasn't going to write off the years he'd spent waiting for her, simply because she had made a foolish decision, had been unable to see the larger picture, blinded by her devotion to her pig-headed father and his decadent music.

But Britain? It was the country they were sworn to throttle into surrendering. Would she starve too, now that she had thrown her lot in with them? He often daydreamed about going to fetch her and bringing her back to Germany. Would their love be the same? He had changed, after all. Now he was a U-boat man. One of a select band, Dönitz's elite, the *Bootwaffe*, comrades under the sea, as familiar with high explosives as he was with the bars and whorehouses of Kiel and Bremen. Gone was any trace of the pimply boy who'd strutted around in the HJ uniform, spouting other people's half-baked rhetoric as though it was freshly minted. That was some shadowy figure he no longer recognised. So why should he expect her to? It had been one of his reasons for breaking the engagement, because he had soon realised that in the *Bootwaffe* the old Erich would wither away and a new one emerge to take his place, one whom she might not like.

Maybe she herself no longer knew the girl who had fled Germany in its hour of need. Perhaps she regretted it. He wished he could write, but no letter would get through to the enemy. And anyway, postboxes were in short supply in the middle of the Atlantic.

'Smoke.' It was said quietly at first, then repeated. It was Petersen, one of the Lords, and now his voice was urgent. 'Smoke on the port bow!'

Five pairs of binoculars swivelled to the south-west, the sea blurring in their users' vision as they swung back and forth until all focused on the same thin smudge hanging over the horizon. Erich felt jittery as Becker lowered his Zeiss field glasses and smiled. 'Excellent. And this time, let's get ourselves a pennant, boys.'

Ross had to walk well back from the coastline these days. The beach was shrouded in wire fences and studded with mines. There were also some radio masts being erected just inland from the shore, and the way past those was now barred by tight curls of barbed wire and surly sentries.

So he tramped through the heather and gorse, walking his five-mile circuit with Bess, nodding to the crews building the hastily thrown-together pillboxes and tank traps. They had been suspicious of him at first, as everyone was of a young civilian

103

male these days, but now he was just part of the scenery. 'Set my watch by you,' one of the sappers said as he skirted the edge of the wood. At one time Ross would have gone into the trees, found the clearing and sat on the rough-hewn bench that overlooked the stream. But now steely bands of wire were draped across the perimeter and inside it he could just make out camouflage netting, with the hard outline of machinery underneath. Tanks, anti-aircraft guns, he couldn't tell, and it didn't do to stare for too long.

It was ten days since he had seen his father. He had thought long and hard about all that the Colonel had told him. He still felt there was something missing, that he wasn't seeing the big picture, but he guessed that was all part of this lonely profession, the one he had joined by default.

Sometimes Ross became angry about that. He was a DI at Scotland Yard, for God's sake, yet he'd been parked here like some glorified janitor. Was this really the best contribution that he could make to the war effort? He was turning this over in his mind for the thousandth time, walking down the lane to his house, and was almost there before he noticed the small Crossley truck. Sitting behind the wheel was a woman who climbed out when she spotted him. She had blonde hair tightly clipped up, steely blue eyes, and a clear, crisp voice that suggested healthy walks in the country, punting on rivers and gymkhanas. 'Hello, you must be Inspector Ross.'

She saluted smartly, then held her hand out, as if to cover every possibility of etiquette. He took it, noting how small and delicate it felt. 'I'm Ensign Blanchard. Emma Blanchard. I'm a FANY.' The First Aid Nursing Yeomanry was a corps of volunteer women dating back to the Great War. 'Your father sent me.'

'Did he?'

'Yes. I have some documents for you.'

'Erm . . . aren't the FANYs nurses?'

'Oh, FANYs are very adaptable, you know.' Ross avoided her gaze, just in case, and followed her to the rear of the truck. She rolled up a corner of the canvas flap. 'Rather a lot, I'm afraid.'

'My God . . .' There must have been a hundred files, of various shapes, sizes and colours. 'Did he say what I was meant to do?'

'Each one comes with its own instructions.'

She let the flap go and Ross stroked his chin. 'Well, I suppose we had better unload them. How long have I got?'

'Five days.'

'Five . . . He's joking.'

'I don't think your father is the joking kind,' Emma Blanchard said solemnly and he laughed.

'OK, let's get them inside.' Ross climbed onto the tailgate of the truck, rolled up the canvas and tied it, then stepped inside. The pile seemed even more daunting close up. He was beginning to wish he hadn't mentioned his boredom.

'Will you come back in five days for them?'

'No,' she said. 'He wants your comments typed. I'm to do it. He said you'd be too slow. I'm booked in at the Dolphin.' She pointed to indicate the local pub.

'Right.' He handed her the first stack. 'Door's open, just dump them on the floor.' Then, in a condescending tone that he instantly regretted, he asked, 'I don't suppose you speak German, do you?'

She looked back at him and flashed a big smile. 'As a matter of fact, I do.'

Erich took up his battle-station position at the torpedo attack computer and the torpedo control board in the small space between the periscopes immediately underneath the open hatch of the bridge. Icy droplets of sea water came splashing down his neck and he shifted his position while he waited for the dive signal to be given, for the Old Man and the Chief to come sliding down from topside as the valves were opened and the ballast tanks flooded, but it never came. They carried on yawing through the foaming waves. Becker, the IWO, who had executive responsibility for the storage and firing of torpedoes, explained. 'We'll lose her if we submerge. Something they've never solved on these boats. How to make them go fast under water.'

Erich forced himself to relax. You couldn't stay wound up so tightly for hours, and the chases could easily stretch through a whole day and night.

'She's seen us.' A yell from the radio room. It was Schnee, the *Funker*. 'She's signalling a mayday.'

Becker ducked down so that he could see Schnee through the open watertight door that pierced the bulkhead and yelled back. 'Any name?'

Prinz, his face glistening with salt crystals, slid down past them into the control room and stood beside the two planesmen on the starboard side, the dive order on his lips. Lutz, the Chief Engineer, had a hand on each of the pair's shoulders, poised to initiate the sequence. He, too, waited for confirmation of the target.

'She's the SS *Cook Star*.'

There was a frantic rush for the *Lloyd's Register*. 'Got her,' said Becker. 'Built at Cammell Laird, Birkenhead. 1929. Freighter. Four thousand BRT.'

The captain curled his lip. Four thousand tons. Not a big prize. He considered for a moment. 'Surface attack.' He pointed at Erich and the IWO. 'Back on tower watch. I want to make sure she hasn't got company.'

'Yes, *Herr Kaleunt*,' Erich snapped back, using the accepted abbreviation of the captain's rank. Erich's spirits sank. Prinz wanted to save his precious, and expensive, torpedoes for bigger fish across the Atlantic. A sub that wasted its eels on small fry early on patrol was no good to anyone. Erich ran down the corridor, bowling through others without an apology, and grabbed his oilskins, passing the bad news to his comrades in the torpedo room, before heading back for the tower.

Outside, the temperature had dropped alarmingly. An easterly wind was blowing, frothing the tops of the waves, and the sun was sinking somewhere behind its shield of clouds. A curtain of rain was shimmering on the southern horizon. This was why Prinz didn't want to submerge. Soon it would be dismal and dark, and there was every chance that this kill would run without lights and slip away.

The Captain kept the binoculars to his eyes. 'She's zig-zagging. But she's slow,' he said. 'Becker.'

'*Herr Kaleunt?*'

'Is she under military direction?'

Prinz suspected a trap, easy prey to draw them in. The IWO shrugged. 'I don't think so.' He indicated the ocean around them. 'There's nothing else here.'

They could see the darkening shape of the freighter quite clearly now. Prinz made a sudden decision. 'Signal the captain that we intend to sink her. We suggest that the crew take to the lifeboats. Tell him we will wait until they are clear.'

Becker hesitated.

'Which part don't you understand?'

'Sir.'

'Tell the second watch officer to get the gun crew ready. How many shells have we got?'

107

'One hundred and twenty.'

'I want her sunk in six.'

U-40 rocked back as the 88 fired its fourth round, a direct hit on the stern of the *Cook Star*, which already had smoke pouring from its front deck. The shell casings were collected and passed down through the deck hatch. Every one had to be accounted for back at Lorient. The crew hastily reloaded under the direction of the *Zweiter Wachoffizier*, the second watch officer. There were two more shots left if they were to follow the captain's orders to the letter.

Erich turned his binoculars on the three lifeboats pulling to get away from the ship. The mayday had been sent out. The survivors had every chance of being picked up by a friendly ship. The IWO voiced mixed feelings about this. True, Prinz was being chivalrous, playing by the old rules. On the other hand, the war was as much about men as machines, surely? Erich agreed, but didn't want to contemplate the alternative.

The fifth shot penetrated the side of the *Cook Star*. There was a pause and then a sharp detonation. A column of smoke and flame spurted up through the deck hatches, sending debris spinning high into the night sky. There was a low rumble and the ship keeled slightly. The sea around the ship flared as spilled oil ignited. She was going down.

'One more for luck,' shouted Prinz.

Now he too sought out the hapless British sailors with his field glasses. He held his gaze on them for a moment, missing the impact of the final 88 shell, which was lost in the fresh wave of detonations racking the stricken freighter.

'Take us alongside the English captain's boat,' said Prinz. 'And break out the brandy from my quarters. The least we can do is give the poor man a drink.'

★　★　★

Ross decided to tackle the files according to colour. Green ones were POW transcripts, red were statements taken from downed *Luftwaffe* pilots and blue were interrogations of enemy aliens with a poor command of English. It was clearly, he realised as he read the first one, going to be more chaff than wheat.

He established a workstation on the kitchen table, positioning Emma on one side, himself on the other. It was gone eleven by the time they finally started. Ross had decided on a system of reports for each document. He would summarise the contents and then pass them to Emma for typing. It soon became apparent that she could type faster than he could summarise.

'Ensign, you have signed the Official Secrets Act, I assume?' he asked after an hour.

'Signed it? Colonel Ross all but tattooed it on my backside.'

Ross didn't ask for proof. 'Well, do you see any problem in you doing the summaries as well? I've got an old typewriter, we can then type them up together.'

She shook her head. 'Well, I'm not qualified—'

Ross laughed. 'That makes two of us. The blind leading the blonde.'

Emma laughed. 'How about I do some and you double-check, see if you approve?'

He nodded. 'I'll make some tea.'

He couldn't fault her. He read while he sipped the scalding drink and admired her conciseness. Truth be told, she was better than him – he was finding it hard to shake the verbosity of police reports.

They carried on through the afternoon, until his eyes started to smart and he became aware of a new noise. Bess, whimpering.

'Shall we go for a walk?'

Neither of them needed asking twice.

The day smelt of early summer and the lanes were suffused with a soft yellow light. He looked up and studied the blurred white lines etched across the sky, the fading calligraphy of the day's aerial combat. Over to the north he could see a ragged flight of Hurricanes passing back over the coast, one of them trailing thin smoke. He suddenly felt guilty, locked up in a cottage with a pretty girl for the last six or seven hours, while men younger than him risked and lost their lives.

'What are you thinking?'

'That I should be doing something more concrete than reading reports.'

As they passed the Signalman pub he slipped the lead back onto a panting Bess and asked: 'Look, shall we have a drink and perhaps a sandwich before we get back to it? The landlord here usually manages to round up something half-reasonable. Cheese and,' he whispered, as if speaking of contraband, 'maybe even the odd pickled onion.'

She wrinkled her nose. 'Not if we are going back to working in the same room, please.'

'No. Fair enough.'

'But the drink and the cheese. Yes, please.'

Twelve

'Depth?'

'Fifty metres . . . fifty-five . . . sixty.'

'We have a leak in the pressure hull in the battery compartment.'

'Bad?'

'Bad enough.'

'Get it plugged. Make sure the protective covers are over the batteries.' If sea water mixed with acid in the electromagnetic cells then the hull would fill with chlorine gas. Lethal and corrosive, it would be the end of them. 'Chief, break out the rebreathers, just in case. Depth?'

'Sixty-five.'

'How many ships?'

'Three sets of screws. All closing.'

'Keep taking her down. All hands to the bow.' There was a stampede of feet. Altering the angle of descent using human ballast was a textbook way of accelerating the rate of dive. Erich sweated at his station, hanging on as the nose dipped further, listening to the exchanges between the Captain, Chief, IWO, navigator, the two planesmen and the hydrophone operator.

111

They'd been spotted silhouetted against the twilight sky an hour after sinking the SS *Cook Star*. For two hours they'd been hanging quietly at thirty-five metres, hoping that the searchers would miss them, but now the enemy were on to them. They could clearly hear the grinding of screws bouncing through their hull.

'Depth?'

'Ninety metres!' It was deep, but still safe.

'How's the leak?'

'It's closed itself.'

'All stop. Level her off at a hundred metres.' This was around the recommended dive limit.

'Both planes zero. Levelling off,' said the Chief.

'What's that damn' noise?'

'Bearing in the propeller shaft.'

'Can't you quieten it down? It's like a drum signal.'

A fine spray at high pressure started to enter a few feet away from Erich. He pressed himself back against the metal, out of the way.

'Boat balanced,' the Chief said, scanning the bank of depth and pressure indicators.

'Now quiet. Let's listen—'

Forty-eight men held their breath, letting it out through their noses in a slow stream, wondering if the others could hear the jackhammer of their hearts.

The thunder started as a low grumble and grew louder, until the world blurred and the boat shuddered under impact after impact, punched in a series of sharp jabs from stem to stern, tossing the crew's heads around until Erich thought his neck was going to snap. He had an urge to scream as more depth charges sank through the water and detonated around the craft.

There was another round of explosions and one of the crew

head-butted a valve, his nose splaying open, flicking blood around the control room. A bulb blew, and the lights died. Flashlights cut through the blackness.

'Fuse!' shouted the second engineer.

The boat shook again as more charges pounded it. Erich felt as if hot needles were being driven into his eardrums. His eyes refused to focus as the pressure waves hit again and again.

'Damn!' Prinz banged his periscope.

The boat settled down, creaking and groaning as she did so. The main lights blinked on.

'They are turning round.' The hydrophone operator started to spin the small wheel in front of him, changing the direction of the detector located on the top deck.

'Relax,' said the IWO. 'Those wabos are fifty metres above us. Just hope they don't reset—'

Becker's teeth chattered the words as another salvo blasted its shock waves through the water. U-40 bucked under the impact, flexing as if she were about to break her back, and the boat filled with the sound of smashing glass and crockery.

'We are going to have to run,' spat the Captain. He crouched down, the better to see the hydrophone operator. 'Do they have us or are they guessing?'

'Guessing.' But his voice suggested that he wasn't certain.

'Take her to one hundred and fifty metres,' Prinz said. 'Then creep speed. Due south.' *Schleichfahrt*, creep speed, meant running the electrical motors at around 100 r.p.m., with a speed of less than three knots. It was the quietest form of propulsion, but agonisingly slow.

'Bow fifteen, stern five,' said the Chief. 'Full left rudder.'

They felt the boat turn and the nose dip, taking it down. New noises rippled through the hull as the plates twisted and settled.

113

There were many rumours and legends about how deep you could go in a Type VII. Two hundred metres, some said, two hundred and fifty, others claimed. However, once you discovered where the limit was, you weren't coming back to boast about it. He hoped that the Chief had checked the welds and the plate bolts properly at Kiel.

'One-forty.'

'Start to bring her out.' The boat responded to the planesmen, but sluggishly, as if unwilling to stop until it reached the ocean floor.

'Planes zero. Boat balanced.'

Erich knew that letting the crew of the *Cook Star* abandon their ship had been a nice gesture of old-fashioned gallantry, but it had kept them in the area for too long. The British had been able to get three ships, at least one of them a destroyer armed with *Wasserbomben* – wabos – on their tail.

Prinz crouched again. 'Phones?'

'He's doing another run, I think. Turning. He's going to pass to the stern.'

'Brace.'

Erich held on to a pipe, aware that he could taste blood in his mouth. He had bitten through his lower lip. The churning of screws seemed to swell through the boat, bouncing off the glistening internal surfaces.

'Wabos in the water.'

Erich pictured the cylinders falling through the water, the pressure triggers bulging until . . .

It sounded like summer thunder in the mountains, a distant warning, something happening elsewhere, to someone else. The shock waves hit the boat, but from the stern, causing a pitching that soon passed. There was the mass sound of breath being exhaled. *Lucky*, thought Erich, as he relaxed his grip on the pipe.

Everyone down here always claimed that a year in a submariner's life was worth five of any other sailor's. Now he knew why.

They surfaced the next morning in the first red-tinged light of day, cautiously bleeding the compressed air into the ballast tanks to bring U-40 up gingerly, the pressure pain in the crew's ears compensated for by the welcome blast of fresh oxygen that the ventilators sucked into the interior.

Erich listened as the diesels started up and one was decoupled to charge the electrical motors. The damage report was long, but nothing too serious. Some of the vents were buckled, which meant the tanks couldn't be blown quickly for an emergency surface. A cover had been ripped from one of the diesel exhausts, which also had a pressure deformation in it. That would need repairing before they could dive again. They had been fortunate. And now the crew of U-40 knew that they could survive a depth-charge attack.

While the repairs were being carried out a short-wave message came from BdU instructing them that they were to stay hunting on this side of the Atlantic. Two big convoys had made it past the East Coast *Rudel* already. U-40 was to position herself at the top of Ireland, and sink them in sight and smell of their home.

Prinz interrupted the gramophone records that Schnee was playing and addressed the crew while the five-man watch in the tower scanned their quadrants, more alert than ever. From now on, he said, no warnings for their targets, no abandoning ship for the targets' crews. He didn't mention the brandy, but he didn't have to. The old type of war that their fathers had fought was over. From now on, it would be the unexpected torpedo from an unseen enemy who would then slip away and be swallowed by the ocean. There was no cheering, only a resigned acceptance of what they had to do next time they found their prey.

Thirteen

June–July 1940

Fritz Walter had guessed, even while they were packing, that the authorities were not going to keep the men and the women together. As they piled their clothes onto the bed, Uli's father had pressed a small leather journal into her hands and told her to read it when things calmed down. She had slipped it into her handbag and helped Fritz pack his battered suitcase one more time, making sure that he had warm clothing. It might be summer in London, but who knew where they might end up?

Uli thought of the book, still unopened, bouncing against her thigh as the ancient bus wheezed into the entrance of the racecourse. She had little idea where they were. All identifying marks and signs had been removed from the course itself, but once inside there were the white poles with their pointed markers from the pre-war meetings, directing visitors to members' enclosures and somewhere called Tattersalls. Presumably knowing which category of racegoer you were would be of little help to invading German parachutists.

The parts of the course that hadn't been ploughed up were

dotted with ugly brown tents of some considerable vintage. Barbed wire was slung around the perimeter, and tin-helmeted soldiers seemed to be everywhere, trying to instil some order into the gaggle of hapless civilians who stood around their new quarters, bewildered.

An open-air altar had been set out at one end of the course and a group of men of all ages with skullcaps or handkerchiefs over their heads swayed back and forth in prayer. A small number of soldiers and other internees stood watching. A few were sneering. Uli spotted what had been scrawled on one of the bivouacs. 'No Jews.' *Even here*, she thought.

There was a long, straggling queue of men waiting for processing outside a building marked Tote. Uli's bus slid past them towards a smaller white wooden building at the far end of the main straight. Here a red double-decker bus was disgorging women, many red-eyed from crying, others with the vacant expression of the shocked and bereaved and a few of them fiercely defiant, fixing their minders with vengeful stares. Some had children in their arms or clutching their skirts, and Uli realised that the women were being further segregated. Her group was clearly made up of those not encumbered by children.

Another small knot of childless women was being escorted by the soldiers to a long, low building, where piles of dirty hay had been pitched outside the doors. It was the stables. They were to be housed in horse stalls.

Uli turned to the young Austrian girl next to her, who was sobbing.

'What's your name?'

'Hilda.'

'Don't worry, Hilda. It won't be for long.'

Uli thought of her interrogation at the police station, the

117

reclassification from 'C' to 'B' – a 'doubtful case' – because, it seems, they had discovered Uncle Otto. How had the British police made that link? He wasn't a real uncle, after all. She hoped that her father would be all right. He had put on a brave show, but she knew that he felt angry and humiliated.

She mainly felt grubby, in need of a decent shower or bath. But, looking at the stables, she guessed that wouldn't be forth-coming for some time.

'Do you really think so?' asked Hilda, finally.

The doors of the old bus swished open and a man's ruddy face appeared. He shouted an instruction that they were to get off and be registered once more, this time at the building labelled The Jockey Club.

Uli smiled with a confidence that she no longer felt. 'I'm certain. You'll be back home within a few weeks.' They both tried to ignore a derisive snort from an older woman nearby. Hilda took Uli's hand and squeezed it as they shuffled along the central aisle to the exit.

Ross found himself growing impatient for Emma's visits. He enjoyed her company. He was still making the transmissions to some distant spot, no longer submarines, probably a base in Holland. He received back a variety of increasingly odd questions which, he now assumed, contained within them a coded subtext, as did his answers.

He wondered if his father was telling him the whole truth. Uli would know, he thought. He wished she was here. At least, he did most of the time. He heard the growl and grind of Emma's truck coming down the back lane, and he placed the kettle on the gas, checked his new haircut and stepped outside as noncha-lantly as he could.

There were fewer files on this occasion, Emma's third visit, so they could take their time with the digests. As usual they worked in silence, except for the occasional question to the other about the exact meaning of a word or phrase.

'What's TVA?' she asked after a couple of hours.

'Sorry?'

'This chap says he worked at TVA.'

'Didn't the interrogator ask him to explain?'

She rustled some papers. 'No.'

'Typical.' One thing had become clear from reading the documents: the standard of questioning by the British was wildly variable. Some – ex-policemen or serving intelligence officers – were excellent. With others, he could almost see the circles that were being run round them. There needed to be some kind of standardisation. He would mention it in his report.

'Who was the subject?'

'Sailor. Picked up in the Channel.'

'Put it to one side. I'll take a look later.'

Emma nodded and picked up another file. Thirty minutes passed to the accompaniment of the constant shuffling of paper and sharpening of pencils.

'Aren't you rather young?'

'I beg your pardon?' Ross asked, taken aback. 'Rather young for what?'

'A police inspector.'

'Ah. Yes. Well, some thought so. Because I had a university degree, one in foreign languages at that, I was allowed to enter the Rapid Advancement Programme.'

'Meaning?'

'Meaning the regulars who have been busy clocking up their service years and diligently taking their exams resented me something rotten.' 'Gentstables,' they called them, anyone who

119

had a decent education before entering the police training college. He'd had his fair share of ribbing over the years about his accent and his tastes in everything from alcohol (preferring wine to beer with meals was tantamount to an admission of homosexuality) to books.

'Yes, I can see that. Do you miss it? Scotland Yard? Blue lamps, whistles, car chases and all that.'

Ross leaned back in his chair, ran a hand through the stubble of his shorn hair and shrugged. 'Well, I didn't get to do too many car chases.' He thought of the blazingly fast Railtons that the Flying Squad used. 'Not enough, really. I did miss it. Yes, I think I still do. It was more satisfying somehow. Than this. More important.'

'You don't know that.'

'You agreed with me before.'

'We agreed that the Colonel must know what he is doing. You don't know you are wasting your time.' Ross wondered if Emma had spoken to his father about his attitude, had been told to gee him along, then dismissed the thought.

'No. But let's call it an educated guess.'

They took Bess for a walk, ate a meal of some suspect sausages that she had brought from London – unrationed, bangers were often more bread than meat – with a couple of potatoes and the carrots he'd foraged in the village. As everywhere, though, real onions were impossible to find. Afterwards they resumed work, but around nine he finally said, 'Well, I think that's it. My eyes feel like they've got half of Blackpool Beach in them. I'll walk you back to the Dolphin.'

'There's no need to do that.'

'No, I insist, can't have you saying I'm not a gentleman.'

'No, what I meant was . . . well, I haven't bothered to book into the Dolphin this time.'

'Oh.' Ross felt himself flushing. He did have a spare room, after all, it just hadn't occurred to him that it might be in any way seemly for Emma to take it, and the bed was cold and dank, the sheets musty.

He explained this to her, and her face broke into a broad grin as she watched him redden and fumble his words. 'What I mean is, a girl could grow old waiting for you to ask, Inspector. I wondered if I could share your bed tonight.'

Uli was billeted in the stables for a week before they were moved again, by slow, overcrowded train this time. The next stop was a half-completed housing estate outside Liverpool, prosperous-looking flat-fronted homes, strangely naked without their garden fences and, in some cases, a full complement of windows. Most of the wire-wrapped estate held men; 'female aliens' were assigned just one street and a close, and Uli and Hilda found themselves sharing a room with five others, including *Frau* Menkel, the older woman from the bus.

There was, however, proper bedding, and running water – not hot, but you couldn't expect everything – and *Frau* Menkel set up a washing rota. Uli was fairly certain that *Frau* Menkel was, if not a Nazi, at least a sympathiser. She caught her looking at Hilda and the other Jews in a way that suggested she would rather not share a room.

The first task assigned by the soldiers – none in the first flush of youth – who guarded them was to organise a blackout. The guards were at a loss about what they should use, so for several hours skirts were unpicked, headscarves unfolded and old newspapers scavenged to seal the light in. The odd precious blanket had to be used as well.

There were no radios and the newspapers were months old, but people gossiped with absolute conviction about the German parachutists who had landed in Oxfordshire and were marching on London, about the destruction of the Royal Air Force, about the British capital having been reduced to smouldering ruins by the *Luftwaffe* in savage retaliation for the pinprick raids on the Ruhr. *Frau* Menkel seemed to be enjoying the rumours, and she wasn't alone. As they settled down for the night Uli heard faint singing from one of the male households. She strained her ears. *'Wenn das Judenblut vom Messer spritzt.'* When the Jewish blood spurts from our knives.

Uli found the notebook that her father had given her and turned it towards the spluttering light of her candle. It was written in his old-fashioned Gothic hand, dense and hard to decipher. It began sixteen years previously. The sentences were short, but were usually followed by a single word or phrase with an exclamation mark. *Thrilled! Wonderful! So proud!* It was his record of her violin-playing, from the first awful scrapes and scratches until days before her accident. As she read it, her wrists began to throb, and pains shot up her arms. *Excellent! A privilege to hear!*

For the first time since she had been taken, Uli rolled over and began to cry, letting tears of shame and guilt soak the thin sacking of her pillow. She never knew, had never realised how he had felt. Such pride and passion leaping off the page. Yet she hadn't been able to detect any of it in her father's face at the time. So much for her damned Duchenne gift. Or perhaps she hadn't been looking hard enough.

She felt a hand on her shoulder and turned, expecting to see Hilda, but it was *Frau* Menkel kneeling next to her, her silver-streaked blonde hair tied into braids, ready for bed. 'Shush. Shush. All will be well, I promise you.'

But Uli suspected that she and the *Frau* had a very different idea of what constituted everything being well.

Fourteen

Robin 'Tin-Eye' Stephens turned from the window overlooking the common to face Colonel Ross. 'Well?' he demanded.

The Colonel stared back at him, making sure that he engaged with Stephens's good eye, the one without the monocle. Officially, Ross outranked Stephens, but expecting Stephens to defer to authority was a waste of time. In fact, the less you did to upset the famously short-fused Captain the better. Ross had read Stephens's reaction to complaints about internees' treatment by men under his command. 'The motives of the complainers are invariably foul. Most of them are degenerates, most of them come diseased from V.D., they are pathological liars and the value of their Christian oath is therefore doubtful.' It was, thought Ross, rather harsh but then Stephens was anything but soft – on his men, his prisoners, or himself.

'I'm not sure—'

'Look, Ross, I know you are probably tied up at Broadway Buildings these days, but the fact remains, you were the best interrogator of men we had in the last war. You speak German, know their minds.' He thumped the slim volume on his desk. 'You wrote the book, goddamn it, and we still use it. At the moment we have to grill internees at Scotland Yard, the Oratory, Wandsworth, wherever they find us a space. My idea is to use this place, Latchmere, solely for the purpose of interrogation, with a crack team, whom I would like you to help train. For crying out loud, man, the whole system is a shambles at the moment. Documents in the four corners of England, no central cross-checking of statements. Most of them written up and left to gather dust.'

Ross knew that only too well.

'Your boys get to question some of the captives, don't they?'

Ross shrugged. 'A handful.'

'Not what I heard. Anyway, here we'd be, the central repository of foreign spies, reporting everything to Five—'

'With copies to MI6.'

A pause. 'Copies to Six of anything deemed relevant.'

'Agreed.'

'I shall have to put it to Swinton, of course.'

'Of course.'

This was the new committee set up by Churchill and headed by Lord Swinton, whose task was to integrate the various security services. All involved agreed that it was needed, even if all dreaded its findings. They were dealing with hard-fought-for spheres of interest, after all, and the blood on the walls was hardly dry in some areas. Stephens relaxed now that he had Ross on the line. All he had to do was reel him in.

'Whisky?'

Ross nodded and waited while Stephens slopped out two tumblers of Glenmorangie.

'Cheers.' Stephens adjusted his monocle. 'You know, I realise that many people think the rounding-up of all the German refugees was . . .'

'Draconian,' suggested Colonel Ross. He had read the reports on the Huyton camp, its poor feeding and sleeping arrangements, the houses full of invalids and the sick who were clearly no threat to anyone.

'Draconian. Quite,' said Stephens. 'But the fact is this. We know, by and large, that somewhere in there we have all of the enemy's agents. We've had to inconvenience a lot of innocent people to do it, perhaps, but the fact remains: we can be certain we've collared the lot.'

'It's possible. There might be the odd sympathetic Fenian at large—'

'And Welsh Nationalist. True. But basically, it's done. If you were Canaris or one of the others, what would your next move be?'

Ross didn't hesitate. 'To infiltrate a fresh batch.'

'Of course. So, any day now, we can expect them, by boat and by plane. Our job will be to catch them and . . .'

'And?'

'Use them.'

'Not hang them?'

'Well, eventually, maybe. But for each one we hang, they'll send another. The trick here will be to . . .' He flicked the pages of the document on his desk. 'What was the phrase you used to use? Ah, yes . . . "to turn the weapon back on the enemy".'

Ross knew he was flattering him by quoting from his twenty-year-old pamphlet on techniques learnt in the Great War. 'When do you envisage this infiltration beginning?' he asked.

Stephens smiled. 'Yesterday. The police picked up a rather interesting Swede, reported because of his strange accent, and he had with him a parachute, a radio transmitter, two hundred pounds in notes, maps, a pistol and an atrocious identity card. He claims he's come looking for his sweetheart.'

Ross felt a shudder of excitement. 'What have you done with him?'

125

'He's downstairs in the cells. Not said a word apart from that stupid story.'

The Colonel drained his glass and let the liquid warm his gullet. 'Keep him in solitary for another two days. I have a few things to wind up over at SIS. I assume I can pick my own assistants? Good. Then . . .' He clapped his hands together. 'The silly bugger is all mine.'

Uli had only just discovered the name of the half-completed housing estate – Huyton – before they were told that they would be moving again the next morning. The women's enclosure was to be redesignated for those with children, although it hardly seemed sanitary enough. She was glad to leave. The ordinary soldiers guarding them were kind enough – in fact, within a few days a black market supplied by the army had sprouted – but the ignorance of the officers, even the so-called intelligence officers, beggared belief. 'What I don't understand,' she had heard one of them say to a colleague, in a booming voice that assumed she and the others around her were deaf, 'is why so many of these Jews in here have sided with Hitler.' She had bristled at such gross stupidity.

It was just after six in the morning when they were roused. Breakfast was, as always, a dollop of pale yellow watery powdered egg and a scrap of bread. Afterwards she repacked her case, having taken down the dress she had donated to the blackout and placed her father's journal on top. She knew from rereading its contents with a less emotional eye that she had been too hard on her father. She didn't think what she'd read in his face was wrong, exactly, just her interpretation of it. Whether she would have reached the top or not, her musicianship had given him great pleasure. She thought that he'd have been satisfied with nothing less than the best. Now, it seemed, he'd have been satisfied with whatever she'd have been able to give.

Uli wondered where Fritz was right now, hoping, praying that conditions were better for him. He was an old, broken man. She had heard rumours about the decaying rat-infested cotton mills they were using in some parts of the North.

She wondered yet again if there was any way of getting in touch with that policeman, Ross, to see if he could help her father. But she'd clearly offended him deeply, despite trekking out to Tempelhof to put things right and giving him her favourite piece of Mörike poetry. If only she'd taken that perfume.

'You all right?'

It was *Frau* Menkel.

'Yes. Yes, thank you.' She quickly wiped her eyes.

The older woman grabbed her hand and pulled her close. 'I feel sorry for you. No, really. You could say I deserve this.'

'Nobody deserves this, *Frau* Menkel.'

'My husband was a steward on the *Bremen*. He has been a courier for the *Abwehr* since 1935. He has an Iron Cross. He was ordered to settle here, as a refugee from the Führer, in Portsmouth in 1938, which we did. His job was to log naval movements.'

'What happened to him?'

'Interned. God knows where. My point is they have every right to do this to me. But you . . . no.'

Before Uli could answer, they heard the ancient buses start up, coughing like smokers in the morning, until the engines settled down to a lumpen clatter.

'Letsbeavinyou!' came the cry.

Uli smiled at her companions. 'Here we go again.'

Ross slipped out of the house just as a late dawn was breaking, its tardiness thanks to the double summer time that the country now observed. Much of the sky was still rich with fast-fading stars as he walked down the lane towards the Mere, Bess at his heels. He was thinking about Emma, who was still asleep in his bed, and about how much he had enjoyed the previous evening with her. She had an attitude to life that he envied, a desire to grab each moment and relish it. He should try and do the same, he decided, rather than brooding on what might have been.

Yet among the elation were grits of suspicion. Could he detect the hand of his father in all this? He dismissed it. Emma was a nice girl, not one to lie back for King, Country or Colonel Ross. As she had said to him, these were unusual times.

He reached the Mere and walked its perimeter, past the village call box, watching the growing sun redden the eddies that played across the water's surface.

He thought of Uli. Had he betrayed her by sleeping with Emma? No – surely, by constantly summoning up Uli's face and figure, it was Emma he was being beastly to. The fading memory of one kiss at an airport, that was all he shared with Uli, whereas Emma was here, real flesh and blood. And they had another day's work to do together. He felt butterflies in his stomach. This would not change their working relationship, he promised himself, then laughed. *As if.*

Ross looked up and saw a brace of fighters climbing into the east, the leading edge of their wings aflame from the sun. They were Boulton Paul Defiants, judging by the gun-turret bulge behind the cockpit, and he cursed the war that was sending up his inexperienced countrymen against the fast and lethal Me 109s of the *Luftwaffe* with their combat-blooded pilots.

Yet this same war, the one that had so effectively isolated him from Uli, had also given him Emma. Surely that was something

128

to be grateful for. In fact, compared to those aircrews searching the skies over the Channel for incoming bandits, he had an awful lot to thank the Lord for.

Ross bent, picked up a stone and tossed it into the Mere, watching the ripples, and set off on the rest of his walk.

Fifteen

A hostile crowd, mostly of women, arms folded and faces set hard, were waiting at the Liverpool dock gates as the old buses wheezed to a halt. Uli kept a tight grip on Hilda's arm as they stepped down and she was aware of the others crowding round, forming into a protective cluster.

She looked around. The whole world here seemed to have been sandbagged – vast walls of them reared in front of every building. Barrage balloons floated over the docks, their cables singing in the wind, and the air smelled of oil and smoke. Other buses and trucks had already arrived, and new ones chuffed in every few minutes. Drinkers from a pub on the corner opposite, its frosted windows thick with anti-blast tape, huddled in the doorway, watching the sport. It was not yet eight in the morning, but these men were already sinking their foul-looking pints with enthusiasm.

A junior officer directed Uli's group towards the gates while his men, bayonets at the ready, pushed them into a ragged line two abreast. They shuffled towards the wharfs.

Someone yelled from the pub in an accent so thick that Uli couldn't make it out. Except for the word 'Nazi', pronounced with a long, soft 'z'.

The women at the gate started chanting insults. 'Go on, fuck off,' cried one of the more ruddy-faced ones, waving an arm the size of a ham. 'Fuck off back to Germany.'

Then the spitting began, a hail of sputum, flying over the women. Hilda shrieked and Uli could feel it hitting her hair.

'You filthy who-ers.'

'Hitler-lovers.'

'I hope they rip the tits off yer.'

Frau Menkel turned around and spat straight into the face of her nearest attacker. The yelling turned to baying. Uli grabbed Hilda to her chest as the kicking started and a sharp stone glanced off her head. *Frau* Menkel had a cut above one eye and there were screams coming from the front. One of the locals held up a fistful of dark hair, waving it victoriously.

The two gunshots caused an alarmed squawking of startled seagulls. Cordite smoke drifted over a stunned crowd. Slowly the attackers withdrew. The column of internees and guards marched through the dock gates and into the grimy complex of warehouses without further incident.

'Eh, Tommy?' came the shout from behind. 'Make sure you give your German bitch one from me, eh?' The locals dissolved into laughter.

'I've been told to ground you,' said Hermann Goering as he sipped his coffee. He watched Heydrich's lips twitch in irritation. The SS man ran a hand through his thinning blond hair. *At least he looks something like our idea of an Aryan*, thought Goering, even if popular rumour suggested otherwise.

'By who?'

A military band began to tune up in the street below. Goering signalled for the window to be closed. They were in the *Reichsmarschall*'s private dining room on the first floor of the

131

House of Flyers, a convenient lunch venue close to the Air Ministry and across the street from Heydrich's Berlin head-quarters.

'By the Führer.'

Now Heydrich flushed with anger. 'What did he say?'

'He said that he did not want his head of Reich Security flitting about the sky simply to add a pilot's badge to his cap. You are too valuable.'

Goering winced as Heydrich spooned several sugars into his coffee. 'That's nonsense,' Heydrich grunted eventually.

'You should be flattered that he cares.'

Heydrich had been flying in secret for months. It was one of the reasons why he was newly enamoured of the air force. He didn't trust the army, which he felt hampered the essential work of his *Einsatzgruppen* in the occupied territories, and he had loathed the navy ever since it had drummed him out for getting a young girl pregnant and refusing to marry her back in the 1920s. Finally the *SS-Gruppenführer* said: 'Who told him? Who told him about my flying?'

'The same person who suggested that you might have Jewish blood.'

It could only be Canaris.

'That is a damned lie!'

'I know,' said Goering, holding up a placating hand.

Heydrich, however, clearly felt the need to explain himself. 'My grandmother remarried after my grandfather died. To a Protestant locksmith called Süss.'

'Unfortunate name.' *The Jew Süss* was a popular anti-Semitic film of a few years previously.

'But not Jewish. I can prove it.'

'You don't have to. You just have to shut him up.'

'I will.'

Goering nodded. He wouldn't put it past Heydrich to neutralise Canaris. The White Fox might be cunning, but Heydrich's men could arrive at your house at dawn and an hour later you could find yourself hanging from a meat hook. Explanation to follow as soon as they had thought of one. But Canaris still had the Führer's respect, so such action was out of the question. For the moment.

'Do you know what he said at the General Staff Meeting?' asked Goering. Heydrich shook his head. 'I quote: "We are up against an enemy that is well armed, with high morale and an excellent air force." I could have strangled him. I am just back from France. I have seen what we can do to their excellent air force.'

'On what does he base this? The *Daily Express*? Is he guessing or does he have many agents there reporting the state of morale?'

'Do you?'

Heydrich laughed. 'That would be against the Ten Commandments.' This was the informal agreement that split intelligence-gathering responsibilities between the SD, the Reich Security Service, and the *Abwehr*. Canaris could send in agents abroad; Heydrich and his master Himmler were meant to operate only within the new Greater Reich, although they could make use of intelligence from German sympathisers, as opposed to infiltrated spies, in other spheres. As an attempt to clarify demarcation lines, it had been an overcomplicated failure from day one.

'Do you?' repeated Goering.

'Not enough,' Heydrich admitted. 'Not yet. Mainly people drawing up arrest lists for when we invade. Although the British seem to have done much of our work for us.'

'Well, Canaris hasn't got many in place either. But this one might interest you.' Goering slid a piece of paper across the table. 'He seems to swear by this source.'

Heydrich glanced down. It was a tightly typed report, with various parts scratched out, including its origin. Goering's personal spy network, the *Forschungsamt*, was meant to have been rolled into his bodyguard or subsumed into *Luftwaffe* intelligence. Maybe the deletions hid the fact that it still existed. Heydrich made a mental note to check.

The document consisted of intercepted transmissions from an agent identified as Cigar who, according to the dates, had been operating in England since before the war. Which made him remarkable, whoever he was. 'How do you know about this, *Reichsmarschall*?'

Goering tapped the side of his nose and the fleshy folds in his face wobbled. 'Never you mind.'

'Where is this Cigar?'

'On the coast. Suffolk. What about – how would you have put it in the navy – a shot across Canaris's bows? Let him know that we know what he is up to.'

Heydrich considered for a moment. The band outside struck up again. It was a parade by the Berlin police to celebrate the victories of their *Wehrmacht* and *Waffen-SS* comrades. If Germany carried on expanding, the police would soon be formed into SS Battalions, perhaps to help subdue Great Britain.

'Short of hauling his backside in front of a People's Court and having him strung up for defeatism, I can think of nothing that would give me more pleasure.'

'What are you flying?' asked Goering.

'A 109.' Heydrich was pleased at the surprise on the fat man's face. A Messerschmitt 109 was not an easy plane to handle for a relative novice, particularly on take-off and landing. Heydrich had had the fighter plane repainted in SD insignia, with prominent SS flashes on the nose. One day, he thought, the security services should have their own air force. He'd want a fighter with more room in the cockpit than the Messerschmitt, though.

'I recently inspected *Jagdgeschwader 26* in Calais,' said Goering. 'The *Hauptmann* of *Staffel 1* is a personal friend. I flew with his father in the last war.' He scribbled the name down and passed it to Heydrich.

'What about this talk of grounding me?'

A lusty chorus of 'We March Against England' drifted up from the street and Goering smiled as he wiped his lips with a napkin. 'My dear Reinhard, this lunch never took place. I'm far too busy crushing England to worry about such things.'

The Mersey wind cut down the estuary and swirled around the quaysides. Uli and her group stood shivering at one end of a ragged concrete pier, just along from the large ship with its newly painted grey hull. The *City of Hamilton*, it was called, and the entryway at the end of the gangplank swallowed column after column of men. Some were, like Uli and her companions, confused, demoralised civilians, wondering what fate was doing to them. Others were clearly German soldiers or airmen. You could spot these because they teased their captors, and laughed among themselves. They thought this was just a temporary measure, that soon their comrades would secure their release by sweeping through these islands.

Frau Menkel had overheard that a boat had broken down in the harbour of somewhere called Douglas. Others knew that Douglas was on the Isle of Man, halfway between Liverpool and Ireland, so that was their most likely destination. Uli hoped that her father would be sent there too.

Her feet began to ache from standing around, but by midday

there was no sign of their packet steamer. They stacked up their luggage to make seats and took turns in sitting down, while soldiers kept a half-hearted watch over them. Soup was issued by the young captain. It was thin and lukewarm, but they all drank it gratefully, except *Frau* Menkel, who complained bitterly. 'How can they win this war? They can't even handle *us* properly, a bunch of women and girls.'

'*Frau* Menkel.' It was Hilda. 'Please shut up about who will win the war. You have no more idea than I have.'

Frau Menkel shook her head, but Uli ruffled the girl's hair. She could see that she was toughening up, no longer jumping at shadows. They were all going to have to adapt to this quickly.

'What the bloody hell is going on here? What are these women doing cluttering up the quayside?'

It was a new officer, more senior than the captain.

'It seems that the *Rushen Castle* has broken down, sir. It's blocking the harbour at Douglas. Repairs are under way.'

'Well, these women can't stay here. I've got seven hundred Eyeties on their way from Wharf Mills. Their ship is already in the pool. Look, there must be room on that.' He pointed at the looming hulk of the SS *City of Hamilton*, whose funnels were starting to bleed increasing quantities of smoke.

'That's mainly carrying men, sir.'

'Well, find them a deck to themselves or a ballroom or something. Come on, come on. Our job is to get them off this island, man. Not book them a first-class passage.'

'Sir,' said the captain.

Within minutes they had been told to grab their cases and were being hustled towards the sagging gangplank. 'Where is it going?' Uli asked one of the soldiers. He shook his head, and she knew he was telling the truth.

'I'll tell you one thing,' said *Frau* Menkel as she looked up at the towering sides of the *City of Hamilton* and its numerous rows of portholes. 'This doesn't look like any Isle of Man steam packet to me.' For once, everyone agreed with her.

Sir John Anderson, the Home Secretary, stood and addressed the House, occasionally glancing down at the paper he held in his hand. 'In answer to the Right Honourable Member for West Derby's question, I do now have the number of females who have been interned under the Control of Aliens powers. It amounts to some three thousand, nine hundred and forty-eight persons. The majority are aged between sixteen and sixty, although some have chosen to take their children with them.' He cleared his throat. 'Three hundred of those had no choice in the matter, being pregnant.' A ripple of laughter. 'They will, by and large, be moved to the Isle of Man, there being no place on these islands sufficiently removed from military installations that we can relax knowing that potential enemies are in the vicinity. They will be held in their own all-female camps on the island, the majority of them in the Port Erin area, until the cessation of hostilities or until they are no longer deemed a risk to these islands. I hope that answers the Right Honourable Member's question.'

Sixteen

It came to Ross in the middle of the night, jerking him awake. Next to him Emma stirred.

'Wassamatter?' she mumbled as he eased himself out of bed.

'Nothing. Go back to sleep.' He took a step, hesitated, turned back and kissed her temple. 'Keep my side warm.' She smiled and snuggled back down. Ross slipped on his dressing gown and went down the creaking, uneven stairs to the living room, shivering. The green dial of the clock glowed softly on the mantelpiece. A good two hours until dawn. He checked the blackout curtains before switching on the light and putting on the kettle. Bess ambled through from her basket and licked his knee.

'Not now, girl. Down.'

Bess slid onto the floor, one lazy eye watching him as he arranged the mug of tea, a notepad, pencils, a German–English dictionary, an atlas and the small pile of documents that they had put aside for further consideration.

It was in the sixth file down. He could see why it had confused Emma. It was a rambling mix of English and German and much of the latter had been copied down phonetically. The man had been a Petty Officer on a submarine that had been rammed in the Channel. It was his first patrol. Before that he had worked for various government establishments in northern Germany. Including TVA at Eckernförde.

Ross picked up the atlas and scanned the Schleswig-Holstein area, and quickly located the town, a dot around thirty miles north-west of Kiel. Ross leapt up and searched the shelf next to the fireplace, cluttered with debris and half-read books. Eventually he found Draper's cigar tube and laughed bitterly to himself. Draper and his schoolboy sense of humour. Ross resolved to call his increasingly elusive father the next day and tell him what he thought his dead spy had discovered.

On board the *City of Hamilton* things rapidly degenerated into chaos. There were uniformed soldiers to guard the women but the squaddies spent most of their time arguing with the ship's regular crew, who seemed ill-disposed towards this invasion of their vessel by German flotsam. The corridors gradually filled with bags and bodies and raised voices. In the midst of the pandemonium, an irascible sergeant grabbed Uli's arm.

'Where've you come from?'

'London,' she said, unsure of what answer he wanted.

'Jesus. Just what we need. You, you and you. Come with me. Bring your gear. Look lively.'

The sergeant ushered ten of them down a chipped, narrow staircase to the lower decks, where every surface vibrated and the noise of the engines grew louder. He pushed open a metal door and hustled them inside. It was a storeroom of some kind, stacked high with boxes. There was a film of greasy water on the floor, a strong smell of fuel and no porthole.

'What's this?' asked *Frau* Menkel, turning up her nose.

The sergeant looked her up and down and said, 'Home, missus.'

Pallets had been laid out on the floor between the boxes, each with a grubby mattress.

'You have to be joking,' said *Frau* Menkel.

'Do I look like I'm joking?'

Uli had to admit that he didn't.

'Don't touch those!' the *Frau* shouted.

Hilda had been about to flop onto her mattress.

'I'll bet those have scabies. Don't you think?' She turned back to the sergeant.

'Like I give a toss. Make the most of it—'

'We'd like to see your commanding officer,' said Uli.

'Yes. So would I.' The sergeant grinned and slammed the door shut. A silence descended and the women felt the chatter of the engines through the soles of their feet.

'Criminals,' said *Frau* Menkel.

'How do you mean?' asked one of the other women.

'Those soldiers, they should be at the front line. Men their age. Yet here they are, guarding the likes of us. I'll bet they are all troublemakers and scum of the earth.'

Uli looked round, already feeling sick from the stench. 'We can't stand up all day.'

'Does anybody smoke?' asked *Frau* Menkel.

'I do,' said a mousy girl who began fishing in her handbag. 'Here.'

'No, not the cigarettes, the matches. Come on, come on.'

Frau Menkel organised the stacking of the mattresses into a pile, ripped some of the cardboard from the boxes and managed to get a blaze going on one corner of the top layer. They leapt back in shock as it crackled fiercely.

'My God, you are going to suffocate us!' came a protest.

Uli wedged open the door, using one of the wooden packing cases. 'Good girl,' said *Frau* Menkel, then, to the rest of them: 'Show some courage.'

Now the smoke was rolling out into the corridor, rising to the ceiling and billowing towards the bulkheads. Uli's eyes began to smart.

The sergeant came bowling along the deck, yelling. 'What the bloody hell is going on—' He skidded into the doorway, unable to believe his eyes. He pointed at *Frau* Menkel. 'What are you doing?'

'Fumigating this place.'

The sergeant disappeared and came back with a red fire extinguisher, which he banged twice on the floor and directed at the flames. Hilda quickly stepped in the way and screamed as the jet of water punched into her stomach.

'For cryin' out loud—'

'Sergeant Dowler?'

They all turned to the officer at the door, a young lieutenant.

'Put that fire out at once.' He waved his clipboard at Hilda. 'Stand aside, you stupid girl.' He waited while the mattresses were reduced to a sodden and blackened mess. 'Explanation.'

'This bedding is unsuitable. These quarters are unacceptable.'

'Are they? And I suppose you were hoping for something from the Hamburg–America line?' The young officer turned to the sergeant. 'Well?'

''S all we have, sir,' muttered Dowler. 'Didn't expect no women.'

'No. Still, I have just come from C deck where a number of the German male prisoners seem to have rather a nice set-up in a lounge. I suggest an exchange of quarters is in order.'

'Sir, those men are prisoners of war.'

The lieutenant lowered his voice. 'I said, I suggest an

exchange of quarters is in order.'

'Yes, sir.' Dowler shuffled off.

Frau Menkel gave Uli a large wink. *This*, thought Uli, her spirits lifting, *is going to be all about small victories.*

There was the distant cry of a steam whistle. The vibration of the engines deepened and the walls seemed to creak ominously. The deck gave a lurch under them. They had cast off.

Erich pulled down his leathers and examined himself in the feeble light in the cubicle. There were specks of blood matted into his pubic hair. He quickly re-dressed and barged out of the forward head.

His face burning red, he pushed through the crowded torpedo room, past the officers' quarters, where the lunch table was being folded away, and found Schnee, the *Funker*, who doubled as the medical officer.

'Have you got a minute?' he asked.

'Boat balanced!' It was the Chief from the control room. They had surfaced, looking for something decent to sink.

Schnee didn't look up and carried on transmitting a message to BdU.

'Schnee—'

'You've got crabs.'

'How do you know?'

'I had my first case last night. Three this morning, another six before lunch. I think you make it a dozen all told. Forty-odd men, all sharing bunks, it only takes one to dip his prick in the wrong place the night before you leave.'

Erich sagged against the doorframe. He was sure his girl had been clean. Or at least, as sure as you could be. 'What do I do?'

'One, stay out of Prinz's way. He's furious. He will not cut short this voyage just because some of you are crawling shitbags.

His words, not mine. Two, the head at the rear has been set aside for treatment. You'll paint yourself with Kuprex. Although there isn't that much of it on board. And I doubt if BdU will send a Condor out just because you are all lousy.'

'I hope you get them, Schnee,' Erich said, resisting the urge to scratch once more.

'At this rate, I'm bound to.' Schnee put on his headphones. 'Which is why I always bring my own supply of Kuprex.'

The klaxon sounded. 'Battle stations. Battle stations.'

Erich's heart juddered as the adrenalin kicked into his bloodstream. Water gurgled loudly into the tanks. They were diving again.

Erich squeezed himself into his position at the attack computer, his throat dry. Around him was the usual cacophony of call and response as depth was marked off and readiness checked. He glanced at the time, trying to imagine what the captain was seeing through the periscope. The sun must be setting by now. He felt as detached from the outside world as he did from the rest of the war. He vaguely recalled some sort of passion about the armed struggle before he joined the *Bootwaffe*, but that had been stripped away to one simple prayer: *Please, God, let me live through this.*

Prinz yelled, his voice thick. 'She's running without navigation lights. Anything else on the phones?'

'No. Not unless there is a water-layer problem.'

Prinz pulled away from the attack periscope and bent down to look at the hydrophone operator in the next compartment. Prinz knew as well as anyone that different densities in the sea played havoc with sound location. 'Don't give me water layers. Give me a simple answer. Is there an escort?'

'No, *Herr Kaleunt*,' came the reply, before the operator

hedged his bets: 'No sign of one.'

Prinz beckoned over the IWO. 'Take a look.'

Becker pressed his eyes to the grubby rubber cups. 'Troop carrier.'

'Possibly.'

'She's a converted liner of some type. She could be fifteen thousand tons.' There was a hint of greed in Becker's voice.

'Nationality?' Prinz didn't want to sink a neutral American ship and provoke an incident.

'If she was neutral she'd be running with lights and a clear flag. She's a legitimate target. But we're trailing her.'

Prinz nodded. They needed to be in a good position, lying ahead of her, letting her steam by for a broadside. He turned and consulted the charts for the area, scribbling figures on a scrap of paper. He drew a line using a set square and tapped it. The navigator at his shoulder grunted his agreement. 'Chief, give me seven and a half knots.'

The Chief telegraphed it through to the *Maschinisten*. U-40 could run for only thirty minutes at that kind of speed. The alternative was to surface and use the diesels, but clearly Prinz wanted to take no chances of maydays being sent. This time it would be a clean kill.

There was little to see from the two tiny portholes in the new cabin, just a monotonous vista of endless waves, blue turning to grey as the light slowly faded. Still, they had achieved the small victory that Uli had hoped for. It was two decks up from the storeroom, had a bird's-eye maple bar at one end – without any stock, unfortunately – red velveteen banquettes around the wall and mattresses of a relatively recent vintage laid on real folding beds. The women set about making it as comfortable as possible. It reminded Uli of one of the BdM camps, all girls mucking in and giggling at the rigours of life under canvas.

A crewman came in, closed and then taped up the porthole, making sure that it was lightproof. 'Can you tell us where we are going?' asked Uli.

The sailor was about forty and seemed to be less aggressive, more assured than the soldiers. 'What, has nobody told you?'

They all shook their heads.

'Well . . . no, no, I can't,' he said. 'Not my place, really, luv.'

'Please,' said Uli.

'Yes, please,' asked Hilda. 'Is it the Isle of Man?'

'Isle of Man? We passed that ages ago. No, we're going to go up and turn left. That's the best I can do. Look, there'll be food in the mess in about half an hour. And there is a door opposite marked "Crew Only".' He lowered his voice. 'Ignore that. It's a washroom. Nobody else'll use it.'

They thanked him. As he left, Uli, who had been trying to remember her geography, touched his shoulder. 'It's Canada, isn't it?'

The sailor hesitated. 'You didn't hear it from me.'

Canada. The other side of the world, she thought. The other side of a U-boat-infested Atlantic.

Erich watched Prinz and the navigator pore over the charts on the table, plotting the expected route of their quarry and using the precious few minutes of extra power to take a chance on cutting across some shallows. Prinz's face was grim, displaying his determination to get this over with, to blood his boat properly once and for all.

'That's about it,' said the Chief. 'You'll be left with nothing in reserve until we recharge.'

'One more minute,' said Prinz, just as a juddering ran

through the boat, along with a high-pitched whine. The Captain threw out a hand to steady himself and said calmly, 'Take her up. Now.'

The planesmen altered the angle of attack to lift the nose and they felt the stern snag on something. 'Get some air in, Chief. Not too much.'

'Blow one, three, both tanks.' The scraping stopped as she lifted free of the sea bed or whatever outcrop was snatching at her. Erich realised that he hadn't been breathing.

'Let's keep her going up slowly. I want to take a look.'

U-40 gently rose to periscope depth and Prinz grabbed the handles. The electric motors whirred and whined as the shaft rotated. 'Can you hear her?' he barked at the hydrophone operator.

'No, sir, seem to have lost contact.'

'How long ago?'

'Just . . . she was there just before we hit the bottom. Faint, but she was there. It could be a temperature band at this depth.'

Prinz spun the periscope column, searching through the increasing gloom, hoping for a shadow, a silhouette, a patch of black against the still-light western sky. He stopped and went back half a degree. The outline of a ship lifted from the background. 'Got her. Yes, that's her. We're well ahead of her. She's coming up fast, though. We should get her before the last of the light goes.'

Schnee suddenly shouted. '*Herr Kaleunt.* She's sent a message to the Irish coastguard.'

'Did she identify herself?'

'Sir.'

'What's she called?' asked Prinz, reaching for the *Lloyd's Register*.

'The *City of Hamilton*, sir.'

146

Seventeen

The food served in the *City of Hamilton*'s old ballroom wasn't too bad, not by the standards the women had grown used to. Afterwards, Uli took her turn in the washroom and enjoyed the hot water while it lasted. She scrubbed her hair vigorously with the shampoo donated by one of her companions, rinsing out every last trace of the spittle from the hostile crowd at the dock gates. By the time she returned to their quarters, she almost felt happy.

Sergeant Dowler and his men came about half an hour later.

They'd been drinking. There were seven of them, their uniforms unbuttoned to reveal grey undergarments, jostling their way into the women's sleeping area and spreading out into a semicircle. One of them held a rifle. Uli could hear commotion from all over the ship. Something awful was happening.

'Now, now, ladies, we don't want any trouble. Just give us what we want and we'll be on our way.'

Uli reached across and took Hilda's hand, pulling the shaking girl towards her.

'How dare you!' spat *Frau* Menkel.

'Shut it, you!' shrieked Dowler, waving a finger in her face. 'There's no namby-pamby officer to save you now. Here – look at this.' He grabbed her arm and showed his companions the shining ring on her finger. 'Do someone some real damage with that. A dangerous weapon. Have to confiscate that for the duration of the voyage.'

Uli watched as three of them wrestled a screaming *Frau* Menkel down while the ring was worked over her knuckle. Uli squeezed Hilda's hand. They were men of the Pioneer Corps and it slowly dawned on Uli that they weren't here to rape them. They were here to rob them.

'We will have to check all these cases for suspicious objects,' said Dowler, breathless from the tussle. 'Then they'll be returned to you.'

'Common thieves,' sobbed *Frau* Menkel.

It was when one of the soldiers lifted up her suitcase that Uli thought of the notebook inside. Angrily, she leapt up and made a grab for the handle, slamming her shoulder against the man. She dug her fingernails into his wrists to try and release his grip. He yelped, and the last thing she saw was the tattooed back of his hand flying towards her face.

'Flood tubes one to four!'

'Tubes one to four flooding.'

'Watch your depth, Chief.'

'Aye, sir. Bow planes up two, stern down two.'

'Flooding complete.'

'I want eels one and three,' said Prinz, 'with a three-degree spread. Have you input the magnetic variation?'

Eric had to compensate for the changes in the Earth's magnetic field if the torpedo wasn't to detonate prematurely. 'Yes, Captain,' he said.

'Keep her steady, Chief. Range sixteen hundred metres. Open valve caps.'

'Valve caps open.'

'Torpedoes to run at four-zero.' This to Erich again.

'Aye, sir.'

Erich's fingers hovered over the controls. He noticed with satisfaction that they weren't shaking.

'Fire torpedoes.'

There was a heartbeat's pause, then a shudder in the ship.

'Tube one fired.'

A second and a half later. 'Tube two fired.'

'Torpedoes running.'

Half a dozen stop watches clicked on and the red hands began sweeping towards the moment of detonation.

'Follow my finger. There. Can you see it. Back and forth?'

Uli's world came slowly into focus. There was a man looking down at her, a kindly man by the sound of him, bald and with a toothbrush moustache. She tried to do what he said but it hurt her eyes just to turn them. She blinked and surveyed the room.

The other women were one step back, all looking very concerned. Hilda had been crying. *Frau* Menkel looked nothing short of murderous.

'I'm Doctor Moravec, Ulrike. I think you are fine. No concussion.' He turned to the others. 'But keep an eye on her tonight. Call me if you have any concern. I am on B deck.' He laughed. 'First class, of course. The purser knows where I am.'

'What happened? Did they take my case?' asked Uli.

'They took all our cases,' said Hilda.

'We'll get them back tomorrow,' said *Frau* Menkel. There was the sound of breaking glass and laughter from somewhere outside. 'Minus any valuables, of course.'

Uli tried to sit up. 'What about – what about their officers?'

The doctor patted her arm. 'Stay where you are. I think most of the officers are more scared of them than we are. I heard some of them protest but . . . It was like a mutiny.' Uli suddenly looked distressed. 'Whatever is the matter?'

Something icy had gripped Uli's heart and she shivered. 'Oh, God. I think something terrible is going to happen.'

'What do you mean?' Dr Moravec asked again, cupping a hand to her forehead. 'Ulrike, what is it? What's happening?'

'Fifty, fifty-one, fifty-two.'

Erich counted the seconds. Prinz had the second set of hydrophones to his ear, listening to the torpedoes run, the sound of their propellers swamping all else. A minute and fifteen seconds. A minute and a half. Two minutes. Too long. Eric saw the torpedo mate hovering in the corridor, biting his lip. Prinz threw down the headset and stormed back into the control room.

'They've missed.'

Prinz looked for someone to blame, and his eyes settled on Erich. The IWO saw what was coming and said: 'All the information was put in correctly, sir.'

Prinz knew that Becker was right. There had been rumours about dud torpedoes, but BdU had blamed everything from poor storage to incompetent crew, never the eels themselves. At twenty-five thousand marks apiece, how could they possibly be at fault?

U-40 would have to go again. The Chief read Prinz's mind. 'We'll never keep up with her underwater. There isn't much left in the cells.'

Prinz called Becker over. 'What do you think? Was it the eels?'

'I hear even Prien has suffered failure.' Becker could see at once that was the wrong thing to say. Bringing up the Knight's Cross winner at a time like this was hardly diplomatic. 'And others. I thought they had cured it.'

'We surface, shadow that ship throughout the night, recharging the cells, and sink her tomorrow.' Prinz pointed at Erich. 'I want the rest of the eels reset for impact detonation. Surface fire. Can you do that?'

'Sir.'

Prinz slammed a fist down onto the metal chart table. 'The *City of Hamilton* is not getting away.'

Cameron Ross waited until he was put through by the operator and pressed button A of the village's only call box, which was down by the Mere. The money fell through with a hollow clatter and the line connected. 'Father? It's me. Cameron.'

'What bloody time is it?'

'Well, it's early, dad.' Ross looked out at a sky that was only now showing the first signs of dawn. Rabbits were skittering on the grass near the water, between the freshly excavated molehills. 'But you're never there these days. I wanted to be sure of catching you. Is it OK to speak on this line?'

'Be circumspect, my boy, whichever line you are speaking on.'

'Draper.'

'Who?'

Ross thought he heard something in the background at the other end. Another person? His father in bed with someone? He stifled a laugh at the thought of it. 'Draper. The man in Berlin. Imperial Chemical Industries.'

'Yes, yes, what about him?'

'I know what he was up to. Have you shown those figures to any naval experts?'

'Yes, of course I have. Draper was in Kiel.'

'Yes, I think he was at or made contact with *Torpedoversuchsan-stalt*. TVA. The torpedo-research people. You yourself said he had a silly sense of humour. It was the shape of the cigar tube that was the clue—'

There was a sigh at the other end. 'Yes, we know.'

'What?'

'A copy of the document went to all departments. Including a few naval chaps. They figured it out about six weeks ago.'

'You knew and didn't think to mention it to me?'

His father's tone became less aggressive. 'Point is, the information was good and bad.'

'In what way?'

'It suggested that the depth-gauging equipment on the torpedoes was faulty. They ran too deep. Which meant that the hulls of the target didn't dip the magnetic primer properly – look, I shouldn't be saying this over the phone.'

'No, I understand. But why is that bad?'

'Because it is absolutely no bloody use to us. What good does it do us? Don't worry if you see torpedo wakes running straight for you, chaps, they'll probably miss anyway? That's scant consolation, isn't it? And we're certain that they've fixed it by now – they've had two years, for God's sake. Look, we'll do this face to face sometime in the next few days. Truth is, I might have another job for you.'

Ross felt a twinge. Would that mean losing Emma? 'I thought this was really important.'

'It is. You'll have to do both. Split your time. How's the girl?'

'Fine. Great help. Picked up on TVA, in fact.'

'Good. Now, if you don't mind, I'm going to go back to bed.'

Ross put the phone down, feeling deflated. *Well, bugger him.* He'd had enough. He stepped out of the box, untied Bess from

152

the railing, and decided to take the long way back to give himself time to think.

The Pioneer Corps squaddies had woken with bad heads and foul tempers. Their haul of suitcases and bundles was stacked on the rear deck, once the games area, of the *City of Hamilton*. A dozen of them were going through the contents of the cases, stripping out anything that might have resale value.

'Look at this. A whole suitcase full of books,' said a disappointed Geordie lad.

'What kind of books?' asked Sergeant Dowler.

'I dunno. German books. Look.'

A sample volume was handed across. Dowler flipped through it. The text was all so much gobbledegook to him and would have been even if it hadn't been printed like something from medieval days. He stood and spun the book into the air, watching it disappear into the foaming wake of the ship.

'Is that the best you can do?' asked the Geordie. 'Here, watch.' He flung another volume, its delicate spine breaking and pages scattering, fluttering among the escort of gulls. 'Damn.'

The contest lasted until the Geordie picked up a whole case and tried to heave it overboard. But it hit the flagpole and burst open, spilling clothes and letters into the water.

Dowler reached forward to the case in front of him and took the small leather notebook that rested on top of the contents. He flicked through it. It was just a diary of some sort and he arced his arm back and watched the notebook fly with the wind, bounce on the waves and disappear. 'I win,' he said. 'Now. Let's add up what we got here.'

'Boat ready to surface, Captain.'

'Surface her, then.'

'Blow tanks.'

There was a deep rumble.

'Boat surfaced. Conning-tower hatch clear.'

'Opening hatch.'

'Equalise pressure!'

Erich waited until the full complement were up there before asking, 'Permission to enter bridge.'

'Come on up.'

He climbed the aluminium ladder and emerged into the chill early-morning air, watching a sea that had the merest swell on it. All five of the watch were searching for the *City of Hamilton*. They'd been forced to dive when they'd seen the lights of a warship, and it had cost them precious time. 'Well?'

'Torpedoes ready for surface fire, sir,' said Erich. 'Impact primers have been checked and double-checked. They won't fail this time.'

'I have her,' Becker said. 'We're astern, just to her port. But look. That headland.' He pointed at a misty finger of Ireland jutting out into the sea. The *City of Hamilton* had been hugging the shore all night, the Captain knowing that it protected her from submarines on one flank at least. 'She's going to head east on a dog-leg. If we cut across her wake and run north-east, she'll turn onto us.'

Prinz nodded. It was worth a try. 'Get the navigator up here for a sighting. All ahead full. I want the second officer and gun crew standing by.' He looked at Erich. 'Just in case those eels are all rubbish.'

U-40 began to buck as she leapt forward, slicing through the green water. Prinz drummed his fingers impatiently on the metal side of the tower. They were crossing the old liner's wake now, although the traces had long since dissipated.

'Debris on the port bow,' said Becker.

'Ignore it.'

'It's . . . well, there's clothes. Suitcases. Look. It must be from the ship.'

Prinz looked at him, irritated. 'We're going to be spotted soon.'

'Let me get a crew down there to scoop it. Five minutes. It'll help in the war diary. We'll know what we've sunk.'

Prinz said reluctantly: 'All stop. Two minutes, Becker.'

Prinz watched his quarry recede through his binoculars, seething. As soon as a few items had been caught by the nets and poles, he ordered the debris taken below and full power again. The boat vibrated along its whole length as the Chief made sure that the diesels gave all they had.

'Think they've seen us?' one of the watch asked.

'No sign of it,' said Prinz. 'No zigzag, no radio. Must be keeping a terrible watch.'

'She's turning. I'm going down to periscope depth. Dive. Clear the bridge.'

They switched to the electrical motors for the final approach as the *City of Hamilton* began its turn out towards the open sea. Prinz would bring U-40 up at the last moment, revealing himself just in time for the kill.

'Flood tubes one to four.'

'One to four flooded.'

'Ready to blow tanks, Chief.'

'Ready, Captain.'

'Depth?'

'Six metres.'

'Range two thousand metres. I want four torpedoes. Five-degree spread. To run at four-five.'

'Sir.'

'Open caps.'

'Sir.' It was Becker this time.

'What?'

Prinz snapped round at his IWO. Becker was pale and shaking.

'Torpedoes ready to run,' said Erich, fingers poised.

'Look, these books.' He held up the soggy pages. 'German. This shirt. It's made in Saxony.'

'Torpedoes ready to run.'

'Ready to blow tanks.'

'What are you saying?' said Prinz, knowing full well what Becker was trying to communicate.

'Everything that came in was German. There are Germans on that ship.'

'Torpedoes ready to run.' Erich's throat felt scratchy. The Chief kept a hand on the blow-valve control, but said nothing.

'Germans?'

'Prisoners of war, probably. Being taken to Canada.'

Prinz grabbed the shirt from Becker and examined the label before throwing it to the floor. 'It could be bluff, Becker. They might have seen us and be playing games.'

'They might be.' Becker thought of U-57, which had accidentally sunk one of its own U-boat tenders in bad weather.

'Damn it, man . . .' Prinz didn't want to believe, didn't want to lose the kill.

'Torpedoes ready to run.'

The words hung in the air. Erich waited the recommended thirty seconds. 'Torp—'

'I know!'

Becker winked at Erich, telling him to stop the reminders now.

After another half-minute Prinz snarled: 'Close caps. Blow tubes one to four. Right full rudder. Two-thirds ahead.'

Prinz pointed at Becker as if it were his fault that the ship contained their fellow countrymen. 'We are not going back to Lorient with any torpedoes left on board. Get me a refuelling rendezvous now. We stay out till we have sunk ships or get sunk ourselves.' He left the control room and they all heard the swish of the curtain being pulled across his quarters.

'My jewellery's gone.'

'What about my books?'

'Where is my case?'

The bleary-eyed soldiers had dumped the belongings into the women's room and left, leaving them to sort out the mess. Uli, exhausted from a fitful night wrestling with unknown terrors, flipped open her brown case. The journal had gone. She felt her eyes sting.

Hilda came over when she saw her. 'Are you all right? Something missing?'

Uli nodded, her lower lip tucked between her teeth. 'A book.'

'Well, absolutely everything of mine has gone—'

The tears came and Uli pulled Hilda close to her. 'You can borrow some of my things.'

'And mine,' said the mousy girl.

'See? It'll be OK.'

'Oh, no, it won't.' It was *Frau* Menkel, hands on hips. 'When you have recovered, I would like you to make a list of all the items that you have lost. All of you.'

'What's the use?' asked Hilda.

'What's the use? Well, perhaps you think this sort of behaviour is officially sanctioned. Well, I tell you, such barbarity would never be tolerated from soldiers of the Fatherland. I doubt that even the British expect their men to behave in such a way. No, we start a list of every breach of common decency.'

There was a knock at the door and it opened. 'Uh, hello. Sorry to disturb you. My name is Baum. A few of us have been talking and we think we may be on this ship quite some time and, well, there's not much to do to exercise the mind—'

'Get on with it,' snapped *Frau* Menkel.

'The thing is, we've found one or two people who know something about Canada – its size, people and so on, and there is a lecture at three o'clock in the theatre. The captain has agreed and has said he'll lay on tea afterwards and I just wanted to say, any of you who wish to attend are more than welcome.'

Uli looked at Hilda. 'Well, if we are going to socialise, we'd better find you something to wear.'

Ross took Bess up the incline to the brackish finger-like pond that ran parallel with the sea. From here he could see his house, the shop, part of the Mere and the beach, but not the shoreline where the sea hissed softly, exhausted, over the stones. That was masked by the ridges of pebbles and the ugly concrete defences. He saw a cigarette flare down in the shadows of a bunkhouse.

That telephone conversation with his father had been the last straw. Ross had risked his neck in Berlin, his emotions were in turmoil – how and why he wasn't sure, but Uli had certainly managed it in the course of two days – and no one had even had the courtesy to tell him what they had discovered about Draper.

He wasn't a spy, he reminded himself, he was a copper, a good one, and as such he ought to get back to it. The tales of looting during the bombing raids that had appeared in the papers were bad enough, but it also seemed that the blackout could be a very handy thing for the criminally minded. Robberies and murders were at record levels, too.

Ross's mind was made up. He'd return to London. Uli was gone for ever, he was sure. He'd settle for the warm openness of

Emma, rather than the sweet mysteries of the German girl, and make the most of it. He had begun the walk down the hill, tossing a stick for Bess to get her to run ahead of him, when he heard the buzz of an aero engine. It was hard to know where it was coming from at first, the sound seeming to swirl around him. It was when the noise suddenly burst over him like a wave that he knew why. The plane had come in incredibly low, skimming the calm ocean surface, and he felt the prop wash of the 109 smack into him as it flashed by and began to climb. The crosses on the side were clearly visible, as was the *Sigrune*, the SS marking, on the engine nacelle.

The Messerschmitt gained height and began to turn, just as Ross heard another plane approaching. This time it was a pencil-thin twin-engined Dornier, its elegant silver fuselage glinting, coming in higher than the smaller fighter had. He looked around for intercepting RAF Spitfires or Hurricanes, but there were none. Ross refused to believe what he was seeing.

Four black cylinders slid out from the Dornier's belly, propelled forward briefly by the momentum of the plane, gave a little wobble, and then began to descend, straight and true.

'No.'

Like a fool he ran down the hill, towards the bombs, arms windmilling as if he could catch the explosives and hurl them away, aware at the same time that the 109 had turned and was coming back towards him.

'Bess! Emma!'

The dog looked back at him, puzzled and frightened by the strange noises.

Ross saw flashes of light flicker from the leading edges of the fighter's wings. The cannon shells tore through the shingle roofs and into the flimsy woodwork of the houses, but the sound was swept away in the roar of the bombs detonating.

The door to his house opened and Emma was there, sleep driven from her by terror, a robe pulled hastily around her. Bess started forward, pounding down the hill, tongue flopping out. Emma held her arms open for the dog, which yelped as it ran faster. Ross followed, then a line of cannon shells danced in front of him and he slowed.

The Dornier had finished its run, one last bomb trailing down, apparently coming right for him, but plummeting straight to earth at the last moment. Ross saw his house transformed into a boiling cloud of smoke, then watched the blackened wood spiral upwards, propelled heavenward by the blast, sucking the interior with it.

Emma and Bess had been swallowed by the dust and debris, and, as Ross raised his arms to protect himself, a fist of metal and wooden splinters punched into him, ripping away his clothes and skin and gouging deep into his flesh, leaving his broken shape sprawled on the pathway as the two German planes circled, dipped their wings and headed back to Calais.

Part Two

1941–2

From the office of: <u>Oberst</u> Karl Boehmer. DATE: 23
OCTOBER 1941.

FORM 03/775. Recommendation for honours. Field Units
of the <u>Ordnungspolizei</u> for the period: January 1941–June
1941.

SUBJECT: <u>Scharf.</u> Axel Schuller. Police number:
2230765/B.

DETAILS OF CITATION: On 8th January 1941. <u>Scharf.</u>
Schuller was leading a ten-man patrol of <u>SS-Polizei</u>
through the village of Grynd in the Czech Protectorate.
Schuller and his men came under intense fire from Jewish
partisans and were forced to retreat into the village,
where other elements fired upon them. Despite being
heavily outnumbered, Schuller organised a breakout from
the town, killing many partisans in the process (see
attached list). Five of his own men were killed, two
wounded. He himself was also wounded. Refusing medical

attention, upon his return to the regional command post he co-ordinated a small force of the SS-Polizei Battalion I and the local Einsatzgruppen to return to the village. The German dead were reclaimed. Over the next two days the village was pacified and cleansed of partisan elements. Schuller took full part in this action.

Schuller has since been transferred to the 11th Company of the German 3rd Battalion of the SS-Polizei Regiment 'Bozen', for duties involving partisan suppression in Italy.

Signed:

OBERST Karl BOEHMER
Kommandant SS-Polizei Regiment 3.
Prague.

i. Recommendation supported by:
Johann Hoehne
Befehlshaber der Ordnungspolizei, Czechoslovakia

ii. Recommendation supported by:
Reinhard Heydrich
Reichsprotektor, Czechoslovakia

Eighteen

Dear Uli,

It seems strange to be writing to you, but I don't know who else to address this to. My father? I have hardly seen him since the war began. My mother? She would only fret at some of the things I have to say. The truth is, I am only meant to stick to general sentiments, not to discuss the submarine or its crew at all. Who enforces this? Well, the cipher clerk, who is a lieutenant. And who is that? Well, me. I was put on a course and promoted – back to U-40, which was a surprise. Captain Prinz asked for me, apparently. Insisted to BdU that I come back. I was very proud.

It is hard work being a cipher clerk, you have to be fast and accurate, but somehow I prefer it to working the torpedoes. It is ridiculous, but when you are the one who lets the torpedoes run you feel as though you personally, not the U-boat, have sunk the ship and killed the men. So you feel the pain and the pleasure more intensely than anyone else, except perhaps the Captain.

We live a life of sounds here. Everything is signified by a

noise – from diving too deep, to an attack, everything has its signature. Like bats, our eyes are poor and our ears compensate for it. I even dream in sounds now, and the noise a ship makes as you hear it going to the bottom is one that will never leave you. You hear the funnels tear off, the back break, the bulkheads implode, the hull smash into the ocean floor sometimes. And in my dreams I can hear the trapped sailors scream as the icy water pours over their heads. I can't, of course, not in reality.

Most of the ships hunting us are equipped with an echo-locating device. You can certainly hear that, searching for you, the ping-pong passing through the hull. It is like cold fingers pushing into your soul. Every three seconds, the piercing noise, over and over again, until they have you. Some hate it more than the depth charges that follow.

There is beauty out here, too. I was on night watch last week with the navigator, a surly Rhinelander. But he noticed it first – our wake seemed to be alive. It suddenly started glowing, like white gold dancing on the thin moon-light, little gobbets of it hanging in the air before it fell down to rejoin the main organism, which boiled and thrashed around. It only lasted ten minutes, but we were mesmerised. It would have been a perfect time for the English to attack, because all five of us on watch were enraptured.

The Captain finally got his Knight's Cross, for when we sailed into the middle of a convoy and picked off six ships – over thirty thousand tons – while the destroyers searched for us. Of course, he wants the oak leaves to go with it now!

It is odd coming back to shore, in some ways. Really, it is like we are fighting a totally different war. We have no proper idea of what is going on at home – only what the radio tells us. We seem to be winning down here. It isn't getting any easier, but still, the British must be losing hundreds of thousands of tonnes.

When I go back to Germany, it is like meeting an old friend you haven't seen for a while – you notice at once the lines and the baldness that have crept up on them gradually. In Berlin I see how many of my favourite buildings have gone, how the coffee has changed, how all the policemen are so old now that they have raised the SS police army, and how my parents have aged. Even in Lorient we see empty berths where friends once stood. U-41, 42, 44, 45, 47 – yes, Prien, the hero of Scapa Flow – and 49 have all gone. And U-48 came back a shambles. It is getting to be a lonely life, being of this vintage.

I am an old-timer on this boat now. It is me who smacks the kids round the head, who shouts at them when the eels aren't greased properly. It is me they leave alone when they see me brooding in the mess. The crew changes all the time – some transferred, some promoted, a few die. We lost someone overboard last week, the second time it's happened. Your line snaps or you slip and . . . you've gone. Each time we come in now, we are fitted with new anti-aircraft guns, or special anti-detection systems. Anything to keep us ahead of the game. It usually gives us an advantage for a month or two, and then the other side shifts tactics to compensate.

I think of you whenever we return to port. We sit there on the bottom, our hull scraping the shingle, a really sickly motion, waiting for the minesweeper that will lead us into the pens safely, past the big anti-aircraft batteries on the island. The band is playing, the boys are thrilled to see the nurses – they always empty the local hospital of the pretty ones when a U-boat comes back from patrol. They hurl fresh flowers at us. The smell of blooms – you wouldn't believe that a scent can start you salivating. It's like feeding a hunger after weeks of smelling the same thing.

Have I been indiscreet? Have I given away too many secrets? No matter. You will never see this letter. In fact, there are many letters being written on this boat that will probably never be seen, for one reason or another.

I thought when I broke off the engagement that it was the noble thing to do. It probably was, but I regret it now. You see, stuck in this steel tube, somewhere under the Atlantic, I now know that I love you and always loved you, and that whereas everything else I was doing and believed in during those last few years of peace – or was it just preparation for war? – now seems false and transient, that still seems to be the truth. The one truth that I can hold on to down here.

All my love

Erich

Colonel Ross stood at the foot of the bed, watching the liquids feeding his son's body gurgle in their glass bottles. The patient was swathed in bandages from head to foot, only his nose and eyes showing. The notes clipped to the foot of the bed recorded his injuries in terms whose meaning Ross senior could only guess at.

'I'm sorry, son,' he said softly, and moved closer. 'I'm sorry. You don't hear me say that too often, do you? It's just like old times for me, this. I never told you, but when you were a child, after your mother died, I'd come in and talk to you. For hours on end. Till dawn once or twice. You were asleep, of course. But somehow it was a way of talking to her. I missed her so much. And it was a way of speaking to you, of saying all the things I couldn't say to your face. Don't ask me why. Upbringing, I suppose. I hope you are better at talking to your children . . .'

He broke off and wiped his eyes. Would this boy live to have children of his own?

'I have to admit I was selfish,' he continued. 'I didn't want to risk losing you. So when the opportunity came to use you as a conduit to Canaris, I took it. It meant you would be somewhere safe, out of harm's way. You were right, that we could have put anyone up there to transmit, but I thought it was a way of stopping you rushing off and volunteering to be dropped behind enemy lines or some such nonsense. That doesn't mean it was a waste of time, son. I know you didn't believe me, but it was important work, even if you felt like a glorified clerk.

'Then, when you got all uppity, I thought the girl might keep you company, the poor thing. You don't even know she's dead, do you? Or the dog, I suppose. And you . . . look at you now. Ironic, isn't it? Listen, Cameron, if you can hear me, I blame myself. There is this place, Bangor, in Wales, where they treat the Spitfire boys, some of whom are banged up a lot worse than you. We'll see if we can get you up there.'

There was a hand on his shoulder and he turned to see a nurse with a finger over her lips. 'Sorry.'

'We have to change the dressings now, Colonel Ross.'

'I need to know how badly hurt he is,' he said.

'You should see one of the doctors,' she said.

The Colonel picked up the clipboard from the foot of the bed. 'What does all this mean?'

'I'm not allowed—'

'Just a summary. Please.'

The nurse hesitated and looked around nervously. She

quickly read down the columns. 'Concussion, possible fracture of the skull, broken leg, damaged ribs, perhaps internal bleeding . . . you really will have to consult one of the doctors. You can make arrangements at the matron's office.'

'Right.' The Colonel turned back to Ross, and said softly: 'I'll come again. Goodbye, son.'

Two of the women killed themselves that first winter. Uli didn't know the first, who hanged herself using her bed sheets from the rafters of the storeroom. But Uli was devastated by the action of Hilda who, even though apparently displaying more and more inner strength, walked off into the woods one day when nobody was watching. The trees were heavy with snow and icicles, the wind pulling the temperature down to minus fifteen or twenty. It snowed again within minutes of her being discovered missing, filling the imprints of her footsteps. By nightfall, the trackers had given up.

Their final destination had been a camp called Kapusak, on the outskirts of a village with the same name, somewhere deep in Ontario. It wasn't the first time that it had been used to house the unwanted and unloved. During the last war the Canadians had interned Ukrainians there since their home country had been part of the Austro-Hungarian Empire. The long, low huts to which the women were confined still bore their graffiti–poems scratched into the timber, or simply initials and a date.

There were two parts to the camp. The women's, the smaller compound, consisted of huts one to four, each containing between ten and sixteen inmates. It was on the western side of the railway track along which, late at night, enormous trains rumbled, their plaintive horns waking all and sundry as they came past. On the eastern side were another twenty-five huts to house the men, of which only nineteen were habitable, and the barracks for the guards, mostly old Canadian soldiers who had last seen service in the Great War and a small group of regular police.

Uli wondered how she got through the winter of 1941–2. The huts had been built by the Ukrainians themselves, and although the logs were thick and well trimmed, there were numerous gaps where the snow piled in. She thought she'd experienced cold in Berlin, but this was of a different order, as was the way the world could blank out in a second, leaving you lost and disoriented. During those times she imagined Hilda panicking, blundering this way and that until, exhausted, she lay down to let the cold claim her.

Frau Menkel, for all her faults, was a fine organiser and she cajoled the military and civilian supervisors frequently and loudly. It was she who got the huts insulated better, who petitioned for more stoves and better lighting. It was Uli, however, who decided that they might as well work, making kitbags and blankets and belts and even canvas shoes. In return, Uli negotiated payment in reading and writing materials.

As the first thaw came and the ground started to turn to a slushy quagmire, they had two unexpected visits. The first consisted of representatives of the Canadian government and the Red Cross, who said that anyone wishing to return to Germany would be repatriated. Each person who wanted to go back would have to swear that their allegiance lay with the Führer, and they would be segregated and, ultimately, exchanged for an internee held in Germany.

All heads turned to *Frau* Menkel.

'Has anybody agreed?' she asked the men.

'Three women from hut three, 'bout a dozen of the men.'

She nodded thoughtfully. 'You know, the only thing stopping me is these girls. Look at them. Hopeless. Without me, they'd probably starve to death.' Uli saw the conflicting emotions flash across her face. 'I will have to say no.'

The second visit came one bright morning as the women were clearing up the worst of the dirty sludge from their hut entrance. Uli looked up as the man entered the 'female' compound and squished over towards them, mud splashing up his trousers as he did so. 'Good day,' he shouted cheerily.

'Good day,' they chorused, welcoming the respite and leaning on their shovels.

'My name's Ernst Uhlman. From across there.' He pointed to the men's camp. 'Taken me all this time to get permission to come over.' He rubbed his hands together nervously. 'The thing is, we are getting some activities together. A camp newspaper. One chap is making greetings cards. To send back home.' He hesitated. 'England, I mean. Not Germany. The commandant has said we can post them.'

Frau Menkel asked: 'Did he say whether they'd get delivered?'

'He reckons so, yes. Just as long as the ship carrying them doesn't get torpedoed.'

'Well, that's a big if from what I hear,' said *Frau* Menkel.

'Would you like some coffee?' Uli asked.

'Yes. Thank you.'

They took Uhlman inside. 'So,' asked Uli, as he sipped the brew. 'Apart from greetings cards . . . ?'

'Well, you would be surprised at the talent over there. And here too, I'm sure. Writers, poets, directors, actors, musicians. We plan to put on a showcase, demonstrate to these lumpen Canadians – I mean, they are very nice, but high art is a young concept here – demonstrate exactly what they have on their hands. Artists, not monsters. And we wondered – do any of you play instruments?'

'Not to your high-art standards,' said *Frau* Menkel pointedly. 'Enough for a decent *Musik Abend*.'

'A decent *Musik Abend* will do just fine,' he said.

'I play flute,' offered one girl.

'Harp – if you can find one,' said another, to a ripple of laughter.

'What about instruments?' asked *Frau* Menkel. 'Can you get any?'

'Oh, the commandant says if we give him a list, he will do his best. The harp might be a challenge. Anyone else?'

'Yes,' said Uli softly, staring into the ripples in her coffee cup. 'I'm a little rusty. But I play violin.'

Nineteen

Ross was sitting in the walled flower garden, enjoying the sun on his face, when he heard someone approaching. Unable to turn his head fully, he looked at his watch. It was six o'clock, too early for the night shift.

A shadow fell across his face and he looked up. It was Harding, who was second in command of the Surgical Division. Harding was around fifty, with thinning hair, brilliantined into place, and deep, sunken cheeks. His hands were remarkable, long and bony as if they had been specifically designed for probing within people, sliding between bone and tissue to pluck out disease and damage.

'Mind if I sit down?' he asked.

Ross shuffled along the bench and pulled his robe around him. 'Be my guest.'

'I thought it was time we had a complete rundown of the damage, what's permanent and what's not.'

Ross steeled himself and said: 'All right.'

'If you feel strong enough?'

'I've been here the best part of a year. I ought to be.'

Harding looked down at a clipboard. 'The limp is permanent.

Your right leg is a half-inch shorter than the left. Not too bad. Can give you a shoe to correct it if you like, but in this day and age a bit of a war wound goes down a treat with the ladies.'

'With respect, Mister Harding, I have a little more than a *bit* of a war wound.'

Ross was taken aback by the flash of anger from the surgeon that came straight back at him. 'Not compared to some of the chaps here, you haven't. Been to the burns unit lately? Seen the pilots who melted in their cockpits, the sailors caught in burning oil? No? Perhaps I should take you there before you leave.'

Ross had glimpsed some of them out in the garden, undergoing painful rehabilitation, faces lobster red, hands shrivelled to useless claws, skin so fragile that it had to be held together with gossamer stitches, mouths without lips, eyes without lids. 'Sorry.'

Harding nodded. 'How's the tongue?'

'Still feels like it belongs to someone else.'

'It wasn't the best one I've seen, I'm afraid.'

After the intruder air raid Ross had been dealt with by soldiers from the shore batteries at Thorpeness, who had found him lying in the road, a bloodied mess. One of them with some medical training had gone through the standard procedure for a broken jaw – putting a stitch through the tongue, then tying the thread to a jacket button to stop it lolling around. Unfortunately, it had become infected.

'The jaw, though, is pretty good, isn't it?'

A section of his damaged mandible had been replaced using bone from one of his lower ribs, and everything had been pulled back into place by a medieval-looking traction device. The science of grafting and tissue 'gardening' – encouraging growths elsewhere on the body for removal and replacement of damaged skin – was being developed in this hospital day by day.

175

'Is it?'

'You haven't looked in the mirror?'

'No.'

'You should. Chest is also pretty good. Don't think the hair will regrow on the left-hand side. Just shave the other to match. If it worries you.'

'It doesn't.'

'You've forty per cent hearing loss in your left ear. Other one is pretty good – perhaps ten per cent, if that. You are lucky that you put your arms up. Protected your eyes. The skin on your forearms will heal well, I think. That stiff neck will go in time, too. Our main problem was the fractured skull, the thing that kept you in pain for so long. That, I am pleased to say, is right as rain now. Just had to shift some of the plates around, as it were. Relieve the pressure. Headaches?'

'Gone.'

'You see? Not a bad checklist for this place.'

'Thank you, Mister Harding.'

'I had a message from your father, by the way. Hopes to get up in the next few days. Says he regrets that he hasn't . . . well, it's a long way from London. It now takes the best part of a whole day to get here, if you're lucky. He's been bombed out twice trying, once when they hit Crewe . . .'

'Can you send a reply?' Ross interrupted quickly. 'To my father?'

'Of course.'

'Tell him I appreciate his efforts to get here. But I would rather he didn't come to see me for the moment.'

'Mister Ross . . .'

'Just tell him I need the time to think. About what has happened, and about what will happen. Tell him that when I was in hospital in Ipswich I heard every word he said when he spoke

176

to me. It's given me a lot to mull over. Tell him it's time I made my own decisions and from now on I will. He'll understand,' finished Ross, not entirely sure that his father would do anything of the kind.

Uli, nervous, sat next to the small stage, waiting for *Frau* Menkel to finish her recital. They were in the town hall of the nearby village. It was packed with townsfolk, all curious to see what the 'foreigners' could do. Things had certainly improved in the months since Hilda had disappeared. If only she'd held on.

As *Frau* Menkel banged her way through some Schumann, Uli rotated her left wrist. It was still deformed, but she had practised long and hard at stretching the tendons, and now she could finger passably well. It still ached afterwards, but she was pleased with her progress. She smiled at the Canadian in the front row, who was frowning with concentration at the music. His name was Dennis. He drove supplies up to the camp once a week, he was big, shy and clumsy and she knew he was sweet on her. She did nothing to encourage him, but little to discourage him either.

She enjoyed the attention. She had forgotten what it felt like. The last time flirting had been so uncomplicated had been . . . She tried to think. Not with Ross, that was for sure, because there had been the shadow of Erich. Where were they now, she wondered? And if they both came through that door, what would she do? *They won't*, she reminded herself. *Make the most of the here and now and the gentle courtship of someone who doesn't know your background, foibles or former suitors.*

Applause crackled out, along with whistling and stamping as *Frau* Menkel finished and took a bow. Uli had asked her why she had refused repatriation. Had she been worried about being sunk on the way back? No, she'd said. It was the size of the country they had seen from the train as they crossed from Halifax to Toronto and then into the hinterland. So vast and fertile. She knew that the Germans could never make any impact over here, that somehow the British government would survive. She now believed her country was doomed.

Uli stood, her cheeks red, trying to recall the youngster who had no fear of performing at her father's music evenings. Half of her wished that Fritz was here now, the other half was glad that he wouldn't see her stumble through the recital. She stepped onto the low stage and cleared her throat.

'Ladies and gentlemen,' she said in a quaking voice. 'Tonight, I would like to perform a few pieces by Mozart.'

There was more applause as she fiddled with the music stand and opened the yellowed sheet music. Uli took a deep breath, put the bow to the strings, closed her eyes, and began to play.

Twenty

Camp 020, Latchmere House, London: 1942

Colonel Donald Ross thought long and hard about silver linings these days. As he waited for the man seated at the opposite side of the table to compose himself, he considered the case of his son. Maimed, unwilling to see him, claiming 'he wasn't ready', whatever that meant.

He wanted to tell his son just how valuable his injuries had proved, to make them seem, if not worthwhile, then bearable. The frantic radio traffic from the *Abwehr* between Berlin and Rotterdam after that strange Dornier raid on the house in Suffolk had provided a valuable tool for ISOS, the signals and cryptography people. For once they knew exactly what the fuss was about and could look for key phrases and place names in the messages.

One of the transmissions proposed a wild theory that somehow Heydrich was involved in the bombing. The Colonel knew Canaris's *Abwehr* were suspicious of Heydrich, but that took the biscuit. As if Hitler would let his top men go swanning round the skies in Messerschmitts and the like.

Still, once the boffins knew what to look for, the code fell surprisingly quickly. With this breakthrough, the *Abwehr*'s transmissions were now routinely decoded and passed to MI5. Hardly a single spy landed in England without the security services knowing in advance. Those that did sneak through usually gave themselves away quickly enough. Ross's job these days was to determine which of the hapless spies should go to the Twenty Committee (designated XX – double cross) for turning back on the enemy and which should be incarcerated and possibly even hanged.

The oily character in front of him was one such hapless spy, ostensibly a Frenchman called Savigny, who had made it to England from Brittany by small motor launch and who claimed he wished to join de Gaulle's Free French. He had gone through the London Reception Centre in Clapham, where all refugees and aliens who made it to Britain were processed. The enemy knew about this centre and had schooled its agents to try and pass through it without arousing suspicion.

Savigny's downfall was that, if he'd made it to England as claimed, his motor cruiser would have had to pass unharmed through several British minefields on its way to the mainland. Like all other suspects, he was quickly dispatched to Latchmere House, which had been rechristened Camp 020.

Savigny had already been thoroughly searched and was now dressed in the regulation Latchmere uniform of flannels and a coat with a large white diamond on the breast. In his instruction leaflet, Ross had postulated that there were two kinds of inter-rogator, the Breaker and the Investigator. They employed totally different skills – the first involved obtaining the confession of treachery and deceit, the second drawing out the background, list of contacts, nature of the mission and so forth.

Ross could do both, although it was best, he found, if interrogators specialised. Tin-Eye Stephens, for instance, was an excellent breaker, but a useless investigator.

Savigny had already been well and truly broken by Stephens, who used a mixture of threats – execution – and psychological menaces. Stephens loved to stoke the rumours about the horrors that awaited those sent to Cell Fourteen which, in reality, was just like any other cell. However, this small room had grown in the fevered imagination of those interned at Camp 020 until it was thought of as the inner circle of hell. The mere mention of it broke some inmates instantly. What none of them knew was that the one thing Stephens absolutely forbade was the use of violence – not because of squeamishness, Colonel Ross knew, but because Tin-Eye maintained that 'it lowered the quality of the intelligence'.

Savigny, though, had not been hard to break: he was another of the *Abwehr* agents whose motives were far from ideological – a mix of money and blackmail had driven him to agree to work for the Germans. Colonel Ross despised him for his frailty, but he couldn't let that show. It was his turn to be the pleasant half of Stephens's 'blow hot, blow cold' technique, whereby a kindly investigator alternated with one who acted like a baying dog.

There was no stenographer present in the room, because they were using 'M' devices, the new recording microphones that were fitted into the light fixtures. Ross wasn't sure about these, but Stephens swore by them. Interviews were taped on the new wire-spool devices that had been bought from the Yanks, and transcribed later. Stephens maintained that the absence of a third person scribbling notes in the corner made for a more conducive atmosphere for obtaining confessions.

Savigny was relaxed now, thinking that the worst was over, and he put his hands on the table and interlaced his fingers, waiting for the interrogation to begin. Colonel Ross reached for the packet of Weights, shook a cigarette out, ready to offer it to the prisoner, and waited in vain for his brain to formulate something. With mounting horror, he realised that, for the first time in his life, he had no idea what his first question should be.

'Torpedoes running.'

Every man held his breath as the shudder passed through the hull. Stares fixed on the clocks, men counted under their breaths. Forty seconds had passed when they heard the dull crump of an explosion.

'Midships,' said Prinz, peering intently through the periscope's eyepiece. A second explosion. 'Stern.'

A ripple of relief ran through the boat. It was an armed British tanker, straggling behind the convoy because of engine trouble. Now they had to get out of there. Gone were the days when the British sent every destroyer in the area searching for a submarine, leaving the merchant ships naked, to be taken at will by the U-boat captain bold enough to slip past the hunters. Now they sent out just one or two escorts, which scanned the area with their damned ASDIC echo-locators, while the remainder corralled the transports.

'Take her down, Chief. Seventy metres. Left full rudder. All ahead full. Give me all she has for fifteen minutes.'

Erich, as cipher clerk, no longer operated the torpedo computer but was a spare pair of hands in the control room to assist with whatever emergencies arose.

Schnee started yelling. 'She's Morsing a distress signal. *Ocean Pride*. Torpedoed by submarine. Sinking to stern. Then her position. She's going down.' A ragged cheer. Another pennant to fly as they sailed into Lorient.

It had been a successful winter patrol. With America in the

war, its ships were now fair game, and the tonnage totals had crept up. Resupplied with torpedoes and provisions by milch-cow submarines, U-40 had prowled the eastern seaboard of the US and Canada, hunting alone and, at BdU's command, in packs when the pickings were rich, making the Allies suffer badly. Now they were feasting in Torpedo Alley, south of Greenland, where Allied spotter planes – either from Canada or Scotland – could not reach and the ships were, therefore, denied air cover.

'Screws. Faint. Astern,' said the hydrophone operator, a panicky note in his voice.

'They didn't waste much time. Launch Bold, Hinkel. Ten-minute delay.'

Erich's job. He ran back to the rear torpedo tubes, issuing orders as he went. 'Break out the Bold canisters. Set for ten.'

Bold was the latest thing in anti-sonar devices. The canisters launched through the rear tubes contained a mixture of calcium and zinc which, on contact with water, produced hydrogen bubbles that could completely fool a sonar operator. They could be set to hover at a particular depth and would throw off bubbles for a good twenty-five minutes.

As soon as two canisters were launched, Erich worked his way back to the control room, through the engine compartment, wondering how much more of this life he could take. He wasn't alone. Prinz himself had begun to say some strange things. He questioned Admiral Dönitz's sanity in adhering to every whim of the Führer and was also depressed by the Americans entering the war. 'I have seen their shipyards,' he said. 'They can build ships faster than we can sink them.'

If they were going to lose the war, what was the point of all this loss of life – both in the U-boats and the merchant ships? Erich knew that Prinz was tired, but the U-40's senior officer had to be careful. The captain of U-154 was rumoured to be under sentence of death for replacing the required portrait of Hitler with a seascape and for making 'defeatist' comments. The old Erich, the Hitler Youth Erich, would have cheered such a decision. Now he thought it idiotic, to waste the life of such a valuable tactician. Perhaps he was just tired, too. Perhaps he just wished he were at home, in bed with Uli, a couple of kids fast asleep in their nursery.

He ducked through to the radio room. The destroyer's screws were still sounding in the hydrophone man's ears, still coming after them, but some distance behind and slowing. Erich checked his watch. He imagined the canisters starting to bubble, the milky cloud dispersing into a long streak, the sound waves bouncing off it.

'He's turned towards the Bold,' shouted Erich. Prinz managed a thin smile. They weren't out of trouble yet.

They all heard the detonations and the submarine shuddered lightly. A whole series of explosions, one after the other, crunched together into a long, continuous rumble.

'Hedgehog,' Erich said to Prinz, who nodded. Underwater cluster-bombs, twenty-four of them, launched in an oval to surround a U-boat, to smash it from all sides. It was a lethal tactic. Another growling in the depths and a ripple ran through U-40 as the shock waves reached it. This time the destroyer had hedgehogged a mass of bubbles. *What happens*, thought Erich, *when the sonar operators learn to tell the difference between decoy and target?*

Part Three

1943–5

Twenty-One

London: 1943

'Ten pounds for the night.'

Ross slowed his step, and turned back to look at the woman. Even in the diffuse glimmer lighting of the blackout, he could make out that she was a tall brunette, with a prominent beauty spot and kohl-ringed eyes. She was dressed in a slightly ratty knee-length fur coat and glossy high heels. The stockings looked real, the crocodile handbag seemed genuine, the diamonds dangling from her ears were paste. She was a beguiling mix of the pristine and the shopworn.

It was getting on for midnight, not far from Charing Cross, and the streets glistened with the evening's spent rain. The West End was crowded with women like this, nearly all of them going for the Americans who could afford their rates. Competition was fierce. But ten pounds? It was double the going price, which usually included a breakfast of sorts.

'Or by the hour,' she said as he took a step towards her, his bad leg dragging slightly. 'Or a short time down here, love.' She pointed to the narrow alley, Two Brydges, a black slit in St

187

Martin's Lane, home, he knew, to one of the dives that served as movable card dens. If the operators changed the venue every night, then they couldn't be charged with having premises used for habitual gambling. He peered down into the blackness. No sign of life.

'Two quid,' she said softly. 'I guarantee you'll leave with a smile on your face.'

Ross hesitated, scratching the beard that he had grown to cover the kink in his jawline, aware of passers-by staring, knowing full well what sort of transaction was in progress. He pulled down his trilby and nodded his agreement.

She led the way, her heels clacking on the paving stones. Ross tried to close his nose to the smell of ammonia that was bleeding from the lower parts of the walls. He watched her sashay in a manner designed to keep a client's stare fixed on her rear, and marvelled at how effective it was.

The alleyway widened out in the centre and it was here that they came for him, from a side passage that led out towards Trafalgar Square. They were big men, not tall, but beefy and they had him by his lapels against the wall in a flash. He felt the air explode from his lungs. One of them held an iron bar and danced from foot to foot, while the larger of the two kept an arm across Ross's windpipe.

'OK, mister, just relax. This won't take a minute.' He was American.

'Hurry up, get it over with.' No, they were Canadian.

Hands were going through his pockets and lifting whatever they could find – his ration book, wallet, coins, watch – and Ross let himself go limp. He knew that if he struggled at all a tap on the head with a makeshift cosh would follow.

His assailant stepped back, breathing hard. 'There, that wasn't too bad, was it?'

As the police whistle sounded, one of the Canadians snapped his head round towards St Martin's Lane and Ross got in a good solid punch that shoved it round even further. The man staggered back.

The second Canadian raised the iron bar, thought better of it and spun round, straight into the arms of a uniformed PC. The alley was soon crammed with cops and the trio of muggers were bundled into a group, each with a pair of darbies around their wrists.

As the handcuffs snapped shut the brunette turned to Ross and said: 'I thought you were a snip. I could smell it. Even with the gammy leg. Should've trusted my instinct, shouldn't I?'

'You should've done a lot of things, my dear,' Ross said evenly. He'd played up his limp to make himself seem more vulnerable. 'Including thought twice about playing the badger game.'

She managed a shrug as the three of them were led away to the paddy wagon waiting on the Strand. Ross bent down and picked up his belongings. The face of his watch was cracked. He wondered if a repair came under police expenses. At least it was still working. Gone midnight. He would have to go back to Bow Street, book the men, deposit the woman with a matron, one of the civilian searchers they employed – this one, like many of them, the station sergeant's wife – then do the paperwork.

The Canadians were deserters, of course. London was full of them, robbing post offices and banks, shoplifting in the under-staffed stores, hijacking coal lorries to sell the precious fuel on the black market. This was the first gang they had come across using tarts as bait for robbery, however.

Ross wangled a lift back to the station in one of the Flying Squad's Railtons, the fast cars that finally meant the unit could live up to its name. The driver was a DS called Jakes, who had been wounded in the Norway campaign.

'You all right, sir?' he asked. 'Not too roughed-up?'

'No. Not really.'

It was a good collar. The tart had been helping the deserters to roll customers for months in a 'badger game' – the old term for having the pimp lie in wait to roll the mug. Nearly all of the victims had required hospitalisation, but only recently had a few managed to drum up the courage to put in a formal complaint and outline the scenario. Ross had drawn the short straw during the decoy-selection procedure, causing much merriment among his colleagues, most of which revolved around where his trousers would be when they arrived on the scene.

Still, it was a proper case, better than the degrading 'nancy boy' patrols in Piccadilly that Vine Street station still ran, arresting some poor unfortunate, bringing him back for the 'test' – rubbing his face with toilet paper to check for make-up – and searching for incriminating evidence such as a pot of Vaseline. If none were found, one would often be provided.

'You on duty tomorrow, sir?'

'No.'

'Any plans?' asked Jakes.

There was a lunchtime concert at the National Gallery that Ross wanted to attend, but it didn't do to say that. He recalled the relentless taunting of the young 'unnatural', as the Section House had it, who had liked Ibsen and Milton and had left the force after two years, disillusioned. His former colleagues still arrested him for lewd acts whenever the opportunity arose.

'Nothing firm,' he said.

'Well, you can have a lie-in, can't you, sir?'

Ross yawned, feeling the weariness in his bones. His idea of throwing himself into work to forget about Emma and Uli and his injuries had been sound, but it was taking its toll physically, simply because there weren't enough coppers to go round these days. 'Yes, Jakes, I think I will.'

The phone in Ross's flat rang at five minutes past seven. After filling in the forms and taking the statements, he hadn't gone to bed till past three, and his eyes felt gummy and his head spun as he heaved himself from beneath the blankets and shuffled into the hallway, where the big chunk of black Bakelite sat on a small occasional table. Ross wondered if he shouldn't move the telephone into the bedroom, as people only seemed to call him when he was asleep.

'Museum two oh three seven,' he mumbled as he put the receiver to his good ear.

'Cameron.' It was his Chief Inspector.

'Sir.'

'Bit of trouble in St John Street. That's your neck of the woods, isn't it?'

About half a mile away. 'Sir.'

'Police constable requested senior assistance. Can't do it from here. Take a look, will you?'

'Of course. Right away.'

'Need a driver?'

'I can walk it, sir.'

Ross hung up, returned to the bedroom and slumped back onto the bed. He counted to a hundred before he rolled off and limped towards the bathroom. His jaw ached. He had been bruxing again, grinding his teeth in his sleep, which apparently wasn't good for his rebuilt mandible. Try to relax more, his maxillofacial consultant had suggested. Chance would be a fine thing. Had the Chief Inspector known it was his day off? Or did he just not care?

Probably the latter, he decided as he squeezed the toothpaste out of its tube onto his toothbrush. It was nearly empty and he reminded himself that he must take the old tube along when he replaced it. The woman in the chemist's had treated him like a Nazi-lover the last time, when he had admitted to having thrown the empty away. He found it hard to believe that the success of the Allies depended on him recycling his metal tube of Kolynos Dental Cream, but he supposed she'd had a point when she'd said that every little helped.

Ross checked his face again. To a casual acquaintance he looked much like he had before the bombing, but he could see the lumps and bumps of the surgical reconstructions. He had asked, and been given, permission to grow a neat beard to hide the irregularity in his jawline.

As he was brushing his hair flat, watching his reflection in the hall mirror, the post fell onto the mat and he quickly checked the stack of letters. The one from his father was at the bottom. He hesitated for a moment, before deciding that he was doing just fine as he was. Ross binned it, unopened, before he left.

The blast from the shotgun reverberated around St John Street, followed by the soft tinkling of glass. The shooter had blown out the window of one of the houses opposite. Ross risked looking out from the side street where he, together with the local constable – a tall, craggy man, one of the Guards inducted into the Met at the end of the last war and happy to stay a bobby – and the medical team of a driver and two young nurses were crouched. St John Street was empty but for the abandoned Morris ambulance, which had been shot at several times, its sides and roof peppered with holes, and a requisitioned taxi and its tender from the Auxiliary Fire Service, which had received the same attention.

Ross turned to the ambulance driver. 'He doesn't want to go with you, does he?'

'He's a right nutter,' the man replied.

'What's his name?' asked Ross.

'Arthur Stokes,' said the constable. 'Fifty years old. Used to be a bookie. Then he started acting strange, like.' Ross wondered if that simply meant that Stokes had neglected to leave out the half-crown for the beat bobby that was the informal 'tax' on bookmakers. 'So they put him away. Was out on a weekend pass, but he didn't go back to the hospital. Neighbours complained he was behaving oddly—'

'Anyone in there with him?'

'Not that we know of. He has a char provided by the Corporation.'

Ross grunted. 'Any attempt to talk to him?'

The constable showed his sleeve, ragged where a blast had sideswiped it. 'In a manner of speaking.'

'Right. Get the army here.'

'The army?'

'The man's got a bloody gun – yes, the army. Tell them to bring tear gas, understand? When they get here, two blasts on the whistle to let me know. Then tell them to throw as much of the gas as they've got into that room.'

'What are you going to do, sir?'

Ross reached over and pulled the constable's gas mask from its canvas bag. 'I'm going over to shove that shotgun up the man's arse.' Ross was too tired to worry about the shocked expressions on the face of the group as he slipped away.

Ross located the house easily enough. It was the one from which a man was yelling and firing into the street every five minutes. The shooter had found that hitting the ambulance tyres made a very satisfying noise, so he had blown out both of those that he could see and was trying to hit the taxi further down the street. Ross tiptoed through the scruffy garden and bent down to pick up a piece of jagged metal, hissing as he pricked his finger. Rocket shrapnel from the anti-aircraft batteries. He let the piece drop and sucked at his finger as he carried on across to the back door, aware of twitching curtains in the adjoining house. He flashed his warrant card.

The rear door to the kitchen was locked, but Ross took off his coat, wrapped it around his elbow and, as the next shotgun barrel fired, smashed one of the panes of glass, put his hand through the hole and turned the key inside. He crept into the kitchen. It smelled of mouldy bread, rancid milk and cats. A big tabby looked at him with baleful eyes from the enamel counter of the green kitchen dresser, as if he too wanted this to end. Precious crockery was scattered across the floor, along with a sticky mass of chicory and coffee essence and the usual framed picture of the king, which had a bread knife protruding from it.

Ross passed through the kitchen and into the dark hall, its chocolate colour scheme making it even gloomier. He could hear the man clearly now, ranting to himself in a low voice, with the odd word, usually a profanity, suddenly emphasised. Ross reached the bottom of the stairs, so intent on the landing above he almost stepped on the woman who lay sprawled across the bottom two steps.

Ross felt his stomach turn several somersaults. She'd been shot at close range, and the top half of her torso was all glistening gristle and bone. The grey hair and the flowery pinafore suggested a woman of a certain age, but there were no features left to confirm it. The char, no doubt. Shot with both barrels by the look of it. He instinctively shooed away the fat flies that had settled on her, but they merely circled lazily and landed elsewhere on the feasting ground.

Ross heard the whistle and steeled himself. A minute or so passed with him frozen on the stairs. Then came a thump and a yelp from the bedroom and the stamping of feet. The tear gas was in. Ross started to put on the gasmask when he heard Stokes rush out of the room, and through the fogged eyepiece he watched as the man tossed the canister over the balustrade. It exploded on the stairs just in front of him, a faceful of the acrid fumes slipping under the mask's canvas hood before he could pull it on.

Ross felt his eyes sting and his chest contract. Above him, more swearing. Ross ripped the mask from his face and leapt back just as the poor woman's corpse received another blast of shotgun pellets, clearly meant for him.

There were shadows at the front door, beyond the glass – army, probably – and he staggered backwards to it as Stokes sprinted along the landing and started down the stairs. Ross felt something snag his calf and looked down. It was an elephant's leg, a three-foot-high chunk of an old tusker, now used as an umbrella and cane stand.

As Stokes came down into full view, Ross swept up the appendage and ran forward, heaving it into the man as hard as he could. Ross was on him before he could recover, his hand locked on the painfully hot barrels of the gun. He had an image of crooked yellow teeth, a three-day growth of beard and crazed bloodshot eyes before he head-butted the man as hard as he could and passed out.

Normality quickly returned to the street. Ross sat on the step while one of the nurses bandaged his burnt hand and swabbed something on his forehead and the ambulance driver tutted at the wreck of his vehicle. The army took Stokes off to a secure unit, and neighbours appeared to exchange doorstep gossip about their role in the Siege of St John Street.

'There,' said the nurse at last. 'It's a bit of an egg, but it'll go down.'

'Thank you.'

'No – thank *you*. You're a brave man, Inspector.'

Ross laughed ruefully. 'No, I just got out of the wrong side of bed this morning.'

'Well, tell the girlfriend to keep you on that side. It does us the power of good.'

Ross smiled indulgently. He hadn't had any dealings with women, certainly not a girlfriend, since poor Emma. Emma and Uli, one killed in front of his eyes, the other very probably dead, a victim of the air raids now pounding Berlin. *Some love-life*, he thought.

Ross groaned when he realised that he'd have to do the paperwork on all this, then decided it could wait until tomorrow. He'd take the rest of his day off, and hang the consequences. He walked back towards his flat as it began to drizzle, and it was only as he was turning up his collar that he noticed the woman driving the Express Dairy milk cart, urging her horse on in a distinctly accented voice. She saw him too, pulled on the reins and stopped the horse. 'Inspector?'

'Hello, there,' he said, still not having placed her.

'It's a good job I've got a journalist's eye for a face. Didn't recognise you with the beard for a second.'

Journalist? It was Gertrud Ritter, the reporter from *Vossische Zeitung* whom he had met at the Walters' house, five years previously.

'You got out of Germany, then,' he said. 'Well done.'

'Ssssh, not so loud,' she hissed. 'All my customers think I am a poor persecuted Pole.'

Ross looked at the cart and the ribby, wheezing nag pulling it. 'It's a long way from journalism.'

Her face, thinner than it had been, with long folds of flesh under her chin, wobbled as she shook her head in sadness. 'It's a long way from home. A long way from the Walters' little soirées. Did you ever run into them?'

'The Walters? They never got out.'

Gertrud looked puzzled. 'Oh, yes they did. I saw them here in . . . I think it was early 1940. Before I got carted off for a six-month holiday on the Isle of Man—'

Ross didn't believe what he was hearing. There must be a mistake. 'Are you sure?'

'Of course I'm sure. I spoke to them. The father and that strange daughter of his.'

Ross's mind whirled, trying to take it all in. Surely his father had checked for him? 'They're . . . here?'

'They were. They may not have got back from wherever they were sent. But they certainly were. Are all you right?'

Ross realised that he was rubbing his brow to try to fight off the headache that was blooming behind his eyes. Could this be true? And if it was, why hadn't he known that Uli was in the country? 'Yes,' he mumbled. 'Nice to see you again, Gertrud. I . . . I must go.'

'Of course. And I have a horse to feed. Goodbye, Inspector.' She made a *tch* noise with her teeth and the beast clopped into motion.

Ross walked home slowly, running the news over and over in his mind. She'd been here, in England, and she was alive. Those few short words made his heart race. Uli was alive.

Twenty-Two

As usual on a Wednesday, Uli washed and brushed her hair carefully and clipped it up. Dennis was coming with deliveries and, as had been the habit since the late spring, he would take her off camp for a picnic with food that his mother – or 'mom' as he put it – had prepared.

It was more or less an open camp now. Fraternisation between the men's and women's sections was the norm. A child had even been born, and *Frau* Menkel had an admirer, which had put a skip in her once leaden step. She had lived through a darker winter than most when she discovered that her husband had been hanged as a spy at Wandsworth Prison two years earlier, at the beginning of 1941. The information had not been released at the time for 'intelligence reasons'.

Her mourning had been hard to watch as she folded into herself, sitting on her bunk, hour after hour, rocking back and forth. Now, though, she had come to terms with it, and either she didn't bear the British too much ill will or else hid any resentment exceedingly well.

Uli had received a letter from her father. He was on the Isle of Man, one of the last ones still interned there, apart from a hard core of fanatics who had been kept behind. Judging by the message's content, he had only received her third and fifth letters, the others having gone astray. She had instantly written a sixth, begging for more information about him rather than news of the wonderful examples of the human spirit's resilience that he had seen and the talented young musicians whom he had met.

She had just examined her face in the mirror – 'no longer that of a featureless young girl' was the best interpretation she could put on the new lines that had appeared around her eyes and mouth – and put the last pin in her hair when she heard the honk on the horn from Dennis's truck and ran out to greet him.

Their picnic spot was on the edge of the pine forest, on a small knot overlooking a lake. Beyond that was a tapestry of wheat and tobacco farms, stretching away towards America. Once the USA had entered the war, the authorities had relaxed the regime at the camp. Now there really was nowhere for thousands of miles that wasn't the Allies' territory. Many of the men had already been transported back to Britain, and the rest figured that if they just bided their time, it would be their turn eventually.

However, the women still seemed to be a mere afterthought. They had petitioned the camp governor for release, who in turn had tried the Alien Office in Ottawa, which contacted the Home Office in Britain, but the fate of a few dozen female refugees was not a priority for the moment. And in her heart, Uli had to admit that, much as she ached to see her father, the thought of crossing the Atlantic again, every nerve alert for the impact of a German torpedo, held little allure.

When they reached their patch of rough grass, they settled down on the blanket and Uli let the sun warm her while Dennis fussed with the meat loaf, ham and fresh bread. 'Mom would like to meet you,' he said softly.

'Well, I would welcome the opportunity to thank her for all this.'

'That's settled, then,' Dennis said, grinning. He unscrewed the flask lid. 'I'll fix it. Coffee?'

Uli accepted the plastic cup. 'Thank you. We do have the little problem of me technically being a dangerous enemy prisoner.'

'Oh, the camp governor is going to start issuing weekend passes soon.'

'Well, yes, then. It would be a pleasure.' A real home, a real family. She wondered if she still knew how to behave in such company. And what would she wear? She was fairly sure that Dennis wouldn't mind if she put on old sacking, but she'd want to make a good impression on his mother. The flowery dress she wore each Wednesday for Dennis was the best thing in her meagre wardrobe, and that garment was faded and patched.

'Oh, and I got this,' Dennis said casually.

She took the newspaper eagerly and looked at the date. The copy of the *Daily Mail* was three weeks old, but she devoured it greedily.

Most of the news confirmed rumours that had circulated in the camp. The Allied landings on Sicily, the Russians pushing back the Germans near Kursk. Elsewhere there were pictures of the giant funfair on Hampstead Heath, items on the relaxing of restrictions on greyhound meetings, the latest rationing news, and the *Mail* had started a campaign to allow turn-ups on men's trousers once more.

Then her gaze caught the name Ross. An Inspector Ross had been awarded the KPM, the King's Police Medal, for his bravery during what they called the Siege of St John Street. Uli scanned the story. Could it be the same Inspector Ross? A hero? Surely not. She thought back, beyond the diffident figure at the airport to the man who had plunged fearlessly into the mêlée in Tiergarten and realised that, yes, the Ross she once knew *did* have it in him. She also remembered the pleasure of the kiss at the Lufthansa lounge, and the effect it had had on him. She'd been a wicked little girl back then.

She leant back against a tree. It was strange to feel a name reaching across from the past and affecting her like that. She could see him now, standing in the hall, offering that well-meaning gift, and she heard her snobbish teenage voice high-handedly turn him down. She blushed at the memory.

'Can I kiss you again?' asked Dennis, sliding his bearlike form nearer, wanting to progress from last week's chaste peck on the cheek.

'No, Dennis. Not this time,' Uli said firmly as she tore out the cutting and slipped it into her dress pocket. 'Shall we eat?'

Torpedo Alley was quiet. Erich had decoded a cipher from BdU which confirmed that a convoy was gathering at Halifax to sail in three days' time. Until then all that the crew of U-40 could do was wait, conserving their energies, wallowing on the surface in a silvery sea. Erich was up top on the wooden deck, along with a dozen others, taking advantage of a soft summer day in the 'air gap', the region where they knew they were outside the range of the marauding Liberators or the Sunderland flying boats of the Canadians or British Coastal Command.

There had been a rendezvous two weeks earlier with a supply sub that was returning to St Nazaire, and most of the crew had handed over their letters to their family and loved ones. Erich hadn't posted his to Uli. What was the point? He had no address, and even if he had, he doubted whether the *Bundespost* sent many mailmen across to London these days. If, indeed, that was where she was. He'd heard that the British had locked all their Germans up in KZs, concentration camps. Would Uli survive that? Yes, she would, he decided. Uli was made of harder stuff than him.

He looked up at Prinz on the bridge. The Captain was wearing his Knight's Cross, getting used to the feeling of its new oak leaves. This addition – a sign that the wearer had won the Cross twice – was by way of a long-service medal, an appreciation of the skill that it took to survive out here for so long. The British had improved their Hedgehog cluster charges and their sonar, and now they had airborne radar and acoustic torpedoes dropped from planes. In response, U-40 had been painted with anti-sonar coatings and fitted with an extra deck, which held an anti-aircraft gun, on the rear of the tower. She also had been given a variety of decoy buoys and new torpedoes that instead of running straight described a ladder pattern, zigzagging through convoys, which made them much more likely to strike a target. Unfortunately, on the early trials the new eels had tended to deploy in a large circle, often coming back and destroying the U-boat that had launched them. Erich was pleased that U-40 had been out on patrol when those prototypes had been deployed.

Despite constant improvements to her defences and operational capacity, poor old U-40 was showing her age. Many of the Type VIIBs had gone. He guessed that few U-boats got to retire – BdU worked them until they broke, taking the crew with them. He had heard Prinz curse Dönitz for this, even, after a few drinks, when they'd been on shore. Prinz thought he deserved a Type VIIC/42, with its more powerful engines and better armament, not to mention its stronger steel hull and less cramped interior. The 42s even had freezers to keep food fresh.

They all deserved that, the Captain felt.

Erich heard a buzzing in his ears. As one, the dozen men on deck swivelled their heads to the west. They'd all picked up the sound of aero engines. 'Liberator!' shouted the *Zweiter* as he found it in his lenses. 'Closing fast.'

Surely they can't get this far out to sea, thought Erich.

'Alarm! All hands below! Clear the bridge!'

Erich joined the stampede. The Liberator could only mean one thing. The damned British and Canadians had found a way to close the air gap.

Twenty-Three

It was, Ross had to admit, a beautiful view. Across from the Ruthen Peninsula where he stood he could see a string of sandy bays interspersed by rocky points. Out at sea, the black pinpricks were seals or sea lions. The houses scattered across the rolling hillsides were pristine white, freshly repainted this summer, and the gardens were neat and well tended. He could almost be on the edge of Loch Sunart, the remote part of the west coast of Scotland where his family originally came from and where a reclusive uncle still lived, rather than the Isle of Man.

Behind him was the row of boarding houses that formed one of the refugee-detention camps, its boundary delineated by a single strand of wire. How different from the imposing fences strung up around the hotels in Douglas, where the men had been kept. The women who had spent much of the war in these houses behind him had had it much easier. And a better view.

Ross turned and faced the tweedy middle-aged woman who strode along the path towards his vantage point. She was the Home Office representative in this complex, which now held a handful of hardline pro-Nazis and a couple of women with no other place to go. She was brusque but sympathetic to a policeman who had used a KPM award to wangle a few weeks' leave to undertake what she clearly considered a wild-goose chase.

Ross had traced Ulrike Walter relatively easily, from Alexandra Palace in North London to Kempton Race Course and on to a housing estate near Liverpool, but he had lost her at the docks. The Isle of Man steamers now left from Fleetwood, not Liverpool. The Mersey wharfs and piers had suffered a pounding by German bombers and there were no surviving manifests of passengers boarded, no proper records of landings for those hectic months three years ago.

Joan Ashley gave him the bad news. 'I'm sorry, Inspector. I've called all the other camps – there is no trace of her.'

'What if she was sent abroad?'

She shook her head. 'No women were sent abroad, Inspector. Men went to Canada and Australia, a few to South Africa. No women. It was not policy. Then, once the married camp was set up, all single female aliens were concentrated on one site.' She waved at the houses behind her. 'If she was on the island then, she'd have come through here.'

'When was the married camp set up?'

'Oh, 1941. The men and women were kept separate until then.'

Ross felt a jolt. *Idiot*, he said to himself. He'd only been thinking about Uli. The transit camps had been mixed, even though the sexes had been segregated. He'd assumed that something similar would work at the final destinations. He'd assumed wrongly. 'Even fathers and daughters?'

'Oh, yes. Man and wife, father and daughter, brother and sister – didn't matter.'

'So Uli and her father could have ended up in separate camps.'

'No "could have" about it. *Would* have. Without a doubt.'

'Or even in a separate part of the world.'

Joan Ashley hesitated. 'In some cases. But as I said, it was the men who were relocated overseas.'

'How many men are left on the island?'

'A few hundred, I suppose. Mostly at Hutchinsons. Those whom the Aliens Advisory Committee still consider a risk. You will have seen Hutchinsons, up the hill from the landing stage at Douglas.' Ross had: a rather bleak windswept collection of houses, cocooned in barbed wire.

'Do you want me to check? I only asked about a Miss Walter at the women's facilities. I can easily check the listings for a *Herr* Walter. If he has been on the island, then the Commandature should have it. The men were looked after by the military authorities, unlike the women, so it takes a bit of time to cut through the red tape.'

'Thank you,' Ross said, aware that he had been rather churlish up until this point. 'I appreciate your help.'

'Don't mention it. You can have a cup of tea while you wait. I think we even have some scones that the inmates baked. Don't worry. They haven't poisoned us. Yet.'

'That would be very nice. Thank you.'

Ross allowed himself to be led back towards the houses, still wondering how he could have been so dumb.

After the Liberator had spotted them, U-40 had turned and run. They had quickly discovered through BdU how the air gap had been closed – VLRs, very-long-range planes equipped with radar to detect them on the surface, and sonar buoys for when they dived. They had survived three attacks so far.

Prinz had stopped to harry three merchant ships, sinking one and damaging another with a gnat, a short-range acoustic torpedo that homed in on propeller noise. It was as though the ships were saying come and get me. And come they did.

Now U-40 had no torpedoes left, and one of the diesels had run a bearing, but she limped on towards home under water, resurfacing at night to recharge the batteries. Erich had coded and deciphered the messages between Prinz and BdU: *send me air cover. Send me a support vessel.* All the replies were curt and to the point: *no cover or supplies available. Head for Lorient as best you can.* It then warned them about Leigh Lights – a combination of radar and searchlights – that enabled bombers to patrol in the dark. Also there was a new radar, which the Metex detectors on the U-boats could no longer pinpoint. The enemy arsenal was expanding and the Germans had no new countermeasures. Erich had never felt so exposed at sea before.

The enemy found them late one afternoon off the north-east tip of Ireland. The phonesman hardly had time to warn them of a destroyer closing fast before the explosions punched through the ship, making her buck. Glass exploded over Erich as dials burst their faces. The lights went out for a second, then came back on.

'Take her down, Chief—'

A cluster of Hedgehogs erupted all around, battering them mercilessly.

'Flooding in engine room.'

'Pumps on full.'

'Second destroyer – damn. Where did that come from?'

Another round of explosions. This time Prinz didn't need to tell them to go down. U-40 began to slide into the depths of her own accord. Erich felt the steel bands of the *Blechkoller* close round his chest, the first time he had felt the submariner's panic in many a month.

'Depth?'

The IWO looked at the shattered gauge and tapped it. A triangular piece of glass fell out, but the needle stayed jammed in place. 'Broken.'

'Flooding in the torpedo compartment.'

'Can you seal it off?'

'Trying.'

'You're going to have to blow the tanks.' The Chief was at Prinz's shoulder, speaking as easily as he could.

Prinz turned on him. 'Pumps?'

The Chief shook his head. 'Working as hard as they can. And the aft pump is failing.'

A surge of water came through the control room, pouring over their boots. Erich could feel the sub starting to roll. If they didn't blow soon, so much water would have entered that negative buoyancy would be impossible. He heard some of the panels start to creak and a rivet popped somewhere. Another pipe burst. More rivets, like gunshots this time. They must be getting deep.

'Rudder full to port!' yelled the Chief. That sometimes acted as a brake. Not this time. The lights went again, leaving only the red emergency bulbs. *We're going straight to hell*, thought Erich.

Prinz prepared himself for one of the final announcements of his captaincy. 'Blow—' he began. A stream of water hit his face and he stepped back, spitting. The gasket rings on the periscope housing had failed. He took off his cap and shook his head to clear the water. 'Blow all tanks.'

The Chief set to work, and Erich stood beside him, rotating the valve handles as quickly as he could. They heard the hiss of compressed air. The sub was still rolling. The navigation aids began to slide off the table.

'All tanks!' yelled the Chief.

U-40 stopped for a second, then gave a little shiver and began to rise. They felt her lift slowly for a few seconds, then begin to accelerate.

'Shit!' said the Chief. 'Too fast.'

The submarine was bobbing up like a cork released under water, liable to break her back and in danger of smashing into one of the hunters above.

'Brace!' yelled Prinz, although everyone had already found something to cling to.

'Fifty metres!' came a distant voice. It was from the torpedo room. Its depth gauge must still be working. 'Thirty-five.'

The lights were restored. The control-room team didn't speak. Several of them had their eyes closed. As the water became less dense they felt the sub rise even quicker.

Then there was the hollow thump of waves breaking over the tower and the deck as U-40 smashed its way into the air, rocking back and forth so hard that it almost turned turtle, flinging its crew across the hull as it oscillated. But the old crate held together.

'Hatch clear.'

'Opening hatch.'

As the Captain climbed the ladder Erich heard the tower crackle under the impact of heavy machine-gun rounds. Prinz slid down. 'Two of them, closing fast.' He looked at Erich. 'Codes.'

Erich sprinted through to the signal room, grabbed the *Kurzsignalheft*, the short-signal book, and the *Wetterkurzschlüssel*, the weather short-signal book, and dunked them into the dirty water slopping around his feet. They instantly began to bleed black clouds, as the soluble ink drifted off the pages. He took the coding machine and, following standing orders, smashed the rotors with three hammer blows before tossing it to the floor. He did the same with the spare rotors. In the mess room he used his key to open the signals locker and took out the dozen letters he had written to Uli, slid them into an oilskin pouch and shoved them into his tunic before dropping the other documents into the water.

As he returned to the control room he saw Prinz at the periscope. 'Schnee! Signal a surr—' shouted the Captain.

They heard the shrieking of metal and sailors yelling followed by the whoosh of sea water cascading its way into the pressure hull. Something had sheered part of the sub's tail off. The boat spun round and tilted once more. Erich could smell burning and chlorine fumes. He fumbled towards the bulkhead where the rebreathers were kept. An explosion catapulted him into the metal. The ship was starting to list. Erich, Prinz and the others didn't need a damage report to know that U-40 had been rammed and fatally wounded. She was going to the bottom.

The Falcon Cliff Hotel sat on a clifftop above Douglas Harbour, its castellated and turreted frontage proclaiming its somewhat grander status compared with the lesser establishments that lined the seafront. Now, though, its lobbies and lounges had been stripped bare of ornament, its carpets torn up, and it smelled of astringent chemicals and the elderly. It had functioned as the main hospital for the internment camps since the first refugees had arrived and the authorities realised that they had interned a large number of people with diabetes, kidney problems, heart murmurs, dementia and even tuberculosis.

Ross followed the nurse along the corridor to what had once been one of the larger hotel suites.

'He's in here,' she said. 'He should have been moved to the

210

main hospital, but, well, he likes it here and we don't have too many patients. Ten minutes, I'm afraid, Inspector.'

Ross smiled his thanks as she held the door open and he stepped into the room. It was bare, apart from the bed and a couple of steel cupboards, the gilded wallpaper was scratched and peeling, and the floor still showed the tack marks where the Axminster had been. The sole patient's wheelchair had been positioned so that he could watch the harbour.

'Hello, *Herr* Walter. Fritz.'

The old man turned his head and Ross tried not to look too shocked at the gauntness and the yellowing of his skin. It didn't seem fair that just five years could do this to a man. 'I . . .' There was the barest glint of recognition. 'No, sorry, can't place you.'

Ross introduced himself and Walter clapped his bony hands in delight. 'Of course. Inspector. My God, that seems a lifetime ago. All that intrigue, eh? Uncle Otto, Canaris. Did it come to anything?'

'Yes. Yes, it did. In a manner of speaking,' Ross said. 'The link with Canaris was broken, though, quite early on.' He didn't add that it had cost the life of an innocent girl.

'Otto and Canaris. They both hate Hitler. Mind you, I'm not sure either of them are huge supporters of democracy, not as you understand it here. But they'd be better than Adolf.' Walter laughed and Ross heard the fluid in his lungs gurgle. 'They don't seem to have done much good, do they? He's still there. Looks like we'll have to rely on that bastard Hitler to destroy himself. Can you pass me that water, Inspector? Thank you.'

Walter took a noisy sip and smacked his lips. 'Thank you,' the old man said again as he handed the glass back. 'It's good to see you. I'm getting a little bored of staring at ferries. Sorry about the state of me. Seem to have gone downhill.'

'Nonsense. It's good to see you, too. I'm actually here mainly about Ulrike.'

'Uli? What's she done?'

'Done? Nothing. It's what we have done to her. And you. Locking you away . . .'

'Oh, that. She was angry at first, I think, as we all were. Furious. But the anger went. You know, for some people it has been a godsend. Some of these camps have allowed talent to bloom. At a Derby Castle concert, I heard these young men. Nissel. Lovett and . . . a Viennese, Brainin . . . my goodness, what playing.'

Ross stepped in as Walter paused for breath, hoping that he had grasped this correctly. 'You heard from her? You've heard from Uli?'

'Eventually. Post awful. Only one censor for the whole island, so letters in and out took an age. And many of them ended up at the bottom—'

'Where is she?' Ross asked impatiently. 'Where is Uli?'

'She's in Canada.'

Ross stated at Walter as if he were mad. No women went abroad. The Home Office woman had been very clear. 'Canada? Which Canada?' he asked, in case he was missing something.

'Which Canada?' asked Fritz Walter, his chest heaving. 'The one five thousand kilometres away, that's which one.'

As the waves broke over his head, Erich forced himself to try to ride higher in his life preserver. The gash on his head was stinging, and one eye had swollen shut. He turned to face U-40. Her bow was out of the water and the stern had dipped below the surface. Men were still struggling clear, hoping she would stay afloat a little longer. Only Prinz and the Chief were left on board now. The sky was darkening and Erich could feel his teeth chattering and his limbs going numb. He wanted to close his good eye and push the pain and the noise and the screams away, erase the memory of the mad scramble to clear the stricken submarine. He hoped he had acquitted himself well and hadn't trodden on others in his selfish haste. He looked away from the boat. He didn't want to see her die.

'She's turning!' someone shouted. 'She's turning back to us.'

It was the destroyer that had sliced off part of their stern, emerging from the billowing veil of rain that was falling a mere kilometre away. He had heard tales of destroyers depth-charging U-boat survivors in the water, the blast reducing their lifeless bodies to sacks of rubber.

He turned to see Prinz, still in the tower, alone now. He was signalling frantically with the Aldis lamp. Erich read off the message: '—Captain U-40. Please save my men, drifting in your direction. I am sinking.'

As he peered through the darkness at the oncoming ship, Erich realised two things: first, the crinkly shapes being dropped down the side of the destroyer were scramble nets for their rescue. Second, Captain Günther Prinz was not going to leave the stricken U-40.

They were waiting for Inspector Cameron Ross at Euston. They were from the rubber-heel brigade, internal investigators into police corruption. They flashed their credentials and nodded towards the black Humber that had drawn up next to the platform. Ross looked around, thinking that there must have been a mistake.

'What's this?' he asked.

'You'll see, Inspector. If I could just have your warrant card?' The speaker was in his fifties and obviously experienced, not about to take any nonsense.

Ross handed it over and was led over to the car. No handcuffs, at least. He removed his hat and slid into the vehicle, grabbing one of the detective's wrists when the man tried to put a hand on his head to push him in.

'Sorry, sir. Reflex.'

They drove south, through Bloomsbury, past the devastated houses of Bernard and Guildford Streets, the jagged scorched outlines a shock again after the unbombed Isle of Man.

The older detective offered him a Woodbine but he refused. They were crossing Waterloo Bridge now, heading towards another flattened area, the warehouses propped up by makeshift scaffolding.

He'd made enquiries about getting Uli back. They couldn't do anything on the island. He'd have to petition the Home Office. They made it sound like a lifetime career. At least she was alive, he thought, a small piece of happiness in an insane world.

The destination turned out to be a dark Gothic mansion, bristling with spires and gargoyles. It was sandbagged and guarded, but there were no signs indicating its function. Ross could guess.

His father was waiting on the first floor, in a room freshly painted military green, furnished only with a metal table and two chairs. He looked up as his son entered and indicated that he should sit. Ross remained standing.

'Is this your idea of an invitation?'

'Would you have come if I'd sent one?'

'No.'

'So I had to pull some strings.'

'Does it ever occur to you, father, that you can pull too many strings?' Ross asked. 'Get yourself in a tangle?'

'I didn't know that Uli Walter been taken abroad. I only just found out when we checked on what you were up to.'

Ross leant forward, trying to hold his frustration in check. 'But you knew she was in the country? Back when I asked you to find out whether she had got out of Germany?'

The Colonel shifted in his seat. 'I knew that there was every chance you'd make a fool of yourself with this girl. They were – are – our enemies, Cameron, something which you sometimes have trouble grasping.'

Ross slumped back. 'I don't know where to begin, I really don't. Some Germans blew me half to pieces. Some of them killed Emma. And you can talk to me about enemies? I know who our enemies are. But credit me with being able to tell the difference between those who are and those who are not on our side, for crying out loud.'

The Colonel looked down at his hands. 'I made some mistakes. Including keeping you two apart.' Then his eyes flared. 'Christ, we all made mistakes. Even Churchill, he laid some eggs at the start, I can tell you. What do you want me to say? I'm sorry.'

Ross paced for a few minutes, letting his anger ebb. 'Well, why am I here?' he asked eventually.

'The beard looks good.'

'Why am I here?' Ross repeated.

'I need your help.'

'You've got some nerve.'

'Yes, you're right. You think I'd ask if it wasn't the only way? I have been asked to head up a new PWIS based at the London Cage. To be run jointly with the Americans.'

'Forgive me if I'm not up with the latest acronyms.'

'Prisoner of War Intelligence Service. It is part of CSDIC – Combined Services Detailed Interrogation Centre, before you ask.'

'What's this got to do with me?'

There was a long pause. 'I need an assistant.'

'And you thought of me? Well, it may have escaped your notice, dad, but I have a perfectly decent job. So, thanks, but no—'

The unfamiliar noise made him stop. He turned and looked at the Colonel's waxy face, his wobbling lip. With a shock Ross realised that his father was crying.

They were allowed up on deck as the destroyer steamed into Liverpool. The air was icy, but Erich enjoyed the breeze whipping against his face, stinging it into life after days below. They hadn't been badly treated by the British, but it was good to stretch his legs and to see a port other than Lorient, even if it was the enemy's.

Erich marvelled at the size and range of the vessels, all sitting out in the open – corvettes and fast torpedo boats, a submarine, several destroyers, one flying a US flag, and a mass of cargo ships. He felt Becker, the IWO, slide onto the rail next to him.

'They have a lot of ships here,' said Erich.

'Looks like we didn't do a good enough job.'

Erich smiled. 'I think we did our best. I think the Captain did his best.'

'Bloody fool,' said Becker. 'He shouldn't have gone down. His place was with his men, not with that old tub of a boat.'

'I suppose it's up to you. To take his place.'

There was a welcoming blast on the horn from a nearby warship and a few gulls took fright, circling lazily before settling back on the grey superstructure. 'His place as what? We don't have a boat any longer – we'll probably be split up. Let's just keep our head down, try and get home for Christmas.'

Erich scratched his head. 'Christmas is a month away.'

216

The IWO shrugged. 'Is it really? Well, next Christmas, anyway.'

All over by the end of 1944. *Well. Amen to that*, thought Erich.

Ross's father took him to a corner pub a few streets away, where he sipped whisky shakily and Ross had a glass of mild and bitter.

'What's wrong?' asked Ross.

'I'm losing my mind.'

'Dad, please.'

'Oh, not all the time. It just wanders. I can't focus. Can't formulate what is coming next. It's . . . unpredictable. There are just times when I forget why I am here, what I am doing. Then, two or three minutes later, I'm back.'

Ross was no expert, but it sounded like dementia of some kind. 'Have you seen a doctor?'

'Why? There is nothing they can do. And I still have work to finish.'

'You can't work like that. You have to take it easy. Retire.'

'That's exactly what I am afraid of hearing.'

'Maybe it's the truth,' said Ross softly. 'It has to come sometime.'

'If the Yanks find out that I'm not firing on all cylinders, I'll be off PWIS straight away. They are looking for an excuse to take it all over. If you were my assistant—'

'What good would that do?'

'You could step in whenever I required you. Nobody need know. They'd just think it was a blow hot-blow cold team.'

'That's ridiculous, dad.'

'The war isn't going to last for ever, Cameron. A year. Two at most. When the Second Front opens next spring, they reckon on thousands of prisoners. They'll need me. I just want to see this through. End it like a man, not some . . . senile old basket case. "Good chap once, lost his marbles before the end" – that kind of thing.'

Ross was embarrassed to see tears in his father's eyes once more. He was frightened. The Colonel was scared of what the future held. 'Please, son. I just need to hold on to things for a while longer. If I retire now I'll be totally ga-ga within six months. I know it is asking a lot. I can square it with—'

'No. Don't square anything for me. I do all my own squaring from now on. This is why I didn't want to see you. I knew I'd get sucked into one of your schemes again.'

'It won't be for long,' the Colonel assured him. 'The war might be over in a year. Please.'

Ross went to the bar for refills, his mind working furiously. He did feel sorry and concerned for his father but this was also an opportunity for the man to make up for some of the damage he had done. As he sat down Ross grasped his moment with both hands. 'OK, dad. I'll give it a go. On one condition.'

Twenty-Four

The SS *Purcell* docked at Southampton on a bright December day and signalled her thanks to her escort and a greeting to her home port with three long blasts on the ship's horn. Ross sat in the vast, echoing processing hall, where passengers had once checked in their trunks for voyages on luxury liners, but where Immigration and Combined Services officials now sat, lining up their forms and their stamps, waiting for their clients to disembark.

As the first Canadian soldiers wobbled down the gangplank and shuffled their way into the hall, Ross slipped outside onto the quay and sat on a capstan, smoking – a new vice – marvelling at the endless stream of strapping, fresh-faced lads who had come to fight on soil far, far away from their homeland. 'God bless the Empire,' Churchill had said. For the first time, Ross appreciated what he meant.

Uli was, of course, one of the last to come off. Ross had been waiting well over an hour when he saw her duck through the doorway into the watery sunlight, her hand clutching a single suitcase.

He threw down his fifth cigarette, ground it into the stones of the quay, buttoned up his jacket and stepped forward before he hesitated. She still hadn't seen him – perhaps she didn't recognise him with the beard – as she stepped gingerly onto the dockside, appearing bewildered and lost. She looked as if the mischievous spirit he remembered had been caged and broken, the flame diminished. Would she want him?

'Name?'

'Erich Hinkel.'

'Rank?'

'*Leutnant zur See.*'

'On U-40.'

'Yes.'

'Do you have any complaints about your treatment so far?' The man's German was good, thought Erich.

'No.'

'You realise that the belongings taken from you and signed for will be returned in due course.'

'Yes.'

'Excellent.'

The Intelligence Captain leant forward. They were in the manager's canteen of a former carpet factory near Lancaster, requisitioned for the war, and now the focal point of the North-West Area Cage. A 'camp' was the final destination, Erich had learned, and it might be in the UK, although many prisoners – a significant number of them from the *Bootwaffe* – had been shipped to Canada. A 'cage' was a holding or transit centre for POWs, where they would be interrogated before being assigned a camp. The NWA Cage consisted of two large lawned areas – a football and a rugby pitch respectively, originally provided for the carpet workers' recreation – studded with Nissen huts, one section for officers and one for other ranks, each surrounded by wire and sentry towers.

The Intelligence Captain offered him a cigarette and Erich hesitated before he took it. He'd thought long and hard how to play this, but the mood in the Cage seemed to be one of resignation. He was berthed with a mixture of soldiers from North Africa and Italy and sailors from the merchant arm and submarines. Play the game according to the rules, they all said, and you'll be OK. Give them just enough, no more.

'What type of submarine was U-40, *Leutnant*?'

'I am not at liberty to say.'

'A Type VIIB, I believe. Old, too.' He looked up from his notes and smiled. 'Or so your colleagues tell me. You did well over the years.' There seemed to be genuine admiration in the voice. 'To survive, I mean. Out there. You must have had a hell of a captain.' He glanced down at his notes. 'Captain Prinz.'

'He was.'

'Did you approve of what he did?'

Did he mean sinking Allied ships? Erich answered warily. 'He did his duty.'

'I thought going down with the ship was rather out of fashion. You can build another U-boat. Men like Prinz are not so easily replaced.'

'I agree.'

'Why do you think he did it?'

'I can't say.'

'We're just chatting, Erich. I'm curious. Would you like some tea?'

'No thank you. I think he did it because . . . I think he thought the U-boat war was over.'

'Hmm. And you? Did you think that?'

Sunderlands, Liberators, the Mark 24 mine – actually a homing torpedo – Hedgehog, Squid, HF-DF, what the Allies called huff-duff, for detecting the U-boats' signals, MACs – cargo ships with short-take-off ramps for planes – all the things Erich had discovered since the sinking suggested that Prinz had been right. 'I am not sure.'

'You must have trained on *Heimsiche Gewässer*.' The code known as Home Waters, or Hydra to the Germans, Dolphin to the British and, as the Intelligence Officer knew, well and truly broken.

'Yes.'

The expression on the IO's face didn't change. He said: 'Well, that's all for now, Erich. Messing is in the large tent over by the football posts. Your particular sitting is on the board outside. We'll speak again.'

Erich had been dismissed, but he stayed where he was and asked: 'Sir – I wondered. Is there any way I can get a letter to someone in England?'

'Who?'

'A German girl who came over before the war. My fiancée.' *Former fiancée*, an inner voice corrected him.

'Do you have an address?'

'No. London, perhaps,' said Erich, realising how hopeless that sounded.

'I'm sorry, you'll need more than that. Especially if she was a German national – they've been well and truly scattered during the past few years. Maybe when it's all over.'

Erich's heart sank. He so wanted Uli to see those letters, especially now they were both in the same country. As he rose he managed to mutter: 'Yes. Of course. Thank you.'

After he had gone the Intelligence Officer wrote on the file confirming that Erich Hinkel was a U-boat cipher clerk, and therefore potentially useful, and stamped across the bottom of the file TRIBI: To Remain in British Isles.

★ ★ ★

One of the ferries had struck a mine. Fritz Walter could tell by the way it was listing and the flotilla of tugs fussing around it. It was limping back into Douglas, taking in water, but it was going to make it. Walter had seen it two or three times from his viewpoint in the Falcon Cliff Hotel. He had also, over the past few months, watched the men march out of Onchen and Hutchinson camps, heading back to the mainland. He would have liked to be with them, but something inside him had given up, poisoning his liver and pancreas.

The nurse came in with some broth, which he sipped briefly, then left the remainder to go cold. It was close to lights out when the Sister and an auxiliary nurse came in and started to wheel him away from the window.

'I quite like to watch the Christmas lights come on,' Walter protested. For the first time in years, there were signs of the festive season strung around the town, a tentative step towards normality. It was oddly heartwarming that a few coloured bulbs could convey such hope and optimism.

'We've got to get you close to the wall,' replied the Sister.

The telephone trolley was wheeled in and plugged into the socket, and all three watched it while the clock edged round to five. The brittle sound made them jump, and Sister picked up on the second ring.

'Hello. HELLO. Yes. He's here. I'll put him on now. Fritz,' she added rather redundantly, 'it's for you.'

Walter put the Bakelite shell to his ear. 'Yes?'

'Father?' the voice was small and distant.

'Hello?'

'Daddy. It's me. Uli.'

'Uli.' His words dried up immediately, jammed in his throat. 'Uli.'

223

'Merry Christmas, daddy.'

'Uli. Where are you?'

'You remember Inspector Ross? The Scottish detective? He found out where I was and had me brought back from Canada. It was just wonderful of him. I'm ever so grateful.' Walter could tell from her voice that Ross was probably in the room with her; she seemed to be playing it up for someone. 'So now I'm in London. I'm back in London.'

'Oh.' He could taste the salt of his tears now, gathering at the corners of his mouth. 'How long have you been there?'

'A few days. A week, perhaps. But I can't come and see you. Something about there being too many hardliners on the island. They still don't trust me. Us. The Inspector is trying his best to get me clearance, but . . . you know how slow they are.'

'I want to see you,' he whispered. All the times he had wished for this, to hear his daughter's lovely soft voice, to speak to her again, and now all he could manage were half-sentences. 'Please.'

'As soon as I can. You know that. How are you?'

'Oh, Uli,' Walter sobbed.

He could hear her crying too, a strange sound echoing down the line. There was a sniff as she pulled herself together. 'Listen. I have something for you,' she said. 'A Christmas present. Keep the receiver to your ear.'

He lay there, propped up in the bed, straining to hear what was happening at the other end.

Then Uli was back. 'Ready?' she asked.

'Yes.'

The sound was thin and weak, the bass notes lost in the carbon particles of the earpiece, but the first few bars of bow on strings filled his heart with pleasure. He could just make out an accompanist in the background. He recognised it, of course.

Handel's Sonata for Violin and Piano in F major, the piece his daughter had been meant to play at the recital before her accident, almost a decade ago. Fritz Walter lay back against the pillow, cradling the receiver, crying as silently as he could, so that he could catch every beautiful note his Ulrike played.

Twenty-Five

Rome: Early March 1944

SS-Obersturmführer Axel Schuller, formerly a mere *Anwärter* of the Berlin *Ordnungspolizei*, watched with pride as the 156 men of the 11th Company of the 3rd Battalion of the *SS-Polizei Regiment 'Bozen'* marched through the streets of Rome, turned along the tiny Via Rasella, and began their final approach to the Macau barracks.

Locals watched with awe, as well they might, marvelling at this well-oiled, battle-seasoned machine. Schuller was pleased with their actions this morning. They had successfully cleared out a whole section of the Trastevere district, where anti-German propaganda had been produced and, he was certain, sabotage against the *Reich* was plotted.

It had been an early-morning raid, as usual, and the dozens of suspects and hangers-on were now heading for the cells, while his men looked forward to a rest. It was time for some leave. Since Berlin, Schuller had served in France, Poland, Czechoslovakia and then Italy for the past two years, in each place waging a brutal war against partisans. He needed a break

226

from the gruelling work to recharge himself.

He stepped aside as a road sweeper squeezed along the pavement, his heavy broom brushing the dust down towards the main street. He could see his men having to swerve around the man's cart, carelessly parked in the road. He thought of admonishing the old street-sweep, but thought better of it.

A rest from the constant punishment-and-prevention actions would be very welcome. However, as *SS-Obersturmbannführer* Herbert Kappler, his commanding officer, said: if they didn't do this vital work, who would? The Italians? Spineless turncoats. Their secret capitulation, the way the Italian soldiers had discarded their uniforms and hidden their weapons once Mussolini had been captured by the Resistance, was despicable. Even Benito had needed the Germans to bail him out – the rescue by *SS-Standartenführer* Otto Skorzeny and his glider force of the hapless Duce from the mountains had become the stuff of SS legend. What a man Skorzeny was.

Schuller recognised that, although he might not yet be a Skorzeny, he was a long way from his days as a callow young *Anwärter* in Berlin. He wondered if he could be transferred to Skorzeny's *SS-Kommando* force, the one that took its assignments directly from the Führer. Kidnapping, sabotage, assassination and mayhem, that was its brief. Could you apply to join such an illustrious band, or were you merely chosen, recommended by a commanding officer? He'd have a word with Kappler.

Schuller felt a sudden flash of irritation about the refuse cart blocking his way. He turned and walked down the slope to where the sweeper seemed to have disappeared. He would box his ears. Everyone knew this was the route to the barracks.

He reached the corner and scanned the street, looking for the shabby little man. He was nowhere to be seen. Then he realised: *everyone knew this was the route to the barracks.*

Axel Schuller dived to the ground as the cart detonated. He felt the heat of the explosion wash over him as the shock wave buffeted him. The men of the 11th Company of the 3rd Battalion of the *SS-Polizei Regiment 'Bozen'* were flung in the air like broken dolls, and Schuller heard the rain of debris and flesh falling all around him. Even as he looked up at the unspeakable horror filling the Via Rasella, he knew that someone was going to have to pay for this outrage.

Twenty-Six

March–June 1944

The house had once been the home of a minor baronet, but, with his servants mostly conscripted, the owner had taken to living at his London residence and Stanhope House had been taken over by the MOD. Located not far from the Newmarket racecourse, it was a splendid Italianate structure, designed by a Venetian who had died before he could make the journey to see what the English had made of his post-Palladian plans. It was surrounded by fine formal gardens, much of which had survived the usual fate of being turned over to growing string beans or onions.

However, the adjoining deer park had been cleared of trees and animals. These had been replaced by huts, a canteen, a chapel, stores, a kitchen, machine-gun posts, latrines and pill-boxes, all put in place along with sodium lamps and the double barbed-wire row that now surrounded the area. Dogs prowled between the fences and searchlights swept much of the perimeter at night. The guards and their superiors were billeted in the house – the former in the warren of basements that had once been the kitchens and wine cellars, the latter in the elegant, light bedrooms with views over the grounds, or in the Dower House, a detached property tucked away to the north of the main house and shielded from the prisoners by a copse of trees. The first floor of the main building also housed interrogation rooms, where each interview was meticulously recorded, either by stenographer or microphone, and the filing centre, which consisted of yards of metal cabinets.

Stanhope House was now Camp 203, just one of the six hundred makeshift encampments built to house the thousands of captured Germans expected to land in the country after the Second Front was opened. Those in Camp 203 had been interrogated and were either awaiting further investigation or were not deemed any real threat. The British were careful to separate the ranks, and the sixteen huts in Compound Alpha that held the officers were more comfortable and better heated than those of their junior comrades.

When Erich finally arrived at his designated camp, after months of being shunted from Cage to Cage, there were 162 officers and 200 enlisted men, culled from all areas of the services. He was one of the few U-boat men, most of them having been sent to Scotland or shipped across to Canada. There were several *Luftwaffe* officers, who had been debriefed at Cockfosters or the London Cage, some sailors, and an increasing number of *Wehrmacht* men who had been captured in the battle for Italy.

Erich was assigned to Hut Fourteen, with a group of the *Wehrmacht*, several of whom were not Germans – there was one from Alsace, two Hungarians and a Romanian. He was welcomed into the hut as a fallen hero and briefed by Werner Dietrich, a young *Leutnant* from Bonn.

As Erich stowed his meagre belongings in the locker next to a

230

double-decked bed, each level consisting of a thin mattress on top of rough-hewn planks, Dietrich kept up a barrage of information: 'The thing is, we are on the same rations as the British soldiers. Which means – we get better fed than the locals! They don't like that, of course. We get almost half a kilo of meat a week, bread, margarine – no butter – vegetables, cheese, cake, jam, tea. Take my advice, learn to like the tea. The coffee is rubbish.'

Erich turned and examined the lad. He was probably the same age as Erich, but he looked younger. 'What is there to be so cheerful about?'

Dietrich shrugged. 'What's so bad?' He lowered his voice. 'You'd rather be back under the sea? Well, I never want to see Italy again. I tell you, we're better off here.' Dietrich went off and fetched some biscuits and offered Erich one. They tasted of chestnut flour. 'Do you play football?'

'A little.'

'There are matches every weekend. Five a side, usually. Each hut puts up a team. We'll see later how useful you are. There are lectures, we have a card school, there is a vegetable garden, and they say we will be able to eat what we grow.'

Erich looked at the little groups huddled around the two tables, playing cards or chess. 'What about work, something more constructive?'

'Well,' said Dietrich, spilling crumbs down his overalls. 'Under the Geneva Convention, the British can't make officers work. Other ranks form construction teams sometimes – they are starting to repair the worst of the bomb damage round here. They pay them four shillings a week.'

'So no work for the officers?'

'Some of us are repairing the tennis courts over the back. We'll be able to use them when they are done. Seems strange,

231

we are trying to repair the hole left by one of our own bombs.'
Dietrich laughed and Erich had an inkling that the lad was
going to be annoying, one of the mouthy types you dreaded
encountering on a submarine, where there was no escape.

'Do you want me to introduce you around? Major Achillin in
Hut Ten is the senior officer. Then there is—'

'No, thanks. I'm tired after the journey here. Twenty-odd
hours on a train. Fifteen to a compartment. I'm going to have a
nap.'

'Oh. Right. Well, if there's anything—'

'Yes. Thanks, Werner. See you later.'

Erich lay down on the bottom bunk and tried to get comfortable. He closed his eyes, blanking out the noise of gossip,
laughter and arguments from his new companions. It wasn't
difficult. He'd been doing it for the best part of five years.
Submarines were perfect training for a camp hut like this, he
thought. Within five minutes, he was asleep.

'He was lying.' Uli's voice was flat, but full of conviction. 'I
would say absolutely. This one.' She tapped the photographs in
front of her. 'Number four was the impostor.'

'Thank you, Ulrike. Can you excuse us for a minute?'

Uli scraped her chair back, smoothed down her slacks – if
Ross hadn't known they were made from dyed blackout mat-
erial, he'd never have guessed – and left the Colonel's spartan
office on the first floor of the mansion that had become the
London Cage. The old man looked at his son. 'It is remarkable,
I will grant you that.'

Ross had arranged for Uli to demonstrate her powers of
perception to his sceptical father. He had insisted that the only
way he would join the Colonel in PWIS was if Uli was brought
back to England to become his assistant.

When the Colonel had objected, he had also explained in detail about her Duchenne gift. Ross senior had simply not believed it. Now, after several tests where four people told their life story – one of them an actor faking it as best he could – he was beginning to think that there was something in it.

'Look, Cameron, it is something special, but it is also a very blunt instrument.'

'Meaning?'

'Meaning that she could tell me which one was lying. But not why.'

'Oh, for God's sake, dad. I said she could detect lies, not read minds.'

'Well, next time try and get me one of those,' he huffed. 'My other concern is that she's a woman.'

'I had noticed.'

'Too bloody much if you ask me. If she'd been a sixty-year-old crone with this gift, would you have dragged her back across the Atlantic? There's no need to answer that.'

No, thought Ross, but it wasn't like the Colonel suspected. Ever since he had met her at Southampton and she had hugged him – the most demonstrative she had been so far – they'd both realised that they had a lot to find out about each other.

'What I mean,' continued his father, 'is that she upsets the dynamic. With the prisoners. Even if she does wear trousers.'

'Can't she be hidden?'

The Colonel scratched his head. 'It's a thought. We could rig up spyholes. Or that special glass, I suppose. Transparent one way only. That's an idea. And I know what she will be perfect for.'

'What?'

'I can't let her loose on intelligence work. Never hear the end of it from the Yanks.'

'Why?'

'Using a German national.'

Ross didn't offer the thought that the Yanks would use any nationality they thought could help them. 'Dad, when will you stop thinking of her as just another German national?'

'What should I start thinking of her as, eh? The future Mrs Ross?'

He felt himself redden. 'No,' he lied.

'Look, one thing the Yanks are keen on these days is war crimes. They want PWIS to report to this new subsidiary.' He searched until he found the document he needed and slipped on his reading glasses. 'Joint Allied War Crimes Investigation Unit. JACI for short, apparently. They are compiling lists of cases pending future prosecutions. I would imagine your girl would be very useful during those kinds of cross-examinations. Tucked out of the way, of course.'

Ross stood up, smelling victory, a rare sensation where the old bugger was concerned. 'She's in, then?'

'I suppose so. I'll find some way of giving her official status. I've got no choice, have I? Bloody hell, Cameron, I hope she's worth it.'

Sergeant Joe Pantole of VI Corps of the US 5th Army Group stirred as the sun came up over Rome. He was stiff, having bedded down on a pavement, and hung-over from all the red wine that the locals had forced on him. Despite his name, and a grandfather from Puglia, he spoke no Italian, and had hardly followed what the excited people had jabbered at him. But it had been late and, after the long slog up through Italy, and especially after the desperate rush through the Alban Hills, he and his comrades were dog-tired, ready to sleep where they fell.

An M4 tank started up across the road, and there was cursing from those still dozing on and around it. The tank crew set about resecuring the sandbags that were roped to the sides in an attempt to compensate for armour that didn't stand a chance against the Germans' 88s. Pantole sat up, lit a cigarette and broke wind loudly.

'Hey, sarge. Go and do that somewhere else, willya?'

Pantole stood up and stretched. 'Fuck you, McCabe.'

'You think we'll get to rest up here, sarge?'

Pantole smiled. The Germans had pulled out of Rome, but they would be regrouping to the north. There were still a lot of mountains and strongholds to slog through, plenty of smaller-scale Monte Cassinos to hold them up, scores of bridges for the Krauts to blow. The Allies were only halfway up the boot of Italy, even if Rome was the big prize. Such a prize that the US commander of the 5th Army had suggested that they shoot any Brits who made it into the city before they did. None of them had. Pantole agreed with what Patton said about the Limeys – the men were as brave as they came, but the officers seemed to lack any get-up-and-go-and-get-'em.

'For a while, yeah,' he said eventually. 'We might get to see how grateful these guys are.'

'Hey, it's not the guys I want to be grateful. I hear a girl costs a quarter. A dollar the night.'

'You'll get your chance, son.' Pantole looked for latrine paper, but ended up grabbing a *Stars and Stripes* magazine and walked away from the troop, heading up the slope, looking for somewhere to take a quiet dump. As he looked back he could see the park where some lucky stiffs had managed to bivouac properly. Beyond the park there was a tantalising glimpse of ancient ruins. He hoped he could get some pictures of the Colosseum before they left, prove to his grandpa he'd made it here.

There were whistles sounding in the streets now, urging them to regroup. Would they get a rest and a crack at the dollar-whores? That depended on what Lieutenant General Mark Clark and Field Marshal Alexander, who commanded the British 8th Army, cooked up between them, once they stopped bickering. His guess was that Clark would give them a taste of the spoils before they moved on.

The first thing Pantole thought when the smell hit him was that someone had beaten him to it. Then he realised that he was smelling more than shit. He took the magazine, tore off two strips and made wads for his nostrils. Ahead of him, the cave entrance was sealed with a mix of jerrycans and rubble from what looked like the aftermath of an explosion. Flies buzzed around the gaps in the barrier.

'Sarge!' came a distant voice from behind him, but something made him heave a dozen of the smaller boulders out of the way. He found the first one just inside. The flesh was largely gone, thanks to the dusting of quicklime that covered most of the body, but the hole in the back of the skull was clear enough. He imagined the man kneeling down, the pistol muzzle against the back of the head ... boom. Pantole waited while his eyes adjusted and took half a dozen steps further in. The cave opened out into a huge main chamber, with side passages running off it. The floor was sticky with bat droppings and congealed blood. As his pupils dilated fully he began to count the bodies, most of them entombed in their sarcophagi of solidified quicklime. He stopped at a hundred and twenty. There were a lot more. All civilians, judging by their scraps of clothing. Slowly, Pantole backed out, trying to keep the bile where it belonged, and ran down the hill to tell the captain about the massacre.

'I am very grateful, Cameron. Really I am.' Ross still marvelled at Uli's new accent: almost all the German inflection had gone, replaced by a mid-Atlantic twang that she had picked up in Canada.

They were lunching in the small bistro off Kensington High Street that had become something of a canteen for those working at the London Cage. The proprietor, Luigi, was a stagy old showman, all big hugs and flowers for the lady, but there was nothing phony about the food, even if the shortage of cutlery meant that couples were asked to share spoons for dessert.

'Is everything all right, Mister Ross, signorina?' Luigi asked, and Ross shooed him away, smiling.

'Grateful?' Ross repeated.

'For getting me back from Canada. For cutting through the red tape so that I could see my father before he passed on.' Fritz Walter had been brought back to the mainland. He had got no further than Walton Hospital in Liverpool. Ross – or at least his father – had arranged for Uli to be flown up to the US airbase at Burtonwood and driven into the city to be at the dying man's side. 'And for getting me something useful to do. Grateful isn't somehow enough, I know. It's more than that.'

'But not the same as I feel.'

Uli pushed her plate away, the *coniglio con rosmarino* half finished, almost a crime in these parts. 'Any girl would be flattered that she made such an impression on a man she met for such a short time.'

Ross laughed. 'Your mother made the same impression on me.'

'Then perhaps you are in love with my mother?' she teased.

'Ah, signorina. Is everything all right? Oh dear. If it is not to your liking shall I get you something else? A little pasta, perhaps?' Luigi looked distraught.

'No, it was lovely. I am just a little under the weather. Really.

237

Some coffee, if you have some, please.'

'Of course.'

As he left, Ross said: 'No, it's not your mother. Can't you tell? Use your gift.'

'I don't trust my gift, as you call it. Not any longer.'

Ross almost dropped his knife. 'You don't trust it? It worked perfectly. Don't start saying that around my father. I've convinced him—'

Uli held his wrist and he was quiet. 'For what you want, it is fine. But I now know that people can lie for many, many reasons. To spare one's feelings, for instance. I once thought each expression was clear-cut – love, hate, lies, euphoria. It has taken me a long time to realise that each category has hundreds of subdivisions. And those I can't read. I don't know if it would help if I could. You know that some people can hear microtones in music? But those people sometimes hear so much detail that they miss the overall picture. The tune, if you like. Understand?' Ross nodded, even though he wasn't sure he did. 'Yes, I think you think you love me. But it's not that simple.'

'Is it Erich?' he blurted.

'Erich?'

'Erich. Yes, your childhood sweetheart. You must remember.'

Uli shook her head sadly. 'I don't even know if Erich is alive.'

'But you hope he is?'

'I don't wish him dead, if that's what you mean.'

Luigi returned with the coffee and Ross asked for the bill. It would be ten shillings for two to fit in with government regulations: anything above that would be made up by a variable 'service charge'.

'No . . . I didn't mean that,' he said. 'Not the way it sounded.'

'I know.' She reached out and held his hand, gently this time. 'Can you wait? A little longer?'

Wait for what, exactly? he wondered, but he said: 'Good God, yes. After all you've been through, the last thing you need is me . . . no. I'm just . . .' He tugged an ear nervously. 'Telling you the truth.'

Uli blew him the tiniest of kisses. 'I know.'

The explosion made them all jump. It was Luigi with a bottle of *prosecco*, bustling from the kitchen, his face alight, bellowing to his customers. 'On the BBC,' he cried. 'Winston has just stood up in Parliament. Roma has been liberated!'

Twenty-Seven

San Croce, Italy: 1944

Sergeant Joe Pantole crouched in the side archway of the church, flattening himself against the bullet-scarred door. Ahead of him was a large cobbled square, which led to the stone bridge across the river that ran though the village. On the far side of the bridge was a four-storey Merchant's House, once the grandest in the village, with its view of the church's elegant edifice, and Pantole was certain he had seen movement in there.

He looked across the street to where the rest of his platoon had taken cover. 'Get me the radioman,' he shouted.

'Sarge!' Arms pointed towards the bridge.

The figure had sprinted from the ruined *trattoria* on the left of the square and was heading for the crossing, zig-zagging as he went. Pantole raised his carbine and squeezed off half a clip, the shell cases ringing as they hit the ground. The bullets struck the cobbles around the German's boots, sending up puffs of grit. There was not enough range for a good, clean shot.

'McCabe!'

The New Jersey boy stepped out from his hiding place, raised his M-1 and took the sprinter out with a precisely aimed shot between the shoulder blades. The German staggered, arms splayed, and fell face down at the entrance to the bridge.

Pantole flinched instinctively at the familiar harsh noise of the heavy machine gun that replied. The stream of shells lifted McCabe off his feet, ripping out his chest as it did so, leaving his corpse smoking and bloody in the centre of the street. Pantole shut his eyes. No need to call for a medic. The enemy fire had come from the Merchant's House. He used his binoculars to scan the glassless windows and the roof, trying to pinpoint the machine-gun nest.

Another burst of rapid firing sounded. Spurts of dust kicked up from the wall opposite and he felt a body barrel into him, almost pushing him out into the street. 'Shit.' He spun round. 'Lieutenant. You wanna take it easy.'

The lieutenant took off his helmet, wiped the sweat from his brow and put his headgear back on. 'What's going on, Pantole? The British are biting our ass back there. We should be in those hills by now.' He pointed ahead to the green and purple foothills that rose in a series of gentle waves beyond the village.

'Yeah, right. You seen McCabe? He always wanted to make it home for Christmas. I think he was kinda hopin' he'd be alive when he did.'

The lieutenant glanced across at the body. He'd seen too many dead Americans lying in Italian streets since they'd left Rome for it to register much. If they'd thought the Germans would pick up and run, they'd been wrong. Progress now was no faster than it had been breaking out of Anzio. 'What do you need?'

'Where are the Shermans?'

'About two miles back.'

'I think we need 'em right here.'

241

'Is the bridge mined?'

Pantole shrugged. They'd come across dozens of blown crossings in the past two weeks. 'I dunno. Can't see no wires. I'd like an engineer to take a look.'

'OK, sergeant.' The lieutenant made to move and Pantole grabbed his arm.

'Before you go, we'd better lay down some cover.'

'Right.'

Pantole signalled to his men and the Merchant's House quickly began to look pock-marked as rounds smashed into the stonework and through the windows, the bullets' impacts dancing across the façade, keeping German heads low while the young officer sprinted down the street.

'I don't think she's wired,' said the engineer two hours later, after examining the bridge from several angles.

'If we knock out the machine gun over there, would you walk across to prove it?' asked Pantole.

The engineer grinned and tapped his name tag. 'It doesn't say infallible, sergeant.'

'Get outta here.'

Pantole wasted another clip trying to hit the Merchant's House as the engineer left, and as he stopped firing, he heard the welcome *squeak-squeak* sound of the tracks of the M4s, the Sherman tanks, edging forward, the noise of their Ford engines reverberating through the narrow streets. He guessed that the Germans heard it too. He hoped they felt sick to their stomachs.

He made his platoon cover him while he dragged McCabe's carcass out of the way of the tanks' tracks, took the dead boy's dogtags and a few personal effects and shoved them in his tunic. He waved the lead tank on and as it drew level it halted, the lid went up, and Pantole explained the problem to the commander.

The M4 jerked forward, the turret and its gun rotating towards the house. Almost immediately heavy machine-gun rounds pinged off the tank and Pantole crouched down, aware that a ricochet could be lethal.

The first shell took out the whole top corner of the four-storey house, collapsing part of the roof. A second *thump* from the tank's 75mm gun and the entire top floor was wreathed in smoke. Two more and the façade gave a loud groan and crashed down, bricks bouncing across the house's forecourt and into the river. There was no more machine-gun fire. Pantole stood up, took a breath, and waved his men out to take cover behind the tank. Now was the time to find out just how fallible that engineer was.

SS-Obersturmführer Axel Schuller watched as the crouching Americans gathered behind the tank, ready to cross the San Croce bridge. He was several hundred metres above the town, on a ridge in the foothills, and had watched the brave machine gunners pin down the Americans for hours. They'd known that resistance against the tank was hopeless but had carried on anyway. His unit desperately needed more anti-tank weapons. He'd requested a dozen of the *Panzerfaust* launchers from the supply dumps to the north but none had arrived.

His *SS-Polizei* were mixed in with *Waffen-SS* artillery along the ridge. On either side of him were his three *Untersturmführer*, Hetz, Kroll and Bauert, who had survived the Rome bombing and helped in the reprisals. Now the house was gone and the trio were waiting for his orders. Bauert had a field telephone clamped to his ear.

The tank rolled forward at walking speed, making sure that the soldiers behind could keep up. A few of the platoon detached themselves and swung over the balustrade of the bridge. Hetz shouldered his sniper rifle but Schuller raised a hand. *Not yet.* The Americans were checking for explosives. There were none.

Halfway across now and Schuller lowered his binoculars. 'Go,' he said quietly.

Bauert repeated the order into the mouthpiece, yelling it three times. Within five seconds the front of the tank peeled open and the turret exploded, popping off like the whistle from a kettle as an 88 round hit it. The mortars that the Germans had spent the previous day so carefully ranging came soon after, exploding around the tank in spheres of shrapnel, slicing through the American GIs. After a minute of this bombardment, the backbone of the bridge shattered and the M4 and dozens of bodies slid slowly into the dancing waters of the river. Hetz fired twice at the couple of Americans who had managed to cross the length of the structure. Both crumpled and lay still.

It was all over in three hundred seconds. A platoon wiped out, a tank destroyed, the only crossing for twenty kilometres rendered useless.

'We'll pull back,' said Schuller.

'Why?' asked Kroll. 'We can pick off the next lot who come to fish out their buddies.'

'Next,' said Schuller, 'there will be an air strike on this ridge. Then shelling. We'd best relocate.'

As they scrambled down from their camouflaged hiding place towards the road, the stench of smoke and oil and burned flesh from the village filling their nostrils, a motorcycle courier pulled to a halt beside them. He undid his chinstrap and raised his goggles.

'*Obersturmführer* Schuller?'

'Yes?'

244

A quick salute. 'I have orders to accompany you and your men to divisional headquarters.'

That was nearly thirty miles away. In the wrong direction. 'I'm sorry, but we have a valley to block.' Schuller pointed into the hills. 'That way.'

The messenger handed over a sealed envelope, which Schuller took. He walked away from the group while the rest of his troop emerged from cover and headed for the lorries. He saw the signature first and felt his heart miss a beat. He quickly read the message, refolded it and turned back to the motor-cyclist. 'I'll be along by seven hundred hours.'

'Sir.'

As the man kicked the bike back into life, Bauert asked: 'What is it?'

'We've been summoned for a special mission,' he said with pride.

'Who by?' asked Hetz.

Schuller couldn't keep the grin off his face. '*SS-Standartenführer* Skorzeny.' The man who had rescued Mussolini. The most daring officer in the SS. It had to be something very special indeed.

Twenty-Eight

London: Late August 1944

'Can you confirm that you are *SS-Obersturmführer* Alex Schuller?'

'Yes.'

'Of the *SS-Polizei Regiment 'Bozen'*?'

'Yes. Police number two three zero seven six five slash B. Your German is very good.'

Colonel Ross ignored the compliments. They were in the interrogation room of the London Cage, once a bedchamber, now stripped and used for the preliminary war-crimes questioning. His son sat to his left, behind them was a stenographer, at the door a uniformed sentry. Sometimes there would be an American observer, at other times a Russian whose presence was a psychological threat – many Germans had such a fear of being sent east that they would break if such an action was even implied. Not this one, though. This one would require more than a bit of bluff.

On the desk in front of Cameron Ross was a box with three lights, which the prisoner could not see. It was called the traffic signal and, at the moment, the light shone green for 'go'. This was the sixth time they had used it, and so far it had been useful, rather than spectacular, but his father seemed happy enough.

'Do you have any complaints about your treatment so far? You have not been physically or mentally abused in any way?'

'No, I have not. No complaints.'

'We have you as being captured in the hills to the north of Rome by the 8th Army,' continued the Colonel. A curt nod from Schuller. 'You were actually stationed in Rome throughout March 1943.'

'I cannot discuss my unit's movements.'

The Colonel handed a mimeographed document across. 'This was recovered from the Macau barracks by occupying troops. Daily Orders for your group on 22 March. You were there, *Obersturmführer.*'

Schuller's face darkened.

'On 23 March the men of the *SS-Polizei Regiment 'Bozen'* were returning to barracks when a bomb placed in a refuse cart exploded.'

Schuller jerked involuntarily at the memory. The man had been there, all right, the Colonel thought. He seemed surprised that his interrogators knew about the event.

'Several of your men died.'

'Twenty-six,' corrected Schuller firmly. 'Sixty wounded.'

'What was your reaction to this?'

Ross watched him closely. MI19, the organisation in overall charge of PoWs, had discovered that, unlike the British, German officers were not tutored in anti-interrogation techniques. It was assumed at the beginning of the war that the Germans would be the ones taking prisoners – or else they would all fight to the death anyway.

'*Obersturmführer*, we know what happened next. We need to

establish what our American colleagues call a timeline.'

'What happened next was that we cleared up the dead and wounded. We treated the latter and buried the former with honours.'

'And then?'

'We went back to our duties.'

The red light flicked on. Uli had seen something even in Schuller's stony face. She was in the old dressing room next door, spying through an apparently opaque glass panel inserted into the door. She would signal to the interrogators whenever she felt that there was deception or obfuscation – the red light – or economy with the truth, which was the amber bulb on the signal box. Inspector Ross raised an eyebrow to draw his father's attention to it. He had still not said a word. *Blow hot, blow cold.*

Colonel Ross began to read from a report, a growing fury in his voice as he recited the facts. 'As we understand it, the commandant of Rome, General Kurt Malzer, went berserk. He ordered the arrest of everyone on the street and in the surrounding area. Hitler, on hearing of the bombing, immediately ordered that thirty Italians were to be shot for every policeman killed.'

'Ten,' corrected Schuller quietly. 'It was later reduced to ten.'

Ross suddenly knew where he had met Schuller before. As a policeman in Berlin. The alley in Neuköln where Draper had been killed. God, the man had only been a kid back then.

His father continued. 'We have in command a certain *SS-Obersturmbannführer* Herbert Kappler. The morning after the bomb, he supervised the transporting of three hundred and thirty-five people to the caves on the Via Ardeatina. Statements from locals say that the shooting began at three-thirty in the afternoon. Most agreed that it had ended by eight p.m. Three hundred and thirty-five people shot in the back of the head, one after another. Four and a half hours it took to reach the last one. Can you imagine that? Awaiting your turn as bullet after bullet was fired into your friends and neighbours.'

'Why do you bring this up now?'

The old man laughed. 'Because—' There was the briefest of pauses. It was strange, but Ross could now detect when his father's brain slipped out of gear, when his creeping dementia took its temporary grip, and he quickly leant forward and took over.

'You won't recall, but we have met before, Schuller. Berlin. Nineteen thirty-eight.' There was no reaction. 'You were just an *Anwärter*. A lad. You've done well. An *Obersturmführer* in five years. Couldn't get promotion like that in peacetime, eh?' The man shrugged. He wasn't going to respond to that. 'Mass reprisals are against the rules of war.'

Ross was taken aback by the fury of Schuller's reply. 'What rules of war? Did anyone bother to tell the Russians the rules, or the Czechs? Or the cowards who planted that bomb in Rome?'

'Were you involved in the executions?' asked Ross.

'No.'

Red light. 'I doubt if Kappler could have done it by himself. In four and a half hours. He would have needed help. A lot of help.'

'I wasn't in the caves.'

Red light.

The Colonel recovered and picked up the questioning again. 'I must warn you, *Obersturmführer* Schuller, that our report will be forwarded to the Joint Allied War Crimes Investigation Unit.'

'You want to talk about war crimes? I suggest you look at the record of the American 45th. Thunderbird, I think it is called. At Comise airfield in Sicily, they machine-gunned forty-two uniformed Germans. Later the same day, sixty Italians. At Buttera airfield, a US Captain of the 45th lined up his forty-three prisoners against a wall and machine-gunned them to death. We have our own records, our own investigations. These men will be brought to trial.'

'If what you say is true, they will be brought to trial by the US Army.'

Schuller shook his head, as if such a thing were inconceivable. 'I think you consider the outcome of this war a foregone conclusion. Germany is not finished yet.'

'Germany has been finished for two years. It is just taking a while to sink in.'

There was a flat *crump* from the east and the windows rattled. A flying bomb, one of the 'doodlebugs' that had been falling on London since just after the invasion of Normandy in June, had landed close by. Schuller smiled.

'I was not in the caves.' Red light. 'I do not approve of such actions.' Red light. 'I am not being obstructive.' Red light.

'Very well, *Obersturmführer*. I would like you to write out a statement of your policing actions in Rome during the month of March. Then we will see how closely it fits the facts.'

'And if I don't?'

Ross's father answered. 'It's going to be a long stay at the London Cage for you, Schuller. A very long stay.' The Colonel stood and leant across the desk, resting on his knuckles. 'And if I'm not mistaken, you can't wait to get back among your own kind, can you? Do you think Germany can still win the war?'

'Yes. Yes, I do.'

Green light.

It was hard and gruelling work, far harder than Uli had imagined. The scale of rumour and accusation was vast. More often than not they had to recommend that an investigation team should be sent out to French villages to gather statements, or that witnesses should be found and brought over for identification purposes. And they were only dealing with Western Europe – most of those who had committed atrocities in Eastern Europe were in the hands of the Russians. Or, more likely, already dead.

Today it had been a barn packed with women and children and then burned down. There was a Commando unit rounded up and summarily shot. News of a crashed aircrew bayoneted to death. Jewish hostages had been liquidated in reprisals. The day before she had heard of Czech women and girls raped repeatedly, executed and then nailed to barn doors so that their corpses could be used for target practice. On and on it went. In the evening, Ross and Uli would retire to the pub on the corner for a few drinks to try and purge the memory of the day's sins. Her country's sins, as they were constantly reminded by Colonel Ross.

They usually sat in a corner seat, partitioned off from the body of the bar by frosted glass, and the ageing bottle-boy fetched them their drinks and refills for a tanner tip. Uli sipped her gin and tonic, without lemon – pubs hadn't seen the citrus fruit in years – and asked: 'Did Schuller make his statement?'

'Yes. Pack of lies. Wasn't there, didn't see it.'

'What will happen to him?'

'Oh, some corroborating evidence will surface. He's being moved from the Cage to Stanhope so we can keep him close at hand for when it does.'

'He's one of the ones who give me the creeps,' Uli said.

Ross took a large gulp of his half-and-half. 'Why?'

'He still believes.'

'That's just bravado.'

251

'No, no. He genuinely believes that Germany can rise from this. He is convinced that everything he has done is justified. He has to.'

'Why?'

'Because otherwise he would have to face up to the fact that he is nothing short of a monster.' She shuddered, downed her drink and signalled the bottle-boy for two more.

'You think that Schuller is a monster? Some other species?'

'Well, I tell myself that,' she said. 'I have to. I'm a German, Ross. Do you want me to say that it's some fault in our make-up? That we are a whole nation of deviants?'

Ross sighed. 'It's about war, not nations. I made some inquiries about the American 45th. Schuller might be right. About the summary executions of prisoners.'

'Somehow that doesn't make me feel better.'

Ross tried to lift their spirits. 'Look, would you like to go to the cinema? Abbott and Costello are on at the Electric.'

'I don't understand Abbott and Costello,' she said. 'They aren't funny.' Another cultural difference to chalk up.

'They are an acquired taste, I'll grant you. Like the Three Stooges—'

'Please,' Uli said, wrinkling her nose in disgust.

'What about *National Velvet*? They say that's rather good. Horses, plucky girl, happy ending. Take your mind off things.'

'No, thanks, Ross. I'm going to go back and have a long soak and then to bed with a good book.'

'Dinner?'

She took the fresh gin from the bottle-boy and shook her head. 'Don't crowd me, Cameron. Please.'

'Sorry.'

Uli smiled at him sympathetically. It was difficult for him, she realised. She wondered how he would feel if he knew that she was spending many of her tea and lunch breaks scanning the lists of captured Germans that were being logged at the London Cage, hoping to find the name Erich Hinkel – alive and well and safe.

Twenty-Nine

It only took forty-eight hours at Stanhope camp for Erich to realise that he was going to go insane if he didn't work, no matter what the Geneva Convention said. The routine programmed into his soul by the years on U-40 demanded it. The thought of endless games of cards, chess or draughts, interspersed with 'improving' lectures, appalled him.

Dietrich turned out to be an asset, rather than a pain in the arse. That puppy-dog enthusiasm could be harnessed, Erich discovered, to help plead his case with the British. Dietrich was on good terms both with the otherwise aloof Carlisle, the camp's Intelligence Officer, and Roebuck, the commandant.

Once German prisoners had finished repairing the tennis courts, Erich was given permission to erect a recreation centre. Rather than having the men crammed in their individual huts, they could then mingle in one communal building. It would have card tables, a billiard table – a refurbished one from the mansion house – and a small library. The timber came from the old tied cottages on the estate that had fallen into disrepair over the past thirty years – one of them also provided a small stove that could be used to heat the place. It was still summer when they started, but there had already been some strong easterlies, chilling the workers, making hands numb and faces throb, a foretaste of what winter would deliver.

As they laid the foundations, their work was always checked by Carlisle or one of his staff, in case the whole project was a cover for something more devious.

While they dug into the earth, Erich often stopped to marvel at the US bombers that seemed to fly daily from nearby bases. The silvery B-17s and B-24s lumbered into the air at first light, returning as the sun started to dip, often singly, many of them with feathered props on one or two engines, perhaps streaming smoke or glycol.

Sometimes they saw Flying Fortresses that had absorbed savage punishment from flak and fighters, the nose cone shattered from full-frontal attacks, the sides raked by cannon from the new German jet fighters, the dying plane skimming the hedgerows, trailing debris as the airframe broke up, the pilot looking for somewhere to put her down. On those occasions, to Erich's shame, some prisoners stood to applaud and cheer the damage inflicted by the defenders back home. The U-boat arm never gloated over a stricken enemy like that.

After they had seen one such plane crash, and watched the column of black smoke dissipate across the sky, Dietrich had said: 'Maybe there is hope yet. They can't keep losing men and planes like that.'

Erich threw down the roof supports he had taken from one of the cottages and picked splinters from his hands. There was too much rot in the wood for it to be useful. 'And tomorrow morning, what do you think we will find climbing into the same sky?'

Dietrich nodded. 'More planes? More men?'

Erich nodded. 'It happened at sea. You think there can't be

255

another tanker left on God's Earth . . .'

'I know. They keep on coming. I saw it too.' Dietrich had been captured in Sicily by the Americans, and had been passed along the line, through Egypt and then the Straits of Gibraltar by PoW transport and finally to England. He had been a regular *Wehrmacht* soldier, promoted as his battalion was mauled and the soldiers were replaced by kids and foreign conscripts. He had been in the Hitler Youth, but only because everyone else had. Erich felt that, unlike him, Dietrich had never actually swallowed all the master-race shit.

'If we get these uprights in here,' said Erich, getting back to work, 'and just hold them in place with a few nails, we can get the opposite walls up. Then if we put a panel— What's that?'

Dietrich had heard it too. They both stopped what they were doing and turned. Somewhere a group of men was singing an old marching song. Erich felt the hairs on his neck stand up. One of the *Luftwaffe* pilots came across to them, shaking his head.

'What is it?' asked Erich.

They could see them now, striding down the driveway, the crunch of their hobnailed boots audible beneath the chorus.

'Oh, we're going to be all right now,' said the pilot sardonically. 'The SS are here.'

A weekend in Brighton might have been a rather obvious ploy, but Ross was fairly sure that Uli had no idea the place was infamous for its Mr and Mrs Smith hotels. They both needed a break from the job and from the doodlebugs, which were landing across London and Kent. The Blitz mentality – a mixture of defiance and fear – was reappearing. Even evacuation had returned as an option. So on Friday he made sure that they finished their work early and then caught the train from Victoria.

They registered at Boyce's Boarding House in Kemp Town and went for a walk along the front, strolling along Madeira Drive, dilapidated, neglected beach huts on the left, the ornate Victorian arches to their right. The beach was still disfigured and out of bounds – rusted, sagging barbed wire barring the way – but they zigzagged between the concrete tank traps on the promenade and marvelled at the two piers, mutilated to prevent them being used as landing jetties, with substantial chunks removed from the superstructures.

'I used to go to shows there when I was a kid,' said Ross, pointing at the theatre sitting forlorn and adrift at the end of the West Pier. 'When we were in England, that was.'

'Such a shame,' Uli said, looking at the missing section. 'To have to do that to such an elegant thing.'

'Did you know that the German 9th Army was meant to storm the beaches here and bring the Panzers with them? Paratroopers were to land on the Downs and join up with them, and head for Portsmouth.'

'I know. You father reminds me of the invasion plans every day, as if I'd had a hand in drawing them up.'

'My father likes to intimidate people.'

'He's very good at it.'

'Not as good as he used to be. He's sick,' Ross found himself saying defensively. 'And without him, you'd still be in Canada.' And perhaps without him she might never have gone in the first place, he thought. His father had finally admitted that part of his campaign to keep them apart had included intercepting their letters.

'Can we have a drink? Somewhere warm?' she asked suddenly. 'I'm getting cold.'

They walked north, past some light bomb damage and rows of boarding houses that had closed, and chose a pub near the

Hippodrome. It was raucous with sailors and soldiers and thick with smoke, but they found space in the snug among the old ladies. Uli took his hand. Hers were freezing and he rubbed each in turn.

'The things we hear from Europe. The world is going to hate the Germans when it all comes out.'

Ross nodded. 'And I think we've hardly scratched the surface.'

'Who will want to admit to being German now?'

'I think those people who can show the world that it wasn't every German who was like that. People like you.'

She sipped her drink, a rum-and-blackcurrant. 'Like me? There I am, helping to interrogate my fellow countrymen, which makes me feel like a dirty traitor. And I have a British boyfriend. Yet the British still think I am suspect. Guilty whichever way I turn.'

Boyfriend? Ross thought. Hardly, not in the current usage of the word. 'It'll be over one day soon. We can get on with making the world whole again.'

She laughed.

'What?'

'Making the world whole? That's rather grandiose, isn't it?'

'But it's what I feel,' he said with as much passion as he could muster. 'Otherwise we'll just tear ourselves apart again. There has to be a reckoning, on both sides, and then some kind of, I don't know, reconciliation.'

'I don't know how we'll reconcile anyone to those execution pits the Hungarian described yest—'

He moved over and kissed her without warning. She pulled away after a few seconds. 'Oh. Cam.'

'Sorry. Only way I could shut you up. No more thinking of all that. Not for forty-eight hours. We'll have a meal, see a show at the Links, stop our minds churning over those horrors. You can't talk about it again. Not until we are back in London. I forbid you, as your commanding officer.'

Uli went quiet and played with her drink. He feared that he had offended her, that one of them would be getting a lonely slow train back to London. Eventually she said: 'Cam?'

'Yes?'

'How many rooms did you book us with Mister Boyce?'

Ross thought of what Emma had said all that time ago about having to wait for ever for him to make a move. He turned his face away as he told the lie. 'One.' He turned back. 'If that is OK? I don't want to crowd you,' he added with a smirk.

This time she kissed him and his whole body tingled. She was tired of analysing things, of battling with her emotions, her remorse about Erich, her concern that her feelings for Cameron were hopelessly entangled with gratitude for getting her back to her father. She was going to have some fun while she could, and she would sort out the mess later.

'Perfect,' she said.

'What are you doing?'

Erich turned and found himself facing a quartet of the newly arrived SS. There had been trouble almost immediately. The dozen *SS-Polizei* and a few *Waffen-SS* had taken over Hut Nine, throwing out the pilots and soldiers who were already there. Erich and Dietrich had kept their heads down and carried on with building their hut.

'It's a new recreation—' began Dietrich.

'I asked *him*,' snapped the leader of the four.

Erich carefully put down his hammer and removed the nails that he'd been holding between his teeth. 'And you are?'

'*Obersturmführer* Axel Schuller of the *SS-Polizei Regiment 'Bozen'*. These are *Untersturmführer* Bauert, Kroll and Hetz. I have assumed command of the officers' section of this camp.'

'There is a Major present. He outranks you.'

'He has been relieved of command. The Führer has decreed that an SS officer outranks any *Wehrmacht* officer. Especially one who has not created a proper command system nor–' Schuller clenched a fist in frustration – 'instigated an escape committee.'

'An escape committee?' asked Erich in disbelief. 'Where the hell are you going to escape to round here?'

Hetz put a hand on one of the uprights and began shaking it loose.

'Hey,' said Dietrich in alarm. As he stepped forward to protest his way was blocked by Bauert.

'You know that officers are not required to work,' explained Schuller. 'Here I find them gardening and building for the British. You will stop this at once.' Hetz tore the two-by-four from its housing and threw it to the ground.

'It's for us, not for them,' explained Erich as reasonably as he could.

Kroll finally spoke. 'By doing this you are helping make the German PoW population docile and pliable.'

'And our duty is to be exactly the opposite of that,' finished Schuller. 'Take it down.'

'Or what?' asked Erich.

'There is a new addition to the camp's roster. Every Friday night, there is a court of inquiry to consider complaints about un-German activities.' Schuller pointed at the half-built hut. 'Take it down.'

After they had gone, Dietrich looked at him, his expression anxious. 'What do we do?'

Erich gathered his jacket and started back to his berth. 'If he wants it taken down, he can do it himself.'

★ ★ ★

It took all Ross's powers of persuasion and a solemn promise to pay in full for the unused room to get Mr Boyce to prepare a tray so he could take Uli breakfast in bed. Toast, jam, a precious boiled egg, cornflakes and tea – not bad at all. She was sitting up in bed, watching the gulls whirl outside the window, and she smiled as he came in.

'Luxury,' she said. 'Thank you.'

They helped themselves in silence while Ross fussed around, pouring the tea, buttering the toast, enjoying the warm self-satisfied glow inside. He remembered the last time he had felt this way, with Emma, and felt a twinge of sadness.

'What shall we do today?' he asked.

'Stay here?'

He kissed her. 'I'd second that. But we're not allowed. House rules. Out by nine, no return until four-thirty. It's the norm at the British seaside.'

'What if it's raining?'

'No exceptions. And it isn't raining.'

'How strange. Well, we'll see the sights, have lunch, cinema, tea—' she began.

'All right, all right. We won't be bored.'

'Oh, so there's a chance I might become boring?' Uli teased. 'So soon after giving myself? You Englishmen. It's true what they say.'

'What do they say?' Ross asked, sliding under the blankets, ignoring the crash of the crockery as the tray slid off the bed onto the carpet.

'Oh, all sorts of things.'

'I love you, you know.'

She cupped his face in her hands and stared into it, lest there be any doubt. 'I know, Cam. I know.'

★   ★   ★

Erich was in his bunk, reading an English detective novel, when he felt every person in the hut tense. He knew what it was. One or more of the *Rollkommando*, the new internal police force. The SS had been at Stanhope camp for two weeks, and already they had bent the entire place to their will. There had been two beatings when some of the men had refused to sign a new oath to the Führer, a kind of get-well-soon card after the Stauffenberg conspirators' attempt on his life, to be sent over to Germany via the Red Cross. Erich had signed. He knew that it wouldn't get past Carlisle, the Camp Intelligence Officer, and his team of censors.

He was startled when Schuller walked over to him. 'Hinkel.'

Erich put the book down slowly. 'Yes?'

'I'd like a word. About the new hut that is, I see, still standing.'

Erich checked whether Hetz, Kroll or Bauert, Schuller's faithful bruisers, were behind him, but they were nowhere in sight. That didn't mean they weren't waiting outside the door to teach him a lesson, though. Erich hadn't touched the recreation hut since Schuller had warned him about it, but the SS man would see his failure actually to tear it down as gross insubordination.

Schuller walked over to Dietrich, who was reading *Die Wochenpost*, the PoWs' newspaper, and tore it from his hands. 'Why are you reading these filthy lies?' Schuller asked.

'I like the crossword,' protested Dietrich.

Before Schuller could answer, Erich swung his legs off his bed, grabbed his ex-British Army jacket and walked outside. 'Are you coming?' he asked over his shoulder. Schuller threw the newspaper to the floor and followed.

As Erich passed into the fresh air he flinched, ready for a

blow, but none came. Schuller ushered him across the open ground, past the latrine and shower block, to where the skeleton of the new building stood.

'This hut,' said Schuller.

'You want it down, get your goons to take it down,' Erich replied, with as much insolence as he dared.

'I don't want it down. I want it built. It's an excellent idea, Hinkel. An excellent idea.'

'I don't understand.'

'The thing is, I want a few modifications.' From his pocket Schuller fetched a folded piece of paper. Erich spread it out and examined it. It showed rough drawings for the recreation hut, but with new dimensions, and some additions that he couldn't follow.

He turned to see Dietrich staring at them. Good old Dietrich, watching Erich's back, even if he was as scared of Schuller's mob as the rest of them. Erich beckoned him over. He saw the look on Schuller's face and said: 'He'll be doing half the work.'

Erich passed the plan across to Dietrich, who also looked puzzled. 'These walls are all about a metre deep. Why?'

'Well, we'll tell the British it is for insulation. Autumn will be here soon, the stoves we have are inadequate.' He looked at Dietrich and said: 'You seem quite friendly with Carlisle. He'll believe you.'

'Not friendly—' protested Dietrich.

'What are they really for?' interrupted Erich, already suspecting the answer. The walls, he now appreciated, were to be so full of cavities as to be almost hollow.

'To hide the soil.'

Dietrich fell for it and asked, 'What soil?'

Schuller slapped him on the back and grinned as if delivering a surprise Christmas gift to a child. 'The soil from the tunnel that we'll be digging.'

Thirty

Wilton House in the Victoria area was one of the many grand London homes that had been requisitioned at the beginning of the war. Originally it had housed Free French officers, then for most of 1943–4 it became part of the Operation Overlord – D-Day – planning nexus that stretched across the British capital. The logistics of supplying beachheads were pioneered in this anonymous stuccoed mansion.

In August 1944, after the Second Front had been opened, it was turned over to the Combined Services Detailed Interrogation Centre, an organisation struggling for space and resources as thousands of German PoWs were shipped across the Channel in special secure barges. It was to Wilton House, in September 1944, that Colonel Ross was summoned for a meeting.

He showed his papers to the sentry on the door and was ushered through to the rear, where two men sat in the conservatory overlooking a sadly neglected garden. Lieutenant Colonel Debenham leapt to his feet and held out a hand. This was to be an informal meeting, clearly. 'Donald. Thank you so much for coming. May I introduce Major Wayne Lillyman?'

'Pleasure.' The American was a tall, handsome man in his

early forties, with that strange growth of velvet across his scalp that passed for a haircut in the US Army. Colonel Ross took the man's hand and made sure he didn't wince when his fingers were crushed.

'Major Lillyman is with the Office of Strategic Services. The OSS.' The Colonel nodded. His old friend Claude Dansey had helped set up that outfit back in the 1930s. 'Now, what can we get you? Tea?'

'Tea would be fine. Milk, no sugar.'

An aide was quickly dispatched and Debenham sat down and indicated to the others to be seated. 'I hope you don't mind me summoning you over here. A bit less public than the Cage in some ways.'

'It's fine. I don't have much time, though, John.'

'No. Well, let's get down to it.'

'Colonel Ross—' the American began. But he was silenced by a glance from Debenham.

'Donald. You have done a grand job over at the Cage. JACI are very pleased with the preliminary reports and recommendations.'

'Very pleased,' interjected Lillyman.

'But?'

'No "buts", Donald. That stands. Ah, tea.'

The conversation was halted while cups were poured and even Lillyman took one. 'The tea's not exactly to my taste, but at least it's not toxic like the damned coffee over here.' He smiled.

'So, Donald. As I was saying, fine work, fine work. However, there are some worrying aspects.'

'Such as?'

'Your health.'

'There's nothing wrong with me.'

'Well, that's not what we hear. Guards and stenographers talk, you know. Canteen whispers.'

'Since when have we dealt in canteen whispers?' asked the Colonel.

'Pretty much always.' Lillyman grinned. 'That's our job, isn't it?'

Ross had to admit that he was right. Rumour and innuendo were the intelligence services' stocks in trade. He'd heard from Dansey that one of the first things that MI6 had done upon learning of the 20 July bomb plot against Hitler had been to start a whispering campaign about the vast number of *Wehrmacht* officers involved, thus ensuring that numerous competent officers – innocent of the charges – were taken out of the German command structure. The number of arrests had reached more than four thousand, including Admiral Canaris who had clearly continued his opposition to Hitler. Now they were hearing sickening rumours about how some of those men had died.

'I'll take a medical,' said the Colonel. 'If you have any doubts. I'm younger than Claude Dansey, y'know.'

'Well, there is more to it than that,' said Lillyman. 'The box on the desk with the lights.'

'Is this more canteen whispers?'

'You have to admit, Donald, it is a bit unorthodox. It's like . . . witchcraft.'

'Now hold on. You just told me that my reports were fine.'

'They are, Donald.'

'But now you are saying that I'm sick and batty?'

'What we are saying, Colonel Ross,' said Lillyman, his patience running out, 'is that the time has come to rationalise the whole service. John and I have had a good look, top to tail, and, while we appreciate what you have achieved, we feel that this is perhaps the best time for you to step aside. We will be recommending the instigation of two-man Anglo-American interrogation teams, using some of your methods—'

'But not the box,' said Debenham, smiling.

'The box isn't what it seems . . .'

'We know about the girl, Colonel,' said Lillyman. 'And we intend to subject her to rigorous scientific tests to ascertain exactly what tricks she was using to fool you. If we find that she is a fraud, she will be prosecuted. If she is a spy . . .' He spread his hands wide, to indicate that hanging would be regrettable but necessary.

The Colonel didn't answer. He was concerned now that he would lose the thread. The cup in his hand was shaking and he put it down quickly. Heightened emotion increased the frequency and duration of his lapses. He had to stay calm.

'When would you like all this to happen?'

'We make a verbal report to the Swinton Committee on Thursday,' said Debenham. 'If they agree, they can have detailed proposals one week from then. The fact is, Donald, once these recommendations are accepted – and they will be – things will move apace.'

'So I should clear my desk now?'

'I would make a start, yes. Don't worry, we'll find something for you to do.'

'And my son?'

'He's a copper, isn't he?' Ross nodded. 'Well, there is always that for him to fall back on. But we'll be happy to find him a position in the reorganisation if he wishes to remain. We need German-speakers. I suspect, though, that once we check the girl out, he might find things difficult . . .' Debenham had already made up his mind about her, of course.

'Do I have a right of appeal, John?'

'No,' said the American flatly.

'I understand.' Ross stood, and said quietly, 'Thanks for the tea, gentlemen.'

When the recreation hut was finished, it had to be inspected by a representative of the Ministry of Works. 'Can't have it collapsing and killing all you Germans, now, can we?' joked Carlisle. Once the papers were signed and a power cable had been run in, Erich and Deitrich were told that they were free to bring in the furniture. It took eight of them to get the billiard table across from Stanhope House itself, and Erich pulled a muscle in his back. They subsequently discovered that the slate was cracked, but Dietrich was sure he could re-cover it in such a way that it wouldn't matter. One of the tankmen offered to make new pockets, and a sapper was given the task of renovating the motley collection of cues.

It was early September now, still warm, and the war showed no sign of coming to a conclusion. Once a week BBC propaganda was broadcast over the loudspeakers. Paris had been liberated. Soon the Allies would be moving across into Germany. Americans and British on the one side, Russians on the other. Erich's country was about to be squeezed to death, unless it tried for a negotiated peace.

Shortly after morning roll-call, Erich went inside the hut to examine his handiwork. The quality of the materials left a lot to be desired, but considering it was reclaimed timber, the structure was good and sturdy. It even had cavities in which to hide the earth when Schuller started digging his escape tunnel. The mad bastard had thought of everything, including a pumping system made from old milk cans to deliver fresh air to the tunnellers.

Every time Erich thought about the tunnel, he felt the steel bands constrict around his chest. It was *Blechkoller*, the submariner's fear, only instead of tonnes of water crushing down on him, it was dozens of cubic metres of earth. Erich wanted nothing to do with burrowing.

He rubbed out the list of tasks on the scoring blackboard next to the dartboard one by one. All done. The last had been the ceiling. He hesitated, looked up and noticed that Dietrich had nailed one of the ceiling strips very badly. It ran out of true and ruined the effect. He was OK, was Dietrich, but his work suffered from sloppy finishing. Erich slid on the heavy canvas work gloves that he had managed to wheedle from the British, fetched one of the sawhorses they had used for cutting the timber and stood on it, using a screwdriver to lever off the rogue piece of panelling. As it came free he saw the wire. It was grey and metallic, not like the striped electrical wire with its fabric covering that they had run to the central light.

He tore off the next strip of wood, then the next, following the wire across the roof space. It terminated next to the central ceiling lamp at a flat green disc, like a shrunken landmine, with a diaphragm in the middle, protected by a fine mesh cage. He had seen dozens of these in his house as a boy. Not exactly the same, and mostly much larger, but he knew that it was a microphone.

He felt a tugging at his trouser leg and looked down. It was Schuller. He put a finger to his lips and pointed at the bugging device. Schuller nodded and retreated outside. Erich quickly put the ceiling strips back in place and followed.

When they were well away from the hut, Schuller spun around. 'What is it?'

Erich hesitated. 'I can't be sure.'

'Take a wild guess.'

'A recording device.'

'Shit.' He poked Erich's chest. 'And you put it in for them?'

'No. That's why they did a building inspection. As a cover. I was just realigning one of the wooden slats. They put one back badly. I thought it was Werner who'd nailed it up.'

Schuller rubbed his chin, pressing his fingers into his flesh. 'Are they in every hut?'

'I don't know. It wouldn't surprise me. It explains a few things, though.'

'Such as?'

'How they managed to break up the black-market trading that Sachsen had going with some of the civilian workers.'

'Shit,' Schuller repeated. 'Would they hear us digging?'

Erich stroked his chin. 'I don't know. You'd have to be very quiet. It's possible. There is something else to worry about, though.'

'What?'

'They could have buried microphones. It can be done. To listen for tunnels. Like the hydrophones we used on the U-boats.'

Erich held his breath while Schuller began to pace in a circle. The truth was, Erich had no idea whether buried listening devices would work, nor if the British had planted any. Much as he wanted to get away and start the search for Uli, he had no desire to be buried alive in the process.

Eventually the SS man stopped and turned. 'Then we think again. You were on the U-boats, Hinkel?'

'Yes.'

'Cipher officer?'

'That's right.'

'You know the island code?'

'I do.' It was a way of inserting messages into apparently innocuous text. 'How do *you* know about it?'

270

'I was a policeman, Hinkel. We had to read people's mail.'

'They read the mail here.'

'Then come up with a decent variation on the code.'

Erich nodded. He doubted they would spot the U-boat version of island code. Not if he was careful. But did he want to be? 'So what's the idea?'

'I want every man to write a letter home. I need you to formulate several of them with island messages inserted. And especially one to your home.'

'Me? Why?'

Schuller repeated some of the information that Skorzeny had given him. 'All incoming mail from PoWs should be checked for messages by the security services at home. It isn't always. But Dönitz insists that it is always done for the submarine branch. Dönitz is absolutely loyal to the Führer.' *Then Prinz was right about him being a fool*, thought Erich. 'You will place a request into a letter and ask for information back.'

'A request? A request for what?'

Schuller put his arm round Erich's shoulder, pulling him close, and walked him towards the wire. 'Repeat this to anyone, Hinkel, and you know what I will do to you. And to your family.'

Erich shrugged him off. 'Don't threaten me, Schuller,' he said with a boldness that he didn't feel. 'What do you want?'

They had reached the perimeter fence. Schuller looked up at the sentry in the watchtower and raised a hand in greeting. The man spat. Many of the British guards had been pulled out for combat duty and had been replaced by Poles. Schuller seemed pleased by this. He spun Erich round and retraced his steps. 'Simple. I want you to get me a submarine.'

Colonel Donald Ross sat at his desk in his office, unable to accept what Debenham had said. There had to be a way round this. He took a deep breath and poured a glass of water. So his mind wandered now and then. With Cameron at his side, it was no problem. And the girl? She was an asset. He'd resisted the idea at first, but she had her uses and by God she made his son happy. Looked like he'd have to get used to the idea of a bloody German in the family. He hoped that Cameron would be prepared for the kind of ribbing he would get, especially if he ended up back in the police force. That was if the damned American didn't hang her.

He heard rushing footfalls up the stairs and was taken aback when the door burst open and Cameron and Ulrike stood staring at him. Both were panting hard.

'Dad. Thank God. I'm bloody well pleased to see you.'

'Are you all right?' asked Uli.

'Am I all right? It's not me who's taken leave of my senses. Not this time, anyway. What are you doing here, barging in like there's a fire?'

'There has been. A gas main exploded,' explained his son. 'Just heard it on the radio. Roads closed, the lot.'

'Where?'

'Wilton House,' said Uli.

'I knew you were over there. I thought . . .'

The Colonel felt his throat constrict. He took another sip of water. 'Anyone hurt?'

'Well, yes. The entire building has collapsed. They're all dead. Anyone who was in there.'

Debenham and Lillyman, he thought. 'Good God. How terrible.'

'What were you doing there, dad?'

'Just a catch-up. They wanted to let me know what they thought about our work.'

272

'What did they say?' asked Uli.

'Well, it's all academic now. But they said—' He coughed, fist in front of his mouth. 'Carry on. Keep up the good work.'

Once the pair had left, Donald Ross asked for a secure line through to Broadway Buildings, the Secret Intelligence Service London HQ. It was five minutes before he got through to Claude Dansey, and once they'd scrambled their phones and exchanged pleasantries, the Colonel said, 'I was over at Wilton House today.'

'Oh. Were you?' asked Dansey.

'You heard?'

'I heard. Terrible.'

'How many gas mains is that – six? Or is it seven?'

Dansey almost chuckled, but remembered himself. 'Yes. Getting to be bloody dangerous out there.'

'I don't think we had six gas mains explode in the whole Blitz, did we?'

'Perhaps not,' mumbled Dansey.

'So?'

'Donald, you know I can't.'

'Or do you think the Germans are sending whole gas mains over now?'

'Donald—'

'Don't "Donald" me, Claude. I was in that bloody building not two hours ago. This is a safe line. I'd like to know what nearly killed me. And don't give me the Victoria Light and Gas Company cock and bull.'

'We think it's a new form of rocket. Like the doodlebugs, only much more sophisticated. The Germans call it the V2, apparently. Thing is, Donald, you can't hear them coming. They fly faster than the speed of sound. The first thing you know about it is the explosion.'

Colonel Ross could hear genuine awe in Dansey's voice at this new development. 'Whatever they are, you can't keep using the gas-main story, Claude.'

'I told Winnie that. He said there'd be panic, but I told him.'

'Told him what?'

'It's their last gasp, Donald. I ask you – what real harm can the Germans do us now?'

The morning runs were instigated shortly after the first letters went out to relatives in Germany, many of them thick with the island code. Schuller had asked permission to keep his men fit with thirty laps of the perimeter fence, and each day, after roll-call, they would don singlets and shorts and lope around in a tightly bunched group, laughing and chatting until the last five circuits when they would put their heads down and sprint with gritty determination. Then it was showers, a few popular marching songs, and perhaps a football match.

On the eighth morning, after his run, Schuller found Erich and brought him out into the open. The SS policeman was sweating, and in the cool morning air steam was rising off him.

'I have just heard that the Red Cross letters are in. You will check each one for a code. Yes?'

'Yes,' the ex-submariner said reluctantly. Schuller was still dropping hints about what would happen to Erich's parents should he fail to cooperate. Part of Erich wanted to call his bluff. Like the rest, though, he feared what the dying system at home could still do to those who crossed it. 'It's a little soon for something to be in this batch, though. Am I looking for anything in particular?'

'Dates. A date for the action.'

'What action?'

'Our escape. Freedom.'

'You'll never get off this island, you know. Nobody ever has.'

Schuller smiled. 'Believe. Obey. Fight,' he said, quoting the old SS maxim. 'You'd do well to remember that. Run with me.'

'Sorry?'

'Come on, run with me. I won't go too fast.'

They broke into a slow jog, hugging the fence, leaving the hut complex behind. Some of the walls of the Stanhope estate had been pulled down to allow maximum use of arable land, and on the other side of the fence there were freshly ploughed fields criss-crossed by hedgerows, and a couple of distant farm buildings.

Schuller nodded at an Austin A10 parked in a lane, around twenty metres beyond the second wall of wire. 'Always there, that car.'

One of the dogs bared its teeth as they came past and Erich jumped away as it flung itself at the fence.

'It's me it can smell. Three laps. Pick up the pace.'

Erich's lungs were burning. He hadn't done this much running since the Hitler Youth camps. There'd hardly been room for morning sprints on the sub.

'Look up. Searchlight. Searchlight. Here. Not here.'

'Flares,' gasped Erich.

'Yes, acetylene flares, but they have to be set off by a guard by hand. This part of the fence cannot be illuminated easily. OK, walk.'

'Schul—' he gasped. 'Schuller, why are you telling me this?'

'Because, Hinkel, you are my U-boat man, my signals officer. You're coming out with us.'

'I don't think so.'

'Again, let's go.' They kicked off once more. 'We can get men out to this fence. We can cut it. Kroll has made cutters from the bars that were on Hut Six.'

'The dogs.'

'Ah. The dogs. Watch.'

On the second circuit, Schuller waited till the tethered dog came for him and quickly threw a handful of dark brown powder in its face. It began to sneeze, snuffling and shaking its head to clear its nostrils. They came round a third time and the dog simply watched them with rheumy eyes, still twitching its snout now and then.

'Curry powder. Deadens their sense of smell. We got it from the kitchen detail.'

'If it doesn't work on the night?'

'We got knives from the kitchen detail, too. I'll personally cut the animals' throats.

'Stop. Enough.' Erich placed his feet apart, put his hands on his knees and lowered his head between them, sucking in air. 'Be careful. To the English, escape is one thing. Killing a dog . . . beyond the pale.'

'The curry will work.'

'What about once you get out?'

'We have papers to prove that we are Poles or Norwegians. The quality isn't too good. We used the badges on the overcoats that the British issued to some of us at Southampton. It will fool the casual person.'

'Let's hope you only meet casual people.'

'*We*, Hinkel, *we*. You'll be going out too. Look, there is more to this than you think. We are in touch with Bridgend, with Devizes, with Lodge Moor, with Comrie, which the British call a Black Camp. You know what that is?'

Erich shook his head.

'The most loyal of us are kept there.' It was where Schuller should have been, except for that nonsense about the reprisals in Rome, which had kept him tethered near London. War crimes.

An oxymoron, thought Schuller. You either had war, or you didn't. 'My plan is for everything to be coordinated. Which is why I need you to read those letters, see if we got through.'

'And when is all this going to happen?'

'That is the beauty of it. It will happen whenever the Führer tells us to go.' Schuller almost snapped to attention as he said proudly: 'We await his command.'

Erich felt the odds against him ever seeing Uli again rapidly clicking over, heading skywards.

Thirty-One

November 1944

As the allies pushed across Europe, Ross and Uli's work load increased. They were temporarily taken off War Crimes preliminaries and sent to Kempton racecourse – now called Number 9 Reception Camp – to help screen the incoming prisoners. As they swept in, seated in the back of a Humber staff car, Uli grabbed Ross's knee. 'My God. I was here.'

'Yes, I know. I traced you here. Hardly a day at the races, eh?'

'We were kept in the stables, like the bloody horses.'

'Don't worry, we'll manage better than that this time.' He lowered his voice so the driver couldn't hear. 'A hotel, with a four-poster, no less.'

The screening was to be carried out in what had been the jockeys' weighing room, with each prisoner being brought in, told to sit, and asked a series of questions. Uli was to keep quiet. Officially, she was a German-speaking South African stenographer. It wouldn't do for either side to know her true nationality. They took the first PoW at midday. He was unshaven and clearly still lousy, judging by the way he rummaged under his shirt, and Ross scribbled a note to change the interrogation order. Delousing first, *then* processing.

After establishing that the man had been a gunner on the Atlantic Wall before fighting rearguard actions in various towns across France until his capture, Ross asked one of the standard questions. 'Do you think Germany can still win the war?'

'Yes, of course I do,' the man replied.

'Why?'

'You are being lured into a trap.' He opened his arms to mimic a pair of jaws. 'When we have you in Germany . . . snap!' He slammed his arms together.

After twenty or more questions, Ross had him taken out by the escorting guardsmen.

'What do you think?' he asked Uli.

'Black,' she said, using the informal colour code of debriefing. White was anti-Nazi, grey neutral, black still pro-Nazi. Whites would often be used as stool-pigeons, infiltrated into the huts to eavesdrop and report on what the Blacks were doing or talking about. In that way, some of the more outlandish last-stand plans in Germany were coming to light.

'I agree,' Ross said. He wrote down the man's name next to Comrie, one of the Black camps. 'Next!'

A sergeant entered, looking pale. 'Sir, sorry, sir, we've been told to lock down all prisoners until further notice.'

'Why?' demanded Ross, looking at the pile of folders he still had to work through.

'There's been an escape from one of the camps, sir.'

'The bloody idiots!' screamed Schuller into Dietrich's face, as if he were responsible, rather than merely the bearer of bad tidings. 'Absolute bloody idiots.'

He punched the wall of Hut Fourteen and stormed out.

279

Dietrich looked at Erich and shrugged. It had cost Dietrich five cigarettes and six squares of chocolate from his Red Cross parcel to find out from a guard why the regime had suddenly toughened. First there had been a lock-down, then increased roll-calls. The guards had been doubled, and the Senior Interpreter and Carlisle, the camp's Intelligence Officer, had plucked people out at random for questioning. Now Dietrich had discovered exactly what had caused the British to panic.

Erich, who hadn't been privy to the whispered conversation with Schuller, said to Dietrich: 'Tell me what you told him.'

'Well, it seems two pilots got out of a camp at somewhere called Devices.'

'Devizes,' corrected Erich.

'They made it to an airfield, got to a plane.'

'What, they got into the airfield? A British RAF base?'

'Yes.'

'My God.' Erich shook his head admiringly.

'They got into two planes, but couldn't start them. They didn't know that British planes often have off-board starters.'

'What's that?'

'Starter trolleys. To fire them up. They got caught in the cockpits, wondering why the engines wouldn't catch.'

Erich didn't know whether to laugh or cry. Now he knew why Schuller was angry. The fact that the pilots had got out and got so close to freedom meant that it could be done. German PoWs could escape. This wouldn't be lost on the British, either. Every camp could expect more guards, more random checks, more suspicion.

Schuller returned and indicated to Erich to come outside, away from any microphones. The ground was still crunchy with the last night's frost as they began another circle of the fence.

'This mustn't change anything. I want you to send another letter asking for a firm date.'

'I'd lie low if I were you.'

'You aren't me,' Schuller said, grimacing. 'Those irresponsible idiots, jumping the gun like that. The British will be all over us like lice. From now on, I want every new prisoner brought in front of the SS tribunal. They'll be sending in stool-pigeons as part of the new security. I want to know who they are – I want them isolated.'

'Why are you telling me this?'

'So that you stay vigilant. So that you don't think of saying anything when Carlisle calls you in for questioning. If you do, I'll kill you. Understand?'

Erich had no doubt Schuller meant it. He nodded.

The sound of engines made them both search the sky. A British Dakota, one of the workhorses that carried supplies and parachutists, began to climb into the darkness and disappeared into the low rain-heavy clouds. Schuller was still staring after it when large drops began to fall.

'Something else in your letter, Erich,' said Schuller, the first time he had used his Christian name. 'See if they can get me an airdrop.'

'Of what?'

'What do you think? Weapons, man, weapons.'

'How is that boy of yours, Donald?' Claude Dansey forked another mouthful of the steak and kidney pudding into his mouth and reached for the claret. His old friend was treating the Colonel to lunch at Rules, which had managed to keep a respectable menu and cellar despite wartime restrictions.

'Fine. Great help these days.'

'Hear he got himself a friendly enemy alien on board. Very

friendly,' chortled Dansey. Uncle Claude, as everyone called him, was deputy head of MI6 by rank, but most people in the intelligence community knew that he was the real power at its Broadway Buildings HQ.

The Colonel nodded. Lunch with his old employer was a rare occurrence these days. Normally they would just swop stories of rampaging through Europe in the days of the old Z Organisation. Today, however, Uncle Claude was more subdued.

'What do you make of this escape attempt?' he asked.

Ross shrugged. Strictly speaking that was MI5's business, not Uncle Claude's. 'At Devizes? A couple of chancers.'

'Scotland is down there,' said Dansey, mentioning one of PWIS's other stalwarts, a man with a South African background like Ross's. 'He's picking up some strange things. Both through interrogation and on the Ms.' This was the code term for hidden microphones. 'Very strange.'

Colonel Ross knew it was no good asking why Dansey had information that should have reached him first. In intelligence, all roads led to Uncle Claude. 'What are you getting at?'

The older man put his knife and fork down and wiped his mouth with a napkin. Ross also stopped eating. They were out of hearing range of the other customers but, even so, Ross had to cock an ear to catch Dansey's words. 'This is in strictest confidence, Donald.'

Ross only had to raise an eyebrow to remind him how far they went back and Dansey apologised. 'We've had a report from the First Canadian Army. They captured signals sent out, by Hitler himself, appealing for volunteers from all arms of the army and the Waffen-SS.'

He paused and took a sip of claret. 'They must be physically A-plus, adept at special tasks, they must be able to speak English. But listen – those who can feign an American accent are particularly sought after. Furthermore, those familiar with silent killing techniques and hand-to-hand combat are also encouraged to apply. There were to be tests at Friedenthal the day before yesterday. Those not suitable will be returned to their unit.'

'And the others?'

'Are to report to Unit Skorzeny.'

Ross shook his head. He had not heard of it.

Dansey looked surprised. 'You remember, Donald. Skorzeny was the joker who rescued Mussolini by using gliders. He's a specialist in airborne operations. Quite a character.'

'Oh, yes. Of course. Christ. So . . . you think the escape from Devizes and this order are related in some way? Hitler is planning a parachute drop in England, behind the lines?'

Dansey went back to attacking the crust of his pie. 'You know, Donald, I bloody well hope not.' He waved the fork. 'But you get security tightened, eh? Just in case.'

Cameron Ross's Fitzrovia flat was too small for Uli and him together but, if he admitted the truth to himself, he was too superstitious to move. After his father's near miss, and with several rockets falling every day, he had this vision that he would settle them into Belgravia or Mayfair and the following day a V2 would come crashing through the roof, killing them both.

So they made do, not minding too much about bumping into each other, about the tiny galley kitchen or the inadequate water heater.

Ross arrived home one Saturday evening with a clutch of parcels under his arms. 'What a day!' he exclaimed.

Uli was lying in front of the gas fire, books and notepad in front of her.

'I managed to find both of us shoes – I've guessed your size.'

'Thirty-seven,' she said.

'Blimey,' he said. 'I'm only an eight and a half.'

'I think it is about a four and a half in your sizes.'

Ross looked crestfallen. 'I got a five.'

'Then I'll pad the toe. Let me see.'

As they unwrapped the string and brown paper, he said: 'And I might have a turkey for Christmas.'

'What sort of turkey?'

'A dead one, I hope. There is this butcher on Goodge Street that dad knows—'

'More of your father's contacts?'

'Look, if it's a proper bird, I'd take it from Hitler himself. We have to go on a list and they are drawing names out of a hat.'

'Well, that's democracy of a kind, I suppose. Lovely.' Uli held up the shoe, which she thought was rather matronly and clunky. But she inhaled the smell of leather gratefully. 'Where did you get these?'

'Cockfosters. Near the Cage up there. Old pre-war stock. Not the height of fashion . . . it's all our coupons gone, I'm afraid.'

'They'll be fine.' She kissed him. 'Thank you. What's in there?' She indicated a small brown paper bag that Ross had tossed onto an armchair.

'Ah. Christmas present.' It was a beautiful antique silver box that he had seen in a jeweller's, just the right size for what he had in mind.

'It's weeks away.'

'Four weeks. You have to buy when you see these days.'

'Can I look?'

'No.' He changed the subject. 'What have you been doing?'

Uli had an atlas open at a map of the United States, and had scribbled down names on a notepad. 'I have been looking at places I'd like to visit when the war is over. Places that won't care too much about me being German. Where the people don't have to know. Look. Alber-kew-kew. What a fabulous name.'

He corrected her pronunciation.

'Well, whatever it is, it sounds wonderful. And Oatmeal, Texas? So funny. Phoenix. What must a city named after a mythical bird be like?'

'Not as exotic as you imagine it, I suspect.'

'You don't know, you've never been,' she said, as if he were spoiling her dream. 'And there's New York, of course. Texas again. Lub-bock. Lubbock.' She rolled the word around her mouth. 'So much to see. I found a New Berlin somewhere.'

He was as gentle as he could be. 'I think they've changed it. All the places called Berlin changed their names in 1942.'

'Oh. Of course. Of course they would have.'

'I can't believe you want to go back across the Atlantic so soon.'

'Only when there are no U-boats.' Uli felt a tightening of her stomach again as she thought of Erich out there, his submarine slipping silently through the blackest seas. At least, she hoped he was there. He hadn't been processed through any of the south-eastern Cages, she was fairly sure, which meant either he'd come in through some other part of the country, or he was still on patrol, or . . .

'Come here.' Ross sat down and stroked her hair as she moved closer to him. They both caught the distant thud of an explosion. 'Uli?'

'Mmmm.'

'Marry me.' He felt her tense, then relax. *She must have known it was coming*, he thought. 'I'll shave for the ceremony. Promise.'

She laughed. He still felt self-conscious about the beard, but

285

she thought it gave him a raffish air. 'Ask me again. When this is all over. Please.'

'You think I won't?' he asked, trying to keep the disappointment from his voice.

Uli suddenly felt very cold. She shuffled closer to the bluish flames of the fire. 'Will we live through this, Cam?'

Ross recognised the feeling gripping her. An icicle in the heart, even though he couldn't know that it was the thought of Erich floating face down in the grey Atlantic that had caused her so much distress. He reached over and pulled her back to him. 'Of course. We've come this far. What's going to stop us now?'

The new guards had arrived at the beginning of December on a grey drizzly day. Mud was everywhere, sticking to boots and trampled on them into the huts. The other ranks' compound, being lower down the slope, was the worst affected, and the authorities had rigged up duckboards, which themselves sank into the quagmire.

The reinforcements were mostly veteran soldiers, either invalided out of the army or too old for combat, but they didn't look like pushovers. If anything, they treated the inmates with even more disdain than the Poles.

On the day after they arrived, Erich was summoned to the SS hut. As usual, he toyed with the idea of refusing, but there seemed no point. Schuller was at the 'executive desk' he had created, near the door. This was where the punishment tribunals were held once a week. Erich wondered if he had somehow transgressed the SS code that the madman was trying to impose. So far there had only been a handful of beatings, but they also imposed shunnings – when it was forbidden to speak to or even acknowledge a fellow prisoner. In the long run it was probably more painful and effective than a straightforward thrashing.

Schuller looked up from his writing. 'Erich. Sit.'

Erich did as he was told. Schuller indicated the half-dozen men in the centre of the room, who suddenly started singing. Swamping the microphone, it was called. Certainly any listener was likely to take a break while the men went through their repertoire of marching songs.

'What are you doing?' asked Erich.

'Notes on every man in this part of the camp. Name, age, background, Party affiliation, if any, willingness to carry on the fight.'

'How do I rate?'

Schuller shook his head. 'You and Dietrich are in the middle. You help, but only when asked. Yet you were in the Hitler Youth.'

'This may seem rather obvious, Schuller, but I was young then.'

'Nevertheless, you felt the call. You can feel it again.'

Erich didn't answer.

'We need some stones gathered. I am assigning one man from each hut to accumulate a reserve of them.'

'Stones?'

'Stones for throwing.'

'You're planning on breaking out with stones?'

'Not quite. You'll see.'

'So I'm our hut's stone collector.'

'Yes. A stockpile. By the weekend.'

Erich stood. 'I've been meaning to ask you, Schuller.' He leant forward. 'How many men do you hope to get out?'

'Here, or from all the camps?'

'Both.'

'Well, here a few hundred. There is a shortage of good material at Stanhope.'

287

'And if you include the others?'

'If the letters coordinating this from Germany have got through to the right people – and I have no reason to doubt it – then about . . .' There was a glint in Schuller's eye as he said: 'Seven thousand.'

The stones were used on the Saturday night. They were flung at the fence, causing the tethered dogs to throw themselves against the wire, yapping furiously. The searchlights flicked on, the precious flares lit. Guards with Lee Enfields or Thompsons appeared, stomped around for half an hour and, grumbling, went back to their warm guardrooms. An hour later it happened again. And again. Then sporadically throughout the following fortnight. After a time, the dogs stopped reacting so wildly, and only one unlucky guard was sent out. The flares were no longer wasted. By the middle of December, the British were thoroughly bored of the prank. Which was exactly what Schuller wanted.

The letter from Erich's father came on the tenth of December. The first two sentences began with 'I', one of the codes that told Erich there was a message within, based on the last word in each line. Decoding was laborious work, but eventually he had it. Snow was falling outside and the ground was firming up under the cold as he trudged towards the SS hut. Inside, they were still singing. Didn't those bastards ever get tired of it? How could you sing about marching towards England when you were a prisoner in the country?

He looked at the message one more time. No weapons were coming. No paratroops, it said. But Schuller would like this message. 'The Führer's Order of the Day. Men of the Freedom Movement. The hour of our liberation is approaching and it is the duty of every German to fight with arms in hand against world Jewry.' Then a date for action. Something was going to happen in just six days, on 16 December 1944.

Thirty-Two

15 December 1944

The hand on his shoulder shook Erich awake. He rolled over to
see Kroll, one of Schuller's thugs, with his finger to his lips.
Several other men had been woken. They all quickly dressed in
their warmest clothes. As Erich pulled on his sweater, he saw
Dietrich staring at him from his bunk. He winked. Dietrich
pressed his thumb between his middle and index fingers in a
'good luck' gesture. So Werner hadn't been chosen. Erich pulled
on his boots and followed the little group as they pressed
themselves into the shadows and shuffled their way to the SS
hut. Inside it was crammed with prisoners, all well wrapped up
against the cold, and the body odour was overpowering.
Nobody spoke. They had discovered that the microphones were
not manned very much after lights out – presumably volunteers
to listen to thirty men farting and snoring for eight hours were
thin on the ground.

'I thought it was tomorrow,' Erich whispered to Schuller.

'That was the general idea. Here. Map. Flashlight. Pass. We
are going out in twos. Your mission is written on the corner of

the map. Read it, tear the corner off, eat it.'

Erich stepped under one of the lamps and read the tiny writing. He was to head east and rendezvous with a submarine that would be waiting off the coast of Suffolk, near somewhere called Dunwich, in three nights' time. He looked at the map. It was crude, but serviceable.

'What have you got?' asked the *Luftwaffe* man next to him.

'East. You?'

'South,' said the airman glumly. 'To London. Sacrificial lamb.'

'What do you mean?'

'We get to bluff the British into thinking it's a strike at London. My guess is that the SS get to the coast meanwhile and zip off back to Germany.'

Erich hated to say it, but that had a ring of truth. 'What are you going to do?'

The man lowered his voice. 'Once I get through the fence? Whatever I feel like.'

Schuller loomed over the *Luftwaffe* man's shoulder but he appeared not to have heard. 'All set?'

'Yes. I need to get my gloves from the rec room,' said Erich. In there were the thick canvas gloves he'd used when building the hut. 'It's freezing outside. Couldn't you have done this in summer?'

'We have more darkness this way. We travel at night, hide by day. First pair go out in ten minutes.'

'Who am I going with?' Erich asked.

'You're coming with me,' said Schuller.

There was a corridor of darkness stretching from the hut compound to the rear fence. The dogs had been heavily dosed with the curry powder, there was no moon and the twin holes in the fences had already been cut by Hetz. Schuller and Erich

291

were the ninth pair to go. The SS man gave a stiff-armed salute to the rest of his men and they were off, crouched low, running towards the wire. The sound of their feet on the icy ground seemed deafening to Erich, but nothing stirred in the towers.

Erich wondered what he was doing. He had stood there in the billiard room, gloves in hand, letting time tick away, considering his options. He had decided that, among other things, at the first opportunity he should give Schuller the slip. He could imagine the fool deciding to go out in a blaze of glory while facing down some English patrol. It was the thought of that which made him act. As he had run down the steps of the recreation hut, he had slammed into Dietrich.

'What the hell are you doing?' Erich had asked him.

'Trying to find out what is going on.'

Erich told him the plan.

'He's quite insane. He has to be stopped. They'll blame us all.' Dietrich had gripped his arm. 'Don't go.'

'I have to,' Erich had said, thinking of how compromised his family were, thanks to the coded letters. 'Good luck, Werner' had been his final words to his friend as he pushed by.

'Here,' whispered Schuller, snapping him out of it. The hole was less than a metre across, with jagged edges from the makeshift cutters, and they had to crawl to get through. Schuller made Erich go first, and then he followed. Erich reached the second fence without problems and as he stepped into the ploughed field the air somehow smelled different. Freer.

'Just think, all over England and Scotland men are doing this,' said Schuller triumphantly. 'Come.'

They started to tramp across the field, half-stumbling over the frozen furrows. Blackness began to envelop them as the weak light from the camp petered out. Erich looked back. He could make out the dark shapes of two more escapees at the hole. 'How do you know?'

'Because this is what we came to England for,' said Schuller.

'How do you mean?'

'Quiet.'

Erich heard a lorry change gear in the distance, then the engine noise receded. They crossed the field, more by touch and instinct than sight. Erich was glad of the thick gloves as they felt their way along a bramble hedge. They located and climbed a stile and felt tarmac beneath their feet. 'This way,' said Schuller. 'Stay close.'

Erich's eyes had adjusted now, and there was enough starlight for him to at least make out the edges of the road they were walking along. 'What did you mean about coming to England for this?' Erich asked.

He listened while Schuller explained that in Italy he had been summoned by the great Skorzeny himself and offered a mission against England. It involved being deliberately captured by the Allies and sent back to England to a PoW camp, where he and his men were to organise an escape committee. At a set date, to be delivered by code, he and the other SS volunteers scattered across the country were to stage a mass breakout of German PoWs. 'The aim is to get as many men from behind the wire as possible,' Schuller concluded.

'And to march on London?'

'March on London. Steal planes from American bases to bomb harbours, fight our way to the sea to be picked up by ships and submarines. A thousand different tasks . . .'

Erich shook his head. 'That's ridiculous.'

'I know.' He heard Schuller laugh. It certainly didn't seem amusing to Erich. The SS man was clearly caught up in a crazy fantasy. 'Here.'

Erich nearly walked into it. It was the Austin A10 that they could always see from the wire in daylight. Schuller bent down and began feeling on top of each tyre in turn. 'There should be keys somewhere. Damn.' He stood. 'Can you get this piece of shit going?'

If he said no, would it all be over? Something glinted in the feeble light. Schuller had a knife. 'Yes,' Erich said.

It took Erich ten minutes to hot-wire the car. He had just got it running when they heard a voice from behind them. 'Hello – what are you two doing?'

Schuller turned and a diffuse beam from a gauze-wrapped blackout torch flashed in his eyes. 'Hey,' he protested.

'Sorry.' The man flicked the beam aside. 'What you doin' here at this time of night?' It was a policeman, but an old one. What they called a Special. Probably the local busybody.

'We are Poles. Guards,' said Schuller, in his heavily accented English. 'Just off duty.' He pointed to the softest of glows in the fields behind. 'From the camp.'

The SS man flashed his phoney ID, constructed from badges on the garments lent by the English and official-looking crests traced from foreign coins. Erich noticed that he kept one hand behind his back. The knife was ready.

'Oh. Right. This your car?'

'Yes. We leave it here most days.'

'I been wonderin' whose it was. OK, off you go, lads. Take care.'

Making sure not to demonstrate unseemly haste they climbed in, Schuller driving, and pulled away, the car jerking as he got used to the clutch.

'Christ,' said Erich, his heart pounding.

'I know. We have to get ourselves a gun. Look in the glove compartment.'

Erich opened it. He could see something under a piece of paper. He reached in and touched the cold metal. 'Nothing,' he said, slamming it shut.

'The cretinous idiots. Their orders were perfectly clear. Leave the keys on the front wheel and a gun in the glove compartment. It's not difficult, is it?'

'I don't understand what you hope to achieve—'

'Maximum disruption. With so many Germans out there, so many different plots, it will be chaos for the next few days. It is timed to coincide with a major offensive in Europe. The British will think it's Armageddon.'

'So what exactly are we doing?'

'Oh, we have a plan. Those of us who volunteered really do have a mission. We are going to meet that submarine.' Schuller slapped Erich's knee. 'Hinkel, my friend, we are going back to Germany to fight for the Fatherland.'

Erich went for the gun, fumbling with the catch on the glove compartment. As the cover flopped down Schuller leant across and elbowed him in the face. Erich felt his cheekbone crack. The car slammed to a halt. Another punch, this time in the side of the head, and Schuller grabbed Erich's collar and thrust him hard into the metal of the dashboard. Erich's mouth filled with blood. Schuller pushed him aside and pulled out the weapon.

'You lying bastard.'

'I don't want you shooting policemen.'

Schuller put the gun's muzzle against Erich's temple. 'It's not *policemen* getting shot that I'd worry about if I were you.' Erich closed his eyes until he felt the pistol's barrel lift away. 'If I didn't need you for the submarine . . .'

He couldn't signal. That was why Erich had been entrusted with the flashlight – Schuller didn't know how to use Morse.

'If we kill anyone they'll hang us,' said Erich. 'That's all I was

thinking. I want to get to that sub as much as you. To get home.'
He put all the emphasis that he could on the next phrase,
hoping that the lie wouldn't reveal itself. 'To serve the Fatherland once more.'

Schuller said, 'Then pull yourself together. We go on. And
don't think. That's *my* job.'

Schuller pushed the gun inside his jacket, restarted the car
and carried on east. Erich wiped the blood from his lips and
touched the swelling on the side of his face. Well, at least he
now had a good idea which of the two of them was better at
unarmed combat.

They ran out of fuel on a country lane, just after they had
skirted Stowmarket. There were probably thirty miles to go to
the coast, but trying to obtain petrol without the proper documentation was highly risky even if there'd been a garage open at
this ungodly hour. It was nearly dawn and the pair of them
pushed the car to the side of the road. Schuller indicated a barn,
several fields away.

'We'll sleep in there today. Tonight, we carry on. Perhaps
there'll be a train we can jump.'

Erich nodded, too tired to argue. They tramped along the
scruffy gravel path that led to the fields, crossed them and
entered the barn. It was sagging in the middle, stank of old
manure and was full of ancient agricultural machinery that
hadn't been used in years. They found some moth-eaten blankets that smelt strongly of animal, and Eric prepared to settle
down.

'Wait,' said Schuller. He had found a length of baling twine.
He tied a loop around Erich's wrist, and then one round his
own. 'Just in case.'

'In case of what?'

'In case I'm wrong about you. In case you lied to me.'

They bedded down as best they could. Erich, despite the chafing of the twine on his wrist, was asleep within minutes.

Thirty-Three

16 December 1944

Cameron Ross had a hangover. Even as he opened his aching eyes, he knew that this was going to be a bad day. Then it started to come back to him what a bad night the previous evening had been. Perhaps Uli was homesick and melancholy. Perhaps, as his police colleagues used to say about a difficult WPC, she'd had the painters in. Whatever the cause, he could have handled it better.

It began with an argument over her violin, after he had fallen over the music stand, which sat in the middle of his living room most days despite the fact that Uli had barely lifted the instrument since her father had died. Then she complained about the pub he had taken her to, comparing it unfavourably to the *Kneipen* in Berlin. His comment that these were probably rubble by now had not been the most tactful way to respond.

There'd been plenty of pained silences during dinner. She'd hardly touched anything. To compensate he'd drunk too much of the rough Portuguese wine.

Now she was a mere foot away from him, wrapped so tightly

298

in the blankets she could be mummified. He knew he had a lot of ground to make up today. Luckily, it was Sunday and they didn't have to go to that bloody London Cage and play cat and mouse with yet more Germans.

Ross could feel his goodwill towards the Germans eroding. He'd argued long and hard with both Uli and his father that you couldn't tar one nation with a single blood-soaked brush, but he was finding it increasingly hard to live up to his own rhetoric.

The telephone, still out in the hallway, started its brittle ringing. Ross swung out of bed, crossed into the hall and put the receiver to his ear. Nothing.

After a second he could sense his father at the other end of the line, trying to collect his thoughts.

'Dad? Take your time. I'm here. It's seven-thirty on a Sunday morning. What's so important, dad?'

He looked back and Uli was sitting up, concern on her face. Perhaps it wouldn't be so uphill after all.

'Fucking hell, Cameron.' He'd never heard his father swear quite so forcefully before.

'Tell me.'

'It's all hands on deck, boy. Get your arse down here.'

'Why?'

'We've lost Schuller. We've lost hundreds of them, Cam.'

Erich awoke, shivering. The temperature had dropped sharply. He levered himself up, teeth chattering. Schuller was sitting a couple of metres away. He'd undone the baling twine round his wrist and was opening a can of bully beef.

'Good morning.'

'What time is it?'

'About eleven,' said Schuller. He passed over the tin and spoon. 'You first. Do you know that you snore?'

299

Erich took a mouthful and handed the tin back. The inside of the barn was still dim, but the shafts of light here and there indicated a bright day outside.

'I'll go and do some scouting later,' the SS man said. 'But I don't think we can move till late afternoon. We should be able to cover a lot of ground tonight if we can stick to the road.'

'Where did you get the map? There are no road signs anywhere. I can't imagine they sell maps to PoWs.'

'It was on the wall in the carriage of the train that brought us from Southampton. What an oversight, eh? More?'

Erich waved the bully beef away.

'Can I take this off?' He held up his wrist, its baling-twine restraint dangling.

'Certainly. If you give me your word that you won't run away.'

'To where, exactly?'

'Back to the British. For a decent breakfast.' Schuller finished the rest of the can and smacked his lips. 'I've eaten worse.'

'How many do you expect will make it to the U-boat?'

'Not too many. Ten, maybe. The rest will be recaptured or killed.'

'Such a futile waste of life.'

Schuller stood and began a series of stretches, paying attention to each major muscle group and tendon block in turn. 'You think I'm just a fanatic, don't you?'

'I don't know what you are, Schuller. I don't even know if I believe that you were sent over here deliberately.'

Schuller knelt down in front of Erich. 'It may be foolhardy but there is a logic behind it. When our counter-offensive in Europe succeeds, and the British and Americans find that they have two armies cut off, surrounded, and there is total chaos in this country too, then the Allies will realise that Germany isn't

300

finished. She can fight on, one way or another. And they will sue for peace.'

'Peace?' asked Erich, shocked. 'Is that what you want?'

'An honourable peace. Not like Versailles. Something that leaves us with dignity.'

They heard a dog bark in the distance, and a whistle. Schuller took the pistol from his waistband and walked across to the door, peering out. After a few minutes he shook his head and came back. 'A kilometre or more away. I don't think they'll come. Look at this place.' He snatched at a cobweb. 'It hardly sees daily use.'

'They won't give you a peace while Hitler is still at the top.'

'You think not?'

Erich shook his head. 'Not a chance.'

'I agree.'

Erich smiled. Schuller wasn't quite the blind fool he had taken him for. 'So, what are the Führer's choices?'

'Exile,' said Schuller. 'Perhaps South America. Like the Kaiser. They let him live out his days in Holland.'

'I wouldn't give you good odds on Hitler surviving to a ripe old age, even in South America. What else?'

There was the sound of a shotgun, again some distance away. A few pigeons rustled nervously in the roof.

'I believe that the Führer will do whatever he has to do to save Germany. If that means taking his own life, I am confident he will have the strength to do so.'

'Let's hope he doesn't leave it too late.'

Before Schuller could reply, they heard a police-car bell sounding in the lane and then the screech of tyres as brakes were applied, followed by the distinctive whine of reverse gear.

'Damn,' said Schuller. 'They've seen the car. They are coming to take a look.'

★ ★ ★

The enormity of the disaster became clear as the morning went on. Twenty-seven camps had seen escapes or escape attempts. In nineteen of them at least one German had got away. The numbers from roll-calls were still coming in, but Colonel Ross estimated that there were three hundred fugitives on the loose. It could have been worse. Things had gone wrong for the Germans – tunnels collapsing, dogs discovering them, alert guards. It looked as though they'd been trying to get thousands out.

Specialist interrogators had been dispatched all over the country, with the big hitters going to Devizes – Colonel Scotland was already there – and Stanhope, which was in Colonel Ross's patch. He drove there with his son and the girl, brooding on the other bad news of the day.

The Germans had started a new offensive. Tanks had blasted a hole through the American lines in the Ardennes Forest of Belgium, focusing on a weakly held section where the front 'bulged' away from Germany. They were relying on more than just regular forces, however. There were reports of infiltrators – German commandos and paratroopers in US uniforms creating havoc by changing road signs and issuing false orders. They were being shot when they were caught, of course, but the damage was already done. He thought back to the lunch at Rules with Dansey. That was what Skorzeny had been up to with his English-speaking volunteers.

They drove in silence, and the Colonel thought he could detect a frostiness between the girl and Cameron. Or maybe it was just the rude awakening he'd given them. Someone, somewhere would get a rocket up their arse for this debacle, that was for sure.

As they branched off the A11 and across the acres of frosted farmland, Cameron Ross finally asked: 'Will this be released to the public?'

'Good question,' the Colonel said. 'If we do broadcast it, then the public will be more vigilant, more likely to report suspicious characters pretending to be foreign workers.'

'And you also risk widespread panic and making the security services look incompetent,' said Uli. The Colonel nodded, not liking to have his thoughts confirmed by her.

'What are the losses from Stanhope?'

'There were thirty-two missing at roll-call. Apparently the hole in the wire was discovered by accident on a walk-round by one of the guards. It could've been the whole damn' lot from the officers' camp otherwise. There've been some recoveries. From goods trains. Railway stations. One cheeky lot climbing over a US bomber base's fence.'

'Leaving how many at large?' asked Ross.

The Colonel dug the list from his briefcase and passed it across. 'I've put a line through those confirmed as appre-hended.'

Uli and Ross both scanned down the list and saw the name, but only Uli uttered a sudden exclamation. Erich Hinkel. Her old fiancé was out there somewhere, making mischief for Adolf Hitler.

'Nothin' in here, sarge.'

'Give it a proper look.'

'I have.'

'Who's that with the shotgun?'

'That'll be Mullins.'

'Oh, bloody hell. Do you think we ought to tell him that if he sees one of the sausage-eaters he shouldn't shoot 'im?'

'He told me he considered any bloody Nazi on his land fair

game. "Not worth any more than a partridge," he said. 'Cept you couldn't eat a Jerry.'

Another boom. 'There he goes again. Let's go and have a word.'

'What about the car?'

'You stay and keep an eye on it. Case they come back with some petrol, like.'

'Sarge . . . what am I meant to do then?'

'You've got a whistle and a truncheon, boy. Use 'em.'

From their perch up in the roof space, Erich watched the two coppers leave, the younger one all but tripping over the empty bully-beef can as they went, and breathed a sigh of relief. Schuller was shaking and Erich realised that he was laughing. 'I suppose all the good ones must be in the army,' he whispered at last.

Colonel Ross's party reached the camp just after midday. Stanhope was in uproar. Carlisle, the camp's Intelligence Officer, was pale with embarrassment at the thought of retribution for his slackness. Roebuck, the commander, was threatening mass punishment for the PoWs, even for those who'd stayed put. The Colonel had to convince them that post-mortems and tribunals were for later. They had to apprehend the fugitives; then they could worry about who had planned this and, most importantly, why.

'How do you want to play it, Colonel?' asked Carlisle, glad to be spared a dressing down.

Ross looked across the compound. All the prisoners were locked in, with four sentries round each hut, except for the structure nearest him.

'What's that?'

'Recreation centre for the prisoners, sir. Out of bounds now, of course.'

'We'll set up in there,' said Colonel Ross, indicating that Uli and his son should go on in. 'Ten minutes with each prisoner, then I want them transferred to the main house to make a written statement.'

'All of them?' asked Carlisle.

'All of the officers, yes. We can piece together a lot from such things, even if the accounts conflict.'

'It'll take weeks.'

'And you're going somewhere, are you, Carlisle?' asked the Colonel.

'No, sir.'

Inside the rec hut, Ross and Uli shifted furniture into the configuration appropriate for the interviews. Ross suddenly stopped and stroked his beard, bothered by something.

'What's wrong?' whispered Uli. 'Look, I know we had a bit of a falling-out last night—'

'No, it's not that,' he said quickly.

'It isn't Erich? You don't think . . . ? I was as shocked as you were.'

'No, don't be ridiculous,' he said, in a tone that he instantly regretted. 'There's something here, in this room,' he said, looking around the hut, 'that isn't quite right. I can't put my finger on it.'

'We'll need that bloody thing moved.' It was his father, pointing at the billiard table. 'Shift it.'

Ross walked across and put a hand under one corner. 'If this is—' He grunted as he tried to lift it. 'It is, it's slate. Take more than Uli and me to move it. And you've got a bad back, dad.'

'Sergeant!'

The sergeant poked his head round the door. 'Sir.'

'Get me six prisoners from the nearest hut. In here. Now.'

The PoWs trooped in, their gazes fixed on the floor. Under

305

the Colonel's direction they heaved the table flat against one wall, making room for him to set up his desks for the three of them plus Carlisle, facing a single chair where the PoW would sit.

As the six were leaving, Ross noticed one of the prisoners glancing at the dartboard and looking puzzled. Ross followed the man's gaze and snapped his fingers at him.

'You.'

'Yes?'

'Yes, *sir*,' Ross reminded him.

'Sir.'

'What's your name?'

'Dietrich.'

'Dietrich, stay behind. I need to talk to you first.'

The Colonel was about to object that he alone would determine the running order when he caught Uli's look and she inclined her head, her eyes flashing a warning. The old man sat down on his folding chair, crossed his arms, and waited for the show to begin.

Thirty-Four

17–18 December 1944

It was on the third night that they finally smelled the sea. Erich and Schuller should have made it to the shore in the early hours of the morning, but there had been roadblocks and troop movements to thwart them. So they spent a cold, miserable day in a lean-to on the edge of a sluggish river that was thick with reeds. To make it worse, Erich's cheek still throbbed where Schuller had elbowed him.

'Do you have a girl, Hinkel?' asked Schuller suddenly in the middle of the afternoon.

'Yes. You?'

'No. Not really. Never settled. Where is she?'

Erich hesitated. If he told Schuller the truth, that he thought she was here in England, the SS man would suspect his motivation immediately. 'Berlin. At least, I hope she is still there. Still alive.'

'She hasn't written?'

'I don't think she knows if I am alive or dead.'

'Have you written to her?'

'Yes,' he said truthfully, thinking of the unposted letters he had in his jacket.

'Tell me about the U-boats.'

A pair of Thunderbolts roared across the wood in front of them, bristling with the drop tanks that enabled them to penetrate deep into Germany as fighter escorts. 'I sometimes wish I'd been up there,' Erich said.

'You think you'd still be alive if you'd been in the *Luftwaffe*?'

'The odds can't have been worse than in the U-boats,' said Erich. 'Towards the end, on the last shore leave before we were rammed, we heard that the losses were at two out of every three.'

Schuller reached into his jacket and brought out a half-bar of chocolate. 'I was saving this. Now is as good a time as any.'

They nibbled at the squares slowly, savouring each bite. Erich told the story of U-40, their stuttering start when they couldn't sink a buoy, the movement into the Happy Time, when the hunting was good, then the gradual reversal of fortune as the Allies became stronger, more numerous and far more cunning.

By the time he had finished the chocolate was long gone. The sun was low in the sky, and an east wind was sending ripples across the river. Schuller held out his hand.

'What's that for?' Erich asked suspiciously.

'I want to shake your hand.'

Erich took it and the SS man squeezed hard as he pumped it. 'You did your bit, Hinkel.'

'What about you?'

Are the rumours true? he wanted to ask. *About what you did in Czechoslovakia and Rome and France? About the things done in Germany's name?* But all he managed was: 'How was it in the SS-Polizei?'

Schuller stood up and stretched his arms above his head. He

308

peered down at Erich. 'I did my bit, too. Come on, it'll be dark soon. Let's see if we can't get you back in a U-boat.'

Erich smiled and levered himself up. How could he tell a man like Schuller that he never wanted to see the inside of a U-boat again as long as he lived?

There were tank traps and pillboxes on the road, the latter either unmanned or their inhabitants asleep, but even so they approached each one as if crack troops were inside, making long, quiet loops around them. It wouldn't do, said Schuller, to fail now. They also avoided the villages.

'What about the other half of the chocolate?' asked Erich. 'That wasn't a whole bar.'

Schuller shook his head. 'I am ashamed to say I ate that the first night.'

Erich grabbed his arm and the two men stood in the lane, listening to the sound of cows rustling on the other side of the hedge. 'You ate it without offering me any?'

Schuller laughed. 'Erich, I didn't like you then. I wouldn't do it now. Two or three more kilometres, I reckon. Let's move it.'

The soil grew sandy and eventually they found a rough wooden walkway that led to some scrappy-looking dunes, full of deep hollows and black crescents in the thin moonlight. Beyond them they could see the neglected defences, left in disrepair now that the invasion threat was long gone. 'Do you think the beach is mined?' asked Schuller.

Erich shrugged. He hadn't thought they'd make it this far. Now he was going to have to go through with this after all. He pulled out the flashlight. 'Ask me when you're scraping me into a coal scuttle. Are you sure this is the right stretch of coast for the submarine?'

The ungauzed torch beam sliced through the night, dazzling the Germans, causing them to step back with hands raised to cover their eyes, and a voice barked from the darkness. 'It would be the right stretch if two destroyers weren't out there chasing its tail right now.'

Erich blinked, trying to see who was beyond the starburst of light.

'Colonel Ross?' asked Schuller.

'And a few dozen soldiers. You're late. About six of the others got here before you. Handcuff them, sergeant. Put them with the others.'

As Erich held his hands out he heard the smallest of explosions, far out to sea, but he felt in his bones the boat buck and shudder under him, the smashing of dials, the hiss of fatal leaks. Depth charges. *The poor bastards.*

Erich was aware of Schuller looking for escape. Colonel Ross noticed it too and shone a torch onto the body lying in the marram grass. Kroll's eyes stared lifelessly into the night sky. 'Your friend made a run for it,' said the Colonel. 'Feel free to do the same.'

Schuller didn't struggle as the metal rings clicked round his wrists. Erich expected to see anger and frustration and fury, but the SS man turned and said quietly: 'It's OK, Erich. We did our bit.'

The rifle butt hit Erich under the chin just as he stepped down from the truck bringing them back to Stanhope. He felt his jaw crack and his teeth shift. He must have passed out for a second, as the next thing he remembered was lying on the ground, with people shouting and hands helping him up. He shook his head to clear it and a lance of pain shot up to his eye socket.

The other recaptured Germans were being pushed into their

310

huts, but he was taken back to the truck and sat on the tailgate. As his vision swam he thought he was hallucinating. Over in the doorway of the rec room, he could have sworn that he saw Ulrike, with a halo of light around hair that had grown much longer.

'Come on, lad,' said a British soldier, as he stepped in front of Erich. 'Sorry about that. We'd better find you a doctor.' When the man moved aside, Uli was gone.

Erich was taken, still handcuffed, to the big house, stumbling between two soldiers. The waves of pain were so intense that he could barely keep his eyes open. He was left in a room with a single bed, handcuffed by one wrist to the frame at its head, and he swung his legs up onto it and closed his eyes, arching his back when the fiery pain in his face became unbearable.

'Hello, Erich,' said a voice.

He turned his head. There was a man with a beard in the room. He was dressed in civilian clothes, but he had a feeling that he'd glimpsed him on the beach.

'Don't try and speak. Doctor'll be here soon. See if you can swallow these things.' The man approached with two large bomb-shaped pills and a glass of water. Erich took them and managed to get them down. 'They should dull it at least. My God, it's nasty. I know how it feels. Had a similar thing myself. We are, of course, very sorry. The man who did it will be disciplined, believe you me. I mean what do you take us for? Germans?' He gave a hollow laugh. 'The thing is, old chap, feelings are running high. Seems some American bodies have been discovered at a place called Malmédy. Somewhere in Belgium. An artillery battalion, overrun by an *SS-Panzer Kampfgruppe*. As you doubtless know, you Germans are push- ing ahead as fast as you can. The last thing the *Gruppe* needed was PoWs slowing them down. So, and you will probably think this very reasonable, they killed them. All eighty-five of them. Buried them in the snow. American units probing the depth of the German lines found them. I know the jaw is unfortunate, but just imagine if you'd been guarded by Yanks, like some of the camps are. You got off lightly.'

Whatever was in the pills had begun to work and Erich felt himself drifting away. He tried to hang on to every word.

'It took us by surprise, that attack in the Ardennes. The Panzers are doing rather well. But not for long. All that the news of the massacre has done is stiffen Allied resolve. Feeling better?'

There was a knock at the door and an elderly man entered, a Gladstone bag in his hand. 'Ah, doctor. Here's your patient.' The bearded man strolled back over and leant close. His face was pulsing in and out of focus, but Erich made himself stay with it. 'Was that your writing on the darts scoreboard, Lieutenant? I knew that something was wrong as soon as I entered the room. But could I spot it? No. Then I saw someone else staring at the chalk marks on the board. The numbers. Not the way you score darts. Certainly not counting down from 301. It took me a while to understand that it was a numerical code. A number for each letter of the alphabet. Simple. Submarine, beach, location. It was you, wasn't it?'

Erich nodded.

'Well, thank you. You saved your own life in a way. That submarine would never have got in and out undetected, even if we hadn't known where to look for it. The seas are ours now, Erich.'

'Ulrike Walter?' he managed to ask, each syllable an agony. 'Is she here?'

Ross ignored the question. 'We have met before, you know, Hinkel. Before the war. When you were in the Hitler Youth.'

The man headed for the door, and Erich remembered. The British Inspector, the one in the Tiergarten, when he'd walked with Ulrike. Did that mean that Uli hadn't been a mirage?

Ross half-turned, moments before he closed the door. 'Funny how things turn out, isn't it?' he said softly, unable to resist. 'I'm sure Uli sends her best, by the way.'

Thirty-Five

LOCATION: Camp 203. Stanhope House. Tape archive.
DATE: 19.12.44.
FILE: KW/990/17
ARCHIVE No.: n/a
SUBJECT: SS-Obersturmführer Axel Schuller.
INTERROGATOR: Inspector Cameron Ross.
ALSO PRESENT: Corporal Harold Pritchett.
RECORDED ON: GE Type 7 wire recorder, Marconi Mk IV microphone.
STATUS: Classified until further notice.

[tape begins 00:00]

SCHULLER: No father? He's letting you out all by yourself?

ROSS: This is just a postscript, Schuller. We've read your statement. I must say, most of it is refreshingly honest. But we need to know who left that car for you on the other side of the fence, sitting in the lane.

SCHULLER: [inaudible].

ROSS: Thank you, Corporal Pritchett. If you will wait outside.

CORPORAL: With respect, sir—

ROSS: I'll be fine. The Obersturmführer and I are old friends. I'll shout if I need you.

SCHULLER: Is this the part where you beat me up?

ROSS: You know us better than that.

SCHULLER: I have two men with broken ribs, one with a smashed jaw. Others roughed up. Hardly fair play. Hardly Geneva Convention.

ROSS: I wouldn't try and pull the Geneva Convention on us, Schuller. You of all people. Feelings were running high. You made us look foolish. And then the news came about Malmédy.

SCHULLER: Propaganda.

ROSS: Maybe so. Pretty effective, though. I'm also here to tell you that London has decided what to do with you. You will be moved to Camp 21 at Comrie in Scotland as of the 26th. As I am sure you know, Comrie is a Black camp. You can rot with your own kind there. Oh, you might be interested to know that not a single man got out from Comrie. Not one.

SCHULLER: But we did elsewhere. It isn't so much that we had to succeed, Ross. It's more that we had to show you people we aren't finished yet. [inaudible] . . . meant to.

ROSS: Oh, I don't think so. Panic and mayhem, you mean? The public heard only that seventy escaped from Bridgend. Some made it as far as Birmingham and Eastbourne. Which is convenient for us. Because now any Germans we pick up, we claim they are from Bridgend. One escape. Not dozens. We got your sub, too. U-876, we believe. Lost with all hands in the Channel.

SCHULLER: [inaudible]. How did you know about the submarine? And the beach rendezvous, Ross?

ROSS: We had our sources.

SCHULLER: One of us?

ROSS: The car? Someone left it for you, day after day, until we no longer noticed it, it became part of the landscape. It's the only piece of the puzzle that we haven't got.

SCHULLER: Are you offering some kind of trade?

ROSS: [inaudible].

SCHULLER: Ha.

ROSS: Well, the car isn't that important . . . I tell you, you'll miss us in Comrie. A right hard crew to look after you up there, by all accounts. We are the sweeties.

SCHULLER: All I know is that it is one of the guards in the other ranks' camp. A Hungarian. Bloody fool forgot.

ROSS: Forgot what?

SCHULLER: He forgot to leave the keys.

ROSS: In which case, I'd bet all my egg ration that he's scarpered. Wouldn't you? He's betrayed us and pissed you lot off by the sound of it. Shot by both sides. In a manner of speaking. So that won't be much use.

SCHULLER: You asked who it was. Not where he was.

ROSS: True, true. In which case, I should keep my side of things. [inaudible].

SCHULLER: Who?

ROSS: [inaudible].

SCHULLER: I don't believe you. That's ridiculous.

ROSS: That's all for now. Be ready to leave for Comrie on Boxing Day.

SCHULLER: You're a bastard, Ross. Just like your father.

ROSS: I'll take that as a compliment.

SCHULLER: [inaudible].

ROSS: Happy Christmas, Schuller.

[tape ends at 00:09]

TECHNICAL NOTE: The wire recorders supplied by the US Army are liable to what they call 'drop outs' if the speaking voice is lowered. Hence the number of [inaudibles] on these transcripts. The Marconi Mk V microphones correct this, but were not available at Stanhope camp at the time of these interrogations. Written manuscripts for many of the interrogations are available, taken by a stenographer, whose presence is indicated by an *S* at the top of the file, and an archive number (SCI/ followed by four digits).

Major Lionel Crawford, Chief Translator and Recorder, Camp 203.

TRANSCRIPT declassified 10.9.2001.

Public Records Office, Kew.

Thirty-Six

24 December 1944

'Come on, it's Christmas. Silent Night. Holy Night. *O Tannenbaum* and all that.'

Erich rolled over in his bunk, looked at Dietrich's beaming face and managed to mutter: 'Like I'll be s-s-singing. You go.'

After five days of ranting – coupled with constant parades and roll-calls – the camp authorities seemed to have finally calmed down, especially once every missing body had been accounted for. Petitions to be able to celebrate Christmas on 24 December, as opposed to the customary English date, had finally received a decent hearing, and a singing concert had been arranged in Hut Six, the most commodious of them all, along with hot, non-alcoholic wine, which, of course, would be spiked with some of the brain-rot that Hut Twelve churned out.

'You could hum,' said Dietrich.

Erich's jaw was wired together. He could speak, albeit slowly and painfully, but he couldn't eat or chew. Soup through a straw was to be his diet for weeks to come.

'If it wasn't for me, you'd be back under the water now, or

freezing your nuts off in Belgium. You owe me,' said Dietrich.

'I owe everyone in this damn' camp something or other.' This was true. Erich had managed to pull together a bribe big enough to get the undivided attention of one of the guards by scrounging every last favour. In return, all the guard had to do was deliver a parcel of creased letters to the interrogators' office, marked for the attention of Ulrike Walter. If that was still her name.

That arrogant English – or *schottisch*, as he preferred – prick Ross. Funny, the policeman had seemed so much older in Berlin, so much more mature and worldly than Erich Hinkel, the gangly Hitler Youth kid. Ross must still have a decade on Erich, but the margin seemed to have shrunk to nothing. In fact, Erich felt as if he were the older man now, being sneered at by a young upstart. Well, there was nothing he could do. The letters would show Uli that there was someone else who loved her and had cared about her during the last five years. Someone who was, unfortunately, on the losing side.

'There'll be schnapps. You can get that past your steel teeth.'

'It won't be s-s-schnapps and it'll make me go blind. So I'll be blind and dumb.'

'OK, you miserable bastard. I might as well give you this now.'

Erich took the crudely wrapped parcel and shook his head. 'I haven't got . . . I'm sorry . . .'

'*Ach*. You've been a bit busy. It's nothing. Just a book I managed to scrounge.'

Erich tore away the brown wrapper and held the slim volume in his hands. '*Emil and the Three Twins*,' he read out loud. It was in the original.

'I tried to get the *Detectives*, but, you know . . .' Dietrich waved his arm around the hut. 'Limited availability.'

'No, this is great, I haven't read this. Thank you, Werner.'

'Are you coming now?'

Erich hesitated, then felt hands grip his upper arms and drag him from the bed. Dietrich yelled a protest but he, too, was grabbed. Four of Schuller's *SS-Rollkommando* roughly pulled them outside into the billowing snow. Erich guessed he was going to the Christmas concert after all.

Ross never did win the turkey in the lottery, which was just as well since the Colonel wanted everyone in the vicinity of Stanhope until the transfers to other camps were complete and the paperwork signed off.

Both Ross and Uli agreed that the main house, with its bare echoing rooms and paper chains put up by the garrison, would be a depressing place to spend Christmas itself, and Ross booked them into The Ickworth, a pub about three miles away. It was a classic country inn, and she had no complaints. There was a big log fire in the bar, decent enough food and a special effort promised for the traditional Christmas dinner.

The publican had joined a Pig Club earlier in the year and, in return for his work feeding and mucking out, was expecting a good chunk of the two beasts that had been slaughtered the previous week. He claimed he boiled his government-issue bran feed and his table scraps with the beer slops, so he was expecting something 'right tasty' from the porkers.

They settled into the rather over-frilly bedroom, Ross went downstairs for a drink in the bar, and Uli said she would join him later. She lay on the bed and thought of other Christmas Eves, those with her father, the music before dinner, then the opening of presents afterwards and the beautiful singing around the tree.

She'd asked to see Erich, of course, but the request had been denied. She'd tried to bluff her way into the camp, but had been rebuffed. Ross swore that it wasn't his doing, but she wasn't so sure. At least Ross hadn't got wind of the letters that the weaselly soldier had passed to her with a knowing wink.

Uli took the little parcel from her bag, untied the string around the letters and sorted them into date order. She sniffed the paper. There was a scent of salt, sweat, oil and fear, so intense that it made her head swim. She caught the sound of a swell of hearty laughter from the bar below, but as she began to read the letters written fifty metres under the sea it quickly faded to nothing. She lost herself to the whirring of electric motors, the ping of echo-locators against steel and the terrifying blast of depth charges.

As they were led into the hut, a strange sight awaited them. At one end, a Christmas party was in full swing, with drinking and singing and joshing. At the other, nearest to them, there was a table behind which sat Schuller, with Hetz and Bauert flanking him. In a semicircle facing the trio, like a human auditorium, were about thirty other men, some of them SS. Erich and Dietrich were pushed into the middle of the crescent and forced to look at Schuller.

'Axel—' Erich began.

'Quiet!' yelled the *Rollkommando* next to him.

'How many men on a U-boat, Hinkel?' asked Schuller.

'Forty-eight. Maybe fifty-two.'

'Let's call it fifty. Fifty sailors dead in the English Channel. Fifty good Germans. Because of you.'

Erich looked down at his shoes. It was true.

'I know all about what happened in the recreation hut,' said Schuller. 'On the pretext of getting your gloves.'

Erich stayed silent. This could be bluff.

'You were overheard.'

'Saying what?' asked Erich through his clamped teeth.

'Telling Dietrich about the rendezvous. Saying it was crazy. That I had to be stopped. We know you must have left some kind of sign or signal behind for the British. You are a disgrace.'

Erich stole a look at Dietrich. He had gone white. He realised how much trouble they were in. Erich watched Hetz and Bauert move away from Schuller and position themselves on either side of the two accused men.

Schuller stood and pointed a finger. 'You stayed behind with the Englishman Ross in the hut! You were seen, Dietrich. You must have helped them with whatever the message was.'

It was a distraction and as Erich turned his head towards his friend the blow from the iron poker came hard and savage. Blood arced from Erich's crushed cheek as he stumbled into the arms of Hetz who thrust him upright. The singing faltered and then resumed.

'No, you're mistaken—' began Dietrich.

'Shut him up,' said Schuller.

A hand clamped around Dietrich's mouth. Erich managed to stand straight, the side of his face white-hot with pain.

'That's right, isn't it, Erich? You told Ross where to find us and the submarine.'

'Nobe,' he managed to say before Bauert hit him with the bar again, spreading his nose across his face. There was a ripple of dismay through the hut now. Schuller glared at the singers, who resumed once more, their voices frail.

Erich tried to speak. He had to save his friend. Dietrich had given away the scrawlings on the scoreboard to Ross but it was he, Erich, who had chalked up the warning message in the first place. They must let Dietrich go.

'Werner did nothing—'

323

The poker swung into Erich's mouth, shattering his teeth and ripping the jaw wire, sending the raw ends into his lips and tongue. Dietrich wrestled himself free. 'For God's sake. Stop this. Stop it!' He shouted as loud as he could, hoping that someone was at the other end of the microphones hidden in the ceiling. 'Stop it. You've got it wrong.'

'Werner Dietrich. You are sentenced by this court—'

'Court? What court? You've gone mad, Schuller.'

'—to be shunned.'

When Dietrich tried to speak again, two of the *Rollkommando* thrust their faces into his and chanted: 'We can't hear you, we can't hear you.'

Schuller pointed at Erich, who was now on his knees, bent over a growing pool of blood on the concrete floor. 'Take him away.'

As Dietrich lunged for his friend, Schuller said quietly, 'And tie this man to his bunk.'

Ross sat near the bar with his father, their faces glowing red with alcohol and the heat of the crackling logs. Despite the shock of finding Erich here, alive, he felt relaxed. His father was easier company these days, and Uli was surely his. He had long worried about Erich, seen him as a great rival, until he came face to face with him once more. Now he wondered why he had been so concerned about the poor boy. He supposed that the ultimate test of his confidence would come when he allowed the two of them to meet. Not yet, though.

Ross even felt confident enough to tell the whole story to his father, from the first meeting at the Walters' party, through his embarrassment in the hallway when he'd tried to hand over the perfume, and the feeling of unfinished business that had haunted him right up until he got Uli back from Canada. His father listened in silence, realising, for the first time perhaps, the enormity of what he had done to his son back when he had intercepted the letters in 1938 and 1939.

It was gone eleven when Ross looked at his watch and said to his father, 'I'll go and get Uli. OK?'

'Absolutely. I thought Christmas Eve was their big night? For presents and so on?'

'You're right.' Ross stood. He would give her the gift tonight, the German way. But first she should have a drink. He stumbled up the stairs, unsteady after four pints. He shook his head to try and sober up. There was nothing worse than a drunk imploring you to come and have some fun. He entered their room and could see her lying on the bed. He stood for a moment, watching the steady rise and fall of her chest. Uli was asleep. He resisted the urge to go over and kiss her. Let her rest, if that was what she needed.

Ross was about to close the door when something about her made him hesitate. He stepped inside to take a closer look. She had a sheet of paper in her hand, and there were others scattered around the bed. Now he could see that her face was red and puffy, streaked with dried tears. She had cried herself to sleep.

Ross picked up the letters from the floor, careful not to disturb her, and retreated to the desk, ignoring the inner voice telling him that this was a despicable invasion of privacy and a betrayal of trust. He clicked on the scallop-shaped reading lamp and sat, reading through the handwriting quickly, his brain snapping into sobriety over the course of the first few pages and forcing him on and on, even though he felt as if razor blades were nicking his insides.

Uli stirred as he was on the fourth of the letters, her moist eyes blinking, trying to focus on him.

'Ross,' she said, pushing herself up on one elbow as she

realised what he'd been doing. 'Oh, God. You had no right, Ross.'

'He still loves you, doesn't he? After all this time. Erich still loves you.'

She nodded. 'Yes, he does.'

Don't ask, you don't want to know. 'And do you still love him?'

There was an urgent knocking at the door.

'Go away,' said Ross. 'Well?'

Uli shook her head. 'You expect me to answer that?'

Another knock and the Colonel burst into the room, his eyes wide, gasping for breath from his sprint up the stairs. At first Ross thought that his father was about to have a heart attack, but the Colonel gulped air and said, 'There's been an incident. At the camp. Carlisle just called.'

'What kind of incident?' asked Ross.

'A hanging. They've hanged a fellow prisoner. The Germans have murdered one of their own.'

Uli put a hand over her mouth.

'Hinkel?' asked Ross. 'Was it Erich Hinkel?'

'I don't know,' the Colonel said, puzzled by the question. 'But we'd better get down there. Happy bloody Christmas this is going to be.'

They had dragged Erich over the snow towards the shower block. Dietrich, who had eventually freed himself from his bunk, could see the dark splashes of congealed blood every few feet marking his friend's progress. Hetz and Bauert must have been beating him as they went, because there were fine sprays of crimson in the churned snow.

He followed the path to the cinder-block latrine and wash-house and paused in the entrance, waiting for his eyes to adjust to the gloom within. Erich was a few metres from the doorway.

They had thrown a rope over the crudely lagged pipes that criss-crossed the ceiling and hauled him off his feet. It was impossible to tell from the mess that was his face, but Dietrich suspected that Erich had died of strangulation rather than a broken neck.

Dietrich knelt down to untie the rope from where it had been connected to a sink's outflow pipe but a voice made him jump. 'Leave it.'

He turned to see Schuller standing over him.

Dietrich said: 'He wrote the message. But I pointed it out to them.'

'I know,' said Schuller. 'Count yourself lucky you aren't beside him.'

'Why, Schuller?'

Schuller looked up at the mutilated face. 'He had to pay for his treachery. It wasn't personal. I liked him, you know.'

'He was a good man, Schuller. A brave man.' Dietrich began to cry. 'He didn't deserve it.'

Schuller acknowledged this with the barest inclination of the head before he said softly: 'I can't hear you.' He walked out into the thickening storm, leaving Dietrich gripping the legs of his dead friend.

'Keep the woman out, for God's sake,' snapped Colonel Ross as they looked up at the body. A dozen of them crowded in the doorway. Even so, the desperate cry he heard told him that it was too late. Ross senior turned to his son. 'Get her back to the hotel. And get her sedated, man. And Cameron—'

'Yes?' Ross turned back.

'How did you know it was Erich?'

'A guess. I just thought that if they put two and two together, he was the most likely candidate.'

The Colonel spoke very softly. 'It wasn't wishful thinking?'

'What?' Ross gasped.

'No. Course not. Go and sort her out, then come back. Cut the body down, Sergeant. I think we have a reasonable idea of the cause of death. Is the MO here? Well, get him . . .'

Ross stepped outside, looking for Uli. There was no sign of her, and the snow had been turned into slush by heavy boots, so it was impossible to know which way she had gone. He strode off towards the main gate and was passing one of the huts when a voice came from its shadow.

'Sir? Mister Ross?'

He peered into the darkness. 'Who's that? Dietrich? There's a lock-down. Get back to your hut.'

'I saw it all. I can name names. I can tell you what happened.'

Ross was torn. He should go and find Uli, but there was a duty to be done here. Uli would be all right, she was a strong woman, she'd survive the shock. His mind made up, he said, 'Come with me. I'll get a stenographer and we'll take your statement.'

He pulled two of the corporals aside, sent one to find a stenographer, ordered the other to check the camp for Uli and took Dietrich over to the reception hut, trying to keep his mind focused on the job in hand.

Nobody stopped Uli as she made her way through the snow to the main house, one hand cupped over her mouth to stifle her sobs. She walked across the hallway and up the darkened stairs to the first-floor interrogation rooms and found one that wasn't locked. She slipped inside, closed and locked the door behind her and switched on the lights. It was one of the transcription rooms, the floor space occupied by six metal tables for typists, each table with a wire-spool recorder next to it, and the walls lined with four-drawer grey filing cabinets.

Uli sat down at the nearest table, and only then did she let her grief consume her. As she cried, she pressed her head down onto the cold surface of the desk, harder and harder, trying to blot the image of Erich from her mind.

Uli couldn't shake the feeling that, somehow, this was all her fault. She was the centre of the events that had started in Berlin with her flirting with a visiting policeman and had ended up here in a prison camp in England.

Yet she couldn't work out what she could have done differently. Even if she had never met Ross, Erich would still have joined the *Bootwaffe*. He would still have been captured, brought to Stanhope and killed by his own countrymen in a brutal reprisal for what they saw as his treachery. To have survived those years under the sea, only to be murdered by his comrades-in-arms – that was a savage irony.

The guilt wouldn't go away even though she knew who was to blame for Erich's death. Those evil men who had taken his youthful energy and idealism and corrupted it, turning him and millions of other Germans into instruments of destruction. Ultimately what was being destroyed was Germany itself.

What would she do now? She couldn't face Ross for the moment. He wouldn't understand why she felt as if a part of her had died out there in the snow.

Uli stood, dried her tears on her sleeve, crossed to the door and pressed her ear to it. There were voices on the landing.

As she leant her cheek against the door jamb, listening to the muffled conversation, she understood that she had witnessed the finale of one small act that would be repeated over and over as the repercussions of this futile war killed the bravest and the best and wrecked countless lives. Including, now, her own.

Ross got back to the hotel just as dawn was breaking. Downstairs stank of stale alcohol and vomit, and there were some diehard revellers lying on the banquettes and on the floor, snoring. Ross climbed the stairs, reflecting on how a few hours could turn your life upside down. One thing was certain. No matter what he felt about Erich personally, the man had been murdered in cold blood. Those who had done this to him would have to be punished.

He crept into his room, but sensed immediately that there was no one there. He flicked on the overhead light. The bed still showed the imprint of Uli's body, where she had lain and read the letters and cried over her U-boat man. Her side of the wardrobe and her sections of the chest of drawers, though, were empty. Her case was missing from its stand. The letters were nowhere to be seen. She'd taken those, too. Where on earth could Uli have gone in the middle of the night on a Christmas Eve? *Anywhere away from you* came the unwanted answer.

Part Four

1945

Thirty-Seven

The London Cage: July 1945

Just a few more minutes, Uli reminded herself, and the trial would be over. The door at the far end of the room opened and the six members of the tribunal marched in. The Presiding Officer, a gaunt, expressionless Guards colonel, nodded as those already in the room rose to their feet, and there was a scrape of chairs and a brief expectant murmur as all sat once more. Uli could read in the tribunal's grim eyes what the sentence was to be, and she glanced over at Schuller and his co-defendants, Hetz and Bauert, for the last time. She imagined first the black hoods and then the intricately knotted ropes passing over their heads and she was surprised that the thoughts gave her no pleasure at all. As a bitter taste soured her throat and her stomach heaved, she rose from her seat and hurried from the court, conscious of the clacking of her heels on the linoleum as the NCOs moved quickly aside to let her pass.

There was a summer drizzle outside. Uli put up her umbrella as she left the building and walked up the path towards the guardsmen who flanked the gate to the street. He appeared between the two giant figures, blocking her way. One of the sentries turned, wondering why she had halted.

'You all right, miss?' asked the guardsman.

'Yes. Yes, thank you.'

'I'll look after her,' Ross said. As she stepped onto the pavement she felt his hand on her elbow, guiding her to the left. 'The Prince of Wales,' he said. 'I need a drink. You look as if *you* need a drink.'

'Cam. I didn't see you in there,' she said, unable to keep the surprise from her voice. 'And I've been there every day.'

'I gave my evidence in camera. Just the tribunal present.'

'Why in camera?'

'Well, SIS don't like their men to be known to the public.'

So he was in the Secret Intelligence Service full-time now. 'You're SIS staff?'

'Kind of.' Ross had spent the first half of the year abroad, working as an interrogator for the various war-crimes tribunals. Now he had accepted an assignment to the German desk of MI6, on condition that his father was allowed to be his paid consultant. It was his way of letting the Colonel fade away with dignity and, if he was honest, of tapping into his vast bank of tradecraft, before it was lost for ever to the hardening arteries of his brain.

'What about the police? I was sure you'd go back.'

'The world is awash with ex-servicemen wanting to stay in uniform. Any uniform. They'll manage without me.'

'You've lost the beard.'

'Yes.' He touched the slight lump in his jawline. 'I thought I'd been hiding behind it for too long.'

'You look good.'

'So do you. Are you playing the violin?'

'Yes. Taking lessons from one of the men whom father met on the island. I'm grabbing him while I can still afford him. He'll be a star once things settle down, and out of my league.'

Uli looked up at Ross as they walked, trying to think what had changed, apart from the beard. A purposefulness, a strength had invaded him. There was no trace of the self-doubt, the vulnerability that she used to sense buried within him. She felt a tremor of fear. They hadn't seen each other since that Christmas Eve when she'd run away. She had sent a message a few days later to say that he shouldn't worry, she was all right, but she wouldn't be coming back to work for the foreseeable future. She needed time alone.

They reached the pub and she collapsed her umbrella as they entered through the etched-glass double doors. Inside, the Prince of Wales smelled damp but welcoming, the bubbling conversation light and carefree, about sport and weather and local scandal. Anything but war.

Ross found them a table and fetched a pint for himself and a gin and tonic for Uli. He shook the rain from his hat as he sat down, placed it on the stool next to him and they clinked glasses. She sipped, relishing the unfamiliar tang of the lemon slice, a sign that normality was returning. 'What have you been doing, Ross? I called Scotland Yard once or twice, Latchmere, the Cage, but they denied all knowledge of you.'

He explained he had been based at the Prisoner of War Intelligence Service outposts in Europe, first in Holland, then in Germany, for the past six months. The war-crimes files that he had helped compile now filled several warehouses, most of which made grim reading. 'You know that they dragged Canaris out naked from his cell at Flossenbürg? He'd been arrested after the 20 July plot when it became obvious that he was anti-Hitler. Strung him up from the rafters, using an iron collar. Took him thirty minutes to die. Slow strangulation. At least Schuller and the others will be spared that.'

'What exactly will happen to them now?'

'Pierrepoint,' he said. When he saw her expression he added: 'Albert Pierrepoint. I don't know why, but we use a publican as an executioner. He'll hang them at Pentonville. In a month or two, probably. It'll be quicker than what the White Fox had to suffer. God, I've missed you, Uli.'

'I wonder what happened to Uncle Otto.'

Something very similar to Canaris and involving piano wire as Ross recalled, but he didn't want to go into that. He wondered why she was ignoring what he was telling her. 'Uli. I said—'

'Ross,' she interrupted. 'There's something I need to know. About the night they murdered Erich.'

'Christmas Eve. Yes.'

'When your father came into the room and said they'd hanged someone. You asked if it was Erich.'

'Did I?' He furrowed his brow. 'I don't really recall. I'd been drinking.'

She smiled. 'Bong. Red light. Yes, you *do* remember.'

He gulped half of the pint in one and wiped the froth from his mouth. 'Yes. I just thought . . . that he'd been found out.'

She felt her throat go dry, but she forced the words out. 'You didn't drop hints to Schuller?'

'Hints?'

'Cameron. Look at me. This has been on my mind. I can't shift it, no matter how hard I try. The thought that you might have . . . Look, it sounds awful—'

'You thought that I might have told Schuller that it was Erich who betrayed them,' he said flatly, recalling that his father had suggested much the same thing.

'Yes.'

'Even before I read the letters he gave you?'

'Yes.'

He lit a cigarette and smoke wreathed his face, blurring his features, as he said: 'It's not true, Uli.'

She picked up her handbag from the floor.

'So,' she said, 'if I take this along to EMI and have it enhanced, I won't find anything incriminating on it.'

Ross looked inside her handbag. It was a wire spool. 'It's incriminating having that, Uli. You stole a recording? Government property?'

'You forget what I used to do, Ross. Sound recording was my business. I didn't steal the original. The night Erich was murdered, I went back to the transcript room at Stanhope House. I flicked through the files. Guess what I found? Your records. I made a duplicate of the interview between you and Schuller, and took a copy of its transcript and tape. I know how to have the parts of the transcript marked "inaudible" boosted.'

'I'm sure you do. And I'll come with you.'

'What?'

'When you do it. I'll come with you. We can listen together. You'll hear me tell Schuller that the traitor was Kroll.'

'Kroll?'

'The man killed on the beach while trying to make a run for it. I put him in the frame. Schuller figured the truth out all by himself, I'm afraid. Our mistake was not getting Erich out, in thinking that moving him would create suspicion and make reprisals elsewhere more likely. We followed my father's dictum – "hide in plain sight".' Strange how the Colonel's once mighty maxims now seemed so arbitrary and arcane. 'That's where I was in the wrong. I should have insisted that we move him, Christmas or no. And that's all, Uli. That's what I have to live with.'

'Oh.' She gazed hard into his face. Uli could see that Ross was telling the truth, and suddenly she felt wretched. All those months of suspicion and doubt gnawing at her, but there was a warmth of relief in there somewhere, too. 'Oh, Cameron. I—'

'Is that why you left? Because you thought I'd had Erich, my rival, taken out of the picture? You really thought that of me?'

'No. Not exactly.' Even if it had been true, she would have thought that in some way Ross's actions were her responsibility, the inevitable result of the triangle of emotions that she had created. She felt that Erich's death was as much her punishment as his.

'I'm sorry, Ross. It was unforgivable. But to have read his letters, and then have him killed on the same night. It left me . . . distraught. And confused.'

'About which of us you really loved?'

'The letters upset me. Mostly because of what he'd been through in the submarine, all the time thinking, hoping, that I was out there for him somewhere. But before you came upstairs, before you read them, before your father appeared, I had already made up my mind. If Erich hadn't been killed, I would have stuck to my choice.'

Ross didn't ask her what that choice had been but reached into his pocket and brought out the delicate silver filigree box he had bought for her Christmas present. He placed it on the table in front of him. 'These past months have been difficult for me, too, Uli. By necessity I have seen a side of the German people that . . .' He shook his head. She must know what he had seen and heard, that Canaris had been the tip of a black iceberg. 'I think I need someone to remind me about Goethe, Schiller and Bach and Brahms and . . .'

'Mörike.'

'Especially Mörike.'

'Don't you want to know what I had decided that night as I

338

fell asleep after reading the letters?'

He should be angry, Ross knew, because of her suspicion, but he couldn't deny the thought had a clear but hateful logic. Would he have sacrificed Erich to keep her? No, not in that way. Otherwise he would have had no right to pass judgement on others these past six months – he would be as damned as them. 'Don't tell me. Just show me.'

From the velvet-lined silver box in front of him Ross removed the bottle of perfume that Max Goldschmidt had made up for him in the autumn of 1938, the label now curling at the edges but the wax seal unbroken and the blue-black ink of Uli's name still glistening as if it had been freshly written. He placed it in the centre of the table, watching her eyes widen as her memory flashed back to the hallway in Alte Westen, and the frighteningly intense desire she had seen in his face that day.

Cameron Ross listened to his heartbeat mark out the seconds before Uli reached out with her hand and placed it over his, and with the other picked up the glass-stoppered perfume bottle and clenched it in her fist, so tight that it was as if she was determined never to let go of it ever again.

Author's Note

Although *Night Crossing* is a work of fiction, much of it has its roots in fact. The passage of the SS *City of Hamilton* is based on a number of incidents. My good friend John Goldschmidt told me about the experience of his father, a respected Austrian publisher interned by the British. He was on the SS *Dunera* in 1940, which was out of Liverpool heading, eventually, for Australia, when it was attacked by U-56. The first torpedo missed (there actually were problems with them running too deep). The second one hit but failed to detonate, the third, again, missed. When U-56 surfaced to sink the liner with gunfire, it found evidence floating on the water of Germans on board – thanks to the ransacking of the cabins, as depicted here – and called off the attack.

In 1941, U-616 fired three torpedoes at a large ship. All three missed. It seems likely that they too were faulty. Only when they reached port did the U-boat crew realise that they had nearly sunk the *Ile de France*, which had on board 2,000 children bound for Canada.

The Rome attack on the SS police and the subsequent brutal reprisals also happened more or less as depicted in this novel.

German SS volunteers were introduced into the British PoW system to try and stir up trouble, although the fictitious Axel Schuller wasn't one of them.

However, Germans really did escape from some of the 600 camps in the UK. There was indeed a plot at Devizes (Camp 23) to free thousands of Germans and create havoc to coincide with the Ardennes offensive, where Skorzeny's *Kommandotruppe*, dressed in American uniforms, had infiltrated the US lines. (Many were shot out of hand; Skorzeny survived.)

The UK escape plot was foiled and the culprits moved to Comrie in Scotland. A German PoW was subsequently beaten and lynched in the shower block and after the war five Germans were hanged at Pentonville for his murder, following a trial at the London Cage.

The details can be found in the book *For Führer and Fatherland* by Roderick de Normann (Sutton Publishing). *The March on London* by Charles Whiting (Pen & Sword) gives a somewhat racier account, but places the events in a larger context. I first came across the incident in the memoir *The London Cage* by Lt Col A. P. Scotland (Evans Brothers), now long out of print. Some of Colonel Ross's background is based on Scotland's – such as the meeting with Hitler – but the character is totally fictitious, as is the son, although PSIW and MI19 are historical fact, as is Tin-Eye Stephens. The book *Camp 020: MI5 and the Nazi Spies* (PRO) is an intriguing look at the interrogation of the *Abwehr*'s agents and details what went on at Latchmere House under Stephens's direction.

The geography of Stanhope is based on Ickworth House, near Bury St Edmunds (there were camps nearby at Newmarket and Bury St Edmunds itself), a fine Italianate building which was never a PoW camp. Part of it is now an excellent hotel, managed by Peter Lord, who didn't mind me requisitioning his grounds, chopping down his trees and moving his sheep. The most successful escape by German PoWs was at Island Farm (Camp 198) in Bridgend, Wales, where seventy prisoners tunnelled out in March 1945. For details see the fascinating website www.islandfarm.fsnet.co.uk.

The background to internment on the Isle of Man, the persecution of musicians by the Third Reich, the ability to read micro-expressions (here called a Duchenne, although that is not a recognised term), Canaris's resistance to Hitler and his attempts to pass information to the Allies at the beginning of the war, and Heydrich's secret flying lessons are also based on fact.

For anyone interested in U-boats, first port of call should be U-boat Net (www.uboat.net) which is run out of Iceland, and is an astonishingly detailed and endlessly fascinating resource. The real U-40, by the way, was sunk in the English Channel in October 1939. Also see *Type VII U-boats* by Robert C. Stern (Caxton), *Das Boot* by Lothar-Günther Buchheim (Cassell), *U-boat Adventures* by Melanie Wiggins (Naval Institute Press) and *The Secret Diary of a U-boat* by Wolfgang Hirschfeld (Cassell).

The background concerning music and musicians in the Third Reich was provided by *The Twisted Muse* by Michael H. Kater (Oxford) and *Trial of Strength* by Fred K. Prieberg (Quartet).

Testimonies of internees on the Isle of Man and other places are widely available, but I would recommend *A Bespattered Page* by Ronald Stent (André Deutsch), *Island of Barbed Wire* by Connery Chappell (Robert Hale) and, on more general aspects of the positive impact of exiles from Germany, *The Hitler Emigrés* by Daniel Snowman (Chatto & Windus).

For Berlin in 1938, I referred to the excellent *A Dance Between*

The Flames by Anton Gill (Michael Joseph), *Berlin* by Giles McDonough (Sinclair-Stevenson), *Blood & Banquets* by Bella Fromm (Birch Lane) and *The Ghosts of Berlin* by Brian Ladd (University of Chicago Press), among many others.

The Third Reich Tour of Original Berlin Walks (www.berlinwalks.com), which meets outside Zoo Station every Saturday and Sunday at ten a.m., is a good taster for what is left standing of Nazi Berlin (the tour commentary is in English). I am indebted to Nick Gay of the outfit for reading an early version of the manuscript.

The golf course at Stoke Park Club (Stoke Poges) is real – it is where Sean Connery took on Gert Frobe. However, I have taken some liberties with the layout and the description of the holes.

Thanks for their tireless support as always to: Martin Fletcher, David Miller, Sabine Stiebritz, Amy Philip, Kim Hardie, Kerr MacRae, Julie Manton, Peter Newsom, Barbara Ronan, Katherine Ball, Paul Erdpresser and all at Headline; Deborah, Bella, Gina and Gabriel; Susan D'Arcy; and to Bill Massey for the invaluable golf tips.